SHELTERWOOD

SHELTERWOOD

A Novel

Lisa Wingate

BALLANTINE BOOKS
New York

Published in the United States by Ballantine Books, an imprint of Random House, a division of Penguin Random House LLC, New York.

BALLANTINE BOOKS & colophon are registered trademarks of Penguin Random House LLC.

Library of Congress Cataloging-in-Publication Data
Names: Wingate, Lisa, author.
Title: Shelterwood : a novel / Lisa Wingate.
Description: First edition. | New York : Ballantine Books, 2024. |
Includes bibliographical references.
Identifiers: LCCN 2023053079 | ISBN 9780593726501 (hardcover; acid-free paper)
| ISBN 9780593726518 (ebook)
Subjects: LCSH: Women park rangers—Fiction. |
Choctaw Indians—Oklahoma—Fiction. | Missing children—Oklahoma—Fiction. |
LCGFT: Detective and mystery fiction. | Historical fiction. | Novels.
Classification: LCC PS3573.I53165 S54 2024 | DDC 813/.54—dc23/eng/20231120
LC record available at https://lccn.loc.gov/2023053079

Printed in the United States of America on acid-free paper

randomhousebooks.com

2 4 6 8 9 7 5 3 1

First Edition

For Kate Barnard and Gertrude Bonnin
For all the women who came early to the battle
And the "little ones" they fought to save.

For Angie Debo,
Who told the story
Before it could fade from history.

For all the scandalous women
Who blazed the trails before us
And refused to take no for an answer.

I have been compelled to see orphans robbed, starved, and burned for money. I decided long ago that ... no citizen ... cared whether or not an orphan is robbed or starved or killed—because his dead claim is easier to handle than if he were alive.

—KATE BARNARD,
Oklahoma state commissioner
of charities and corrections, 1907–1915.

SHELTERWOOD

Oklahoma, 1990

Possibly the old man made up the stories he told as he sat on the bench outside the Dairy Queen in Ada, Oklahoma. He'd spin whoppers while carving twigs with his pocketknife, a bone-handle Barlow with the blade almost worn through. Whittle and talk, and so people called him Whittles.

Sergeant, the state-champion football boys added in 1962, shortly after the old man first appeared in town. Sergeant Whittles, a joke about the worn-out tanker jacket with army patches on the sleeves. But Whittles could weave a tale that would make a kid's hair stand on end, and so the name became a moniker of genuine respect. As Whittles told it, he'd been a miner, a treasure hunter, a Wild West show performer, a horse thief, and too smart for his own good before he joined the army in 1914 to avoid prison time. He'd served in World War I, World War II, and Korea.

He understood the folly of youth, the allure of it, and the potential consequences of its naïve recklessness. He'd felt the odd thrill of cheating death, tempted it, and walked away from it more than once.

He spoke of it in ways that indelibly marked his young listeners, some of whom remembered those oversized tales for years after they'd left Whittles, and hanging out at the Dairy Queen, behind.

For that reason, when two former MVPs of the 1962 state championship football team found themselves driving through the Winding Stair Mountains, almost three decades older and three hours west of Ada at the slow pace of a delivery van, the topic of Sergeant Whittles came up.

A debate ensued about the veracity of a story Whittles had told them on Halloween night of their senior year. The driver thought it *was* true. The passenger was certain Whittles had merely been pulling their leg. The debate led to an argument. After a few hotel-bar beverages on their overnight run, the argument led to a bet. The bet led to the engagement of a local guy who, for a few more beers, thought he could pinpoint on a map the area they were looking for.

The map led to a stop on the return trip, and then a hike, and then a climb.

"Hey, I see somethin'!" the driver yells.

The passenger stops, surprised to have fallen so far behind. "Yeah? What'd you find up there?" He wheezes, thinking maybe he'll stop where he is. The bet, the late night, the beer had been stupid ... although old Whittles probably would've gotten a kick out of it, two middle-aged guys clawing their way up a mountain, miles from anywhere, all because of some crazy story from years ago.

"There's a ... a little cave ... I think," the leader answers. "Like Whittles said."

The skeptic freezes.

That can't be, he thinks, *can it?* He stares upward into the sun while rocks tumble and bits of brush fly. His companion disappears into the side of the mountain, but he doesn't make a move to follow.

Because according to the way Whittles told the story, what he saw in that cave as a kid haunted him the rest of his life.

CHAPTER I

Valerie Boren-Odell, Talihina, Oklahoma, 1990

When our ancestors first came to southeastern Oklahoma one of
the first things they set their eyes on were the beautiful, forested
Winding Stair Mountains. They are our Plymouth Rock, our
Mississippi River, our Rocky Mountains, our Pacific Ocean.

—RON GLENN, WINDING STAIR MOUNTAIN
WILDERNESS BILL, S. 2571, CONGRESSIONAL HEARING, 1988.

Dear Val,

*Why mince words? Dreams are wonderful things, but a single mother
needs to be practical. Please tell me it isn't too late for you to return to
your job at the Arch in St. Louis?*

*Have you lost your mind? Talihina, Oklahoma? I can't even find it
on the map without putting on my glasses. No wonder you didn't tell us
ahead of time. Kenneth has been around asking about you, by the way.
You know he thought you two were becoming more than just friends. I
understand grief, my dear, but you can't cling to it forever, and let's face
it, if you remarried, you wouldn't have all these financial struggles. If
you don't call Kenneth to iron things out, I'm telling him where I sent
this postcard to.*

*Put Charlie in the car and drive home. I know you have always been
a free spirit, but it's time to grow up.*

—Gram

I read the postcard for the third time since grabbing it from the
mail on my way to work, then survey the breathtaking valley below

Emerald Vista turnout and try to decide how much trouble I'm in. My grandmother taught high school English for more than a half century. She does not end sentences with prepositions.

. . . where I sent this postcard to.

She is in a mood. This note is meant to tear me up a bit, and it does. To unsettle me slightly, and it does that, too.

I am in the backwoods of southeastern Oklahoma, where after a rain, the morning shadows linger long and deep, and the mountains exhale mist so thick it seems to have weight. The countryside exudes the eerie, forgotten feel of a place where a woman and a seven-year-old boy could simply vanish and no one would ever know.

A puff of wind slides by, unsettling the folder I pulled from my day pack to extract the postcard. A mockup brochure and a half dozen high-end paper samples tumble to the pavement and slide away like fallen leaves. I should chase them down, but instead, I stand frozen. My mind drifts all the way to Talihina, where a cheery yellow house offers the only acceptable daycare willing to watch over a boy whose mom's new job will sometimes entail rotating days off and working odd hours.

Just go get him, I tell myself. *Pick him up and pack everything back into the car and go. This is crazy. All of this is crazy.*

Instead, I pull a slow breath. The morning air is thicker, greener, and warmer than I'm accustomed to in May. It smells of summer. Summer, and earth, and damp stone, and shortleaf pines. Different from St. Louis in a way that whispers something so compelling my heart quickens.

The yearning for wild spaces is as much a part of me as my father's gray-green eyes and thick auburn hair. He fostered that passion in me even before a stint in Vietnam quietly severed my parents' ten-year marriage and made the backcountry the only place he was at peace. Knowing him at all after that meant spending time in the woods, so as often as she could, my grandmother drove me from the Kansas City burbs to the Shawnee National Forest, where her only surviving son guided hikes and raft trips. Gram made those journeys seem like a gift rather than a burden, so I saw them that way, too.

I thought she, if anybody, would understand this job transfer from Gateway Arch in St. Louis to the newly minted Horsethief Trail National Park in Oklahoma's Winding Stair Mountains. But now I wonder if she sees history repeating itself—another thirty-year-old parent running from pain instead of dealing with it. Another helpless kid caught in the tailwind.

Is this relocation a reckless escape attempt or a smart career move? The position here is a GS-9 level job. At the Arch, developing programs and exhibits, shuffling tourists around patches of grass and concrete, I was doing what amounted to grade-level 5 tasks, which was all I could handle when Charlie was three and suddenly without a father. I didn't have the mental space to care about career advancement. But it's time now. This is my chance to step back into park law enforcement. I never thought I'd get the position at the new Winding Stair unit, and I still don't know why I did. But here I am.

It isn't selfish, I assure myself. *It's necessary. If Joel were here, he'd tell you to go for it.*

Just the thought fills me with a bittersweet mix of warmth and longing. I wish he could share this stunning morning view. Joel liked nothing better than a mountain he hadn't yet climbed. Nothing.

"Hey . . . your stuff!" The voice seems remote at first. "Hey, Ranger, you dropped your papers."

I come back to earth and Emerald Vista overlook, where suddenly I'm not alone. From the path to a nearby campground, a spindly adolescent girl sprints across the pavement, snatching up my runaway brochure sample on the fly. She's eleven, maybe twelve. A few years older than Charlie. Wiry with long, dark hair.

Clutching the folder to my chest, I gather the pieces still at my feet. When I straighten, the girl is on her way over with the rest of the escaped papers in hand. She's dressed in raggedy cutoffs and a washed-out T-shirt that reads ANTLERS BEARCATS BASEBALL. I search my memory for where Antlers is located. Someplace farther south along the Kiamichi River. I've seen it on the map.

"Here ya go, Ranger," she says with a childlike admiration that reminds me I'm wearing my Class A Field uniform for the first time since the move. My start at the new unit has been frustratingly slow, my daily assignments for the past two weeks alternating between familiarizing myself with park trails and facilities, performing menial office tasks, and stocking brochure pockets on shiny new notice boards. I donned the uniform, gear-laden duty belt, and Smokey Bear hat today to make a point. I'm ready to do the job I came here for. But once again I find myself tasked with the same busywork.

The girl draws back upon getting a full frontal look at me. "Hey, you're a *girl ranger*!" She blinks as if a UFO has landed. One of the advantages of being tall—I can almost pass for one of the guys, but the *guys* at the station have been quick to remind me that I'm not. A female law enforcement ranger wasn't something they'd imagined here at Horsethief Trail.

But this little girl likes it, and so I immediately like her. "That's *cool*," she says.

"Thanks." I recover the paper samples, spreading them like a deck of cards. "Got a favorite? I'm working on print materials for the park's official opening ceremonies." More busywork from my new supervisor, Chief Ranger Arrington. *You know, give you some time to get up to speed.* He came just short of patting me on the head when he said it.

"Looks like the park's already open," the girl observes. "The church field trip bus just pulled right on into the campground down yonder after some kid upchucked all over the place. Nobody's camped down there, but the gate's not locked or stuff."

"Opening ceremonies aren't for a week and a half yet, but, yes, the facilities are already available to the public." The park is an eclectic combination of WPA-era recreational areas built over fifty years ago and fifteen million dollars in additions and upgrades funded by the congressional designation of Horsethief Trail National Park.

"My grandma told me they were making all kinds of new trails and stuff up here," the girl chatters. "She said she'd take me to see everything."

"Great idea. It's a beautiful time of year."

"Except she can't right now." A hopeful look slides toward my patrol vehicle. "But somebody might take me around, since I'm stuck for the summer. In stupid Talihina. Where I don't got any friends."

She's laying it on thick, but I nod sympathetically anyway. "I bet we'll be hosting summer opportunities for kids, once we're fully staffed here." Visitor programs aren't in my purview, but the cultural and historical features of the region include ancient earthen mounds left behind by prehistoric Caddo-Mississippian cultures, Viking rune stones that are either genuine or forged depending on whom you ask, French and Spanish treasure legends, rumors of hidden outlaw loot, Civil War sites, the 1830s-era military road, and the Horsethief Trail, by which stolen animals were moved between Kansas and Texas back in the day. "These mountains have a lot of history."

"Yeah, my grandma knows all that stuff. She's been around here since, like, forever."

"Interesting." Grandma might be a good person to meet, as I'm trying to acquaint myself with my new neighborhood.

I'm about to inquire further when a car veers in, the sky-blue-and-yellow seal of the Choctaw Nation of Oklahoma emblazoned on the driver's side door. The fresh paint testifies to the fact that tribal police are increasing their resources in the region. In the past few decades, with changes in federal policy regarding tribal nations, the tribe has begun reconstituting infrastructure gone since the turn of the century. Their law enforcement arm, once the Choctaw Lighthorse, is now the Choctaw Nation Tribal Police.

Horsethief Trail National Park lies amid the ten and a half counties that fall within the jurisdictional area of the Choctaw Nation. Even in my short stint here, I've picked up on the tenuous relationship between the tribal authorities, state politicians, area residents, local law enforcement, and the federal government. The designation of any new park stirs some controversy, but this one is a political cherry bomb. Reclassification of thousands of acres has cramped the business bonanza of timber companies that've had easy pickings on federal forest land. Shady deals and backroom handshakes allowed the decimation of huge swaths of trees. From almost any ridgetop, the view is scarred by patches that look like the surface of the moon.

The tribal police officer leans out his window, elbow hooked over the frame. I'd guess him to be around my age, thirtyish, with dark hair cropped short. "Sydney, you better scamper back down that trail." He thumbs abruptly toward the campground.

"There's puke all over the bus." Her retort has enough vinegar in it to marinate a salad. "They'll be cleanin' that up for, like, a hour."

"Might help if they weren't wasting time looking for you."

"Whatever," she huffs. "I told some kid where I was goin'."

His cheek twitches a little. "You don't watch it, you'll be in hot water when you get back to Granny Wambles's place." He pumps the thumb again, this time with fingers clenched so that the muscles in his forearm flex. He has the red-eyed look of an officer coming off a long shift. "Go."

She shrugs my way. "But I was helping *her.*"

"Sydney." His chin jerks to one side, straight white teeth gritted. He'd probably have a nice smile, except he's not smiling. "You need me to walk you down there, or what?"

"Geez." She punctuates the word with an exaggerated sigh. If that were Charlie, I'd be putting his skinny behind in the car right now and offering him an earful all the way home.

"See you later," I say to urge her on. "Thanks for catching those loose papers for me."

"No prob." Brazenly edging closer to the drop-off rather than the campground, she cranes toward the mountains as if she's considering bolting into them. "You see my brother out there?" A beseeching look turns my way. I sense it as the first emotion that isn't a performance. "He's got red hair, real tall and skinny and stuff? Might be he's lost."

"In the park?" Lost-visitor reports are usually false alarms.

"I dunno ... maybe."

"Did he come here with you this morning?"

"No. But he didn't visit me at Granny Wambles's place when he said."

"Oh, I see." My mental dialogue shifts from potential park incident to *family issues,* and then, *this poor kid.* "I'll keep an eye out for him."

"Tell him to come get me at Granny Wambles's."

"If I see him."

"He's got red hair."

"Yes, you told me."

The tribal officer intervenes, instructing her to quit messing around and march herself back to the campground.

Sidling closer to me, she lingers unabashedly, then finally says, "That one," and points to one of the paper samples atop my folder. "It'd look best."

I glance at the pale green parchment-style square. It's suitable for materials meant to impress state political muckety-mucks, their local counterparts and constituents, and whoever the Department of the Interior sends our way.

"Thanks. Great choice." I muster some brochure fervor for Sydney's benefit.

"See ya," she mutters, dragging her sneakers and kicking stones as she crosses the pavement. I sympathize with her mood. My hopes for this job transfer are like a kite struggling to catch air. Up, down, sideways.

The tribal police officer's fingers drum the metal just above the Choctaw emblem, pulling my attention. "You the new addition at Horsethief Trail?" No doubt he already knows the answer. Everybody here seems to have heard of me in advance, just not in a good way. I've been trying to let it roll off, but my Gore-Tex is wearing thin.

"I am. Got here a couple weeks ago. Staying in a cabin over at the Lost Pines Tourist Court until park housing is available. It's not bad. Gives me a chance to learn my way around Talihina."

"Well, that won't take long." The joke comes with a suppressed yawn. Spattered mud on his shirt testifies to the fact that his shift in the tribal jurisdiction hasn't been uneventful. "Watch out for Sydney," he offers out of the blue. "She's . . . been known to tell some tall tales."

The mom in me bristles. *What an unkind thing to say about a kid who's dealing with a bad day, bad week, bad . . . whatever.* "Sounds like she's missing her friends and her brother. Kind of a tough way to spend the summer when you're just . . . what . . . eleven or so?"

"Twelve, maybe. A couple of my nieces are on the same church field trip down there, so Sydney must be about their age. Mrs. Wambles drops all her group at the church every time the doors are open and someone's there to watch them for her." His tone holds an undercurrent, but I can't decipher it.

"Well, I hope her summer gets better."

His fingers drum the car door again. "So, you're the new park LEO?" Again, the question is rhetorical.

I nod anyway, affirming that I am the new park law enforcement officer.

The tiniest smirk plays on one side of his mouth. "Looks like they fixed you up good." A quick chin jerk indicates my patrol vehicle, which required a jump-start before being issued to me. I have less than affectionately nicknamed it The Heap. It came complete with wobbly mismatched tires and an AC that only works when it's in the mood. I feel like I'm being hazed.

"Looks that way," I reply.

"Not surprised."

I shrug. "I can handle it. I know my way around cars. Although I'll admit that one is a dinosaur."

He puts his shiny new cruiser in gear. I swivel away, resigning myself to returning to the ranger station. Working on brochures and picking out party plates and plastic silverware for the opening ceremonies can't wait forever. We have no public information officer here yet, so Mindy, the clerk typist at the station, and I are it.

To my shoulder, the tribal officer says, "They tell you about the bones yet?"

"Bones?"

"Figures," he grumbles, and then he's gone.

CHAPTER 2

Olive Augusta Peele, Pushmataha County, Oklahoma, 1909

Practically unlimited power was put into the hands of many guardians who were unfit for such a trust.

—*Muskogee Daily Phoenix*, April 26, 1915.

He comes into our attic room quiet, the way a rat sneaks into the corncrib, afraid the tabby cat will waken from its slumbers. It's me he's worried about. Me he doesn't want to know what he's up to. Me and the old black dog. Least not till he figures out what to do about the both of us—how to get rid of us, or keep us quiet.

The black dog that belonged to my daddy barks too much . . . and me? Just like my sainted daddy did, I talk too much.

I know what you did to Hazel, I told him when I saw Hazel's seat empty at the breakfast table last month. *You try that with me, I'll cut your neck some night when you been heavy on the bottle. I helped my daddy butcher hogs, skin deer, hunt squirrel and rabbit up on the mountain. And I got my daddy's big knife, too. It's hid where you won't ever find it.*

Maybe I shouldn't've opened my mouth, but once Hazel went missing, I was afraid Tesco Peele would come again in his night wanderings, while Mama slept heavy from wildcat whiskey and her opium powders, quiet as the dead till sometime the next day.

You got a big imagination. Tesco laid a hairy hand like a tarantula atop my head. *And a big mouth. You oughta watch what you say. It ain't becomin' of a young lady. Might be we need to send you off to one of them schools for manners and such. Back there in Kansas City, where your mama come from, maybe. What'd you think of that, Ollie Auggie?*

I bit my teeth together. That pet name for me didn't belong in his mouth—*Ollie Auggie* was what my daddy called me. It was bad enough, losing my real last name and having to use *Peele* after my mama married Tesco.

Send me off to a school, like you did with Hazel? I spat out. I wanted him to say yes, that was what happened to her, so I'd know it wasn't something worse.

He just laughed and said, *Mind your own business, Ollie.*

I twisted out from under his grip. *You keep away from me!* I told him. *Or I'll tell Mr. Lockridge about what you did to Hazel. You leave me be . . . or else.*

I hoped that'd be enough. With Tesco in good as the foreman on Mr. Lockridge's big ranch, I didn't figure he would risk any trouble. Even a snake knows enough to stay still when it's landed in a bed of roses.

But a snake like Tesco Peele can't keep from slithering round in the dark, and tonight I see him cross the attic room, right past my bed to Nessa's. He stands like a ghost in the moon's white glow, looking down at her.

She's just a little girl, six years old, and nowhere close to getting womanly like her big sister, Hazel, was. Nessa's been with Mama and me half her life, since back when we lived with my real daddy in a high-mountain valley of the Winding Stairs. There, the cool, clear water ran straight from the rocks, and the old shelterwood trees watched over us. That cabin was where Daddy came home toting two Choctaw girls, one a couple years older than me and one a few years younger. *I brung you somebody to play with, Ollie Auggie,* he said. *This is Nessa Rusk and Hazel Rusk. They got no more family left in this world to look after them. They'll stay with us now.*

My daddy never could turn down a need when he came across one in his travels. Before that, he'd took in a half-grown boy he found living alone in a squatter shack, but the boy tried to steal our pack pony, then ran off into the woods. So, when Daddy carried home Hazel and Nessa, all I saw was two little girls that'd leave pretty soon. Their quiet ways of whispering in their Choctaw tongue piqued me some, as it did my mama. That's why Hazel and Nessa and me weren't ever real friends, especially after Daddy left on one of his prospecting trips, and a full month later, his calico-spotted pack pony wandered home alone. The pony was still loaded down with all Daddy's gear and goods, but Daddy never came back.

Without him, Hazel and Nessa were another burden to bear when Mama gathered up her broken heart and took us down the mountain to the Commercial Hotel in Talihina, just ahead of winter's first snow. By then she knew Daddy had met with a bad fate. If it'd been just Mama and me, we could've got by in town, like we did in Kansas City when I was small and Daddy was gone in the army. But with three girls on her apron strings, Mama had to settle for somebody low as Tesco Peele.

I blamed Hazel and Nessa for it, but that didn't mean I wanted anything bad to happen to them. Especially not little Nessa, who mostly moves silent around the corners of the world, trying to stay out of the way.

My body goes bowstring tight while I hug the sheet close and watch Tesco. I think about Daddy's knife, hid behind a loose piece of chinking in the log wall. If I try for it, he'll hear the rope springs groan under my mattress, and then he'll slap me flat and take the knife.

I see it in my head, the way I sometimes conjure things that haven't happened yet. I see my daddy's knife in Tesco Peele's hand.

Squeezing my eyes shut, I try to take my mind someplace else, same as I used to when he'd come to trouble Hazel in the night. I try to turn my bed into a magic carpet like in the storybook, then Nessa makes a sleepy sound, and I can't help but hear it.

I peek out, watch Tesco lift the quilt and stare down at her. Nessa rolls over and pulls her knees up under her nightdress against the cold.

I sit up in my bed quick enough that the ropes and feather tick mattress make a racket and even the floor creaks. Stretching out my arms, I feel around in the moonbeams from the window. "D-Daddy?" My voice comes whispery and raw.

Tesco drops that quilt so fast it falls all the way over Nessa's head.

I see him out the corner of my eye, but I keep pretending a spirit's got me. Tesco's a superstitious type. He's troubled by the tales a Choctaw cowboy on the ranch told him about witches and giants that roam the deep woods, and the na lusa falaya that looks like a man, but has long pointed ears and slides on his belly like a snake. Tesco's also bothered about the Choctaw freedmen, the ones who used to be slaves on the Choctaws' farms before the War Between the States, and the conjures and curses they make. First thing Tesco did when we moved into Mr. Lockridge's foreman house was paint the ceilings of the porches blue, hang witch balls over the windows, and nail a horseshoe above the door to scare off the haints and boo hags. This log house and all the Lockridge land belonged to some Choctaws before Mr. Lockridge took it over. Tesco's worried them Choctaws might still haunt the place.

"D-Daddy? Wha ... what ... you mmmm ... you-u-u s-say?" I crook my fingers into witch fingers, scratch the air.

Tesco stands there, froze up.

"Ollie?" he whispers.

I moan thick and gurgly, crawl up onto my knees, and wave around in the moonlight, like I'm dancin' with somebody. A giggle rises from my belly, and I let it come out, low and deep. "Dad-deee, Dad-deee," I whisper-moan. "Clos ... closer. Hear ... can ... c-can't he-e-earrr."

Tesco coughs in his throat. "Git ... now git on back to sleep, Olive."

I giggle again, high and trilly as a bird this time. The noise echoes off the quiet walls, but doesn't sound one bit like me. I wonder if maybe there's ghosts in the room after all. The old roof timbers a Choctaw man carved after his people got moved west from Mississippi to Indian Territory moan so loud it's all I can do not to jump.

Tesco jerks up quick, like whatever liquor he drank tonight just burned off in a wink. He looks at the timbers while he crosses to the attic stairs. Must be his bare foot lands on a splinter in the plank wood floors, because he cusses under his breath.

I'd laugh, but I don't dare, so I sigh and melt down backward into my bed. The last thing I say, just loud enough for Tesco to hear as he heads down the steps is, "Trrr . . . Treas . . . Treasur-r-re?"

That'll get him thinking. He'll wonder if I know something about where to find one of them French gold mines, or that outlaw loot Daddy and me were always looking for. Maybe I can string Tesco along till I figure out what else to do.

After he's gone, I look at the moon outside the window, and tears spill onto my pillow. I don't stop them because there's nobody else to see. I want my daddy . . . and my mama the way she was in that cabin on the mountain, before Tesco, before she took to the powders and the drink. That beautiful hanging valley was the happiest place ever.

If we could go back, I say to myself, watching a moth fan his wings on the window glass, so that he makes a shadow ten times bigger than he is, *Tesco would never find us there.*

I smile while sleep takes me away, because I think I hear my daddy singing someplace far off, same's he always did as he'd come up the mountain from his travels, almost home.

When I wake, morning's barely graying the attic window, and Nessa's standing over my bed, bumping her knees on the frame. Her arms are wrapped tight because the spring air's still cold at night.

"Get back in your own bed." I'm mad that she woke me and took me from the old place in the Winding Stairs.

Her eyes blink, big and brown, till finally I pull back the blanket. "Well, get in already."

She does, and she's back asleep pretty quick. I don't rest again, even though I want to. Instead, I think on how to get us out of here, and whether I dare try to make Mama come, too. I picture her like she used to be, with her smooth pretty skin and the dark hair and eyes of her Polish people, same as I've got. When she laughed, the light danced against those eyes like sparks from a fire. If I could take her away from Tesco and the grave of the baby boy they made and lost together, she'd do better. We'd start again.

Wouldn't we?

I work it toward true in my head, and I make plans, one step at a time, to get us free. And home.

Home free. The words've just gone through my head when Tesco hollers from downstairs, "Breakfast! Y'all two git to the table."

Nessa's up and flying down the attic stairs before I can even stop her to get her dressed. If you don't jump when Tesco says, he'll make you wish you had. I hurry into my good blue ribbon-sash dress with the high collar and long sleeves, and I button every button, even though the collar is tight and starchy from the washing and ironing we do with Mr. Lockridge's kitchen women. It's the most grown-up thing I have, except for my red dress with the plaid pinny. Both dresses got passed my way after Mr. Lockridge's daughters were done with them up in Oklahoma City. They're better than anything Tesco could buy, even if he wanted to.

Tesco's waiting at the stove when I get down there. He's got himself all cleaned up, and he's wearing a fresh pair of brown pinstripe pants, high boots up to his knees, and a tan shirt. His hair's combed, and he's shaved that long, pointy chin of his, which must mean he's headed over to Mr. Lockridge's house, or might be he's driving Mr. Lockridge down to Antlers for business with the lawyer or the judge, or to catch the train. Mr. Lockridge doesn't light anywhere for long; he's got more houses than he can dirty the floors in.

I smell the fatback and eggs and notice the table is all set. Even though I know Mama won't be there, I look anyway, but she's still in bed, like usual.

Tesco scoops a fry cake and puts it on Nessa's plate. She blinks and smiles up at me like I had something to do with Tesco being nice, of a sudden.

"Well, good." Tesco plops a fry cake onto a plate for me. "I's beginnin' to wonder after you, Ollie. Ain't like you to miss breakfast." He slides into a chair. "I even got us some cane syrup from the big house yesterday." He's sweet as that thick brown syrup, and my neck hairs prickle because that's how he'd started talking to Hazel a while back. He'd bring her candies and pretty clothes that Mr. Lockridge's daughters had tossed out. *Awww, go try it on, Hazel,* he'd say. *You're too growed up for little girl things anymore.*

And Hazel, who wasn't used to having any fine thing to call her own, would run off and do it. She didn't see that Tesco's kindliness is like a poison dripping on your skin. You don't know it's there till it seeps in.

Pushing the red-and-white-speckled syrup pitcher my way, he says, "Here. You first, Ollie, gal. And fix up our lil' Nessie there, too."

I do what I'm told, then slide the pitcher away and put my hands back in my lap. My mouth wants that syrup cake pretty bad, but there's a long wood spoon laying by Tesco's plate. Tesco can give you fry cake one minute and whack you across the face for touching it the next. Depends on his mood. So far, I ain't sure which way it is this morning.

"Have a good sleep all night, did ya?"

Goose pimples run from my toes to my head and back.

Nessa bends toward her plate, her lips clamped over the two front baby teeth she's lost.

Tesco's not waiting on an answer anyhow. "I's wonderin', on account of I heard somebody cryin' up there last night, so I went to check. Which one of you was that?"

"I dunno," I croak out, then take a chance on grabbing a drink of milk. "Maybe me. I dreamed . . . some."

"That so?" But he doesn't ask about treasure, so my plan didn't work like I hoped. "Well, if you gals got trouble sleepin', I can give you a pinch of your mama's medicine. Them opium powders go in remedies for teethin' and such. Help you sleep like a baby."

The milk I just swallowed tingles on the way down. *Did that taste funny?* I look over and watch Nessa drinking hers, and all I want is to get us away from the table. "I think we been doin' all right . . . sleepin'."

"Y'all eat," Tesco says.

I cut off a bite and put it in my mouth. I don't dare do anything else.

"Good, ain't it?" Tesco asks. "Sweet and fine."

"Yes'ir."

"Slide that syrup over this way, Ollie gal. Mine's a might dry. Been a while since I had me some sweet, sweet syrup. Too long. I'm hungry for it."

When I push the pitcher across the table, his fingers close over mine. The skin feels rough as a cat's tongue. I make myself take my hand away slow, just like normal.

"Y'all surely done a fine job on this butter," he says while he pours more syrup. "Good as your mama used to." His eyes cut toward the bedroom door that always falls open a bit. The gap shows rumpled linens and Mama's foot hanging off the edge. She's facedown this morning. She'll crawl out sometime after Nessa and me head off to the school the Choctaws built along the Black Fork in the old Choctaw Nation days. Now that Oklahoma and Indian Territory got joined in the statehood, the school has to take white kids, too. President Teddy Roosevelt said so last year.

"Nessa did most of the churnin'," I mutter. "Extra's in the springhouse to go over to the Lockridges'." That's part of the foreman work here, milking the cow, skimming off the cream, and churning some into butter, gathering up the eggs from the chicken coop, and sending plenty over to the big house. Mr. Lockridge likes his goods fresh when he's at the ranch.

"Speakin' of the big house . . ." Syrup drips off Tesco's mustache. "Thought I might take you over there with me today, Ollie. Nessie can find her way to school on her own."

My fork lowers to the plate with a quiet *tink*.

Why's he trying to get me off by myself?

"You know that palomino show pony Lockridge got delivered all the way from Tyler, Texas, for when the missus and the girls come down?"

"Yes."

" 'Scuse me?"

"Yes'ir."

Tesco grabs another forkful of butter for his cakes. "Well, that sorry rascal's got too much spit and vinegar for Lockridge's girls. The old man said, 'Bring Olive here and let her get after that pony a few times. Now, that girl is a fine hand with a horse.' I told him, 'Sure enough our sweet little Ollie Auggie can ride anythin' with hair on it.'"

Smiling, Tesco reaches across the table and rubs my hand. He figures he's got me like a fish on a hook. Fry cakes, syrup, ponies instead of a school day.

Tesco Peele is courtin' again. He's looking to get his hands on somebody. I'd sooner be dead in the grave.

Nessa and me have to leave this place. There's no more time to wait.

I pretend to choke on my food, then grab for my milk to shake him off me. "Be all right to wait till tomorrow about the pony?" My mind runs faster than the Lockridges' new Buick roadster as I wind up a tale. "Teacher's got us to do times tables contests in school today. She won't be happy if I miss."

Nessa's head comes up and her doe eyes scrunch. She knows there's no contest.

You keep your mouth shut, I tell her with one look. And she does.

Tesco studies on her a minute. "S'pose I could take Nessa with me today, instead. She's a fair hand on a horse. Pony's too small for a grown man, or I'd whip the fool outta that spoiled brat myself."

Nessa's face goes still. Her cheeks hollow out like she's chewing them on the inside.

"But can't it wait till tomorrow about the pony? I'm stronger than Nessa by a lot." I try to sound bright and sweet. "The younger kids do their addition tables in the contest. Teacher will ask me why Nessa missed out."

"Reckon." Tesco's not one bit happy. "We'll do it tomorrow, then. You and me."

"Tomorrow. Yes'ir."

Only I won't be here tomorrow, and neither will Nessa.

I think on a plan while we finish up breakfast and clean the table, then wait for Tesco to saddle his horse and ride off over the hill.

Soon as he does, I grab Nessa. "You listen at me now," I say while we stand in the doorway like we're headed for the barn chores. "And do everything I tell you. We ain't got much time." *Tesco could circle back by here. Mama could waken. The ranch hands could come for supplies out of the barn.*

Nessa tucks her head in that bashful way of hers. I grab her chin and pull it up. "You listen real good. We have to get away from here. Tesco's got something bad in his mind. We can't stay here, or we'll end up like Hazel. You understand?"

Nessa's face drains, and her mouth trembles. She shakes her head, looks back into the house.

It's then I notice that Daddy's big black dog ain't barking by the barn this morning. The tie rope's just sitting there in the dirt with nothing hooked to it. The dog has disappeared, same as Hazel did.

Shivers run over my skin.

"Nessa, we've got to go away from here *now.*"

"To ... to the school?" The word travels up and down singsong, with a trace of the Choctaw tongue, which was the only language she spoke when Daddy brought her up the mountain. "To Teacher?"

"Teacher can't help us, you hear?" Anybody in this town will send us right back to Tesco. "You have to do what I say. I'm headed to the barn to get my daddy's old camp packs and rucksack and catch his calico pony. We'll need old Skedee to carry our traveling supplies. You go into the house and gather up just what I tell you."

I count out on my fingers, telling her the things we need. Food. Fire matches. Clothes. Our coats. Some blankets. Daddy's hunting knife. The blue pot that sits up top of the stove. Coins, if there's any in Mama's cracker tin ...

"You remember all that?" I ask, and she nods the littlest. "And watch out the windows while you're in there. If Tesco comes back, you hide under the bed, and I'll hide out here till he's gone. Careful you don't waken Mama."

"Where?" The word whispers through her missing front teeth. "Where we goin' to?"

"The woods. Back to the old place in the Winding Stairs, so nobody can find us. You remember it? Where we lived before Tesco?"

She nods, and I'm glad. I thought she might've forgot, being as she was only four and a half when we left.

"That's where we're going, Nessa. Just you and me."

Her eyes get wide and fearful, and she looks into the house again. "B-but, Ollie ..."

"Maybe Mama will come later and be with us, and maybe Hazel will, too. For now, we've got to go there first and get everything ready. It'll be a long way through the woods, across the river, and up the mountains. Lots of walking. Camp out at night. You make sure and get matches. Plenty of them."

I turn to go to the barn, but she catches my skirts and hangs on.

"Do what I said!" I snap. Lightning crackles inside my body. "There's no more—"

"B-but ..." The look on Nessa's face stops me short. She points across the pasture to where the tall pines float in a brew of morning shadows and fog. "But, Ollie, they're gonna git us in the woods," she whispers. "The elves."

CHAPTER 3

Valerie Boren-Odell, 1990

The trail there was called Horsethief Trail and went from Texas to Kansas. It crossed the Winding Stair Mountains and passed close to Talihina.

—George Lewis Mann, 1937, aide to US marshal, Indian Territory. Indian-Pioneer Papers Collection, interview by Grace Kelley.

Human skeletal remains—that's what my co-workers have been keeping from me while I've been *acclimating myself* here at Horsethief Trail. The bones of three children, silted in and partially decayed. Based on pelvic structures and teeth, the eldest was around the age of puberty, but small. The other two were younger, one with permanent front teeth only partially grown in, one at the stage of second molars.

A smattering of forensics and archaeological training runs through my mind as I squat on the cave's cool, sandy floor. *So much of a society's history—and an individual's—is wrapped up in how people are buried,* a visiting antiquities specialist once told me when Joel and I were wide-eyed newbies at Yosemite. *The story is there in ceremonial items, burial shrouds, the way in which bodies are placed. Bones don't talk, yet they speak.*

There was no pageantry in the placement of these poor little ones, however, only the nestling of bodies side by side. The bones aren't ancient or recent, but somewhere in between. Chances are, the dry

environment inside the cave has kept them remarkably well preserved. Slabs of stone had been propped against the wall, hiding the
remains through seasons and decades until the cave was found by a
couple of truck drivers who stopped off for a hike while working in
the area—at least that was the story told by a woman who called in
an anonymous tip, saying she heard some guys talking about it in a
local bar.

The accidental discovery of this place seems implausible, considering the cave's remote location and well-hidden entrance. It's more
likely that someone came here treasure hunting. Loot legends make
great campfire tales and tourist fodder, but they also bring in diggers
looking to turn a buck by stealing artifacts from federal land. There
are some theories that if the guys *were* truck drivers, they were local
and familiar with the mountains, maybe working for the county
road service or Parker Construction, which operates a nearby quarry.

What else was here when someone first disturbed the site? Anything? If not, why were these children laid to rest this way? There's no
evidence of funerary or comfort items having been placed with the
bodies. No bone or metal buttons or buckles left behind after clothing decomposed. Not even names scratched into stone, yet the bodies seem to be protectively wrapped around one another, eldest to
youngest. *Thirteen-ish . . . ten or eleven . . . five or six years old maybe . . .*

I carefully bypass *seven*, Charlie's age, and try not to imagine his
thin arms and legs, cracked and battered like this, never allowed to
mend. Time ran out for these little ones. Somehow they ended up in
a cave. Alone. In the dark. Forgotten. Hidden.

These were *somebody's* children.

A partial hole in the smallest skull makes me wince, even though
I've been told about it ahead of time. According to the tipster, when
the truck drivers finally noticed that one of the skulls had been
bashed in, they got spooked, ran all the way back down the mountain, and went for drinks to get over the experience. They weren't
willing to report the discovery because their boss might fire them for
goofing off on a workday.

None of that explains the condition the site is in now. Based on
the variety of fresh shoeprints, any number of people have tromped

through here in the past twenty-four hours. No real effort has been made to preserve the scene, even though the discovery of human remains on federal land is a sensitive issue. From what I've been able to glean, Frank Ferrell, my second-shift counterpart, didn't take the call-in tip seriously and failed to act on it at first, and Chief Ranger Arrington—who's away on personal business for the second time in two weeks—is mainly concerned with figuring out how to handle the whole debacle quietly.

I'm only learning about the bones after having cornered the most naïve staff member available—a twenty-one-year-old summer seasonal named Roy—and pretending I knew about the burial site already. I convinced him that I needed to take a look, and Roy filled me in while we drove the overgrown forest road up here. Along the way, he let slip that I had somehow elbowed out several local applicants for my slot at Horsethief Trail. I'm still probing for the reason I was selected, and why the crew here treats me like a redheaded step-child . . . but one they must handle with velvet gloves. It's not just because I'm female, which in general does you no favors in the NPS system. If you're harassed, hazed, ogled, propositioned, whatever, you're expected to tough it out, deal with it yourself, grow a thicker skin, and move on.

I'll get the details out of Roy sooner or later. He is a typical college boy—talkative, friendly, unguarded. I know a bit about him from listening to daily chatter over the radio. His mother is Choctaw and his father is Australian, a horse trainer, but out of the picture. Roy is fond of doing the Okie version of an Aussie accent to make people laugh. He's eager to be liked and is giddy about his first seasonal NPS gig. He's especially keen on the uniform and service vehicle. He knows a lot about power players within the Choctaw tribe and other various area folks, factions, and history. Apparently, lost graveyards and hastily discarded human remains have never been all that uncommon up here. Back in the day, these mountains were frequented by loggers, hunters, prospectors, whiskey runners, dirt-poor squatters, and outlaws looking for places to hide or to run riot. Jesse James, Belle Starr, and a host of others took advantage of the seclusion and rugged terrain. Roy has also given me the lowdown on what are locally referred to as the Dewy trees. According to Roy, Dewy was a notorious bootlegger of wildcat whiskey who carved his name into trees to warn others to keep off his territory . . . or else.

Such sordid history could explain three children suffering a violent death before the turn of the century, and even well after.

"It's not a Choctaw grave, though." Roy interrupts my thoughts. He's already mentioned the general concern that laws giving tribal authorities ownership over Native American remains and funerary objects are expected to pass through Congress any day now. If the bones *were* indigenous, that could make this whole thing a sticky ball of wax.

"How can you tell just by looking?" Someone with advanced skills might be able to establish a racial identity based on skeletal characteristics, but Roy doesn't have that kind of training.

"Choctaws wouldn't have . . . well there's a lot of respect for the dead, you know?" he says quietly. "Especially in the old days, they'd be buried near the house and there'd be a pot with some food, change of clothes, blankets, maybe a toy, that kind of thing. Bones mean a lot to Choctaw people. It's in our heritage." He waves his flashlight toward the bodies, the beam bouncing around. "This is white people stuff, just dumping somebody in a cave and piling rocks over the top. Poor little girls."

"Girls?"

"They are, aren't they?"

"You can't be sure, based on subadult skeletal remains." I point to the eldest of the three, placed farthest from the wall. "Postpuberty, you can tell by the sciatic notch and the shape of the pelvis— adaptations for childbirth. This girl was still really young, though. Maybe twelve or thirteen."

Roy leans over me, his breath ruffling the loose hairs at the back of my neck. I fight the heebie-jeebies. The tragedy here feels fresh, even though it's not.

I duckwalk sideways, then stand to get a better look at him. The first thing you learn in interviewing witnesses—body language doesn't lie. His evasiveness is evident despite the fact that his features are hard to make out in the haze beyond the flashlight beam. "Any reason you assumed all three were female?"

"Huh?"

"You called them *girls.*"

"Yeah ... I dunno."

A rumble presses through the cave's entrance. Storms come spotty and fast around here, bearing torrents of rain, hail, and sometimes tornadoes. I've learned that much just by chatting with the owner of the cabin court that is my temporary home.

Roy retreats a step. "We better get back down to the truck."

Another reverberation adds urgency, and somewhere in the rock surfaces around the entrance, the wind moans plaintively through a gap.

Roy is out of there without waiting to see if I'm following. Only after he's crab crawling through the entrance do I remember the camera in my pocket. It's an inexpensive one I take hiking, but it has a flash and it'll be better than nothing. I should inherit Ranger Ferrell's files when he goes on medical leave for a knee replacement in a couple of weeks, but based on his sloppy job so far, there's no telling how the site was originally processed. For now I want to send some pictures to an archaeologist friend and ask if he's ever seen anything like this.

"Right behind you." I grab a few shots, then follow.

When I emerge, Roy casts a nervous look at the camera, but he's too young and far too junior to question me.

"Has anyone contacted a specialist at the region office to come look at this?" I ask while we reinstall the sloppy barricade over the cave's entrance.

"Uhhh ... you better talk to Chief Ranger Arrington. I guess he'd know." Either the weather or the camera has Roy really spooked. "I think he's back after the Memorial Day weekend."

I'm dumbstruck. I can't imagine any chief ranger *anywhere* who'd remain absent after the discovery of human remains in his park. Horsethief Trail may be new, but Arrington has been a chief ranger before. He must know better.

Wind stirs the canopy of oak, elm, and shortleaf pine overhead. Nearby, a widow-maker branch crashes to the ground. Roy starts downslope, grabbing saplings as his boots slide in the moss and leaf litter. He reaches the truck with impressive speed for a big kid with a linebacker's build. He's in, with the engine fired up, before I yank open the passenger door. A clump of pine sprigs smacks the windshield as I take the passenger seat. Both of us jump.

"Dang." Roy stretches to get a glimpse of the sky. "We better move out before a tornado picks us up and drops us in the next county."

"That'd be a lousy end to a second week on the job, wouldn't it?"

"Yes, ma'am."

We bounce along in silence, debris pelting the truck. Leaning forward, I squint through the window. The whole tornado thing isn't new to me—we get them in Missouri—but not like they do here.

"Those're just regular clouds." Roy nods definitively. "You can take my word on that. I got a B-plus in meteorology last semester at MIT."

"MIT? I thought you were local."

"Murray in Tishomingo." He points in the direction of the college east of here, Murray State. "MIT."

"That's a good one."

"It gets used a lot. Outsiders fall for it every time," he admits sheepishly.

"Noted. I'll quit falling for that one. I was military, so I'm pretty adaptable to new locations."

"You live a lot of places?"

"Four countries. Seven U.S. states. Eight if you count this one."

"Dang, that's a lot."

"That was some years back, for the most part." I leave out *before my husband died,* but the usual knot of emotions tightens anyway. "Gateway Arch in St. Louis has been home for a while now."

Roy's brows form a knot. "Huh . . . I thought somebody told me you came from DC."

"DC?"

"Yeah, brass, you know?"

"What?"

"They said that was why you got the LEO job."

"*They?*" I'm irked to be the subject of water cooler gossip, even though I've sensed it all along. "And why DC?"

"*Boren*, your last name, you know? Senator Boren was one of the bigwigs behind the Winding Stair unit getting designated, right? He's been senator for long as I can remember. You're related, huh? That's why ... well, I mean ... Chief Ranger Arrington sort of got his pick of who he wanted for everybody else, but I heard Region sent you. Ferrell said why else does a woman keep two last names, except that she's trying to pull stri—" Roy's lips snap closed. "Crap," he mutters.

"Strings? Trying to pull strings?" *That's what they think?* How dare they! I kept my last name and added Joel's with a hyphen, in homage to my father, who passed away shortly before Joel and I married. *Our* Borens definitely had no political connections. There was no sports-car when I turned sixteen, so I learned to fix up a junker. No money for college, so I went military intending to use the GI Bill.

"Everything I have, I earned," I say, but somebody's mistaken assumption about me explains a lot. In the NPS system, political connections are the golden ticket.

"Crap," Roy says again, hammering the steering wheel. "Crap, crap, crap." His outburst rattles him. "Sorry. My stepdad says I talk too much."

"Don't worry about it." I feel a sympathetic kinship. My mother remarried when I was a teenager. My stepfather and I still haven't figured out what we are to each other.

"I didn't mean anything by it. I mean ... I don't think ... well, that women shouldn't work and stuff. My mama works for the tribe, and my grandmama has worked at the courthouse in Antlers, like, since forever. I'm all the way modern about stuff, and ..."

"Roy, we're fine. Really. I'm better off knowing what people say."

He focuses on piloting the vehicle through a water crossing. "Don't tell anybody you heard it from me, though, K?"

"I won't."

"Or that I brought you up here. I maybe wasn't supposed to."

"Understood."

"It's just ... I need this seasonal at Horsethief Trail. These slots are hard to get, and also there's not tons of good summer jobs around here and I can't ask Mama for college money. She's got enough to pay for with my little sisters and all their cheerleading uniforms and junk. When I make it through college and hire on full-time with the Park Service, I can help out. But I've gotta get the degree first, put in some seasonal hours, then hire on at a good unit, where I can move up."

A hopeful look slides my way. I feel guilty for not disabusing him of the notion that I'm loaded with helpful political connections, but right now, I need all the advantages I can get. Let people assume what they will about my last name. "Everything you said stays with me, Roy, I promise."

"Whew," he sighs. "Man, me and my big mouth. My stepdad's right."

The mother in me resists the urge to tenderly pat his shoulder. "Don't listen to that stuff. The whole stepparent thing can be rough, even when everybody's trying hard."

"Yeah, my stepdad's not real into trying."

"Then listen even less."

"That's what I tell my sisters."

"Sometimes it's good to take your own advice."

Roy straightens in his seat. "Yeah. Yup, that's true."

We wobble along, the wind drowning out any further opportunity for small talk, until we're back to the empty parking lot where The Heap awaits. Gusts sweep leaves across the pavement and oversized raindrops pelt the glass, harbingers of an oncoming deluge. Even though it's early afternoon, the boiling sky gives the feel of evening. Something primal in me recoils at the idea of three children, side by side in eternal sleep, alone in the storm.

I touch the camera in my pocket without thinking.

"You might be careful about getting those developed," Roy warns over the noise. "Chief Ranger Arrington wouldn't like it. Smooth opening for this park matters a lot to a bunch of people . . . and a bunch of those people matter a lot, y'know? It's not that everybody doesn't think those little girls oughta get treated respectable . . . just that they want it to be done quiet."

I sigh, looking down at my hand. Maybe he's right. Most likely, the deaths occurred a century ago, and if the grave is over one hundred years old, it can be excavated and relocated without many complications, particularly if there's no means of identifying the remains.

Roy squints through the rain as lightning claws the jagged peaks across the valley. "Best to just let it go. Pretend you never went up there."

"Noted. But, Roy . . ." I wrap my fingers around the door handle, preparing to step into the storm. "Why do you keep calling them *little girls?*"

CHAPTER 4

Olive Augusta Peele, 1909

Mr. Whiteman, evidently, fearing to lose his grip on his ward, demanded the child, and Ledice Stechi, child of much abuse, was returned to custody of her legal guardian.

—GERTRUDE BONNIN, 1924, RESEARCH AGENT, INDIAN WELFARE COMMITTEE, GENERAL FEDERATION OF WOMEN'S CLUBS.

Before me and Nessa can see anybody coming, we hear horse hooves on the road Mr. Lockridge had gravel paved, so he could drive his new Buick roadster all the way to our little timber town. The last time Hazel and me helped the kitchen women serve a fancy supper at the big house, Mr. Lockridge promised his businessmen friends he'd soon put roads everywhere. Too long the Choctaws had been wasting these fine lands, he said. With Oklahoma Territory and Indian Territory now married together into the forty-sixth state of the nation, it was time to fit the area for modern industry and folks of a higher type.

That same evening, while the men ate ice cream on the porch, Mr. Lockridge had surprised Sheriff Gowdy with a fine blood bay gelding and saddle. It was a reward for putting down some rumbling by the Snake Band, which were Choctaws mad at the Dawes Commission for breaking up the tribe's land and making each Choctaw have his own separate parcel. Gowdy had arrested two troublemakers and let everybody know there'd be no cattle killings, barn burnings, pry-ing up the train rails, or lighting fire to timber piles in Pushmataha County, from here on out.

That new saddle was so stiff you could hear the leather squeaking all the way from the horse barn, plus the horse had a loose shoe that popped every fourth step. That's how I know who's coming up on us from behind. Two girls and a spotted pack pony can't hide, so I start thinking fast.

"Nessa, don't say a word, except the same thing as I say, you hear?"

Her hand quivers when I grab it to move us aside, hoping Sheriff Gowdy will pass on by. I start singing, so we won't spook that flighty horse when it rounds the corner.

Did you ever see a lassie,
A lassie, a lassie?
Did you ever see a lassie,
Go this way and that?
Go this way and that way,
Go this way and that way.
Did you ever see a lassie,
Go this way and that?

Nessa squints up at me as I try to smooth out the shaking in my voice and the knots in my chest. "Did you ever see a laddie, a laddie, a laddie . . ."

That big gelding has the snorts before he even gets close. He fights the bit when old Gowdy pulls up the reins. "Is it Saturday?"

"No, sir, it sure ain't."

"You truant from school? Because you know, with that new compulsory education order from the statehouse, it's the *law* now." Old Gowdy is red-faced and sweaty, spoiling toward a fight. "Tesco lettin' you two go truant, is he? Because that'd be a legal matter." Gowdy doesn't care about school or the law, but he'd love to get a charge on Tesco. Gowdy wants his own no-account son to have the foreman job at Mr. Lockridge's place.

Nessie sidles behind my skirts. I squeeze her hand harder till she stops that. "We ain't truant . . . sir. We're off on a project for Teacher."

"Teacher." He spits the word and a chaw of tobacco all together. "What kind of schoolwork you be doin' out here, needing that lil' rat of a Texas pony in tow?"

My mind scrabbles like a chicken after a cricket. "A leaf collection." In our log schoolhouse building, Teacher presses the leaves flat, then pins them up with a paper tag telling the name from a book of the sciences. "And butterflies, too."

"You need a pony for that?"

"Oh no, sir. But we're collecting rocks, also. Interesting ones. When we're done, we'll send it for a statehood display at the World's Fair."

Gowdy's eyes go to slits, and I know my story just grew too big. "What say we go on and . . ."

The rest gets swallowed up by the timber train whistle. The noise and the rumbling sends Gowdy's new gelding dancing sideways into the brush. A dead branch catches on its leg, and that horse goes to crow hopping back toward the road and plows right into my calico pony. Skedee scrambles over the top of Nessa and me, the lead rope rips from my fingers, and we hit the gravel hard. Next thing I know, my calico pony is off at a gallop, the pack saddle's panniers slapping his sides and his white tail flagged in the air.

Our rucksack lays busted open. I hurry and scoop stuff back in, and Nessa snatches up a handful of mud and spilled matches.

"We gotta get after the pony!" I yell while Gowdy's still fighting his horse, then I grab Nessa by the arm and tell her, "Run!"

I don't even look back. I take to running and hope Gowdy gets dumped clean off that new saddle. Behind me, I hear Nessa pounding along the gravel on her short, stout legs. The sound gets farther and farther away as I jump over puddles and dodge wagon ruts. I'm fast, even carrying the rucksack. Finally, there's only wind in my ears, and all I want to do is keep going and never stop. I could, too. Mama used to say I could run forever. She liked that about me before she took to the drinking and powders. When I run, I can go anyplace, leave behind anything, keep anybody from catching me.

Nessa calls my name, and at first I think I'll just keep running. But Nessa's voice is all begging and tears and snot and pain. I figure Gowdy's got her by the scruff, so I skid to a stop and double back. But when I get to her, she's laid out where she tripped and fell, and she's trying to tell me something, except she can't catch her breath.

I hear the roar and sputter coming up the valley and that lets me know what she's saying: *motorcar.* Big cities have lots of them, but there's not many around here. Two are Mr. Lockridge's.

"Come on!" I yank Nessa to her feet, but her ankle gives out, and she screams. Pulling her up again, I drag her to a cedar patch, and we crawl to the thickest part, afraid to breathe while that motorcar blows and coughs and spits like a tired old bear trying to climb the hill.

It's past us a bit when it lets out one loud bang, a big ol' sigh, and a long, high squeal . . . and that's all it'll go.

Lifting my head, I peek through the branches. It's not Mr. Lockridge's roadster, at least. This one's the older kind that looks like a horse carriage, but with no horses to pull it. The driver sits up high on the seat, wearing a tall, round-topped Stetson hat. Smoke circles him in a cloud, and he goes to hollering over the engine's hiss. At first I can't untangle the words, but then I know he's talking in Choctaw and must be one of their number that's made out good on timber and oil money. Lots of the Choctaws around us just have plain little cabins with some garden fields, but others own stores and ranches and timber mills. Tesco hates both kinds of Choctaws, but he hates the rich ones most.

A boy about my size jumps down from the seat to try the engine crank. When that won't work, he and the man get behind the car to try pushing it up the rest of the hill. If they can get it to the other side, they'll let it roll down, gain some speed, and then start the engine. I've seen it done.

That motor carriage could carry us out of here quick, I think to myself. *And we need to get gone, bad.* Now that Skedee is free, he'll head cross-country toward the home barn. Whenever Tesco finds him there with the halter and pack saddle on, it'll be clear enough what we're up to. Tesco will come after us, and it'll be the devil to pay.

Cupping my hands to Nessa's ear, I say, "Let's ask, can we help push that car, and . . ." The sound of new saddle leather and a horse with a loose shoe stops me short. Gowdy's back on our tail.

"Ssshhh," I whisper, and bend my body around Nessa's.

Gowdy passes by, then goes to ask the man and the boy if they saw two girls and a bay-and-white pony. The man shakes his head, and Gowdy and him talk in English some more. Pretty soon, Gowdy ties that motor carriage to his horse with a lariat rope and starts dragging it like a big ol' black bull, up the hill, while the man and the boy push. At the top, the men shake hands. The only reason the sheriff would be that neighborly is because that man does business with Mr. Lockridge.

I know right then it's a lucky thing we didn't ask for a ride.

Our luck's bound to run dry, though, because Gowdy's on his horse again and headed toward town at a high lope. When he doesn't see us farther up the road, he'll go to the school and check with the teacher. Then he'll track down Tesco and be right pleasured to say we're truant.

We've got to be far from here before that happens, go deeper into the woods. But without the pony, I don't know how we'll get by. Every single thing that's in Skedee's packs, we need for the journey.

"You stay right here and rub on your ankle," I tell Nessa when we scrabble out of the cedars and uphill into the trees. "Maybe Skedee stopped for grass someplace near. Maybe I can find him."

Latching on to my arm, she shakes her head with big, scared eyes.

"I'll come back. Stay right here," I tell her, but I have to pry her hands loose.

Hugging her knees, she buries her face in her skirts. That's the last I see of her as I make my way quiet and careful through the trees till I find where Skedee left the road. His hoofprints don't turn toward the home barn like I thought they would. He follows a game trail past a spring creek, up a slope, then he heads back down through a shallow valley. I finally end up almost right back where I left Nessa.

Except she's not there.

A hitch knot yanks in my belly.

"Nessa?" I whisper.

The wind breathes through the trees like a mama shushing her baby, like a voice. I hear someone, and I turn, then turn again, then again, but there's nothing except pine straw, mossy gray rocks that rise like tombstones, and branches making long shadows that trick my eyes.

I see somebody, then turn quick. There's nothing.

"Nessa? Nessa, it's me. Come out."

A rustle stirs the branches. I whirl around, feel eyes on me, but if they were Nessa's, she'd answer.

Ollie, they're gonna git us in the woods, her voice whispers in my mind. *The elves.*

My head fills with the stories Tesco tells about boo hags, and haints, and the elves with shiny black stones for eyes. They come to your house looking like ragged children, beg for food and a warm place to rest. But if you ask them in, they'll kill your goats and chickens, drink the blood, and carry your children off in the night. Tesco loves that tale, says he's seen those elves for hisself.

"Nessa . . ." I press my back against a tree. "Nessa?"

The smallest scrap of color flutters against the brown of last year's leaves. Rose pink. Nessa's dress. I circle toward it, careful and quiet, till I spot her curled in the washed-out roots of an elm tree with her face hid in her skirt.

For the tick of a minute, I think, *What if this ain't her at all? What if the elf children already got her, and this one's wearin' her dress?*

She stretches one arm toward me with the fist closed. Something red drips between her fingers and down her arm. I stop where I am.

"N-Nessa?"

Her fingers open. The palm of her hand has mushed dewberries, at least a half dozen.

"Nessa Bessie, you look at me." I need to make sure her eyes are people eyes, not all black and shiny as glass. The breath hangs in my chest till I see them come up regular, just red and weepy. "Can you walk?"

She nods, and I get her on her feet. The ankle troubles her some, but she wobbles along after me, and we pick up the game trail, where pony tracks lie right over the top of deer tracks and bobcat tracks and coyote tracks and a pile of bear scat that gives me shivers.

But at least Skedee is headed away from Tesco's place, and so we follow, keeping our eyes peeled and listening out for anybody . . . or anything . . . coming after us. Skedee goes right around town, and on to the north and west. I don't figure out why till after he leaves the game trail for a ox road made by the timber haulers. We've walked it a long while and hid from a man passing on a horse before we come to a fork where signs nailed crooked on a tree point to Stanley one way, and Clayton the other. Skedee's prints turn north toward Clayton, and it's then I know that Daddy's old calico pony is bound for the stable all right, but not the one at Tesco's house. Skedee means to get to the Old Military Road and follow it to the Winding Stairs, just the same as he did when some terrible difficulty fell on my daddy, and that calico pony came back home alone.

"The river can't be very far." I try to prod Nessa, but she's been limping along for hours now, and she's wore out. "I bet Skedee will stop for some fresh spring grass by the water. Then we can catch him, and, come suppertime, we'll have more than just the half a fry cake that's in my rucksack. How's that sound?" I'm so hungry my head hurts.

"Uh-huh."

"We gotta keep movin', Nessa, or Tesco will find us."

"I know."

"The river's close. I bet we can catch a fish for our supper. Big ol' fat perch, or a mudcat, or a mooneye, or a shiner, or a bullhead, or . . ." I go right on naming off every kind of fish I can think of, to keep Nessa hopeful.

I've long since run out of anything to say before the shadows go deep and the day turns toward waning. The air's cool and the night bugs sing in the trees and the ox trail starts downhill toward the sound of running water. Coming through the brush, we land on the banks of the winding Kiamichi, its waters as pink-painted as the spreading sky.

In the sand down below, I can see where Daddy's old pony walked up and down, looking to cross, but it's too deep and fast here. His trail wanders back up the bank and disappears into the cedar brush and redbud trees. "Bet Skedee's found us a camp place already. He likes a good river camp, just the way my daddy did when he was prospecting for gold. I like a good river camp, don't you, Nessa?"

"Uh-huh." Nessa never argues with anybody. Tesco's made her too scared to.

I hunt up a long stick to scare the snakes, and we push our way through the brush till finally the dark hides Skedee's trail, and there's no choice except stopping. The rotted bones of a canoe half buried in leaves and moss give us a camp place for the night. There, we open the rucksack and drink from Daddy's canteen and eat the last of the fry cake Tesco left by the stove at breakfast. I don't even tear off the place where Tesco bit into it while he was cooking. I'm too hungry to care about Tesco's spit. The wind dies down, and the air carries the smell of woodsmoke and sound of men laughing and yelling. There's a town or a timber camp not far off.

"Ssshhh," I whisper to Nessa. "We can't let them find us."

When Daddy and me had a river camp once, three woodcutters came to our fire to share food and wildcat whiskey. They laughed and told tales a long time instead of bedding down. Before first light, they tried to gather me up in my sleeping blanket and carry me off, but Daddy stabbed a man and they ran away.

I lay that same knife near my head before I cover us up with Daddy's old wool army blanket. It still carries the smells of leather and hay and Daddy's oilskin slicker. We pull the blanket all the way over our heads, and I feel for the sewn-on patch that has the words RADLEY, SPANISH-AMERICAN WAR, 1898.

The year I was born.

Sleep takes me while I think on his stories about fighting with Teddy Roosevelt and the Rough Riders.

In the morning, I waken to Nessa shivering and the sound of Tesco calling my name. Sitting up, I clamp my hand over Nessa's mouth, whisper, "Ssshhh."

He's close by. Other men, too.

Nessa's eyes go wide, but she doesn't make a sound while we both listen and try to figure out which direction the voices are coming from. She points, and I nod. Then I slip the pack and the blanket over my shoulders, and we start crawling through the thicket. Cold dew-drops fall over us, so I know we're rustling the branches. Tesco will hear when he stops yelling.

We have to go faster, but if we stand up and run, they'll be on us in no time.

A crashing in the trees stops me short. I grab Nessa, push her into a willow bush, but it's not enough to hide us. He's coming. He's right beside us. I fold myself over Nessa, and Daddy's blanket falls over both of us.

Something brown busts from cover not three foot away. A doe. Just a yearling. She jumps sideways when she sees us, then turns in one quick move, burrows under a stand of buttonbush, and slides down the riverbank toward the water.

"Over that way!" one of the men yells.

Nessa and me go belly-first after the doe, through the buttonbush and down the riverbank till we hit a gravel bar at the bottom. The yearling snorts at us and bolts back up the bank into the thickets to escape.

Voices scatter all around, come from everywhere.

"We've gotta cross the river," I whisper into Nessa's ear. "We have to now."

Ahead of us, the Kiamichi lays fingered with rocks and gravel bars. The channels at the edge are shallow, but the ones farther in could be deep and fast. Down past the riffles, the water is wide and sits full of fresh-cut trees. Muddy slides run like slug trails along the bank, where timber cutters push their logs in to float to a sawmill some-place. If we get washed into that log run, the loose timber will smash us to pieces.

But we can't stay here.

"Get your boots and stockings off and tuck your skirt up high," I whisper to Nessa.

My fingers shake so bad I can hardly undo my laces, then tie our boots and stockings tight to our bodies. Finally, I undo the sash bow on my dress and knot the tails round Nessa's wrist. "Keep your legs under you. But if you go down, hang on to this and kick hard. You're a good swimmer. I'll help tow you across."

Nessa nods, and I grab a long piece of driftwood with some roots on the bottom, to steady us against the current. I hope I can do it, but the truth is, what happens now is up to the river.

The water is cold as walking bare naked through snow, but we make it to the first gravel bar easy. The next channel is deeper, lined on the bottom with big rocks, slippery and sharp. I feel ahead with the stick, pull Nessa with me. *Poke, step, pull. Poke, step, pull.* I think small thoughts. Cold ones. I want to look back for Tesco, but I don't.

My whole body's shaking when I climb onto the next bar, dragging Nessa up by the strings. We balance together on an island just big enough for us two. Water runs on all sides, so loud the whole world is a river. I stop worrying about what's chasing us and start worrying about what's ahead.

The blue-black water means the next part is deep, moving fast. I poke the stick in, and it goes all the way to my hand without the roots touching anything. Just off the island, the channel's eddied up against a big, flat rock that's a few inches under the surface. If I can jump to it, I might could pull Nessa across.

If I miss, I'll go down the river and take her with me.

My heart pounds while I untie the sash from her wrist and put it in her hands, lean near her ear, and tell her, "You hang on, but if the river sucks me up, you let go. Fast. You hear? You let go."

She nods, but her eyes tell me how scared she is.

Please, please, please, I think, and lay down my drift stick, run two steps, and try to fly over the water. The jumping's easy, but landing's bad. I slide down, my feet kicking in the current while it pulls at the rucksack and rips Daddy's blanket from my shoulders. The blanket skims over my legs, and my fingernails bend backward, scratching across moss and rock. Finally, I catch hold, claw my way up till I can get my knees under me and look back for Nessa.

Sash tails float loose in the water between us like long blue ribbons. I've got no way to pull her to me, and I can't get back to her from where I am now. She's too little to make the jump.

I've left her all alone in the middle of the river.

She grabs my drift stick like she means to walk across, but then she stops at the island's edge, holds the roots, and tips the other end toward me, so that it topples like a tree. I reach up to catch it, and it lands in my hands, making a bridge between us. All she's got to do now is hold on tight while I pull her toward me. Sitting down on my rock, I brace my feet to make ready.

A sound like thunder cracks above the noise of the water, then echoes down, and down, and down the river. Back the way we came, there's smoke in the air and Tesco's wading from the shore with a pistol held above his head.

Nessa takes one glance over her shoulder and catches sight of him. Next thing I know, she jumps, but I'm not ready, and the weight of her pulls me loose from my rock. The world turns into water and sky, clinging to that stick and trying for air. I kick and fight and yell to Nessa to hold on, but she can't hear. I see trees, water, rocks rushing by, and Tesco. Then he's gone, and we're tumbling sideways into the log trap. The eddy at the bottom catches us and spins us round, then spits us out.

We spin, and spin again, and hit backward against floating timber. The breath goes out of me. Everything's black. Water closes over my face, but it's quiet under there. Something pulls my feet, and I think of the Choctaw stories old Isom Mungo told when I helped him at the Lockridges' horse barn. The okwo naholo, the white-people-of-the-water, take children and make them into water spirits you can see right through. *Little children need'a be mindful round water,* he said. *You remember that, Ollie.*

I'll let the water people have me. It's better than Tesco.

The air trapped in Daddy's rucksack tugs me toward the surface like a float, and I come up beside Nessa. She catches my hand and pulls it to the drift stick, and I clamp on again. The logs close in all around, ramming against each other. I try to grab on to one, but it rolls and starts to suck me under. I push away from it. Another log bumps it, and it comes back, and we're stuck between two cut tree trunks, the roots of that piece of driftwood the only thing keeping us from getting smashed to bits or pinned underneath the log raft.

I wrap my fingers over Nessa's, look into her face, think, *Don't let go. Don't you dare let go.* Water floods in my mouth. Nessa's head bobs under and comes up again. Timber presses the rucksack to my back and pins my chest till I can't get air. The river loosens its fist, tightens it again. Nessa goes under, fights her way up. My feet touch bottom, drag over a rock, then it's gone.

The river runs down, and down, and down, and we run with it. The world goes bright, dim, bright. The logs push in, let up, push in, finally the logs spread out and the current slows. A red-tailed hawk flies over, circles lower, then lower. He dives, disappearing into the log run till he comes up again with a fish.

Under, I think. The red-tailed hawk is a messenger bird, a protector. *Here, where the river is slow and wide, swim under,* that's what the bird came to tell me. *You might not get another chance.*

Around us, tree shadows dot the water, which means we're by the shore. Pulling close to Nessa, I tell her what we have to do, and I point toward the branches. Her eyes say how scared she is to try it, but she nods, and I grab the back of her dress. One big breath and we dive under the logs, swim for all we're worth. My lungs are burning before we touch sand and the river coughs us up in the roots of a hornbeam tree. All I want to do is stay there and feel the ground under me and grab air, but I know we can't.

"We have to keep moving." I spit words and water all together. "Away from the river."

"T-Tesco," Nessa coughs out, shivering.

We put on our wet shoes and stockings, stumble through trees, and meadows, and more trees. I keep the morning sun at our backs till the train whistle sounds in the distance, telling me we're close to the Old Military Road that follows the Frisco tracks toward Talihina. With any luck, Tesco gave us up for dead at the river. But we don't dare walk on the road, so we follow along it, staying in the cover of the trees. Now and again, the train whistle, or a wagon jangling, or a horse's whinny lets us know we're not alone.

We walk, and stop, and hide to rest, and walk again, following the road. My teeth quit chattering when our clothes finally dry and the day warms, but my head hurts from hungry. All we find to eat are a few dewberries and a handful of the fairy potato roots under tiny pink spring beauty flowers.

By the end of the day, I can't feel my feet, and Nessa limps along so slow we're hardly going anywhere, but there's been no more sign of Tesco Peele. Might be he's still looking for dead bodies at the river. Might be he's gone on home.

Before the light gives out, we stumble onto a dirt cave under a rotten log, where some charcoal shows that a hunter or traveler has camped before. With our matches ruined, all I can do is bust up the charcoal and spread it all around, so if a bear wanders by, it might smell that and not us.

The evening's chill gets us to shivering again, but the river took Daddy's blanket, so we cover ourselves with leaves and pine straw.

Nessa's so tired she's asleep right off.

I hold the big hunting knife in my fingers, listen at the sound of coyotes howling someplace far off. A barred owl calls out, *Who, who cooks for you? Whoooo . . .*

The air smells of stone and water, like the caves Daddy used to take me in, where he'd strap a candle lamp on my head and his, then light the hand torches and say, "Just like miners. Don't be scared now, Ollie Auggie. There's boys young as you that go down in the mines round here. Breaker boys that pick the slate out of the coal on the conveyors, and trapper boys that sit down in the dark all alone, to open and close the air doors. They ain't scared, and so you ain't scared, either. A Radley girl is least as tough as a miner boy, right? Hold that torch for me now."

I close my eyes, and I'm a trapper boy way down in a mine. I open a door and fall right through.

A noise rouses me sometime in the night, and I feel for the knife, pull it closer while coyotes yip and howl and run right over our hiding place.

Once it's quiet, I drift away again. I'm not a trapper boy this time. I'm a sunfish, shiny and slick. All the colors in a rainbow. Then I'm a girl, but I'm a girl who can fly. I sail over the whole countryside, and everywhere my wings touch down, mountains rise from the ground. Trees grow on the mountains. Birds and animals fill up the trees, and finally I fold my wings and settle in the branches to rest, but the dark won't stay quiet.

I dream about bears, and Hazel, and Tesco, and elf children with all-black eyes under their hooded cloaks.

When I waken beside Nessa, I see three of them watching us.

CHAPTER 5

Valerie Boren-Odell, 1990

Mystery surrounds the death of little Ledice Stechi, girl millionaire, as she lies buried in the silent hills of McCurtain County.

—GERTRUDE BONNIN, 1924, RESEARCH AGENT, INDIAN WELFARE COMMITTEE, GENERAL FEDERATION OF WOMEN'S CLUBS.

"Look, buddy, the sign says only thirty-seven more miles to Paris. That's not so bad, huh?" I glance over at Charlie, securely buckled into his booster seat. "I always promised your dad we'd bring you to Paris. That's where your dad and I fell in love, you know? Paris."

The highway sign refers to Paris, Texas, so it's kind of a lame joke, but seeing the word pulls threads of memory. Joel and I were wild child one and two, pals in Paris celebrating the end of our military careers and embarking on a couple weeks of backpacking and rock climbing in Europe before going our separate ways. We ate French food, got sauced on French wine, looked at one another under the soft civilian light of a Paris moon, and got married.

"Kenneth or my real dad?" Charlie's face turns far too analytical for a boy newly graduated from the first grade.

"Your *dad.*" Suddenly I'm uncomfortable in my own skin. In my fog these last few years, I've been unfair to Kenneth, Charlie, and Kenneth's teenage sons. I let Kenneth quietly slide into the stepdad role for Charlie, the five of us living as back-fence neighbors and functioning as an unofficial blended family. Little League games, movie nights, Fridays at ShowBiz Pizza. Charlie has no memories of Joel, other than whatever misty impressions can be retained from birth to three, or learned from stories I told him early on. At some point, I let the door drift shut on that history, because it was easier.

Charlie looks out the window, a trail of brown freckles scrunching beneath his curly blond mop. "Paris, like in the *Aristocats* movie?"

"That's the one." Finally, he's perking up after being fetched from daycare just in time for a ninety-minute car ride. Given Roy's warning about my photos of the gravesite, a one-hour photo store far from home seemed the best option for developing my film. Hence the road trip to Paris, Texas.

"Could we buy *Aristocats*?" Charlie senses an opportunity to make it worth his while.

"We'll see. Depends if the Walmart Supercenter has it and how much it costs."

He snorts a noisy sigh, which brings to mind the girl at the overlook this morning, Sydney. I want to track her down tomorrow and find this Granny Wambles, the one who knows everything about everyone and all things in the Winding Stair area. The sooner I begin networking locally, the sooner I can be effective in my job.

I have a lot to prove here. I was in park law enforcement in Yosemite. This is my chance to get back in the game. A study of the photos and some back-channel archaeological consulting could help me contribute to solving the mystery of the bones.

Unless having the pictures developed blows up in your face. The thought hits like a sudden slap. *Get caught snooping around someone else's investigation and you'll end up dealing with skunks in dumpsters, vandalized pit toilets, and other noxious situations for the next six months—every bit of it meant to remind you to keep your nose to yourself.*

A few more miles spin by as I mentally review contents of the film roll—the rental cabin at Lost Pines, me in my uniform (taken by Charlie), the two of us by a Horsethief Trail sign.

The film tells exactly who I am. Then it ends with three sets of bones, frozen in time.

What if the photo machine operator isn't just running batches through in a rush? What if that person actually looks at the photos?

This drive to Paris is a bad idea. The reality asserts itself as we pass the final turnpike exit. I hit the off ramp toward Hugo, Oklahoma.

"Hey ... Mom?" Charlie protests. "It's Paris, that way. The sign ..."

"I know," I admit as we merge from the exit onto the rural highway. "Let's go to the little Walmart in Hugo today. There's no one-hour photo in this one, but we'll get the film developed some other time."

"Cool!" Charlie is all for a shorter trip ... until he isn't. "But we were gonna send Gigi and Gram pictures of the cabin and stuff, remember? You said."

The kid is too smart for his own good. He has sensed the family strife caused by our move, and he's eager to show his grandmother and great-grandmother that we're having loads of fun here. "How about you draw pictures of the cabin for them? They'll be thrilled to get those in the mail."

Charlie's face sags, taking his body with it. "When're they comin' to visit us?"

Guilt stabs. I don't know how to fix the mess I've made of these past few years. "Tell you what, since we're not getting photos printed today, how about we grab film for your Cool Cam, and you can take instant pics to send to Gigi and Gram?"

"Radical!" Charlie loves the neon-colored Polaroid camera, an extravagant birthday present from Kenneth and a reminder of the lifestyle he could have offered us. I love-hate the camera because the refills are pricey.

But it does have a flash, and the film doesn't require developing. A new approach to the cave bones solidifies as we park at Walmart and exit the car. Charlie threads his fingers through mine, propelling our arms in a happy, wide arc while we walk. He's not the least bit embarrassed to be holding hands with his mother in public. It's so sweet, I hate the fact that I'm about to drop a mom-bomb. I hold off until we're in the camera section.

"So, I need you to save four shots on the roll for me to use, all right?"

"Mom. That's . . ." He finger-counts while I grab a box. "That's, like . . . *half*. We could buy a double."

"Have to conserve our funds, bud, remember?" My NPS salary here, even with nominal upgrades for law enforcement, coroner, EMT, and critical-incident counselor certifications, isn't a spendy level of income. "So . . . all right, then, let's say . . . three pictures for me?"

"Ohhh-kay." He turns the cart, filled with a few snacks and household necessities, over to me, so he can work the fingers and count out loud, "Eight, take away three . . ." That keeps him busy until we've picked up *Aristocats* and are headed toward the cash registers.

"Hey!" His boisterous greeting surprises the middle-aged checkout lady. The boy will talk to anything that stands still long enough. It's one of the quirks I love and an issue that set him uncomfortably apart from Kenneth and his kids. Charlie's nonstop questions drove them nuts. I found myself constantly trying to tone Charlie down.

In the Hugo Walmart, I'm relieved that I haven't shushed the life out of my little boy. He's curious and unbounded like his father. That's okay. In fact, it's beautiful.

"What's eight minus three?" he asks the cashier.

"Five." Her accent stretches the word, *fi-i-ive*.

"But if the counter starts at ten, but the first and last are blanks, but you gotta save *three* for your *mom*"— eye roll—"is it still five?"

I palm my son's curly head like a basketball, steering him toward the bagging area. "The Polaroids are for his camera. We're sharing a pack."

"I getcha." The cashier focuses on Charlie. "Then, yep, still five, lil' man." Bagging the film separately for him, she winks and says, "I'd do some negotiatin' with your mama, though, being as it's your camera and all. That's almost half."

"See!" Charlie protests as I hand him a sack and we depart, weighed down like pack mules.

A weird feeling slides over me when we exit the store. I'm being side-eyed by a handful of men gathered around a rusty pickup truck in the loading zone. At first I think they're gawking at my uniform— preparing to offer up some unwelcome *lady ranger* jokes. Then I realize I'm not in uniform. Normally I enjoy the anonymity that comes with civilian clothes, but just as I move out of earshot, the words *ranger* and *Thief Trail* and *fed* drift by me, and I glance back. A guy with his boot hitched up on the bumper and his elbow resting on his knee catches me looking and tips his ball cap.

The others jostle and tease. He tells them to cut it out, only not in such polite terms.

I hurry on, reluctant to engage, but I can't shake the feeling I should know who he is ... or that he, at least, knows who I am. It's unsettling, because I have Charlie with me, and if any law enforcement guff is going to come my way, I don't want it to involve my son.

I hustle him into the car and he hugs his new videotape, smiling blissfully out the window as we leave Hugo and the miles roll by, first on the turnpike, then on the two-lane past Antlers. The drive at sunset is stunning, the peaks of the Kiamichi Mountains and the Potato Hills sketching torn-paper lines against the sky.

Near Talihina, we pass the Sardis Shores Café, which I've caught mention of at work. The lopsided sign out front offers a $4.95 catfish special. Charlie and I can split that and it sounds so much better than frozen pizzas.

As I veer into the parking lot, Charlie perks his curly little head, showing signs of almost having drifted off, which makes the stop an even better idea. If he naps now, bedtime will be rough, and tomorrow won't be pretty, either. In the morning, I want to get back to the gravesite to snap my three Polaroids before anyone else is out and about.

"Hey, catfish special tonight." I nod toward the ramshackle building. "Let's grab a bite, and then head on home."

Charlie licks his lips and murmurs, "Mmmm," as we exit the car and walk hand in hand, taking in the shimmering waters of Sardis Lake. A rust-spotted pickup truck rattles into the lot and parks next to the café's front door. I ignore it until we run into the truck's passenger and driver at the entrance.

"Y'all got here first," one of them says. I glance up, but he's backlit by the light overhead. *Was that the truck from Walmart? Are those the same guys?*

Charlie and I slide past with a quick thanks.

Not until we're inside checking out the menu do I hear one of the guys drumming absently on his tabletop, then catch a side view of him as he removes his ball cap. Finally, the mental connection comes through. Emerald Vista overlook. The tribal police officer. Maybe he stared at me in the Walmart parking lot because he was piecing together why *I* looked familiar.

After each putting in our supper orders, he and I end up at the salad bar together.

A curious, overly studious look comes my way, like he's still figuring me out. I save him the time and say, "I met you at Emerald Vista overlook. Tribal police, right?" Laying a splay-fingered hand on my chest, I add, "Park Service."

"I know." He has a nice smile. Friendly, genuine . . . I think. "I figured it out. The little spud threw me off at first." He nods toward Charlie in our booth.

"That's my second-shift backup."

He chuckles, deep-chested and melodious. I don't want to like it, and I sure don't want to seem warm to it, but it's . . . well . . . easy on the ear, and I'm looking to build rapport around here. In law enforcement, relationships will take you further than any other investigative tool.

"Looks like he could do the job." A speculative glance flicks Charlie's way.

"Future ranger. His dad was a ranger, too." *Way too personal.* I push forward, fast. "Hey, speaking of kids, I was wondering if you could tell me where to find the girl from the church field trip at the overlook—Sydney, right? Before you drove up, she'd mentioned that her granny—was it Granny Wambles?—knew everything about the families around here and the history of the area."

"Granny Wambles?" he chokes out. "Unless you're looking for gossip or whatever happened on the soap operas this week, she won't be much help."

"Well . . . Sydney said her grandmother . . ."

"Ahhh." He takes a plate off the stack and extends it to me like I'm a houseguest. "Sydney probably meant her real grandmother, Budgie

Blackwell. Budgie was a state representative for years, so she kept up with everyone and knew their business. She'd give you her opinion on it, too. Only a certain kind of woman earns a nickname like Budgie, you know?"

"I can imagine. I'd love to look her up, maybe chat a little. Get more acquainted with the area." Someone with long-term knowledge might lend context to the bones in the cave. Was there ever a town near there, a lumber mill, a mine, a church, a house?

The tribal officer focuses a curious look. "Doubt that'll work out. I heard Mrs. Blackwell's not been well, and she couldn't raise those grandkids anymore. They're not Choctaw, so they're not eligible for any services through the tribe. Didn't have much of a safety net, I guess. Sydney ended up at Mrs. Wambles's foster shelter, and Sydney's older brother was living with a family friend and working for him, last I heard. Braden's seventeen, maybe close to eighteen? A high school senior next year. They were good kids, far as I ever knew. That's to Budgie Blackwell's credit, because Jade, their mama, had issues. Really rough for Braden and Sydney to lose their grandmother. That was all they had."

I feel a pinprick for lousy situations children end up in through no fault of their own. "Oh." Loading up the salad plate, I rethink potential avenues for understanding the burial site in the cave. "Is there a historical society around here?"

"A historical society?"

"Or a museum? Or library? Someplace that would have records from this area? Maybe old newspaper archives?"

"Hmmm ..." He follows me along, laying claim to nearly everything I leave behind. The teenager coming our way with a plastic tub will have light work breaking down the salad bar. The officer's plate needs sideboards. He also likes ranch dressing. A lot. "Pushmataha County or Le Flore or McCurtain?"

"Either. Maybe all three."

"There's the museum in Poteau, and the Push County Historical Society in Antlers Depot, and the train museum in Hugo. Libraries, too, of course. You looking for old Choctaw Nation era or after statehood?"

"Not sure."

We lock eyes, then, and I wonder if he knows what's on my mind.

In a dusty file somewhere, is there a newspaper story about three missing kids who were never found?

It's not impossible.

With our salad plates filled, I feel the window of opportunity closing. "How did you know about the bones?"

His eyes, a deep walnut brown, dart away, then back. "Caught a little scuttlebutt."

"Why did you tell me about it?" Is he trying to clue me in ... or trying to use me to start trouble between tribal authorities and the park?

"Mom!" Charlie beckons as the server delivers our order.

"Hey, Curtis," the guy at his table calls. "Food's here."

Curtis, I remind myself just before he catches my gaze and says, "I figured you should know."

The atmosphere feels strange after we part ways. The café staff cleans around us while Charlie and I wolf down a mountain of fish, then wait for a to-go box. The tribal PO and I share a clumsy wave as he passes by on the way to the door.

I study the exit for a minute after he's gone.

The waitress, a solidly built young woman who's maybe twenty, sets two Styrofoam containers on our table. "Watch out for him," she says, then darts off without further explanation.

CHAPTER 6

Olive Augusta Peele, 1909

The "little people" make their homes in the trees of the woods and those homes can be distinguished by extra thick growth and small twigs of branches in the trees, but the homes cannot be found in every tree. If no trouble is given to the little people, they do not harm one.

—MOSE LASLEY, 1937. INDIAN-PIONEER PAPERS COLLECTION INTERVIEW BY BILLY BYRD, FIELD WORKER.

They look like small, skinny children, squatted outside our sleeping place, except that ain't what they are. Can't be. Not way out here in the woods, prowling before first light comes into the trees. Hoods hang over their heads to hide their all-black shiny eyeballs.

Come in with the fog, ridin' on it, them elves do. Reach out a bony hand and gitcha! Eat your juicy little livers and your soft little hearts, drink your blood and boil the eyeballs. They love eyeballs 'cause they ain't got any, Tesco says in my head.

Skinny fingers stretch toward us, and of a sudden I know Nessa's already awake. She's reached behind and grabbed my dress to rouse me.

Cut off the hand of the thing, Tesco whispers, *send it howlin' back into the fog.* I feel for Daddy's knife, sift through the pine straw. It's not there.

That hand almost has Nessa. Her breath comes fast, and she trembles against my stomach.

The fingertips touch her. It'll get her heart unless I do something.

I push hard into the straw again, find the knife scabbard. My palm settles over the deer antler handle.

Nessa whimpers.

Cut off the hand! Tesco says. *Do it. Now!*

In the turning of a minute, I'm up over Nessa, squashing her into the ground. My head knocks the dead log that's our ceiling. Light sparks around my eyes as I bring down the knife. It cuts through something, slices all the way to the dirt.

"Get-way!" The scream comes rough and low, like an animal's growl, and then I know it's me yelling. "Get away! Git! I got a knife! I got a knife!"

The sound dies in the fog.

Wings fan the air just above our shelter. Something takes flight. Something big.

They fly, just like Tesco said. *They fly on the mist. But I cut one. I got its hand.*

I don't want to look, to find out if they bleed, but I raise up and try to see into the dim. No blood. No cut-off hand.

No sign of the elf children.

A downed branch. That's all it was. Sliced clean in two by Daddy's knife.

It smells of pine sap bleeding out. A good smell. A safe smell, like the Christmas tree Daddy and me cut in the Winding Stair, and Mama decorated with paper snowflakes and homemade angels with hickory nuts for heads. I want to close my eyes and let the smell take me back there, but I can't. All I can do is huddle with Nessa against the dirt wall of our hiding spot, and hold tight, and wait on morning to come.

When I can see around us, I whisper to her, "Stay put." Then I crawl out with the knife, stand stiff and shivering in the morning cool. Down the slope twenty foot or so, the fog lies thick as buttermilk in a bowl, but around us it's clear enough to see that nothing's near except one big ol' crow resting on a branch. He wouldn't be there if danger was around.

Maybe I dreamed it all.

"Nessa, did you see them? Them things that wakened us?"

She answers *yes* in Choctaw, which'd get her a swat on the hand from Teacher, or a whipping if Tesco heard it. Choctaw talk ain't allowed, but I never told on her and Hazel for doing it. Sometimes I listened to see how many words I could make out when Hazel whispered stories to Nessa in bed.

"They're scared of my daddy's knife, at least. This knife's got magic in it. Big magic." I say it loud enough that if those elves are someplace in the fog, they'll hear.

When I look down, tracks are all over the ground. Little barefoot prints, smaller than Nessa's, just like a person would make. Three trails go through the silvery dew on last year's dead leaves. The elves didn't turn to fog and fly away from here after all. They ran, one right after the other. I can see their path cross the hillside, and go down.

"We best get our necessary done, then move on," I tell Nessa. "It's all right now. Elves can't come out in the sun." Tesco told us that once when he'd got us too scared to walk from the house to the barn.

"Okay, Ollie." Nessa's tummy growls as she teeters on her feet. "We ain't seen no berries in a while, huh?"

"Yeah, I know." I'm so hungry my head feels like it's floating off my body, but I can still feel the hurt all over from the logs in the river. "We'll find some soon, I bet."

Looking at the footprints in the morning dew, I wonder where they lead.

Take the game trails down the hills into the hollers, Daddy used to tell me when we'd camp out in the woods, hunting turkey or squirrels or rabbits while we looked for treasure caves. *Wild things know where the water runs and where the forage is.*

Is an elf a wild thing same as a bird or a bobcat? Or is it a spirit, a whiff of smoke?

It makes tracks the way wild things do. *Anything that makes tracks has to eat.* Daddy taught me that, too.

Nessa and me get ourselves ready, cold and sore, then start across the hill, and down till finally the mist swallows us up. My heart beats fast as the ground turns slippery and wet, and I have to put the knife in its scabbard, so I won't cut myself if I fall.

Anything could be hiding in the fog.

The dew trail turns sideways again, goes along the slope to where the elves stopped at a clear-water spring dripping from the rocks. Nessa and me drink and drink, then fill the canteen and move on, because the dew's melting fast and so's the trail. It takes us down the slope and into a valley, where the last of the fog meets the morning sun. The elf tracks turn through a meadow grown over with cedars, green briar vines, and blackberry bushes budding with spring leaves.

I figure out where the trail's going before we can even see it. Off in the distance comes a low, steady rumble. We're headed toward the Frisco train tracks.

What would elves want with a train?

But their trail sign takes us right to a tall, round water tower marked SLSF for the St. Louis–San Francisco Railroad. Beside it stands a little section-workers' tool shed. A scruffy black cat waits on the doorstop like it's a passenger with a ticket.

Looking up at that tower makes me think of Daddy taking Mama and me on the train when he brought us the final leg from Fort Smith to settle in the Winding Stairs. Mama smiled so big while he told us about our new place in the high-meadow valley and how we wouldn't be able to breathe when we saw it, because it was just that pretty. Spreading oaks as old as the hills, and cliffs with moss and maidenhair ferns and wild violets growing from their rocky faces, and a stream where you could catch all the fish you wanted, or dip your feet in the dead of summer and feel the cold springs from deep underground. I remember Mama's laugh, and our basket of cheese, and salt meat, and bread, and apple butter, and pecans Daddy had shelled for the trip. And I remember how happy we were.

The Frisco train gets closer and the memory further off. The slow *chinka-chunk-chink-ssshhh* says the engine is bound for a water stop at the tower.

"Get down in the brush, and don't move unless I say," I whisper, and Nessa and me take cover. "Best that nobody sees us." Tesco could be on that train, or Sheriff Gowdy, or any of Mr. Lockridge's men. But a plan's starting in my mind. If I can figure out how the Frisco comes and goes, maybe when one passes through headed the other direction, we could sneak onto it and be miles from here in no time, even all the way to Talihina.

Across the track, the brush rustles, and two more cats come out, a brindle and an orange tabby. The tabby's got kittens. They sit down at the edge of the gravel and wait.

The bushes move some more, and I think, *How many cats are in there?* Then for just a second, I see a face. A person face. A small one.

I think it sees me, too.

Soon as it's there, it's gone, but I keep watching for it till the Frisco rolls to a stop betwixt us. The train's a short one with only freight, timber, and tanker cars. No passenger coaches. That means Tesco can't be riding it. If we sneak on a train, we need one like this, with not many eyeballs aboard, but ours has to be going north.

The fireman hurries to the tender car. Quick as a sneeze through a screen door, he pulls the tower's waterspout down to the hatch, then yanks the chain and here comes the water. While the tender fills, the engineer climbs out on the steps. The cats trot up, and he makes some fun out of throwing bits of food to them from a square tin plate. A handful of crows fly in, and the fireman pulls a poke sack from his pocket, then tosses scraps for the crows to catch in the air. The cats jump up, trying to grab it first, and fight the crows. Train men laugh and point, yelling over the noise of the engine and the water, making bets on who'll get the food, till finally the fireman shuts the tower valve and sings out, "She's a' fu-u-ull up!"

The waterspout is just raising toward the tower when I hear him holler, "Har! Har! Git away from that, ya sorry devils. Git!" Right quick, he runs to the fuel bin and starts pitching chunks of coal at something, but I can't see what it is he's after. Laying my head on the ground, I look under the train, and there're three little kids with matted black hair, scampering around, fighting crows and cats for the scraps. They're barefoot, and one's more naked than dressed.

"Har! Har!" the fireman calls again. "That ain't fer you! Git, ya useless mud larks!"

Coal flies everywhere. Crows scatter, and cats hiss and yowl. The kids duck and dodge and keep grabbing food, till finally a coal rock hits the smallest kid on the head, and it yelps and topples over.

"I got me one!" the fireman cheers, starting down the ladder. "I'll teach you to dally round railroad property!"

The two bigger kids try to get the little one away, but they're not fast enough, and the fireman is almost on them.

Next thing I know, I'm up out of my hiding place, running at the engine and hollering, "Hey! Hey, you there!"

All the commotion stops, and the fireman and the engineer look at me, standing in the middle of the tracks waving my arms.

Their jaws hang open like they just laid eyes on a ghost.

CHAPTER 7

Valerie Boren-Odell, 1990

The National Park Service (NPS) is looking for its next generation of law enforcement rangers—those trusted to protect the country's most precious resources.

—NATIONAL PARK SERVICE JOB POSTING.

"With Ranger Ferrell going on medical leave soon, I'd like to get up to speed on the investigation of the human remains." I grip the clipboard in my lap so tightly I'm surprised my fingers don't punch holes through fifty sheets of paper, plus one hidden Polaroid from my second visit to the burial site. There was no need for more film, because the skeletal remains had been bagged and removed, the site swept clean.

My attempts to find out who sanctioned that have been fruitless. Frank Ferrell avoids anyplace he and I might cross paths during shift change. Chief Ranger Arrington has returned from the Memorial Day weekend in a surly mood. The rumor is that his "personal business" trip involved trying to minimize the fallout from a romance with a co-worker at his previous duty station.

I hope that's not true, but I know better than to engage in gossip about it.

Now I've been sent on a daylong trip to Oklahoma State University, wearing my hot, sticky Class A Service uniform, to hand out

NPS literature at a college job fair. Joining me is Arrington's supervisor, our park superintendent, who co-manages Horsethief Trail and a national recreation area in the center of the state. He's here to speak at an afternoon gathering of politically significant people, once our three-hour job fair stint is complete. Normally, this would offer me a perfect opportunity to fish for information about the unorthodox handling of the grave site. Nothing that significant is ever kept from a park superintendent. If it were, heads would roll.

"That's in law enforcement's purview, as I'm sure you know." His nonanswer *is* an answer. Our superintendent isn't on the commissioned law enforcement side of the NPS system. Being a noncommissioned employee, he intends to lay the responsibility at law enforcement's feet, if trouble arises. "Ferrell is local, as I understand it. He came over from the Forest Service and has a longtime relationship with the sheriff's office and other interested parties. I'm assured that he'll wrap this thing up before going on leave." He sips his coffee.

"I realize we're not dealing with a scene that's recent, but that seems . . . overly ambitious. I'd like to be ready to step in as needed. I've been on incident teams for more death investigations than I care to remember. My second year at Yosemite, we had seventeen, including the climbers struck by lightning at Big Sandy Ledge on Half Dome." I cringe inwardly, even though invoking prior incident involvements is standard procedure when establishing credentials at a new unit. These things are like gory badges of service, but I hate politicking.

Aside from that, bringing up Yosemite strays dangerously close to the larger truth—I was in the thick of it for less than two years before Joel and I slipped up, got pregnant, and became parents. I moved to more benign duties, which allowed for predictable work hours and staggered shifts. That was the only way Joel and I could afford childcare, the government rent for our meager park housing, baby formula, and diapers. My career backstep was supposed to be temporary, until Charlie was school-age.

"You were in on that Half Dome thing with the lightning strike?" For the first time, the superintendent seems genuinely impressed.

"The rescue and recovery. " I skirt the fact that I was topside, not one of the rescue climbers. Normally I would've been pushing for my chance to go down the rope, but I had a secret. I knew I was pregnant. "I was field medical at the scene, then the liaison with the families of the deceased climbers. It's rough stuff, dealing with that much grief all at once."

The superintendent levels a jaundiced look at me over the top of his glasses. With his graying burr haircut, he seems a relic from another age.

Be glad you're drawing a paycheck and wearing the uniform, little lady. He wants to say that, and ten years ago, he would have. With the passage of more workplace antidiscrimination laws, he knows he can't. He's probably had to sit through endless seminars on this very subject. Doubtless, he hated every minute of it.

"Well—" He drawls the word, pointedly turning his focus back to the tabletop. "We're not quite Yosemite around here, are we? Some hundred-year-old bones, unmarked in a cave, don't exactly compare. Wait around, Boren, maybe we'll have a real dead body for you, next go."

"It's Boren-Odell. I use both," I say, but don't dispel him of the illusion, if he's under it, that I might be some relation to Senator Boren.

"Noted," he replies flatly. "Hang in there, *Boren-Odell.* We get some dead bodies—suicide or two, hiker goes over the edge on one of the overlook trails, heatstrokes, drownings, ATV rollovers, base jumper takes a gainer off the electric company's high-line poles. An escaped convict killed two campers in the Ouachita a few years back." Straightening a stack of brochures, he looks down his nose at the information sheets, picks up one of the free ink pens. "Wait around. We'll get you a chance to use all those . . . skills and all that . . . *critical incident* training." Smiling, he nods at the pen, well satisfied that he's put me in my place. "Not like there's any grieving family to liaison with on a bunch of bones that've been lying there at least a century."

I struggle for a response. Twice now he's pushed the *century-old* timeline. The cave bones have been conveniently filed in the category of *cleared for relocation.*

"Hundred years ago, the area was still Choctaw Nation, Indian Territory," he goes on, watching the door for the next influx of students. "Up in the Winding Stairs . . . why, all those mountains, was an outlaw haven. Jesse James, the Rufus Buck Gang, Belle Starr, Booly July, whole bunch of others hid out in the old Indian Nations. The tribal courts didn't have jurisdiction over outsiders. The only thing the Choctaw Lighthorse could do was boot them from the territory, or try to get them handed over to federal custody. Federal marshals could go into Indian Territory after somebody, but there weren't nearly enough of them—not ones with the guts for it. Ever read *True Grit*? It's set in the Winding Stairs. The real-life Tom Chaneys and Lucky Ned Peppers were many . . . and the Rooster Cogburns were few." For the first time since I joined him in the booth, his eyes light up.

Something stirs inside me, too, sending ripples of unexpectedly deep and tender nostalgia. "That was one of my father's favorite movies." I hadn't made the connection that my new job was taking me to the land of Mattie Ross, her faithful pony, and the hunt for her father's murderer, Tom Chaney. In Yosemite, I nicknamed my first park patrol horse Little Blackie in homage to a Saturday matinee my dad and I attended for my eighth birthday, right before he shipped out to Vietnam.

My tide pool of memory swirls until the superintendent says, "Not the film, the book. The original. By Charles Portis. You read it? They filmed the John Wayne movie in Colorado, of all places, not where it should've been. You'll get questions about it from park visitors. Portis's story is fiction, but at this point, it's part of the history. A tourist attraction."

"I'll read it. Thanks."

"We all know how it is." His eyes go dull again. "Happy tourists mean dollars—local business dollars, park concessionaire dollars, funding dollars from Congress. The brass wants smooth sailing. No controversy. No messy media headlines. No hullabaloo about deaths in the park."

"Yes, and I do realize those skeletal remains aren't anything recent, but . . ."

I can't even finish the sentence before he rises, preparing to greet students who haven't yet entered the room. "Anyway, back in the day, you had dirt-poor squatters and land speculators by the hundreds, looking to rent or pilfer tribal land. And immigrants passing through on the Old Military Road, too green to know they were in dangerous country. Plenty of shenanigans went on there—none that the government wants to revisit at this point—but plenty of things that could've happened to three little girls there, a hundred years past."

"I see." *Three little girls* and *a hundred years.* "I'm wondering how we *know* the remains are over a hundred years old. Has an archaeologist from district been—"

"That'd be in the purview of law enforcement."

"Do we know they're nonindigenous? Because the archaeologist might be able to . . ."

That earns me a long, fixed stare. "I'd say Chief Ranger Arrington and Ranger Ferrell have a handle on the issue."

"Has anyone investigated—"

His sharp intake of breath stops me cold. "On occasion when a dog is on a bone, he's better off letting it go before he . . . or she . . . chokes on it. This is one of those times, Ms. Boren . . . Odell."

Students push into the room, so I retrieve my Smokey Bear hat from the table, stick it on my head, and muster a smile. The afternoon passes in a blur of telling starry-eyed kids, especially the girls, what incredible career opportunities await them in America's national parks. I feel like a cardboard cutout—fake and one-dimensional—but my presence sends the desired message. Park Service jobs are for *girls,* too.

Afterward, walking across campus to The Heap, I attempt to put my mind in a better place, but it's useless. Despite the crush of students hurrying by with backpacks, loneliness reaches in and grabs me in the gut. It's so quick and so strong I'm completely unprepared.

What am I doing in Oklahoma, so far from family, working with people who don't know me and don't want to? The thing I thought I could reclaim—that sense of adventure and wildness, and purpose, and endless possibility—is gone. My time of mad young love and blissfully living in camp tents and crappy single-wide trailers is over. It ended when Joel died.

He took all of that with him, and he took the best part of me. He didn't intend to; it just happened. It happened because he was dedicated to his job, because he loved search and rescue, because we had a little boy of our own, and the injured hiker's ten-year-old son had run for miles to get help after his dad fell into a narrow canyon with no foot access. The helicopters were unviable due to the weather. The only way in with a haul bag of emergency medical supplies was over the edge, down the rock—but the rock was icy, and at seven thousand feet, the conditions were getting worse by the minute. The victim was in shock. We needed to medically stabilize him and prevent hypothermia until we could extract him in the morning. The incident commander wanted that rescue. Joel went down. He never made it back.

He didn't mean for our perfect life to end that way, but it did.

Sinking onto a bench, I stare at the wide sky over the university's stately brick buildings, and I beat myself up with questions. *Why am I here?* Life with Kenneth would be easier in so many ways. But can I let Charlie be raised by a man who sees him as a square peg—too talkative, too inquisitive, too boisterous, mildly annoying? It's not fair to anybody. Charlie doesn't need a replacement dad. He needs a fresh start. We both do. If the powers that be are determined to make me a token at Horsethief Trail, the requisite female on the crew and nothing more than a paper ranger, I'll fight that battle as it comes. Charlie and I will have our adventure—exactly the sort we boasted of in the Polaroid hiking, fishing, and cabin photos we tucked into letters over the weekend and sent home as a peace offering to my mother and grandmother. Charlie can spread his wings and fly here, just like Joel would've wanted.

The chimes of the bell tower stir me from my reverie. Looking up, I realize I've missed my turn toward the parking lot and stopped in front of the university library. Squinting at the building, I chew my lip, contemplating my next move. A long drive home awaits me. I should get going. I should heed the park superintendent's advice. I could get to the station in time to clear up some leftover relocation paperwork, and yet . . .

Dog on a bone, I think, and laugh under my breath as I proceed toward the graceful old building with its arched windows and towering white steeple. I have no student ID, but I've learned that a National Park Service uniform will get you in almost anywhere.

The Edmon Low Library is no exception. Within fifteen minutes, I have my own courtesy card plus an eager graduate research assistant, Heidi, who is more than willing to guide me. She'd be happy to set me up in a study carrel, where I can spread out the material on whatever subject I'm here to research.

"What *are* you here for?" she asks in the delightfully blunt way of a college kid. "I could maybe snag you a subject librarian if I know what you're after."

"Choctaw Nation area, statehood era, Winding Stair Mountains. Trying to brush up on local lore, separate history from tall tales, that kind of thing. But I only—"

"You need Mr. Wouda." My eager-beaver assistant is off at a goodly pace before I can add that I have an hour at most. I don't know whether to follow or wait where I am, so I jog after her. We make our way through staff-only doors and along hallways lined with dusty file cabinets and unused card catalogs, up two floors, then back down, asking after Mr. Wouda. Finally, we locate him in a tiny staff workroom.

As Heidi explains my reason for being here, Mr. Wouda cranes up at me. He's a diminutive man in a beige cardigan, plaid polyester pants circa 1975, loafers, and a tweed fedora. With thick bottle-bottom glasses magnifying eyes of a bright amber hew, and a bulbous nose, he looks like a cross between Mr. Magoo and Tom Landry. A library ghost come to life.

I find myself opening with an apology, which isn't like me—my grandmother taught me that women shouldn't habitually apologize for taking up space in the world—but Mr. Wouda has an intimidating way about him. "What in particular about the Winding Stair?" he demands curtly. "Your local libraries or museums could offer a concise overview. Little snippets to tell the tourists."

"I'm sure ... but I was looking for deeper context on a particular story." I fumble. "Something I ... heard around town."

"I'm listening."

"I don't know exactly how to classify it. A ghost story, legend ... folktale?"

"About?" A craggy hand wheels in the air between us, as in, *Move along. Busy, busy, busy.*

"Human remains buried up in the mountains. Unmarked."

His chin disappears into his neck and he peers over the top of his glasses. "That *was* a perilous area, as I'm sure you know. Creeks and mountainsides, horses and wagons, accidents and diseases, predators, both animal and human. Graves could be anywhere and undoubtedly are. We walk over history, unaware, every day in all places. We sleep atop it. When we rest our heads at night, we've no way of knowing who may have been laid to rest beneath us."

A chill scuttles over my shoulders. "Was it typical to bury someone without personal effects, though? No clothing or grave goods? No funerary objects of any kind?" Heidi raises a quizzical eyebrow, and so I add, "That's the way I heard the story."

Mr. Wouda considers the question, lips moving as if I've fed him gristle. "Not *typical,* but if travelers were waylaid, a smart thief might remove items that could identify the body. Clothing, shoes, a pocket watch, a wallet, a blanket, a cookpot, those things were also valuable resources in the time." He checks my reaction. The barest hint of a smile alters his no-nonsense demeanor. "Many a wandering spirit likely travels those mountains looking for his boots."

Again, the chill. Again, I hide it. "Children, though?"

Mr. Wouda's mood sobers instantly. "Go on."

"Were there towns ... or someplace families would have lived?"

"In the valleys." The answer is careful, measured. "Timber towns sprung up from the 1910s through the thirties, until the land was so cut over and burned the only bidder willing to take it at auction was the US government, for $1.42 an acre, over forty-eight thousand acres. Once again, as I'm sure you know."

"Yes." That tidbit is printed on our brochures and wayside exhibits. "But on the high ridges out of the way? Child burials?" Heidi gasps, and I realize I've strayed way too close to the truth. "Or is that just a creepy story to keep Boy Scouts in their tents at night?"

Mr. Wouda adjusts his glasses, eyes me as if he realizes I'm not really here asking about a campfire tale. "Perhaps you should know about the women."

"The women?"

"Yes." Drawing out the word, he interlaces his hands, steepling the index fingers. "And what was once obtusely referred to as the Indian Concern. Of course, no one would use such a crass term today, but your ghost story might lead there . . . to Kate Barnard and the club-women, and to Gertrude Bonnin, who came a bit later. Bonnin was herself Yankton Dakota Sioux and a well-known writer when she came to Oklahoma as a research agent for the Indian Welfare Com-mittee of the General Federation of Women's Clubs. Have you heard of this? Or read Angie Debo's work on the subject, perhaps?"

"I haven't." I feel as though we've jumped the tracks somewhere, but I'm along for the ride, wherever it leads.

Mr. Wouda's golden-brown eyes gain intensity until they glitter with it. "My aunt, Alva Grube, was a prominent member of the Okla-homa Federation of Women's Clubs. She raised me alongside her stepson, Beau, after my mother died and my father left me. Auntie was a bit of a scandal, really. She championed the clubwomen's horse-wagon library, and sometimes drove it through the hills and dales to the tiny towns that had lacked for books. It was quite a bold under-taking for a female in the days when decent women didn't stray from home alone. She knew Miss Kate *and* Gertrude Bonnin and was a fan of women who stepped outside their place. Scandalous women. I was at her hip so much of my boyhood that I adored those women and was quite a fan myself." Mr. Wouda peers through the bottle bottoms at my badge and name tag, smiles in an approving way that tells me I've been accepted into the club of women willing to step outside the lines. "How long are you here today, Ranger Boren-Odell?"

I check my watch, wincing. "Maybe fifteen or twenty more min-utes at most, unfortunately." Mr. Wouda looks instantly dashed. My level of regret is equivalent, but unavoidable. "I have a three-hour drive home and my son to pick up."

"Ah, life," he sighs. "I cannot gather the needed materials for you as quickly as that. They are somewhat obscure at this point. Forgotten in the dust of history." He whisks toward the door, his sweater lifting like a superhero's cape. I think I've been dismissed, until he adds, "Leave your contact information with this young one here. I'll send a packet to you—the writings of Gertrude Bonnin, Angie Debo, a few others. But not immediately. I'm off on a walking tour of Europe next week."

Without another word, Mr. Wouda blows out the door, leaving Heidi and me standing like two people in the wake of a tornado, shocked to find ourselves still in one piece.

"I told you," she says finally. "You needed Mr. Wouda."

Grinning, I pull out my pocket pad and jot down the cabin mailing address and phone number, then hand it to Heidi. "I guess I did."

Leaving the library, I feel fifty pounds lighter. I'm no longer an outcast, but a member of the secret society of slightly scandalous women. I walk in the places where they walked. I like the notion of it.

The idea settles my head, and even a long, sweaty trip in The Heap can't dull the shine. I pass the miles home, rocking out to oldies on the radio and singing as out of tune as I please. Outside, the landscape morphs from cedar and prairie grass pastures, to hills, to slopes and tall pines.

Finally, the Winding Stairs rise in the distance. For the first time since moving here, I have the faintest sense of belonging as the mountains close in around me.

I'm barely within range when dispatch comes over the radio, and I jump halfway out of my skin before catching that power company workers have discovered a Ford LTD sedan abandoned in a tiny parking area at one of our trailheads. "Anybody round there?" Mama Lu drawls out. "On that ten-thirty-seven, it's been three days now that car hasn't moved. There's keys on the seat, door's unlocked, no flat tires, but no sign of the driver. Over."

I've got the mic in my hand before my brain even catches up. The trailhead is in a remote corner of the park's 26,500 acres, but I'm fairly nearby.

"Seven hundred ... five-four-nine, I'm in the area. I'm on it," I say.

"Five ... four ... who?" Lu, the dispatcher, asks. She has already made an impression on me, based on the daily radio chatter. She mothers everybody, but not in a soft and fluffy kind of way. She doesn't take guff off anyone. The guys call her Mama Lu, but only behind her back. "Oh, five-four-*nine*," she says, making sense of my newly issued call number. "You sure? Hon, that Keyhole Loop parkin' lot is wa-a-ay back in the twigs. I don't think those electric comp'ny boys are still down there ..." She leaves the sentence open-ended, intimating that it might not be safe for me, a female all alone.

This is the polar opposite of talking to Mr. Wouda. Not that some measure of concern isn't warranted. Abandoned cars in out-of-the-way places generally indicate something bad—lost or injured hiker, drug deal gone awry, wildlife poacher, emotionally disturbed person who has taken to the woods, fugitives from the law, or a suicidal individual seeking the right location. The Keyhole Loop hiking trail eventually leads down to Holson Creek, which flows through hundreds of acres of waterfowl preserve, then into the Fourche Maline River, and finally Wister Lake. The territory has flooded to the extreme during recent rains. We could be looking at a drowning.

"I'm ten-seventy-six. Over." A mild adrenaline rush hits me as I wheel The Heap around. I've missed this feeling.

"You sure, five-four-nine? You'll likely lose radio down at Keyhole Loop. Let me check who else might could meet up with you there."

"No need. I'll update once I've taken a look. Five-four-nine, out." The abandoned car has been sitting there for three days. *It's hardly a hot scene,* I remind myself as I veer off the blacktop, then grind along a gravel road, The Heap squealing loudly enough to flush a pair of foraging deer. Anyone at the trailhead will be amply warned of my approach.

Anyone alive, that is.

The parking area is quiet when I reach it. No sign of the electric crew, other than tire tracks and a discarded Mountain Dew can. The silver Ford LTD sits in one corner of the lot, trunk and passenger door wide open. A flock of crows roosting in a tree nearby hints at an uninhabited scene, but crows also love dead things.

I exit with my hand resting on the butt of my service weapon, then take a few steps toward the car as the birds scatter. Mirror tint obscures my view through the car window. Drug dealers favor mirror tint, but the vehicle isn't tricked out in any other way. It's only a few years old. Well kept.

Who opened the door? If the electric crew found it this way, door and trunk open, surely they would've told Lu. She would've passed on that information.

Who's been here since the power-line workers left?

Scanning the woods again, I move in a wide arc toward the vehicle, every nerve in my body on high voltage.

"NPS Law Enforcement!"

I watch, listen. No answer but the crunch of my boots on gravel.

I've nearly got a bead on the car's interior when three telltale marks near the door handle and an empty Pringles can in the dirt tell me all I need to know.

"A bear," I whisper to exactly no one. "Okay."

Black bears know how to open unlocked doors, operate trunk latches, lift unsecured windows on cabins, open coolers and containers of most types. They are quick learners and masters at all maneuvers that might lead to food.

It's almost funny, a bear break-in sending me into full alarm mode, except for the fact that it doesn't explain the Ford LTD. The interior is clean, free of signs of blood or struggle. A crocheted lace angel dangles from the rearview mirror. A little girl's barrette rests on the floorboard, rainbow colored with a unicorn in the middle. This is a family car, the type someone's dad might drive to work at the bank or the insurance office.

Moving to the woods, I look for footprints at the trailhead but find no signs of recent use. At the lot perimeter, a slide indicates that someone half walked, half slipped down a mossy, duff-covered slope. Following the trackway a short distance, I carry out a hasty search, calling, "Hello? Anybody out here? Park Service." No answer comes, other than my own voice echoing off a boulder-strewn slope where the trackway ends. A circle back toward the hiking trail yields nothing more than the paw prints of a sow bear with cubs.

The shadows lengthen as I return to the parking lot to search the car and inventory the contents. I'm squatting to check the Pringles can, just in case it contained something other than potato chips, when I look up, past the door handle, past the bear claw digs in the vinyl door pull, past a perfectly positioned dried-mud paw print on the steering column, to the sun visor.

A photograph has been tucked under one corner. I recognize a face in it.

CHAPTER 8

Olive Augusta Peele, 1909

The case . . . is one, so far as the guardian was concerned, in which it appears that he was interested chiefly, if not solely, in the estate of the Indian ward . . . and that said child . . . died by reason of starvation and neglect.

— REP. P. R. EWING DURING THE ANNUAL MEETING OF THE MUSKOGEE CREEK INDIAN BAPTIST'S ASSOCIATION, AUGUST 18, 1923.

Me and Nessa stand there watching the train chug away while the cats grab the last scraps off the ground. No need in us fighting them for it. We're holding a flour sack with ham and sausage in it, plus an empty Kellogg's Corn Flakes box with some fried corn pone biscuits inside and a tin can of water to drink. It wasn't hard to get those railroad men to hand over some of their foodstuff. After the story I told, they felt happy about it, even. One thing about people is they love a story that makes them feel like they did a good deed.

My daddy taught me that. Keyes Radley was better at stories than anybody. He could spin a tale that'd get a shopkeeper to throw in an extra yard of fabric for no charge, or give a kid a bag of penny candy, or get us moved up to the train car with the velvet seats, even though our passes were for regular coach. "Give me a minute," he'd tell Mama and me. Then he'd rub me on the head with his big, strong hand or kiss me on the hair. "Now, y'all stand here and look awful sad. Like you lost your favorite pup. Can you do that?"

"Sure we can," me and Mama would say. She'd pick me up and

hold me, and I'd hang over her shoulder like I was sickly, while Daddy talked with whoever he needed. He was good at that, and a looker, too. Folks wanted to like him and he made it easy.

"Keyes Radley, you are a magic man," Mama would say.

"You do me too kindly, Sadie Jane," he'd answer. "You do me too kindly."

The Radley magic is still with me now. Those trainmen were glad to help out two mannerly girls who were headed to town, fetching medicines and supplies for a sick mama, when of a sudden their calico pony got spooked and bolted.

"We know the way," I promised the men. "Once we get to my uncle's farmstead near Tuskahoma, he can help us. It's just . . . the pony ran off with our packs and food. We had to spend the night in the woods, and we're awful hungry." I made big eyes at them while they studied on me. They could tell by our muddied clothes and scratched-up arms and legs that we had been through a fright. They frowned at Nessa, because she looked like the kids they'd just tossed coal rocks at, only Nessa's wearing good clothes, even if they are soiled. Makes a big difference in this world how you're dressed. Daddy never told me that. I figured it out on my own.

"She's a orphan," I said real quick. "My mama looks after her, on account of she's all alone in the world and barely six years old. She's a real sweet child, except she's hungry and cold just now, and that's from my mistake, letting the horse get away."

The men went to checking their watches because we'd already slowed them down. Quickest thing they could do was scrape together some food.

The engineer patted me on the head just the way my daddy used to. "You girls take care on the road. Heard there's been trouble with a gang of bad men up by the Arkansas line. Night raidin' and waylayin' travelers. They might run down this way next."

"I'll be mindful, and thank you kindly for the warnin'. We can get to my uncle's farm okay, even afoot. That rotten old calico pony, he's probably back in the home barn by now." I thumbed over my shoulder. "The rascal."

The man laughed, his belly bouncing. "If we was goin' that direction, I'd put you on the train. Be safer, with them bad men about. You hurry on to your uncle's place, now, y'hear? And watch out for them lil' flea pickers that was grabbin' after the cats' food while ago. They come near, you throw a rock or get a stick and swat at 'em."

"Oh, yes, sir. We scared them off once already." That part was true, but we thought they were elves who would eat our livers.

I hugged that Corn Flakes box and told him he was sure charitable as a saint. Even though I didn't mean to, big ol' tears rolled from my eyes. After almost two years of Tesco Peele, it felt good for somebody to be kindly like that. I was sorry to see him get on the train and roll away.

"There's even some corn flakes left in the bottom of the box," I tell Nessa, and the back of my mouth waters. I want those corn flakes bad. Somebody's chewed-on cigar butt is mixed in, plus a couple used train passes, so I guess a passenger left that box on a train. I'm too hungry to care. I toss out the cigar and stick the train passes in my dress pocket, even though they're used up. "It's a lucky day for us, Nessie. We'll eat for a while now."

"Yes'm!" Nessa's pink tongue swipes across her missing teeth. She looks over toward the cedar brush, nervous when it rustles.

"We best move off from these train tracks before we stop for breakfast." I put a hand on Nessa's shoulder to get us going. "We can eat a fry biscuit on the way to tide us a while."

The cedars shift again, and I can just make out some eyes and noses and matted hair. For a half second, I wonder if Nessa and Hazel looked like that when my daddy found them. Daddy never said. By the time he carried the girls home to my mama, they were cleaned up and fed, but they still looked nervous and scared.

The remembering is why I do the one thing Tesco would hate. I set three little fry biscuits on the grass before I take out two for me and Nessa. Then I stuff the Corn Flakes box down the front of my dress, stick the poke sack down Nessa's, and grab the tin can of water to take with us.

We start out, both Nessa and me biting into our biscuits, but we're barely round the bend when I look back and see three skinny kids and one big yellow tomcat following us.

"Y'all git!" I shoo a hand at them. "Go on now, before you wind up lost!"

They all four stop, three kids and the tomcat, and stand there looking at us. The old cat's been in so many fights he's got two bobbed ears and only half a tail. The kids are just as raggedy. Their hair is tangled with weeds and twigs, till it sticks out all around their heads. The oldest one, who's not much taller than Nessa, is trussed up in what's left of a too-big woman's dress that might've been pink once. It's tied on with twine to cinch up the waist. Her eyes are big and dark as a deer's, and her cheeks suck in under the bones. Her dress hem's all tore off, and her stick-thin legs end in dirty, scuffed-up feet.

The two littler kids are still in shirttails, their legs and feet bare, but the shirttails are just mill sacks with holes cut out for the arms and neck. All three have thready homespun blankets tied on their backs. That was what I thought were hoods when they scared us this morning—those blankets over their heads to keep warm.

The smallest one's a boy. His hair is as long as the girls', but he fists the front of his shirt, and I can see he's got boy parts like Mama and Tesco's baby that died. Rubbing his tummy, he looks at my dress where it bulges from the Kellogg's box, then he brings his fingers to his mouth, makes like he's chewing and calls out, "Halito!"

"Kil-impa!" the middle kid says. I'm pretty sure she's a girl. Her front teeth are missing like Nessa's, but she's skinny and small.

"Yakoke!" the biggest one says. She's got her grown-up front teeth.

I only know a few words of Choctaw, but I pick out *Howdy,* and something about *eating,* and that last one from the big girl is *thanks.*

I nod and grab Nessa's hand to get gone, but before I can, Nessa rattles out Choctaw talk faster than I can keep up with, and here those kids come. All three, and the tomcat.

"Nessa!" I snap. "We don't need them tailin' us."

But they're already talking, and Nessa's chattering back. She's got more to say than in the whole time I knew her. Tesco Peele would knock her into next week if he heard.

"Tell them . . . tell them we'll give them three . . . no . . . two more corn pone biscuits if they'll let us alone." I squeeze Nessa's arm a bit. "Tell them that, and then quit all this talking. We *ain't* friends. We've got to move on and get away from these tracks before another train comes by. The next one might have passengers looking through the windows."

Nessa squirms out of my grip and reaches down her dress for that sack of salt pork and ham.

"Don't you pull that out." I grab for it, but that spills the water can down my dress and stocking. Growling, I try to brush drops away before they get into my shoe. When I look up, the tomcat is gone, and those three kids are running for the trees. Nessa takes right off after them.

"Nessa!" What's she doing? "Nes-sa! You come back here!"

She only stops long enough to give me a quick look, then she grins, and away she scampers, dodging blackberry bushes and last year's dry thistles.

"Nessa, stop!" I kick into a run. What choice have I got? There's one of her and three of them. They might do anything to her so they can get at that food.

They all disappear through the brush and brambles, heading toward a rocky slope that goes up into the big trees. Just before we get there, the way opens onto a creek where the water gurgles through big flat rocks. They're stacked so perfect, you'd think giants piled them up on purpose. The three kids go scrambling up the tower, and Nessa climbs after them.

"Nessa, you come down. *Now.*" Fisting my hands on my hips, I stand at the bottom, red-faced mad.

"Ollie, come look," she pants while she's hiking her belly up to the flat place on top and shinnying over. Her and those kids walk around and chatter and point at things far-off distant. I hear a few more words I know in Choctaw, *tree, bird, house, food.*

"We ain't got time to play, Nessa. They could push you off of there, and you'll be broke-neck dead." I squint into the morning sun. The wild-haired boy leans over the edge and sticks his thumbs in his ears and makes monkey faces at me. Next thing, he smiles and stretches his arms out like he means to pull me up, then he squats and pats the rock. His boy parts show again. Nobody gives it a care, and he sure doesn't.

"Oh, hang." Grabbing my skirt, I bring it through my legs and loop it into my sash so I won't trip. I guess I *do* want to know what they can see from up there.

The rocks are moist from fog, and my boot soles slip, but I'm the biggest so the climb ain't hard. It's worth the trouble. Up on that rock, we're like pirates on the wide ocean. I can see over the cedar bushes, blackberry brambles, honeysuckles, way down to the Frisco water tower and past it. In the other direction, the tracks cross a wooden train trestle over the creek, and travel on down the Kiamichi River Valley. Along that way, I spot what might be a chimney.

"That a house?" I ask the oldest girl. Now that I look at her, I think she might be more my age, but she's so puny she's hardly taller than Nessa. "That where you live?"

Her eyes turn where I'm pointing, but I can't tell if she understands me. She looks at Nessa, and they talk in Choctaw.

"A house, but it ain't her place," Nessa says.

"Whose is it?"

Another answer. "Ohoyo achukma," and I make out achukma, which means *good*.

Nessa says, "A good woman."

"Where do they live?" I nod at the kids, and Nessa asks in Choctaw.

The girl turns a full circle, sweeping her thin fingers toward the valley, the sky, and the hills that round upward on either side like the ribs of a giant whale. "Al-l-l." She says the word so slow I can barely sort it out. If she's ever been to school, she ain't been much. The schoolteachers only let kids talk English. It's a rule. "Al-l-l."

"Where you sleep, though?" I make a pillow with my hands, lay my head on it, and close my eyes. "Where's your ma and pa?"

The little boy frowns at the pink-dress girl. The middle girl hugs her shoulders up, then lets them fall. The pink-dress girl stares off across the valley toward the hills, then up into the sky.

Nessa and me frown at each other. "Oh," I whisper, and we all go quiet. Now it figures why these three look so poor and why nobody sews them some clothes or combs their hair. Whoever is watching after them can't care enough about orphan kids to be bothered.

"Where do you stay at night, though?" I make the sleeping sign again, because there's a plan working in my mind.

The big girl answers in Choctaw, and Nessa says, "She might could show us after we eat, okay, Ollie?"

Of course, that girl wants our food, and I don't like it, but I know it's a right thing. It's what my daddy did—help folks he came across in his travels. Be kindly. Not like Tesco Peele.

The rag kids sit down on the rock, and so does Nessa, and they look at me, waiting.

"Oh, all right," I say. "Guess this is a pretty good place." At least we can see anybody coming from a long way off, and the wind is fair, and the rock has warmed from the sun. I hand Nessa the tin can and say, "Get us some water to drink. Those fry biscuits go down dry as paste. Sure wish we had a cookfire to heat up the meat. It'd taste a whole lot better that way."

Nessa tells the big girl, and pretty quick, they all go to rustling around, and turns out we're not the only ones with goods stashed under our clothes. Those kids carry hollowed-out brown gourds on a neck string for water, and the big girl keeps a ladies' drawstring bag in her dress pocket. The little purse has been used so much the blue velvet is patchy as a mangy dog, but there's a tin of matches, a knife blade with no handle, a bent-up dinner spoon, and a saint's medal of Mother Mary on a broke necklace chain. I ain't surprised about that, since lots of the Choctaws are church folk, and hold their own gospel meetings at churches and brush arbors, and even have bibles and hymns written in Choctaw. I reckon these kids' parents must've been of the Catholic persuasion, but I don't ask.

The little kids scramble down to the creek and come back with the gourds and the tin can filled, plus a bunch of twigs. Right there on Ship Rock, which is what I name the place, we light a tiny fire. The big girl puts a hand on her chest and gives her name, *Tula*. Then she gathers some flat stones, and we wash them off for plates and set them up with a few wet leaves for napkins.

Looking over that long cedar-and-bramble sea, we have us a breakfast on Ship Rock. While we're eating, I find out that Tula's twelve years old, just one year more than me, and the two smaller ones, Pinti and Koi, are five and four, just shy of Nessa's age. They're sisters and a brother.

Tula watches while the little kids scramble down to play in the creek.

"That was a right nice breakfast," I tell her.

She smiles and nods, so I guess she understands. "Yeh." She rubs her belly, and I see that it sticks out like a muskmelon, even though her arms and legs are bony. The other kids are like that, too. I can tell because when they're down to the water, they strip off their sack shirttails and scamper around the stream naked as the day they were born, even though that water must be cold. I don't say anything about it, but I do wonder if those kids have worms. Skinny body, saggy belly, dried-up hair. At our school, Teacher would dose them with pumpkin seed and wormwood and hold their mouth till they swallowed it. The bully boys always said Teacher bought that from some Choctaw witch woman, and it was poison, but I never saw anybody die of it.

"What you got wrapped up there in your blanket?" I ask, because I see she's packing something in the low part where it hangs across her hip like a sling.

Her eyes sparkle, and she pulls out something black and smooth. I know it right off. I saw the train men throw it just a while back.

A laugh comes up my throat and busts past my lips. "You took their coal?"

Tula's grin stretches across her whole face. "Yeh."

I laugh again.

"Man," she says, and makes a motion like she's pitching a rock.

"Well, he did that." I nod and we laugh some more. "You're pretty smart. That'll make a right good fire later." Ain't the first time I've seen kids pick up spilled coal from the trains, but it's the first time I've seen kids trick railroad men into throwing it to them on purpose.

Tula nods, still grinning.

We have another giggle together over it. I like Tula. She's chummy and fun, not quiet and sad like Hazel was. If me and Tula met at school, we could be friends . . . if Tesco would let us, which he wouldn't.

While the other kids splash in the creek, Tula and me lie back and look at clouds and birds and the spring butterflies. We point at the pretty ones. It's nice up on Ship Rock, and for a minute I wish we could stay, but Nessa and me don't dare. "Guess you oughta show us where you live now." That matters for my plan.

Tula sits up and says, "Yeh. Come . . . see?"

We two clean up Ship Rock and have some fun stacking our pretend plates in the middle, but before we climb down, I pick up the whole batch and toss them off in the sand. Best not to leave any signs behind, in case Tesco didn't give us up for dead at the river.

We gather the little ones, and it's plain enough that pretend plates are the least of the worries. We've left boot tracks all over the mud along the creek, plus there's barefoot prints from the other kids. Anybody coming through here could read that trail sign.

The longer the day goes on, the more trail sign I see. Tula, Pinti, and Koi have got paths from hither to yonder, and they drag us all over the place, me all the while telling Tula she promised to take us to where they *live*. "Where y'all sleep at," I keep saying, but we end up climbing a sycamore tree to look for eggs in a bird nest, then getting a big mess of wild dewberries, and gathering up some dandelion greens. They don't eat any of it, so I guess they must mean to take it back to whoever looks after them.

Finally, I figure out we're headed toward that chimney I saw off down the way. Tula already said that wasn't their house, but I figure maybe some Choctaw folk live there, and I can work my plan with them in trade for the six nickels Nessa grabbed from Mama's cracker tin. I hate to let go of those nickels, but it can't be helped.

The house ain't fancy when we get there. Still, it looks good enough, and the animals are fat and tended. There's a chicken coop, a spotted milk cow, plus a kitchen garden, and some acres of field crops sprouting up.

Tula and the kids stop in the brush cover and squat down.

"You know these people here?" I ask.

Putting her fingers to her mouth, Tula quiets me.

I don't like the looks of that, and I start wondering if we're here to steal something.

I reach for Nessa because I don't need that kind of trouble, but Tula grabs my arm, then points through the branches as a woman comes out the back of the house to dump a wash basin. She's a tall lady with blond hair, not fancy dressed, but respectable in a blue chambray skirt, brown blouse, and button shoes. Her sun bonnet hangs down from the ties round her neck. She ain't young nor old, either.

Tula wraps her blanket around herself, then hoods her head and hurries across the yard like a shadow. Once she gets to the porch steps, she opens the bundle of our pickings, lays it out so the woman can see. The woman takes Tula's goods into the house, and Tula hides beside the steps till the woman comes back with something, hands it to Tula, then shoos her off. Once Tula's gone, the woman looks around like she's worried if anybody saw.

Soon as Tula gets back to our hiding hole, it's clear she got the best end of the deal. She's carrying three hard-boiled eggs, some cheese, and two heels of bread. That's a lot for a few handfuls of dewberries and dandelion greens.

At the house, the lady shades her eyes and stands looking toward our hiding spot.

CHAPTER 9

Valerie Boren-Odell, 1990

Lucky Ned Pepper had been seen three days earlier at McAlester's store on the M K & T Railroad tracks. His intentions were not known. . . . Rooster said we would be better off if we could catch the robber band before they left the neighborhood of McAlester's and returned to their hiding place in the fastness of the Winding Stair Mountains.

—MATTIE ROSS, 1873. *TRUE GRIT*, BY CHARLES PORTIS.

A sudden change in the weather steals the late-day sun as I drive back to Talihina. Milky clouds shroud the higher elevations, obscuring all but the next few feet of road. The underbrush of dogwoods, redbuds, sumac, witch hazel, and sassafras disappears along with road signs warning of steep grades and S curves. In the valleys, I punch through the cloak. Wooded lowlands, trickling clear-water creeks, and boldly painted spring wildflowers emerge like woodland fairies.

The Heap's radio goes silent, and it is as if I depart from the world, then reenter, then vanish into the clouds again. The experience would be tranquil, but I'm pondering the abandoned Ford LTD. The face in the photo tucked under the visor was familiar because the same girl, Sydney, chatted me up at Emerald Vista last Friday. The photo captured her standing beside an athletic-looking teenage boy in camouflage pants and a T-shirt. He's a redhead, so I'm guessing that's the brother she mentioned at the overlook.

You see my brother out there?

He didn't visit me at Granny Wambles's when he said . . .

Braden. Sixteen or seventeen, now adrift in the world. Absent father. Bad mother. Grandmother had a medical crisis and couldn't take care of him anymore. Little sister stuck in foster care. The car is registered to an LLC owned by the grandmother, Budgie Blackwell. It hasn't been reported stolen.

"So a high school kid leaves a car in the trailhead lot—" I mutter to myself as I roll into Talihina. "Wanders off into the woods . . . and then never resurfaces. Why?"

Not for any good reason I can think of. That's what scares me.

"But no one reports him missing . . ."

Is he okay? Mentally? Emotionally? Is he in some kind of trouble?

Might be he's lost.

I dunno . . . maybe.

Tell him to come get me.

Is Sydney telling the truth, or is she just desperate for a way out of an unhappy foster home situation?

She'd have motivation, if what Charlie told me over the weekend is true. Mrs. Wambles and her wards are the source of epic daycare chatter. *Kids get sent to Granny Wambles's house to be locked up, and at school you should watch out for them because they'll steal your stuff. They are bad kids and they lie and get other kids in trouble, plus they smell bad and use cuss words, which can make the whole class have to sit out recess.* That's the gist of it from a first-grader's perspective. It's a horrifying mischaracterization of an emergency shelter and why kids go there. I've tried to clear it up so Charlie won't feed the rumor mill, but he likes the creepy Hansel and Gretel version better.

I'll have to wait until tomorrow to find out more. There's zero chance Frank Ferrell will waste his remaining knee power on an abandoned car and the murky word of an adolescent. He'll pass the hours until midnight clocking motorists with the radar gun, looking for illegally parked ATV trailers and horse rigs, and handing out a few campground citations. Meanwhile, my shift was over forty-five minutes ago, and Charlie is probably more than ready to head home to a frozen pizza and the 998th consecutive showing of *Aristocats.*

When I arrive at the daycare, he's singing the theme song and playing an imaginary saxophone. The daycare owner and her assistant think it's cute, and so they're egging him on. I apologize for being late, but they assure me it's fine. The owner's husband is with the county sheriff's office. They're accustomed to unpredictable shifts.

Charlie leaves singing "Everybody Wants to Be a Cat" and feeding the nonstop ear worm in my head. He quickly moves to the latest news on the street. He'd like to sign up for T-ball, maybe soccer, Boy Scouts, and when it's time for his birthday in September, he wants a dinosaur birthday party with a dinosaur costume he can also wear on Halloween. Dustin James will be having a Batman birthday party in three weeks, and can Charlie go? Can he spend the night afterward? Also, can we have mac and cheese tonight instead of pizza? Is mac and cheese nutrition-ous?

How much money do I think a dinosaur party will cost? Can we have it at the lake? Make s'mores? Swim? Look at fossils and rocks? Do I think all the kids know how to swim like he does?

Can kids come if they don't know how to swim? Will it be too cold to swim by his birthday? Or does it stay warm around here all the time? Because it's really hot here already compared to St. Louis, don't I think?

"Hey, bud?" I say finally. "Why don't we sing the cat song?"

And so goes our foreshortened evening—mac and cheese, carrots, and broccoli to doodle in the leftover sauce, *Aristocats*, bath, jammies, reading time, bed. Up in the morning to shuffle the grouchy, groggy, less talkative version of the boy child off to daycare. We share a long, sleepy hug and cuddle before I set him free.

From there, the day takes on a life of its own, beginning with torrential rain and an on-the-fly crew meeting about bad-weather contingency plans for the park's official dedication ceremony at the end of the week. My abandoned car is briefly mentioned. I say I'm following up. Nobody's very interested.

Morning is almost over before I have time to seek out Mrs. Wambles's place. The paint-bare gray house fits Charlie's maudlin lore perfectly. Overgrown holly bushes cloak the front windows. Partial sets of shutters hang askew, resembling crooked teeth. A netless basketball hoop leans over a weed patch by the gravel driveway, and behind the backyard chain-link fence, faded plastic yard toys lie scattered like flood debris. The smell of cat urine mixed with cigarette smoke chokes the air as I approach the house.

A thin, thirtysomething woman in cutoffs and a tank top preemptively emerges from the front door. "Mrs. Wambles ain't here. She took the kids down to town." Curling her lip, she squints at my uniform. "Oh, you're a park ranger. Sorry. I thought you were from the sheriff's department. What'd you want?" A baby fusses somewhere inside, and she fidgets nervously. "I gotta get back. One of them's sick. We just got her last night. She come in that way."

I apologize for interrupting and quickly seek clarification as to Mrs. Wambles's whereabouts. Fortunately, the worker is as eager to have me gone as I am to leave, so she is more than happy to point me to a nearby church.

The door snaps shut and the dead bolt turns before I'm halfway to my vehicle. A chill runs along my spine as I drive to the church, where the atmosphere turns out to be as bright and cheery as the daycare was grim. Some sort of kids' activity camp is happening. The front walk has been decorated with vines, cutouts of jungle animals, and a Register Here sign, but activity on the playground in back draws me there instead.

I don't even get the chance to ask after Mrs. Wambles before I gather the attention of children who assume I'm part of the jungle entertainment. Questions fly from all directions.

"Are you the police?"

"She's the game warden!"

"Are you a lady ranger?"

"Do you got a ranger horse?"

"Where's your truck?"

"My mama saw a bear in the backyard!"

"Can you come git a snake from under our house?"

"What's a armadillo eat?"

"Guys! Guys! Quiet down." A helper chastises the gaggle. She jogs toward me like a first responder bent on performing a rescue, but a streak of blue jeans, orange T-shirt, and flying hair cuts her off before she can arrive on scene.

"Hey-eeee!" Sydney hits me at high speed, wrapping me in a hug, or a wrestling hold. I'm momentarily pinned, arms at my sides, before she turns me loose, casts a warning look at the other kids, and says, "She's *my* friend."

One of her hands slides into mine. The other encircles my wrist, and she leans backward, lolling against my arm. "I been wonderin' when you were gonna come by," she says as if the two of us had plans together.

"Uhhh ..." The motherly part of me goes squishy and warm ... and sad all at once. I want to be the special visitor for this kid who will undoubtedly have no one else stop by to share her day, but that's not why I'm here.

"Did you do the color I said?" she inquires. "Of the paper?"

"Actually ... well ... yes, I did."

If she's worried about her brother right now, it certainly isn't showing, which makes the drama at Emerald Overlook seem to have been an act. "That's the best one." She offers her approval of the paper choice. "It'll look *so* good. What else you need me to help with?"

"Hmmm ... Let me think about that." *There's probably something. Isn't there something?* A few parks have at-risk teens serving as volunteers. They monitor trails, offer directions, warn people about heat stroke, bears, and weather threats, but Sydney is too young for any of that.

The hand clasped around my wrist breaks free to swat away a small boy who's trying to touch the flashlight on my belt.

"Get back! She's *my* friend, I said."

"Sydney!" The playground monitor, who is authoritative but probably not far past teenagerhood herself, closes in. Grabbing Sydney's arm, she tugs the girl off me, then gets in her face with a pointed finger. "You better keep your hands to yourself, or I'll tell Granny Wambles, and you'll be sittin' home tomorrow, understand?"

"Yes. But she *is* my friend. I knew her before." Sydney turns to me for vindication. "Right, huh?"

Law enforcement habits kick in. De-escalation. Always. Begin by separating the parties involved, then gather information. "Yes, we did meet. And thanks for the help. It's good to see you again, Sydney. Right now, I need to have a quick word with—"

"Joanie," the attendant fills in. Up close, I realize I've met her somewhere in town.

"Joanie. Maybe if there's time, I can answer questions from the other kids later. You probably already know more about it than they do, right, Sydney?"

"Yeah." She brightens slightly before being shooed off.

"Sorry about that," Joanie says. "They didn't tell us you were coming."

We position ourselves side by side, watching the wild rumpus on the playground. Nearby, Sydney loiters under a covered walkway. One hand around the support pole, she rotates like a lazy tetherball, eyeing us on each new turn.

"They?"

"The highway patrol, or . . . where're you from? We just had the firemen yesterday for the kickoff parade. They didn't tell us somebody was coming today, too."

"National Park Service, but I'm not here to—"

"Makes sense." She nods toward a few cardboard animals and vines taped to the church door. "Jungle and nature stuff and all. But I thought there was a park ranger person talking Friday." Frowning, she checks a printed schedule from her back pocket. "Yep, it says Friday."

"I'm actually not here to talk to the kids. I'm looking for Mrs. Wambles."

"Uh-oh." Offering a conspiratorial look, Joanie leans closer, ready for the dish. "What's gone on now?"

"Quite possibly nothing, but I'd like to ask a few questions of her, and our friend Sydney, over there."

Joanie chews her lip. "She tells tales . . . a *lot.*"

Nearby, Sydney stops circling the pole and directs a wrinkle-nosed sneer our way.

"They're fairly basic questions." I redirect the conversation.

"And once Myrna Wambles drops these kids, she scoots. She's not back till it's time for afternoon pickup."

"So, about Sydney..."

Across the playground, a dispute over a swing is brewing. Joanie yells, "Y'all cut that out at the swings! Cody and Cole, stop it right now or I'll sic this police officer on you!"

I stiffen instantly. It's maddening when people invoke law enforcement to threaten children.

"Sorry." Joanie winces apologetically. "That pair is from Mrs. Wambles's place, too. Hers are always the troublemakers. That one on the left, he..." She spills the sad history of both boys, whose mother is an addict who *can't get herself straightened out.*

It's heartbreaking and more than I want to know. I hate problems I can't barrel in and fix. "Actually, you might be able to answer some of my questions. I'm looking for information on Sydney's brother. Any idea where I might find him?"

"Braden Lacey? No, ma'am." She studies me curiously. "You might could ask the ladies in the office... or Mrs. Wambles whenever she comes." A quick wristwatch check, and then, "It's just a little more than an hour now... till we're done for the day. We've gotta get back inside for our last rotation."

"Do you know Braden?"

"Well, not much. He dated a cousin of mine one time. I couldn't tell you how to find him."

"I see." I let the silence stretch. Silence bothers people. They feel a need to fill it. With information.

"I mean, last I heard, he was living over in Antlers with his grandmother, old Budgie Blackwell. That family's got land all over three counties. They used to raise tons of cattle, but maybe they quit after Budgie got old. I really don't know. Budgie's husband died way back years and years ago... and their one son, too. Both of them got carbon monoxide poisoned in a hunting cabin way up on their land someplace."

"Oh. That's awful." I go silent again, waiting for more information. If the Blackwells are property owners of means, with a ranch down in Antlers, it's even more inexplicable that no one would be tracking Braden's whereabouts and that Sydney would be in Talihina, in a foster care situation. How did that happen?

"But then I heard Old Mrs. Blackwell died and the government took a bunch of her land for the park, so now they're broke, and she had to be buried in Oklahoma City because it's free, since she was in state politics way back when."

"I see." That tranche of factoids is at least 80 percent nonsensical. No land was taken from private citizens for the park. We haven't put anyone in the poorhouse, and I doubt that former state politicians get free burial plots in Oklahoma City. "So . . . you don't know where Braden has been living recently?"

"No, ma'am. I mean, I heard he was workin' for Parker Construction and living out there at the equipment yard." Her eyes dart off. She pinches an earring, plays with it. "They don't look alike—Braden and Sydney. They're only half relations. Braden's redheaded as all get out. Not a *little* red in the sunlight, like yours. I mean, *real* red. You'll know him if you see him."

"Good tip. Thanks." I adjust my ball cap and make ready to slip away without attracting the kid herd again, since they've forgotten about me. Even Sydney has finally wandered off.

"Sorry I'm not more help." Joanie checks her watch again, takes a couple of steps toward the playground, then stops to look back. "Is he in trouble? Braden?"

"Do you have reason to think he is?"

"I just hope not, that's all. I never heard he was bad or anything. Kind of quiet and brainy, into military stuff, but nothing bad. He isn't . . . is he? Into anything bad?"

"Not that I know of, but I would like to talk to him about a vehicle left in one of our parking lots." I hand her a business card. "If you think of anyone who might know where to find him or his grandmother, could you call me? Or if you're able to get a message to him, have him call me directly."

"All right." She tucks the card away for safekeeping. "You might give Mrs. Wambles one of those."

"Good idea. Thanks for the help."

We part ways, Joanie rounding up the kids while I proceed to the playground gate. A nearby lilac bush comes to life as I reach for the latch.

"Hey, Lady Ranger," it whispers. "Over here."

I stop, rest a hand on the fence. Sydney partially emerges, squeezing herself between the greenery and the church wall, to avoid line of sight from the playground.

It's funny, but not, but it is. "I heard you say Braden's name. You find him at the park?"

"I haven't. But I would like to talk to him about a car that was left in one of our parking areas, a Ford LTD belonging to your grandmother. I'd also like to talk to her about it. Do you know where she is under medical treatment or how I can reach her?"

"No, ma'am. Nobody tells me anything about that stuff."

"Have you heard from Braden since you and I talked at the overlook last week?"

"Nope. But he's probably just workin' a lot. He's gonna pay a lawyer to bust me outta the Wambles's place. He promised."

My confusion level creeps upward a bit. That doesn't sound like a kid who'd head to the woods to do himself in. He was making plans. Promises. "I saw a picture of you two in the car. Did he say he was going camping in the park . . . or say anything about exactly where he planned to be, or for how long?"

"Nope."

"You told me the other day you thought he might have gotten lost."

Sidling along the fence, she checks to be sure the coast is clear. The playground has gone quiet, other than the rhythmic tapping of a metal flag clip against a pole.

"He said he might be gone awhile." Cupping a hand beside her mouth, she adds, "He's treasure hunting."

"Braden is?"

"Yeah."

I'd discount that as tale telling, per Joanie, except that Sydney seems so earnest about it. Her brown eyes widen with enthusiasm. "Braden's gonna get the treasure and make some money. Like, *tons*. Then he won't have to work for Parker anymore, diggin' ditches, and mowin' grass, and helpin' at the rock quarry. He's gonna get his GED and skip senior year in Antlers High School. Then we'll move over to

Ada, and he can go to East Central for college, unless if he gets in army flight school. Either way I'll be out of the stupid Wambles house. That place is—"

"Sydney Potter!" The shout is so shrill and sudden it jerks us to attention like string puppets. I turn to see a dilapidated twelve-passenger van, of the sort that might've once been a hotel shuttle, pulled to the curb. A heavyset woman in a hot-pink muumuu and tennis shoes traverses the sidewalk at a goodly pace. From the salt-and-pepper bun and the authoritative manner, I'm guessing this is Mrs. Wambles.

Glaring at Sydney, she stabs a finger toward the building. "I do *not* know *what* you think you are doin' out here, but you better *git* your sassy little self up in that buildin' right this dang minute!"

Sydney flees like a gazelle, leaving me alone to face the wrath of Mrs. Wambles.

Fortunately, the wrath disappears as quickly as the kid.

"I am sorry, Officer." The muumuu woman presses one hand to her chest, chubby fingers outstretched, her head tipped forward so-licitously. She can't be more than five feet tall—a good eight inches shorter than me—but her voice packs a punch. "I am Myrna. Myrna Wambles. It's so good to meet ye-ew. I am so, so, so sorry for that little mess there. She should not have been botherin' you. No she should not. We've only had her a couple weeks, and hadn't got her lined out yet. It takes patience. Lots of patience. That's what these kids take. Lots of patience till they settle."

"I'm sure."

Peering up at me, she tries to decide whether I'm buying the ten-der act. Sweat glistens under a thick layer of pancake makeup. Fetch-ing a wadded Kleenex from her dress pocket, she mops up a bit. "And at first, oh Lordy, they will walk up to any-*body* and ask about their mamas, or their daddies . . . or when they can go home. They'll tell all *kinds* of stories to get you to take them places or buy them treats. They'll latch on to anyone. They all started callin' me Granny years ago, because they are *that* terrible lonesome for family. But I am sorry, so, *so* sorry, Officer, that she bothered ye-ew."

I'm possessed of a sudden, fierce need to defend Sydney, maybe get in a minor swatting match and wreck Myrna's fresh manicure. I grip the gate instead, because of course I know better. "I asked her a question, actually. And she was no trouble. It was my fault she didn't go in with the other kids."

"Do say?" Mrs. Wambles draws back, eyeballing my uniform. I have a feeling she's just realizing I'm not city police or county sheriff's office—as in someone who'd be checking up on complaints about a shelter. "A question?"

"Yes."

"Oh, honey!" Cackling, she tosses her head. The Kleenex hand flops down and lands, damp and squishy, over my fingers on the gate. I'm revolted. "Oh, darlin'! You cannot listen to a word that one says. She is very manipulative."

CHAPTER 10

Olive Augusta Peele, 1909

The valley is bounded on the west by the Buffalo and Potato Hills
Mountains, the latter having a sawtoothed appearance against the
western skyline, on the north by the Winding Stair Mountain.

—GOWER GOMER, 1938. INDIAN-PIONEER PAPERS COLLECTION.

The thing about the elves is, they ain't elves at all. Maybe I wondered again for a minute when I saw their camp. They live in a big tree that's old as these hills. Its twin trunks grew up side by side till they joined into one. Where the roots push out of the ground, Tula and Pinti and Koi tunneled the dirt and built a pretty good dugout shelter. With dead branches, stripped bark, and cut pine boughs laid over it, the place is real cozy.

Elves in a fairy book would have a house under a tree like this, but these kids used to live in a cabin with their ma and pa, plus their granddaddy and grandmama. Their ma was Choctaw and their pa was part-blood, and the land was theirs from when the government divided up the Choctaw parcels a few years back. The land was hilly and not good to farm on, so their pa took to hunting wolves and coyotes and turning in the pelts for bounty money. Plus, they hunted deer, trapped rabbits, caught fish, and gathered other food from the woods. Sometimes they were hungry a little, but they never did starve.

A sickness came one summer, and the old folks died right off and then later the ma. When they lived with only their pa, a man came and said the judge in the new court had wrote a paper that the three kids couldn't stay with their pa alone, and the man was there to take the kids off to a school, where they could get educated and have good food every day.

Their pa didn't like what the man said, and so he told the kids to sneak off to the woods and stay there while he traveled to Poteau to see about the judge, and maybe get a wife to help keep the family.

That was the last day they ever saw him. The stranger man stayed in their house. For a while, Tula would sneak back at night to take eggs from the chicken coop, and nipi shila jerky from the smokehouse, but the man got a dog, and when the dog barked, the man shot his gun, so the kids ran off. The man and the dog tried to track the kids, but they kept running and walking a far piece, and wound up here at the Twin Sisters Tree. That's what I named this place after Tula told us the story yesterday.

Tula says they see other kids like them sometimes. That spot where Nessa and me held up under the rotten log, and Tula, Pinti, and Koi scared us—it used to be the camp of two brothers who were mixed-blood Choctaw. They taught Tula about getting food from the train and the Good Woman's house. But one day they disappeared.

"Tula says they're gone on the train, maybe. Them brothers," Nessa tells me as we sit together in the morning chill, while overhead the Twin Sisters Tree lifts her branches to a pink sky. "Or the man got 'em." Nessa adds a worried frown.

Tula looks up from picking twigs and leaves out of Pinti's hair and tossing them into our little morning fire. She's already told us that sometimes there's a man at the Good Woman's house, and when he's there, you don't dare go near. He's tried to catch these kids once already. Tula says there's other men around who catch kids, too. She heard about it from those two brothers who disappeared.

The Twin Sisters Tree might look like a storybook, but it ain't one. Hunters roam the valley. Child hunters.

That's why I know Nessa and me can't stay around here long enough to work my plan and find somebody who'd take our six nickels in trade for food and traveling supplies. It's too risky. Tula hasn't got any people looking after her like I hoped, and at the Good Woman's house, the man came home last night.

"Time for us to move on," I whisper to Nessa.

Koi's tummy grumbles, and he grins like it's funny, then while he's got everybody looking, he belches and grins again. "Fesh?" He swims a hand through the air, then brings it to his mouth. I just got him saying *fish* yesterday evening, and he taught me nvni, which is how the Choctaws say it. We used the hooks and lines from Daddy's rucksack to rig a pole and catch perch, then we ate a right fine supper of three small fish and six fat crawdads, plus boiled eggs and some berries.

"Fish 'n' tr-ain." Tula nods in the direction of the train tracks, then makes legs from her two fingers and walks them down her arm. She circles her chin toward all of us with a big ol' smile. "Fish 'n' tr-ain. Kil-ia!"

Her grin falls when I shake my head. "Nessa and me can't go fishin' or to the train with y'all. We gotta be moving on."

"Fish 'n' tr-ain," Pinti pops out, then slaps a hand over her mouth and giggles like the words feel strange in her mouth. Her and Nessa been cooping up together and chatterboxing every chance they get, making dolls out of twigs with leaves for clothes. "We . . . go."

Pinti's got *we* and *go* down for sure. Between us learning their words and them learning ours, we're getting better at talking already.

"We go!" Koi jumps up and lands like a frog, which fits, since he never holds still. "We go! We-go! We go-oh-oh!"

The sound echoes up through the big tree, and Tula clamps a hand across his mouth. The worry that passes over her only makes me more sure that Nessa and me can't stay here. This place ain't safe for three kids, much less five.

I lean back and grab Daddy's rucksack. "Nessa, you tell them today's our day for moving on, and that's that." I talk slow on purpose, because Tula hears a whole lot more English than she speaks. "Tell them we can't go fishin', but I can leave them a couple fish hooks and lines from my pack, and I'd be awful happy if we could have some matches from their tin, since all ours got wet and ruined. We don't need a bunch, just five or six to get us through a few days."

Nessa sulls up and crosses her arms. She's got herself a new friend and ain't happy to leave. She's never had a friend before, except her sister, Hazel.

"Nessa Bessie, you *tell* them what I said."

Turning her face away, she pokes her nose into the air.

"Well, I guess you can just stay here ... then. I won't miss you one bit. I ever come back this way again, I'll stop in and see how you're farin'." But I picture myself alone in the woods at night. Tales about the giants and the k<u>o</u>wi an<u>u</u>ka asha, the little people that live under rocks and trees, come to mind. Plus bears, and panthers, and coyotes ... and bad men. "That is, if the witches or boo hags or elves don't get you first. Just 'cause these kids ain't black-eyed elves don't mean there's no such thing."

I make a show of opening my pack and sorting out fishing hooks. *You mark my words, Ollie Auggie,* Daddy whispers in my mind, *the first rule of relations with mankind, womankind, horsekind, and any other kind is to get folks to do your bidding by making them think it's their own wants. Every critter looks to its own wants first. No shame in it. It's just what's true.*

I dillydally with fishing lines and wait for Keyes Radley's first rule to work itself out, because it will. Daddy was the rightest person I ever knew.

I've poked myself on the hooks, plus Tula has started helping me before Nessa finally speaks up and says our piece. Tula never looks away from the fishing goods. She wants those real bad.

Her voice is soft when she answers Nessa's question.

"She, after we fish, says," Nessa tells me. It takes me a minute to switch the words around. Nessa sometimes lines them up in a different way now, like the Choctaws do.

"Well, all right, but tell her to bring some extra matches along. Once we catch a few fish down at Ship Rock, we'll each take some, then trade matches for fishing lines and be on our way. We best not stay long by the creek with the Good Lady's mister at home." I don't say it, but I've got a trouble feeling about today.

That bad feeling covers me like a shadow while I follow Tula and the other kids back down to Ship Rock for our last fishing trip.

Something's not right. We all see that soon enough. The game trail through the cedars is wider than it's been, and once we hit the mud, there's no mistaking hoofprints. Lots of them. Shod hooves and barefoot hooves, both.

Riders have been all around the brush patches, the creek, Ship Rock, and even the sandbar where the kids play. Tula points across the water. The tracks travel up another game trail that leads straight toward the Twin Sisters Tree.

"That ain't good." I'm glad I carried all our things with us, planning to leave out from here. "Y'all can't go back up there. Not for a while anyhow." I grab Tula's arm when she squints in the direction of their camp. "Whoever's riding around here is hunting something... maybe hunting some*body*. From up on that ridge, they could see you down at the creek."

We sidle back into cover and sit there, looking and listening. Even Koi is quiet. He blinks at me and holds his tummy, and I know he's starved for some breakfast. We shouldn't have eaten everything we had yesterday.

I try to think on a plan, but I'm hungry, too. It's hard to think when you're hungry.

Tula points off toward the Good Woman's house and makes finger-legs and walks them across her arm.

"We can't *go* there," I whisper. "The Good Woman's mister is home, remember? Just as likely *he's* the one been riding around your trails this morning already. What if he circles back to the house while we're over there getting food? He'd catch us and then..." I don't know what might happen then, and I don't like to think about it. "Y'all can't be near that house till he packs up and leaves again."

Nessa tells her all of that in Choctaw, but Tula waves off what I said. Then she makes more hand signs, and the meaning's real plain.

Not all of us together. Just you.

"You want *me* to go over there? Well, I ain't doing it. No, sir, no, ma'am. Nobody can go there with the man home. You said so yourself."

Tula's mouth puckers, and she snatches the empty flour sack poke that's stuck in my sash, shakes it in her fist. She sweeps a hand in front of her face, does the same to my face, then pinches the lace on my ribbon sash dress and gives it a tug.

"Tr-ain," she says. "Men." She acts out the way the men threw rocks at her but gave me food.

"Like at the water stop," I whisper.

She nods slow, and all the while our eyes stay knotted together.

"I might could." I can't even believe I'm saying it. "Maybe that'd work. I could use my same story from the train." The only trouble would be if Tesco or Gowdy's been by here, but that don't seem likely after what happened at the river. Maybe the folks in the house would even sell me the supplies Nessa and me need for traveling. That's worth a risk, even a big one.

We make a plan for Tula and the rest to go farther down the creek and see if they can find someplace safe for fishing. I'll try the Good Woman's house with my tale of the runaway calico pony, and then we'll meet back here at high noon, but stay hid in the brush, in case somebody's up on that ridge overhead. If everything goes right, which I hope it does, we'll have some food goods to split.

Before we part ways, I hold Nessa's hands and say, "Now you listen at me. You do as Tula says today, all right? And be careful. And if you see any men, run into the woods. You hear?"

"You comin' back, Ollie?" Tears shine in her eyes, and I'm glad to see she doesn't want to part ways with me, after all. Even if she did make a new friend in Pinti, I'm the one who knew her the longest.

"Course I am." I try to sound sure about myself. "I wouldn't leave you, Nessie, okay?"

"Okay, Ollie." But Nessa's shaking her head at the same time.

"I'll be back. Promise."

"Hazel promised, too." A drop runs over her bottom lashes and down her cheek, silvery in the morning light.

It shames me that I never thought about how much she must've missed Hazel these past weeks. Hazel was her sister, and they loved each other.

I wipe her cheek with the palm of my hand, hold it there. "Hazel couldn't help it. She'd never go and leave you behind on purpose." A lump swells in my throat, because even though I don't want to believe it, I know the only reason Hazel would leave Nessa behind is Hazel's dead. "But, Nessa, listen real hard. If something happens—it won't, but if it does—you don't let *anybody* take you back to Tesco Peele. He is a bad, bad man. You understand? If you ever get caught, you tell them you're Tula's sister. Make up a name, but don't say Nessa Peele or Nessa Rusk, you hear?"

She sniffs and rubs another tear against my hand, and I hope she's big enough to understand all that.

We go opposite ways, till we disappear from each other. Before I leave the creek, I sneak down under the water oaks and wash my face and hands, comb my hair with my fingers, then take out my bonnet and put it on and tie a nice bow under my chin. I smooth my dress best I can and even black my scuffed-up boots with a half-burned stick from under Ship Rock.

Once I look respectable enough, I climb the bank and start through the scrub and brambles. Cottonwood trees pop and rustle along the water, and I feel alone in the wide world, but it's a bad kind of alone. I think about bears and panthers and bobcats and bad men and child hunters.

The more I walk, the more dangerous the plan feels.

"Radleys always figure a way," I say, like Daddy used to. "You are Olive Augusta Radley." That name tastes like honey in my mouth. I'll never be Olive Peele again. I hated that name as much as I hated Tesco for making me use it. He said if I told anybody he wasn't my real daddy, he'd whip me into next week.

Now I can say it all I want. *Olive Augusta Radley. Radleys always figure a way. Olive Augusta Radley. Radleys always figure a way. Olive Augusta . . .*

When I step up on the porch and knock, I nearly let those words slip out at the opening of the door. "I'm—" I catch myself, then say the first thing that comes to mind. "Hazel Rusk. Good mornin'! I am so, so very terrible sorry to trouble you . . . ummm . . . ma'am . . ." I stop and grab a breath soon as I see it's her and not her mister. There's a baby on her hip. It gurgles a oatmeal-drippy smile at me. "Oh, good mercy! That is the cutest little . . . is it a girl? Those blue eyes are too pretty for a boy."

"A . . . a what . . ." The woman blinks at me like she'd sooner have expected to see a circus elephant on her porch.

"And those eyelashes. My lands!" My knees go stringy, and my words shake more than I'd like, but I've learned a lot from serving lemonade and tea cakes in Mrs. Lockridge's ladies' parlor. I know all about the chatter women make together. "What's her name?"

"Beau. It's . . . he's a boy."

I play peekaboo behind my hand with the baby, and he giggles. "Beau! That was my granddaddy's name. What a dear man he was. Straight up and godly as the day is long. Charitable, too."

The woman stretches side to side, looking past me into the yard and trying to figure how in the world I came to be here at this hour of the morning . . . and why.

Not good to let folks wonder too much, Daddy warns in my head. *Wonderin' gets them suspicious, and they start explaining things with their own minds. You tell them what to think. You write the tale, Ollie Auggie. That's how it's done.*

"I am so regretful for taking up your time, and I can see that I have interrupted breakfast." I say that last part to Baby Beau, and lean close, and he giggles again. "But I have walked quite a distance, and I'm afraid I am in a terrible fix."

I tell her about my sick mama back at home, and how I was headed to Talihina to get a special medicine for her, and some supplies for my baby brother, and how it fell to me to do it, my father being away working on the railroad. And, yes, I know the way, of course. Why, yes, I have done this before, but this time my daddy's pack pony, which I was riding, got spooked by a copperhead snake and threw me off and ran away with all my traveling provisions, except what's in my rucksack.

"So, I guess as you can see, ma'am, I am in a terrible fix. Otherwise, I would never, ever bother a stranger." I flatten a hand to my chest like the ladies do in Mrs. Lockridge's parlor. "Although I do believe a stranger is only a friend you have not yet made acquaintance with, don't you?" I follow on with a sad face and let my chin quiver like I'm trying not to cry.

It's working, I can tell. The woman looks me up and down, from my good lace boots to my ribbon-sash dress. It's mud spattered and wrinkled, but getting dumped from a pony explains that.

"You poor child." She's got real sweet eyes, sort of a golden-brown color. She's not a comely woman like my mama, with a tiny waist and a face like a china doll. This lady's big built and *coarse headed*, as Tesco would say, but I catch myself wishing *she* was my mama. I remember having a mama like this. One with clear eyes that smile at you, steady and strong and kindly. "What's your papa's name, dear?"

"Mr. Keyes Rr-Rusk."

"And where have you come from?"

"Up the valley from Adel. About a day's ride." I spit out the first thing that comes to mind from Daddy's travels. He went to Adel to trade for a horse once. "On a little farm."

"On a farm, but your papa works for the railroad?"

"He does both farmin' and railroadin'." *Pay attention to your mouth, Ollie.* I've let the story grow so many legs it's running all over the place.

"What does he do for the railroad, child?"

"Puts water in the trains." I make sure not to squirm at all. "And coal."

The woman nods and smiles. One front tooth's crooked sideways, so there's a gap in the middle. "My husband may know him. Mr. Grube is quite involved in the railroad brotherhoods." Quick as a whistle, she turns over her shoulder and hollers into the house. "Mr. Grube, would you kindly come to the door? A girl here needs our help."

Before I can even say not to bother her mister, here comes a man.

CHAPTER 11

Valerie Boren-Odell, 1990

It is said that all animals have some outstanding weakness. The bear is no exception. He, too, has his weakness. There is no danger to which he will not expose himself when a feast of wild honey may be had.

—GOWER GOMER, 1938. INDIAN-PIONEER PAPERS COLLECTION.

The Saturday evening business looks brisk at the Sardis Shores Café, even though the place is out of the way for the growing herd of nature enthusiasts checking out the new park. I'd anticipated pulling in to see only a few local cars, maybe a fisherman or two coming off the lake. The evidence of a supper rush causes me to sit indecisively twiddling the car keys, wishing I hadn't let Charlie cajole me into driving over here. I'm not in the mood for noise this evening. Or company. Or human communication.

It's been a long day at the end of a six-day workweek, going on seven. The full moon and a heat wave, coupled with violent thunderstorms, have whipped up a surge of what feels like mass insanity. My quiet new job has seemed more like the summer rush at Yosemite— five cases of heat stroke on hiking trails; a middle-aged equestrian who tried to swim her horse across a rain-swollen water crossing and nearly drowned; a temporarily flooded campground; branches down everywhere; three calls for skunk removals; one rattlesnake relocation far, far away from the campground bathrooms; a massive rockfall event that took out one of the new hiking trails; and a mama bear who's decided the easiest way to make a living for herself and her three cubs is to raid coolers or cars. She slashed her way into a tent and left behind a perfect Z, which has earned her the staff nickname Zorra the Bear . . . unofficially, of course.

I was the one who jokingly called her Zorra, and the name stuck. Naming a bear you'll probably have to target for relocation is against policy, but the fact that my moniker sticks is a slight sign of approval from my new co-workers. Being insanely overtasked has also made them more willing to hand over jobs like attending to minor medical emergencies, lecturing campers on fire safety, and monitoring naughty bears.

Frank Ferrell has gone on medical leave, which has helped improve my situation, as has the fact that I'm no longer the most recent addition at Horsethief Trail. Edwin Wilson, our newbie as of two days ago, is just a year out of school somewhere in the Northeast and is as green as a spring leaf. He and his young wife have moved far from the family home in New Jersey to begin the arduous quest for a full-time-with-benefits ranger job, which generally involves multiple relocations and working your way up. Edwin's wife is a photographer who has fantasies of plying her trade in the backcountry of the Yellowstone or Rocky Mountain National Park units. She and Edwin remind me of Joel and me, back in the day. Wildly in love. And just wild.

They're living in a tiny single-wide mobile home, just like Joel and I did. Shellie has done her best to make it cozy. She's also lonely, and happy to babysit Charlie anytime. That came in handy when I sensed an unscheduled shift coming on, during which I'd be doing an introductory patrol with Edwin. Today was complicated, and the hours got long. Tomorrow I'm on weekend patrol with Edwin again, hence tonight's conciliatory catfish dinner with Charlie. Now that we're here, I'm so tired I can hardly face exiting the car and going in.

"And Shellie can draw *all* the Transformers and the Ninja Turtles. And Smokey Bear, too. It's so awesome," Charlie can't stop chattering about the day with Edwin's wife. "She's gonna teach me how."

I feel the vague sting of having missed Saturday morning cartoon time, and then the afterburn of working-mom guilt. "I'm glad it was fun. You can never have too many Smokey Bears, right?"

"Yea-uh!" He stretches the word with enthusiasm.

My head lolls against the seat. "Hey, did I tell you we've got a nuisance bear in the park?" Charlie loves wildlife stories. "She slashed a Z in a tent, so we're unofficially calling her Zorra the Bear. Zorra like Zorro, you know?"

"Or Zorra the Zombie Slayer, like in the movies." He does creepy fingers at me, wherein I give him the stink eye.

"How in the world did you hear that? You're not allowed to watch scary movies. Ever."

"I know," he sighs. "Somebody told me about it at daycare is all."

"Future reference, anything with *slayer* in it is totally off-limits."

"Ice cream slayer?"

I stand corrected.

"Sock slayer?" He props a foot onto the dash. The hole in his sock heel is so big I can see his grubby ankle above the sneaker.

"You are that. Charlie Joel Odell, Sock Slayer. It has a ring to it."

Laughing, we exit the car while Charlie tries out more *slayer* options. The game continues, the two of us jostling and teasing until we sink into a booth with a view of the lake. Outside the window, the full moon rises over the trees, swollen and red-orange, vibrant and clear. I breathe in the serenity of stars and silver-tipped water as I pull off the NPS cap I forgot to leave behind when I changed out of my uniform. The cap might smell faintly like skunk, or I might. A few scrutinizing gazes seem to turn in our direction.

"Does she got a radio collar or a tag?" Charlie prods me from my absent-minded reading of the room. I'd been entertaining the thought that Curtis might be here. I'd like to ask if he's heard any updates on Braden Lacey. I've been too busy all week to dig into it much. A stop-by visit to the Parker Construction headquarters—where Braden was reportedly living and working—yielded little new information.

Alton Parker, the owner, seemed oddly unconcerned about the whereabouts of his young employee. *Boy's a flighty sort,* he said, rocking back in his chair to counterbalance a midsection that tested the fabric of his Parker Construction polo shirt. *Likes to go off in the woods sometimes. He'll turn up when he's ready. Kid's nearly eighteen. Not a crime for a man to go missing, is it?*

Not if it's by choice, I admitted, but my skepticism must've shown, because Parker assured me that as a close friend of Budgie Blackwell's, he knew Braden very well, and had been finding work for *the boy* to keep him *out of trouble.* Parker wasn't concerned about Braden spending time in the woods, and I shouldn't be, either. Budgie wouldn't have a problem with it, though she would have *chewed his butt* for forgetting to lock the car and take the keys. Last Alton Parker had heard, Budgie was undergoing some specialized medical treatment out of town, but hadn't offered any details. She was very private about it.

I asked if I could take a quick look at where Braden was living, in case he left a note or other information, and Parker shrugged, pointing out the window toward a portable office shed nestled between a defunct bulldozer and a backhoe with a missing tire. *Help yourself on your way out,* he said, and so I did.

The shed, hot and stale inside with the window air conditioner off, smelled of old grease and a chemical odor I couldn't identify—bug spray or herbicide, maybe? A quick search yielded nothing but a few used food containers, an empty spiral notebook on a crate upturned for a nightstand, three Parker Construction T-shirts thrown over a chair, and one pair of cargo pants folded on the narrow cot-style bed. The only thing specifically connected to Braden was a pay stub from Parker Construction. Forty-four hours labor, $4.50 an hour, so Braden had been working full-time before he decided to check out. Other than that, his life was a mystery.

"Mo-m-m-m," Charlie protests my lag in the conversation, drawing me back. "Does she *got a collar?*"

"What . . . collar . . . who?"

"Zorra the Bear. Does she got a radio collar or a tag or a BIMS report? Because if she was in trouble before, she would, right?" A worried look follows. He knows that a bear who becomes too comfortable around humans only gets a chance or two at relocation and monitoring. Two strikes, maybe three, and you're out.

"Nope. Zorra didn't have a record." *She does now.* Zorra's first Bear

Information Management System report went in this past week, but I don't share that with Charlie.

His lips purse as he exhales a comfort breath. "That's good."

"For sure." Propping an elbow on the tabletop, I rest my chin on my hand and lose myself for a minute in looking at my son. He is so cute, and his tender spirit shines through the silvery green eyes that are a Boren family legacy. Daycare and babysitters or no, he's more open and unstressed now than he has been in a long time. My dad would approve. Here in this place with just the two of us, there's no pressure to stop asking questions. Stop openly wondering about life, and the world, and how everything works. Stop being himself.

The freckles on his nose compress as he squints at me. "Mom?"

"What, buddy?"

"I don't need a haircut yet."

"Huh?"

"A bath, okay. Not a haircut, though."

"W-what?" A laugh puffs out. I have no idea where this is going.

"'Cause that's how you looked at me, like—" Rising to his knees, he juts his chin in a comical imitation of my scrutiny.

"I'm looking at you because you're *cute.*" I tussle the unruly blond curls.

Ducking away, he grins. "Cute like Zorra the Bear?"

"I don't know if Zorra's cute. I haven't seen her yet. But I don't imagine she's cute if she's slashing a hole in your tent in the middle of the night to grab your groceries."

"Only dummies put their groceries in the tent."

"Hey, that's not a nice word. We don't call people that."

"Except it's true. Tie the food on a tree branch, or keep it locked in a bear can. Put rocks in the tent, and if Zorra the Bear comes"—he acts this part out—"you throw the rocks and say, 'Get out, bear!'"

The performance grows loud enough that it draws eyes our way from a large group of what appear to be local folks gathered for Saturday evening victuals. They're making a goodly racket themselves, but judging by the narrow glances, Charlie and I have annoyed them.

I put a finger to my lips, giggling. "Use your inside voice."

Charlie rolls a puzzled look toward the loud table, then asks permission to go to the restroom. ". . . just *me* by *myself*," he finishes. He's at the age where I struggle not to apprehensively hover outside doors, thinking of NPS reports about perverts stalking campground bathrooms. Parks are not exempt from society's problems; in fact, pavement brings those things to the countryside.

"All right. Hurry, though." Fortunately, the facilities here are singles with locking doors.

Off Charlie wanders in his big-guy mode, head bobbing as he checks out the weird assortment of wildlife art and bric-a-brac on the walls.

The waitress shows up, and her smile is familiar. "Hey! I remember you," Joanie from the church playground remarks cheerfully. "Lady Ranger."

"Just ranger. We don't make any gender distinctions. Not if we can help it."

"Awesome. That's *boss*. For real. Every place oughta be that way." Joanie offers a look of female camaraderie that brings to mind Mr. Wouda's comments about the generations of scandalous women who blazed the trails before us.

"You're right. Every job should be that way. But I guess we change it one place at a time, right?" I hope the day arrives when younglings like Joanie can chart any career path they want without having to fight just to do the work, and men like Frank Ferrell and Chief Ranger Arrington no longer get pats on the back for shoddy work and bad choices. Ferrell closed the file on the bones before he went on leave, and Arrington is so busy dealing with his own problems he was happy to let it go with a wink and a nod. Unless some new piece of information comes in, that's the end of that. The superintendent is probably relieved, as well. I'm angry in ways I am too busy to contemplate.

"Darn straight," Joanie agrees, then we get back to business.

I order the kids' catfish for Charlie and the chicken-fried steak special for myself, compensation for Fritos-and-soda lunches on the run all week.

"You got it!" Joanie twizzles her pen, then points the clicker at me. "Hey, I thought you were coming back to talk to the kids at vacation

Bible school. My girls are outdoors kids. They might could be lady rang— I mean *rangers* in a few years."

I'm taken aback. Joanie can't be more than twenty.

"I'd be happy to talk to your girls sometime, but I was only at the church last week to ask about Braden and the abandoned car."

She nods grimly. "I guess since Budgie Blackwell's down sick, Braden's got one of the cars from the ranch. Budgie's real particular about her things. She'd have a hissy fit at Braden if she heard about the car being left like that."

"Didn't you tell me Budgie Blackwell died and the burial was in Oklahoma City?"

Joanie blanches. "I hear so much stuff around here, I forget who said what." Leaning closer, she adds quietly, "You might could talk to Alton Parker . . . at the construction company? He's been a friend of the family for a while, I guess."

"I have. Mr. Parker seemed of the opinion that Braden needed a little time to himself and would show back up for work when he was ready."

"Hmmm." Skepticism is written all over that very short response. My tired brain perks up. "Well, I guess Parker oughta know. He or Mrs. Wambles. She tell you anything?" Casting an over-the-shoulder glance toward the table of locals, she shifts her weight foot to foot.

"Like . . ."

"If she knew where Braden went after he came by her place Wednesday a week ago?"

Braden was at Myrna Wambles's a week ago Wednesday? So, theoretically not long before he left the car in Keyhole Loop lot? Interesting that Myrna didn't mention it. "Did Mrs. Wambles tell you that?"

"No, but Sydney was bragging about it at the church. I think it's real sweet that Braden wants to get a place so he can look after his little sister."

"That's a lot of pressure for a seventeen-year-old." The heartbreaking dichotomy hits me as I watch my son wander aimlessly back from the bathroom with seemingly not a care in the world.

"It's sad." Joanie absently jiggles the collection of pens in her apron pocket. "I think Sydney heard me saying to the church ladies that I wanted to rent out the little camper behind our house. She might've thought her and Braden could move in there. Sydney is always workin' the angles."

"Hey, Mom?" Charlie pipes up as he slides into his seat.

"Just a minute, buddy."

"But, Mom—"

"Charlie, in a minute. Joanie and I were talking." I give him *the look*.

Unfazed, he turns to our waitress and sticks out his hand for a shake. "Hi. My name is Charlie J. Odell. I'm seven."

Clamping my lips together, I smother a laugh. Where did he come up with that?

"Glad to know you, Charlie J. Odell, seven." Joanie returns the handshake. She tells him that she has a daughter his age, and maybe they can play together sometime.

"I like girls okay," Charlie allows.

"Well, she's pretty much a tomboy. A tomboy and a cowgirl, so she likes to do boy stuff and ride horses."

Charlie pops onto his knees. "I like boy stuff *and* horses! My mom had a patrol horse in Yosemite once. I only sort of remember 'cause I was little, but there's a picture. His name was Blackie, and—"

"Okay, Charlie, that's probably enough. Joanie has work to do." While there are a plethora of Blackie tales to be told, most of them cast an embarrassing light on me. Blackie was the world's most hapless patrol horse and had a mind of his own.

"Oh-kay." Charlie sinks reluctantly into his seat. "Hey, Mom? What's a pine pig?"

Joanie's eyes go wide. My mouth drops open and my skin boils. Joanie and I stare at each other before I swivel toward Charlie. "Where did you hear that?" *Pine pig* is the sort of term that gets thrown around by lowlifes you're about to ticket for public intoxication, smoking weed, or poaching in a national park. *Pine*, as in park ranger. *Pig* as in police.

Joanie is clearly familiar with the term, which means it's being bandied about town.

"That guy over there told me it." Charlie points across the room at a bearded dude in a ripped-up T-shirt. "He said, 'Your mama a pine pig, boy.'"

"He *what*?" The sow bear in me rears her roaring head. "He *said* that to you?"

"And then he asked if I was a pine piglet." Sandy-brown brows rise over innocent green eyes.

My teeth grind together. I shift to slide out of the table, but Joanie's in my way. I know I shouldn't get up. Members of the public can dish out all the name calling and bad attitude they want, but we are not supposed to return it. Ever. That kind of blunder can lead to chief rangers and park superintendents having to write simpering apology letters to congressmen whose constituents have bellyached about bad behavior by a federal employee.

"Don't pay them any mind." Joanie keeps up the blockade. "They're just a bunch of idiots. When I was a kid, they hollered about the government damming up Jack Fork Creek to make Sardis Lake, and it'd kill all the fish. Then after there was a lake, they hollered that the government was going to let Tulsa and Oklahoma City suck all the water out of the lake—well, might be right one of these days. They also hollered about the highway getting repaved, I can't remember why, and then about the tolls going up on the Indian Nation Turnpike."

She flicks a narrow look over her shoulder. "They've been hollering about all the new stuff with the park since the very first big public meeting. They said it'd take away the logging work and put all the post companies and pulpwooders in Push and Le Flore counties out of business, and Washington politicians don't know jack, and would stand around hugging trees, and outlaw clear-cutting timberland while the pine beetles ate everything down to the ground and then a fire burnt what was left. They said the government wouldn't let dozers come in to put out the fire, just like what happened in Yellowstone Park, and it'd burn fifty thousand acres or more. I thought Congressman Watkins was going to snatch himself bald before that meeting was over."

I rest my hands on the table, breathe. "We have all the tools for proper land management, and of course we'll clear-cut acreage if the

trees are diseased, but if the forest is healthy, we'll insist that the timber companies practice uneven-aged cutting, letting some of the
shelterwood stand and ..."

"They're never going to listen to you," Joanie warns.

"They need to hear it."

"They're stuck in their ways, especially about new things ... or
outsiders. Trust me. You'll end up like Congressman Watkins, wanting to pull your own hair out. And that'd be a shame, because you've
got real nice hair. It's so thick and a pretty color, like Julia Roberts. I
wish I had your hair."

She shrugs toward the rabble-rousers' table. "I don't know who's
been stirring up all the talk against the park lately, but that bunch
over there is just ignorant and cranky. They'll get used to Horsethief
Trail eventually. For now, it's best if I just tell them they shouldn't
have said that to your little guy. That it was mean and they need to
tone it down."

"We *know* how to manage a forest," I grind out. After the week I've
had, I'm on my last nerve, and now it's smoldering.

She lays a hand on my arm. "Please don't start a wrangle, okay?
Pretty please? We can't afford to lose regulars, especially not locals
that come year-round. The owners need the money, and I need the
tips. How's about I bring y'all a free strawberry shortcake?"

Charlie perks up. "I didn't care if he said it, Mom. I like pigs. Pigs're
smart, ex-pecially wild pigs. They live in twenty-three United States
now, but they'll get in all fifty pretty soon. Pigs have babies very fast.
That's what I told the man."

I want to laugh and cry and hug him all at once. Instead I tell
Joanie, "You don't have to bring us a strawberry shortcake. It's not
your fault. Thanks for offering, though."

"But it's my *favorite*," Charlie interjects, which isn't true. Choco-
late pie is his favorite.

"You got it, pal." Joanie gives him a high-five and leaves, dining
room brawl averted. A few minutes later, I see her talking to the ki-
bitzers' table. I hope it doesn't cost her tips. I should've just told her
to let it go.

Turning to the window, I watch the moonlit water resting in a silver-rimmed pitcher of pine and post oak, elm and cypress. The night and the scene are too beautiful to be wasted hating the people across the room. Hate is a thief that will steal everything and return nothing if you let it.

I'm glad when the complaint department clomps off to the parking lot just as Charlie and I are finishing up. Joanie insists on bringing us two strawberry shortcakes to go.

"You need your leftovers boxed, too?" she asks.

"Please." Across the room, a teenage worker drops an empty salad bar container, and the noise sparks a thought. "Hey, I ran across a tribal police officer here the first night Charlie and I came in. Curtis . . . something."

"Enhoe. Curtis Enhoe."

"Any idea how I can get ahold of him . . . without bugging him at work, I mean?" Joanie looks a little too curious about the request, so I add, "I thought he might know someone who could take charge of Braden's vehicle, if it comes to that. With the weather this past week, plus the park dedication ceremony and tours for politicians and whatnot, I've only been able to drive by a couple times to monitor the car. I'll leave it in place for now so Braden won't be stranded if he returns, but it can't stay there forever."

"I could try to find you somebody." Joanie offers sympathetically. "But if you want to call Curtis, grab one of the phone number slips off that flyer on the bulletin board. That's his. The blue paper about puppies."

Charlie picks that exact moment to surface from finger-sampling his dessert. His thick brown eyelashes fly upward. "We're getting a *puppy?*"

CHAPTER 12

Olive Augusta Radley, 1909

Just the menfolk went to town. The women gave them a list of
what they needed and the menfolk bought it.

—JOE M. GRAYSON, 1937. INDIAN-PIONEER PAPERS COLLECTION,
INTERVIEW BY GRACE KELLEY.

He ain't a mean man, the Good Woman's mister. Don't know if
he's a nice man, either. I ain't figured him out yet. I was scared that
soon's he had a look at me he'd decide I was a stray and run me off,
or worse. But all he saw was a little girl in good clothes, with mannerly ways.

That's what I am to the Good Woman and her man. He's Mr.
Grube, and she's Mrs. Grube. And that's how they call each other,
too. I don't know anybody's first name except the baby, Beau. I don't
aim to be around long enough to find out, but I can't leave till I get
my calico pony back.

Mr. Grube's been tracking old Skedee since yesterday. Said he
heard from a freight wagoner that there was a rangy Texas pony running loose around here, still wearing a pack saddle, halter, and dragging a broke-off lead rope. Poor thing had blood trails down both
flanks, where a panther tried to get him. If somebody didn't catch the
pony soon, it'd either end up as food, or snag the halter on a tree and
break its neck trying to get free.

That's how I know Mr. Grube ain't a bad man, even if he does have a temper. Big as he is, he could break an axe handle in two, but he doesn't want that pony to die. Especially now that he knows who it belongs to.

"We get him in the mornin' now, ja?" he says while we sit with the night lamps burning. Mr. Grube talks like the German who shod the Lockridges' saddle horses, but I think he's something else, not German.

"Yes, sir. We will." I stack blocks on the braided scrap-cloth rug for Baby Beau to knock over, and I try not to think about Nessa. The best I could do for her was to sneak away with a few of the lunch scraps while the Grubes worked in their crop fields. I tied the scraps up in my flour-sack poke and put it where Tula and Nessa would spot it when they came hunting for me. "That naughty calico pony will find the bait food and hay you left out, Mr. Grube, and we'll have him caught. All I need is to get close to him. He knows to come to me."

"Ja. Dat is good." Mr. Grube goes back to rocking in his chair and smoking his pipe. I hope those hoofprints at the creek were from him tracking Skedee, and I hope that while I'm out hunting Skedee, nobody's out hunting kids.

But Nessa and me need that pony and the goods in those packs. It's worth any chance I have to take, even leaving Nessa in the woods without me.

"I do wish I could go along to help," Mrs. Grube says. "I cared for the horses in my father's stable when I was a girl. I loved them so."

"You got the baby to be tendin'. You are his ma, ja?"

Mrs. Grube's face goes red and blotchy. I already figured out she ain't that baby's mother. She told me she just married this past fall. She must've got a husband and a baby all at once, because that baby looks like him.

She goes back to knitting with fine mohair yarn. She's making socks. She's got a basketful by her chair already. Don't know how they'd need so many socks, but if she ain't busy with farm chores or the baby, she's reading or knitting. Mrs. Grube ain't a idle woman.

Mr. Grube likes that about her. He watches what she does sometimes and nods to hisself.

"I only wish to help, Mr. Grube." She's getting peevish now.

"You got the cow, and the chicken, and eggs, and the hoein' in garden, and the onions for picking."

"My goodness, *such* important things. Heaven forbid they wait a day or two." Her hands and the knitting drop to her lap.

"Wife . . ." Mr. Grube slaps his chair. "Nee. We'll speak no more of dat."

Baby Beau goes to fussing and I hop up real quick, because I want out of there. "I can get him in a fresh diaper and put him down for the night. I'm good at babies. I'd be pleasured if y'all would let me do it." I pick up that rolling-fat boy and cuddle his head under my chin. "I surely would. And I believe I'll turn in myself, if that's all right. I'm wore out after that good meal."

"Certainly," Mrs. Grube answers. "Yes, that will be fine. And thank you."

"Oh, it's me who's thankful to *y'all* . . . for all the trouble over me. You folks are surely helpin' out a stranger in a fix. The good Lord will mightily bless you for it. Yes, he will."

I sweep Baby Beau away to the small closed-in porch off the back of the house, where his cradle is. Mrs. Grube has set me up on a little rope-tie bed in there. With the warmth coming off the back of the stone fireplace, I should be snug as a speckled pup, but Nessa's on my mind, so it'll be hard to sleep.

Baby Beau doesn't fuss when I lay him in the cradle to rock him and sing the lullaby songs my mama sung to me when I was a little girl in Kansas City, and Daddy was gone soldiering. I like to think of her the way she was then, not how she is now, pale skin laid like sheer cloth over bones, her eyes so far away most days they don't even see you.

When Beau nods off, I blow out the lamp and sit on the rope bed, my head rested against the warm stone wall.

". . . the most wonderful letter from Everly Waters," Mrs. Grube is saying. "You remember—I've told you of her, I'm certain? Everly was my dearest friend back home in Oklahoma City. We were at St. Joseph's Academy together, before my father suffered his terrible difficulties."

"I think you said dat, Mrs. Grube, ja. Everly . . . a strange name, dat is."

"It was a family name, I do believe."

"What does dat letter say, Mrs. Grube?"

"Well . . . the most exciting news, and . . ." There's a quiet spell, while Mr. Grube's chair groans and the iron poker stirs the fire logs right behind my back. Mrs. Grube waits till he's done before she goes on. "Why, it's news that has implications from here to Oklahoma City and beyond."

"Dat so?"

"Indeed. The Oklahoma ladies have won acceptance into the General Federation of Women's Clubs, and come May, it will be official. National recognition for the ladies of our fledgling state! Isn't that quite something?"

"Dat so?"

"Yes." Mrs. Grube goes on about the women's clubs, and how there's women's magazine clubs, and women's literary societies, and women's charitable circles that'll now become part of the international organization, and powerful, too! Her voice gets louder while she talks about all these women who felt the inner stirrings of their underdeveloped powers, and now they'll have a means to chart those seas together and follow the call to a more enlightened and educated womanhood.

She chatters and chatters while Mr. Grube says, "Dat so?" or, "Ja." He ain't listening, of course. I can't blame him a whole lot, because she talks up a storm about how federated women believe in charitable work for the poor, and how they have speakers come to give education lectures for better minds, and how they're sponsoring a horse wagon library to go to the tiny towns where there's hardly a book in any home.

She sounds like the ladies at Mrs. Lockridge's tea circles. That's the kind of things they yammered about on the wicker porch chairs in their pretty dresses and fancy hats with colored feathers and flowers and ribbons. Mrs. Grube ought to be at the Lockridges' house instead of out here in the woods, taking care of a baby that's not hers and a man who doesn't listen.

I wonder if he's nodded off by the time Mrs. Grube says, "And Everly informed me a club is to be chartered right in Talihina! Can you imagine? Genuine advancements in culture and refinement, even in this far-off corner of the world? Only three days from now, they'll hold an official ceremony *in* Talihina. It's to be quite the to-do, with a visit from the Oklahoma Federation's mobile library and a political speech by none other than Miss Kate Barnard. She is an extraordinary speaker and making quite a name for herself as the state commissioner of charities and corrections. Do you know of her?"

"Ja." So, Mr. Grube is still awake, after all. "The Good Angel of Oklahoma, dat is how she is named by the Brotherhood of Railway Trainmen. We voted her to office for the first state legislature. She fights for workers, for the better life." He's more stirred up about that than I've ever heard him.

"Yes, indeed. I knew Kate Barnard as a young teacher. *Now* I wish I'd come to know her better. Who could imagine a woman elected to such a powerful position, and when women have no vote? It is simply magnificent." Mrs. Grube's voice goes loud enough to stir the baby, and I rock him with my foot while I listen. "I thought perhaps to go to Talihina for the festivities and reacquaint myself with her."

"Nee, Mrs. Grube. I have only one day before I am away on trains again for seven."

Baby Beau makes a whimper, and she stops to listen at him before she answers. "Good heavens, Mr. Grube, I've lost count of my days. They're all the same out here. But it is no matter; I can easily hitch up the horse and go on my own. And we've some supplies to purchase for the summer garden."

"Alone to Talihina?"

"The supplies will come at less expense there than in Albion, making it well worth the trip, and—"

"Nee, Mrs. Grube."

"*Mr. Grube,* I cannot sit *endlessly* on this patch of ground, with chickens and cows for company, and naught to occupy my mind or—"

"We'll speak n'more of it." His chair squeaks, and he gets up so fast it snaps back and hits the wall. I rock the baby harder. "These bein' just the sort of misthinkings dat comes of women gathering for prattle when they best be tending to the home and children."

"Did you *not*, moments ago, speak with admiration of Miss Kate Barnard, a *woman* elected to statewide office?"

"Dat Miss Kate bein' only a maid woman. Past thirty, and with no husband, Mrs. Grube. You bein' a married woman, the place for you is at home. I'll speak n'more of it!" He moves through the house like a bull, and a minute later their bedroom door slams shut.

Mrs. Grube sits up for a long time, her chair going back and forth, back and forth. When it finally stops, I slip under my quilt and pretend I'm asleep. She opens the door and stands there like she's thinking to bed down with Beau and me. I'm glad when she finally leaves, and the house goes quiet for the night.

Come morning, loud voices and pots banging around the cookstove waken me. First light has broke outside the window, and Baby Beau is gone from his cradle, so I must've slept deeper than I thought. The door's slivered open, and a blade of flicking lamp glow cuts across the room.

"Something must be done, Mr. Grube," she's saying. "Even *you* must admit that. Children cannot simply be left to fend for themselves in the wild. And there are more and more of them all the time. Children, off on their own. In the woods, following the train tracks, on the road, along the river."

"You'll niet feed them, Mrs. Grube. And I'll niet have them steal from us. Eggshells, I found near the creek. They have been in my henhouse."

"I threw the eggshells out for the birds and the raccoons, Mr. Grube, and the animals carried them off, no doubt."

"You'll niet give the children cause to linger. The railroad wouldn't like it, and the railroad is our livin' and our home."

"Yes, you've told me . . . in no uncertain terms—the railroad does not want them begging at the water stops and stealing from families in the railroad section houses. But one cannot expect children to graze on the grass and sleep in the field like wild deer. Perhaps if someone would investigate the problem of all these feral little ones, we could solve it at its source."

"Gather the thieves, and take them to the workhouses and orphan asylums. 'Tis right dat a man protect what is his own."

"And more little wanderers will come until we discover *why* this problem has grown so quickly. If I attend Kate Barnard's speech, Mr. Grube, I might speak with her and raise her awareness of the issue."

"The Indians will niet farm the land allotments to feed the families proper, and so dat is the trouble."

"Surely the Indians have for centuries had children and raised them quite admirably, or there would be no more Indians, Mr. Grube. It is also quite evident the Choctaw people, and indeed all the five tribes, have made a success of themselves here since being removed to Indian Territory. What has changed recently? *That* is the question."

"Many children must work for bread, Mrs. Grube. You work, you eat. No shame in it. The mines, and the mills, and the laundries have need of able hands."

"The mines, and the mills, and the laundries and factories are a scourge. I saw it myself in Oklahoma City after Papa's financial misfortunes lowered our standing. In the parts of town where the working class lives, the call whistles blow before daylight, beckoning the youngsters to their stations. Bone-thin waifs dragging their feet through the streets, toiling from dawn's breath to dusk's sigh. Everly reports that despite the state's new child labor laws, the employers often lie about the children's ages, or send them down south to states that still allow little ones to toil. I'd sooner see children live in the wild."

"Better there than on land of mine."

"Surely in this modern age we have the means to sort out the orphan problem without such cruelty. Everly writes that the clubwomen ..."

A chair scuffs across the floorboards. I hurry and stick my feet in my boots because I'm afraid Mr. Grube will go off after Skedee and leave me behind.

He's already out the door by the time I skitter from the bedroom, blinking and rubbing my eyes so Mrs. Grube will think I slept through their fight.

"Sit down for some breakfast," she says, and tries to smile at me. "He can wait."

"Oh, no, ma'am, but thank you, ma'am. I'll just take a biscuit and a bit of ham and get along. That rotten ol' pony might go after our bait food anytime this mornin'. I didn't mean to sleep so long, but that bed and quilt was just so comfortable. I thank you for your kindness." I stop at the table for a swig of milk from the cup that's been set at my place. "It's more charity than a careless girl like me deserves. You got a real big heart, Mrs. Grube."

"Take the sweater by the door. It's cold this morning." Turning her back, she rests her hands on either side of the sink. Her head sags between her shoulders, and I pretend I don't hear her sniffle. Instead, I tease the baby into a giggle and stuff my pockets with dewberry muffins, which I'll drop at the meeting place for Tula if I can. Then I put on the sweater and hurry to the barn.

Mr. Grube is already mounted on his horse and waiting. He reaches down and swings me up behind the saddle without saying a word. As we plod off through the mud, I think on what he said about getting the kids off his land. If Tula, and Pinti, and Koi stay around here much longer, he'll hunt them down for stealing eggs they traded for, fair and square. They can't keep living at Twin Sisters Tree.

The poke sack is gone from the hiding place where I left it, at least. A short piece of twine from Tula's dress hangs there to show that they made it back from the creek yesterday. I pull the dewberry muffins from my pocket and drop them into the cedar bush when Mr. Grube ain't looking.

While we wind through the brush and briar patches in the morning cool, I start thinking about how to get away from here with Nessa once I have Skedee in hand. I'll need to go on down the road a piece, then circle back somehow. I can't let the Grubes see me. Mr. Grube doesn't strike me as the kind of man you cross.

I'm still pondering that when he points to the spring pool where the bait food and hay was laid out. There's Skedee, regular as you please, helping himself. He's beat up, with scabby claw marks over the white patches on his flanks. The pack saddle hangs sideways, but it's in one piece, and so is my pony, and that's a wonder. He snorts and raises his head on catching wind of us, but perks his ears when I call his name. I guess Skedee knows he has got himself in a fix and needs help, because no sooner do I slide down from Mr. Grube's saddle than that calico pony limps over and puts his head against my chest to have his ears scratched.

"You old rascal," I whisper, resting my cheek against his forelock. "Don't you ever do that again, you listenin' at me?"

Today is your lucky day, Ollie, I say to myself.

But soon as I try to lead that pony out of the creek, I know I'm not quite so lucky as I thought. He's so stove-up from the panther fight and from being in the pack saddle all that time he can hardly walk. The trip back to the Grube place is slow, and it's plain enough that my pony won't be carrying any packs till those saddle sores get salved up and have some time to heal.

I can't stay here, but I can't leave, either.

It's a muddle, and I don't know what to do about it, but the muddle works itself out, as muddles sometimes will if you give them their own time.

With the pony caught, Mr. Grube decides he's tired of putting up with Mrs. Grube's mad, so he leaves out early to go catch the train for work. Once he's gone, Mrs. Grube says to me, "I've been thinking, Hazel, and given a day or so to rest and recover, that horse of yours should be well enough to make the walk to Talihina ... if he weren't carrying the pack load, that is. What I mean to say is, if the pack load were carried in the wagon. Then once you've finished your business in town, and with an extra blanket to pad the pack harness, your pony would be fit for duty."

"But ... how would the wagon get ..." I don't even finish before I look at how her eyes are fixed on that wagon by the barn, and I know what she's got in mind. She's going to that meeting, whether her husband says she can or not. I ain't sure it's a good idea for her, but I say, "Yes, ma'am. That is so. And since you can drive that wagon on your own, that's a right fine idea."

"Indeed." Mrs. Grube's eyes sparkle, and her crooked teeth make a big ol' smile. "I do believe it is the *best* idea. We'll depart day after tomorrow in the morning once we've fed all the animals and stocked up the hay and water and milked the cow. She has a calf on, so if she's not milked daily, it's no matter. We'll have a picnic at the old stone chimneys where Prairie Creek runs out of the Potato Hills, then cross the river at the ford, and travel on. I'll pack for a wagon camp in Talihina, as Mr. Grube and I often do. Then I'll return home after attending a women's club event that's to be hosted on the meeting grounds. It's to be quite the exciting gathering, Hazel. Not to be missed."

"Yes ma'am . . . if you're sure of it."

"I am."

"Right fine, then." I feel bad for the trouble I might be helping her into, but every mile toward Talihina is one mile farther away from Tesco Peele. And the next thing after Talihina is the Winding Stair Mountains, and home.

Only problem now is how to get Nessa on that wagon with me.

And Tula and Pinti and Koi, too.

Because none of us can be here when Mr. Grube gets back.

CHAPTER 13

Valerie Boren-Odell, 1990

I have studied personalities. It was part of an officer's training and work and I know human nature for by watching a man or knowing him for two or three days I can tell if he can be trusted or if he will bear watching.

—GEORGE LEWIS MANN, 1937, AIDE TO US MARSHAL, INDIAN TERRITORY. INDIAN-PIONEER PAPERS COLLECTION, INTERVIEW BY GRACE KELLEY.

The vintage sandstone home looks like it belongs on a postcard rather than across the street from an out-of-business auto repair shop. A pack of adorable black-and-white border collie puppies frolic under a sycamore tree in the fenced yard, which lends to my conviction that I'm at the right place. Curtis Enhoe's house appears as orderly as an accountant's desk, everything clean and tidy.

As weird as it is to show up here uninvited, every time I've called I've gotten a recording about puppies for adoption. Leaving a message seemed awkward, so here I am. I don't want to let this thing with Braden Lacey drag on any longer. Four more days have gone by with no progress. Joanie from the café left me a message yesterday, saying that Braden had missed another weekly visit with his sister, and she wondered whether I'd gotten in touch with Curtis. For reasons I don't want to contemplate, she wanted me to know she didn't mean it when she told me to watch out for him, in regards to Officer Enhoe. Curtis is *really a good guy*, and *about my age*, and has *been divorced a long time*, and the girl he was married to was *so citified and spoiled she would've gone running home to her daddy no matter who she was with.*

Next time I see Joanie, I will definitely let her know that my interest is job related only, but for now I'm reaching out wherever I can to pin down the facts regarding Braden's whereabouts and welfare. I've burned through every search mechanism available: department of motor vehicles and National Crime Information Center, state resources, county sheriffs' departments, and municipal jurisdictions regionally. Not a hit anywhere. Braden isn't in jail. He hasn't gotten a speeding ticket. He's not in a hospital. No one has filed a missing person's report on him, or for that matter, his grandmother. The powers that be at our county sheriff's department are confident that if Alton Parker vouched for the situation, I can take that as gospel.

I ran across one of Parker's crews out working on a culvert along the road and asked a few questions of the three men. The general response was *Braden is flighty and unreliable.*

"The boy's got some issues, y'know?" one guy said, winking at me while pretending to toke a joint. "He'll turn up when he feels like it and Parker'll hire him back. Family's friends, y'know? We been tryin' to line the boy out." Covertly, he cast a grin at his cohorts, and then they went back to leaning on their shovel handles.

"We find him, we'll let him know a good-lookin' rangerette's after him," another worker chimed in. "That oughta flush him outta the woods."

The innuendo was as galling as the dreaded *rangerette.* Rangerettes do dance routines and baton tricks in parades.

Locking my fingers around my duty belt, I resisted the urge to step closer and say, *Hey, speaking of weed, I think I just caught a whiff of something. That rangerette sense of smell, you know? You got anything in your pockets that shouldn't be there?*

I let it go instead. I was upwind of them, and couldn't really get a bead on the smoky-sweet scent. The guys being Alton Parker's people, I didn't want to make accusations and be wrong.

With all my other efforts coming up empty, my little blue puppy paper slip and Curtis Enhoe seemed like the best possibility left. He came across as a straight shooter in our brief conversations. Maybe even a nice guy. He knew the Blackwell family and had offered some concern about their situation. I didn't think he'd mind my catching him with a few questions.

Now I'm feeling awkward about stopping by, and find myself reconsidering whether this is an unwarranted intrusion on his personal time. Officer Enhoe ends my mental debate by appearing on the porch in his gray-and-black uniform, a soda in one hand, chips in the other, and his patrol hat sandwiched loosely under an elbow.

Dropping my flat hat onto my head to backhandedly indicate that this is an official call, I proceed to the antique garden wire fence, where he and I meet up. He rests his elbows on the gate but doesn't open it. "Joanie called me yesterday." His preemption catches me by surprise. "Said you were still trying to track down information about Budgie Blackwell and her grandkids."

"I am." I don't want to contemplate Joanie acting as a go-between. The last thing I need is an amateur matchmaker tromping around my investigation. "You heard anything?"

"Possibly."

Squinting as the midday sun presses under my hat brim, I wonder at his answer. Is he intentionally being coy? Has Joanie dropped some unwelcome hints about me? Or is there a territorial thing going on here? Federal law enforcement, tribal, and local don't always mesh. "And?"

"I did some checking, but I didn't come up with much." He runs a hand over his scrub brush hair and every last strand falls into exactly the same configuration. "I called a friend whose land neighbors Budgie Blackwell's place down in Antlers, asked him if he'd heard anything about her. He said no. He wondered if I knew where or how she was. The way he told it, old Mrs. Blackwell and those two grandkids were there, and then they weren't. At first, the neighbors assumed they went to visit family, or to a funeral. Budgie knew a lot of people in Oklahoma City from her politics days, and she had a couple sisters around Tulsa someplace—they might've passed on by now, though. Budgie kept pretty private about family stuff, especially after her daughter took up drugs and lowlife boyfriends and left

Budgie with the two grandkids to raise. Jade's issues caused a lot of embarrassment and lost Budgie an election. It's hard when you're a well-known name in town and your life goes wrong. People make hay of it, you know?"

A shadow flickers over him—empathy, sympathy, the sting of an old wound? Was that how it was for Curtis when the *citified, spoiled* wife went back to her daddy? People made hay of it?

"Last time I saw Jade," he goes on, "she was getting hauled out of the Choctaw Labor Day Fest in Tuskahoma, so stoned she couldn't see up from down. Sydney was a little thing, and Braden was a half-grown kid. There was a boyfriend involved, biker dude . . . and not the harmless type, either. First time I'd ever seen somebody hopped up on crystal meth. It took four guys to get cuffs on him. All the while, there was Braden, maybe ten or eleven, holding his little sister and bawling his eyes out. It was a sad deal."

"The worst kind." I picture the scene, even though I'd rather not. "When the kids are parenting each other, it tells you everything you need to know about the adults." Parks aren't immune to domestic drama. No place is. "Given that history, though, do you think Braden would leave his sister so he could go on a recreational junket in the woods? And while she's at a place like—" I bite back my critique of Myrna Wambles. "In an emergency foster situation? I mean, Sydney seems convinced that Braden was working to earn money and get her out of there."

One dark eye squints shut. Tiny crinkles line the rim. I form the impression that Officer Enhoe is someone who laughs a lot in his off-duty life. "You've got to be careful about investing too much in what Sydney says." He adds a rueful chuckle. "I ran into her when I visited vacation Bible school to see a couple of my nieces singing, and she told me you were going to make her a ranger helper for the summer and she'd ride around with you in your truck."

"She *said* that?"

"She was convincing, too." He adds a smirk. "That kid'll make a good living in sales someday. Or politics, like her grandma."

"Sounds like it." I don't know whether to be offended or amused.

"She also told me her brother has a treasure map, and as soon as they get the chance, they're going to go dig up the treasure and have all kinds of money."

"She told me something similar. But aren't they already well off . . . if they own all that land?"

Curtis shrugs. "Maybe. Maybe not. Lots of these old families have had their places since the tribal land was allotted into parcels eighty-five, ninety years back, or since homestead times, but there's not much ready cash coming in, especially if there's no oil and gas money. The surface brings in some grazing or leasing for cattle or hay. It's hard to make a living that way these days."

"I see." I'm reminded again of what an outsider I am. The tumble-down houses and sagging trailers around here tell a story. I just haven't wanted to hear it.

"Everything looks easier from a distance." He hangs his hat on the gatepost and fishes up a puppy that's tugging on his trouser leg. "You stand up on one of those overlooks, stare out over miles, it's like staring at a painting. Rich grass and timber . . . except for the clear-cut patches, that is. You spend a little time, focus in, you'll find the wide view is a lot easier than the narrow reality."

The words are profound enough that I find myself studying him while he bunches the fluffy black-and-white bundle under his chin, and croons, "You little rat. You eat one more uniform, you're outta here."

Glancing up, he catches me . . . staring. I quickly shift my attention to the puppy, afraid Officer Enhoe will see the deeper question running through my head. *Where does that perspective come from? Who are you?*

I take up the puppy's case instead. "How can you talk that way to something so cute?"

"You get good at it after a while. It's time for these guys to go." He tries to offer the puppy over the fence while it wriggles in his over-sized hand. "Here, you want him?"

"Oh no. No no no no no, nooooo." Lifting both palms, I retreat a step. "Joanie pointed out the puppies flier when I was in the café with my son. He hasn't shut up about it since."

"A boy needs a dog."

"Not this boy. Not right now anyway."

"These'll be good dogs . . . well, at least half, anyway. Their mama's a peach. Found her wandering around a convenience store a couple months ago. Not sure what the father is, but she's a full-blood border collie, or mostly. Dumped, I guess. Nobody ever came to claim her." He nods toward a weary-looking black-and-white dog trying to catch a nap under the front porch while puppies pester her from all angles.

"Poor girl." She lifts her head when I say *girl*, as if that's what she's used to being called. "I don't understand how people do that, just walk away from something instead of taking care of it."

"Me either." Curtis's face sobers, then he dangles the puppy so that its fat little rear swings back and forth over the gate. "They're really soft."

I cross my arms, shut my eyes, and shake my head. "If I pet it, I'll want it."

"That's the *idea*." When I crack an eyelid, his face and the puppy's are side by side. They're both grinning at me.

I can't help myself. I chortle, "S-stop."

"But it's working, isn't it?" All of a sudden, he has the impish look of the class clown in high school. I never would've guessed this to be part of his personality.

"Definitely-y-y . . ." I draw out the word, and I know I shouldn't because it sounds too familiar, or friendly, or maybe even flirty. Women in the military and law enforcement must resist blurring those lines. Always. He may be trying to blur the lines. He may be just a friendly sort of person. I have no way of knowing. "*Not*. Sorry, because I'd love one, but we're still in temporary housing at the Lost Pines Tourist Court. No place for a puppy."

"Mama dog's adoptable, too. She's low maintenance. And she loves kids—boys especially . . . about . . . yea high."

He means Charlie.

The handheld radio on my belt breaks in before I'm forced to produce an answer. "Five-four-nine . . . seven hundred. Five-four-nine . . . seven hundred. Ten-eighteen. You out there?"

Dispatch is routing an urgent call my way? Everyone else must be out of range or have their radios turned off, because nothing that important ever comes to me.

On the other end, Mama Lu is uncharacteristically breathless.

Grabbing the radio, I respond, "Seven hundred ... five-four-nine, go ahead."

I listen, vaguely aware of Curtis leaning closer as Mama Lu reports, "Somethin' of a critical nature that needs to be seen now. *Right now.*" A few things aren't to be spoken of over airwaves that can be picked up by anyone with a scanner. Dead bodies are top of the list. Reporters and curiosity seekers are complications you don't need while processing a death scene. Mama Lu goes on to do an impressive job of covertly letting me know that *the problem* was reported by off-trail hikers along a backwater not far from the waterfowl refuge. I'm snatching the notepad from my shirt pocket and trying to get my pen to work while she spills out a slew of details as if she were describing a live suspect. "You'll be looking for a male, no shirt, camo shorts, missing his shoes, at least from what they could tell at a distance. They got out of there pretty quick. It was a bad deal. Poor thangs."

Mama Lu's drawl stretches the news like chewing gum. Then she apologizes for sending this to me, but she hasn't been able to raise any of *the guys,* except "... our summer boy, Roy, but he's not certified, and the new fella, Edwin, but he's at home. He wouldn't know where to go anyhow. He just started last week."

My jaw stiffens at the fact that Mama Lu feels compelled to apologize for asking me to do my job. It's even harder to abide coming over the radio, and in front of a fellow law enforcement officer. "But I called both of them," Mama Lu assures me. "And I'll get them up there soon's I can, with *supplies.* The hikers will meet you at the trailhead. They're pretty shook up, but they'll tell you where to go, hon."

I clutch my pen hand over my forehead. "Ten-four. I'm ten-seventy-six from Talihina."

"All ri-i-ight, hon ..." Lu's uncertainty echoes off every word.

"Five-four-nine, out." I shut down the conversation before she can call me *hon* one more time.

"Mind if I tag along on this one?" Curtis asks. He has soundlessly deposited the puppy and slipped out the gate. His posture is all business.

When I don't offer an immediate affirmative, he hesitates. "Not trying to get all over your turf, but I've got a bad feeling I know who that might be."

My mind speeds immediately to Braden Lacy. Blood drains from my face, hands, feet.

Curtis's head tilts as if he's wondering at my reaction, but he doesn't inquire. Instead he says, "I'm missing a motorist from a couple weeks back. Some local boys got it into their heads they could drive through a flooded low-water crossing. Two were enrolled Choctaw Nation. Two weren't. We pulled a passenger out of the front seat, still belted in the truck, drowned. Plucked one from a tree downstream. One made it to the bank on his own. Still haven't found the driver. Truth, I was hoping he ran off somewhere and he's been staying gone on purpose. I know the family. They'll be pretty broken up if it's him."

"Man, that's hard. I'm sorry." Drowning calls are tragic in any number of ways, the worst being that the victims frequently come in multiples and try as we might, we can't always locate the bodies. "Crossed my mind it could be Braden Lacey. We've had some serious rains lately, and that's down water from where he left his car."

"I hope you're wrong." Curtis meets my gaze, and a taste of grief passes between us, a brief sensation like a scent on the wind—one potent enough that it harbors for an instant in your mouth. As quickly as it's there, both of us close ourselves to it. There's no other choice.

"We'll find out." I turn toward my patrol vehicle.

"Behind you," he says, and in truth I'm glad. Whatever we find in that backwater, it won't be pretty.

My mind shifts to clinical mode because that's how it's done. Get to the scene, secure the scene, process the scene. Photos, measurements, grid, notes, sheriff's personnel, body bag, transport to morgue, death notification, incident report.

Step-by-step, like marking off a checklist. You can't let yourself slide down the well of imagining your own eyes staring blankly skyward as that sturdy zipper closes out the light, the air, the world. You can't let yourself picture your family receiving the news. You must not contemplate the fragile veil between life and death, clear like glass, so that you can be face-to-face with it, and never even know.

Under the porch, the patchwork dog lifts her head and looks my way. Rising, she moves about the yard protectively gathering her wandering young, as if even she senses the lifting of the veil.

CHAPTER 14

Olive Augusta Radley, 1909

It took courage to be a clubwoman in those days. Customs were
not, as we so casually take them now.

—Tabatha Milner, 1929. Texas Federation of Women's Clubs newsletter.

The stars have barely grayed out, and the sky's pinking with the
coming sun when I back the Grubes' horse twixt the wagon shafts.
Mrs. Grube hooks him on, but then she just stands there knee-deep
in the fog, looking around the farm. Maybe she's thinking what Mr.
Grube will do if he finds out about this. Half of me wants to get on
the road before she changes her mind. The other half worries that
she's got us starting out a lot earlier than she said. Unless I can slow
her down some, the plan I made yesterday with Tula and Nessa will
go wrong. Bad wrong.

Mrs. Grube unties Baby Beau from the sling where she carries him
on her back, and she gives him a long kiss on the head. Squaring
herself up, she says, "Well, I guess that's everything."

"I could check all the hay and water one more time before we go."

"We'd best get on with it." She nods toward the wagon.

I climb into the seat and she hands me Baby Beau, and then up she
comes and takes the lines, chucking the horse to get him moving.
Skedee fights his lead rope at first, plowing furrows in the dirt with

his hind hooves, but he's no match for the wagon. We roll forward while Mrs. Grube worries her lip, and I bounce my knees under Baby Beau's bottom to get him giggling, so maybe Mrs. Grube won't commence to talking again. She has wore me out, jabbering about the Federated Women's Club and Kate Barnard and all the politics in the new state legislature up in Guthrie.

I've got bigger troubles to think on, but Mrs. Grube's chatter has been taking all the mind in my head since yesterday.

We're barely round the bend before she starts again. "We'll go the first three hours." She squints at the dawning sky from under the wide-brimmed farm hat she's put on for the trip. Her good clothes are hanging in the wagon with mine, washed and ironed. I helped her do all that yesterday, and she fixed me up an old blouse and skirt to wear. It's big enough for two of me, but we just rolled the sleeves and skirt waist, and Mrs. Grube made me a yarn belt to cinch it in. With one of her hats over my head, I look almost like a old woman that shrunk inside her clothes. Not a living soul would know me if they drove right by.

"Then a stop for lunch at the old rock chimneys, where Prairie Creek flows down from the Potato Hills." Mrs. Grube goes right on talking. "From there, we travel to the ford, cross the river, and go the remainder of the way. Have I told you that already?"

"Yes, ma'am." That woman is jumpy as a grasshopper on a griddle. She should be. "Seems like a real sensible plan and right pleasurable, too. There's nothing so balmy to the spirit as the sound of runnin' water. It's like quiet, only prettier."

"Indeed." She snaps the driving lines and chucks up that poor old horse. "And I must say, Hazel, you do have a lovely way with words for someone your age. Your parents must have you reading quite a lot at home."

"Oh, yes, ma'am. We love a good story." *That ain't a lie.*

"I simply adored my well-read students. I was a teacher for some years before coming here to marry Mr. Grube."

"That's a real fine occupation for a lady. None finer. Maybe I'll be a teacher someday. I haven't gave it much consideration, thus far yet."

"What a wonderful idea. Or a librarian perhaps? Why, with the

Oklahoma State Federation of Women's Clubs on the mission, we'll have libraries everywhere one day. But until then, a wagon library can serve the purpose. A town without a library is no town at all."

"I'd like to be a library ... what did you call it? A library-anne someday ... I think." Really, I don't know what a library-anne is, but I have seen a library *room* at Mr. Lockridge's big house, and it's a eyeful. I'm guessing a library-anne dusts all those books.

"What are some of your favorite stories, Hazel?"

"Well, my daddy knows quite a few, since he meets lots of folks in his travels. And I know some Choctaw ones from a old man I helped in a horse barn sometimes. Anybody ever tell you about the Soul Eater, or the white-people-of-the-water, or the little people of the forests? The Choctaws call them the kowi anuka asha, and they look just like people, but they only stand high as your knee and will throw a rock at you in the woods, mostly just to tease you, though. Now, Impa Shilup, the Soul Eater, he's more of a worry. All you have to do is think bad thoughts and he climbs right inside you. He can get anybody, anytime, anyplace ... not like the white-people-of-the-water, which the Choctaws call oka nahullo. They're only around lakes and streams, but are see-through like glass, so you can't hardly spot them before they grab you and ...."

"I don't know that we need to talk about such things while we're traveling." A shudder ruffles her gray wool shawl, and she pesters the wagon horse again. "Indeed, I was intending a discussion of literature. What do you like to read, Hazel?"

That poor old horse would slow down if she'd just let him, so to take her mind off the driving, I answer, "Well, ma'am, I do like *Black Beauty* very much ... and *The Adventures of Mabel*." I try to think of what other books Teacher read to us in school. She only had a few, and we couldn't take them home for ourselves. "And there's *McGuffey's Reader*. And, of course, the *Blue Back Speller*. And there's the Good Book. That's what we read at home mostly."

"How wonderful that your parents encourage it. They have certainly raised you into a sharp-minded, capable girl of fine character."

"Thank you, ma'am. It pays to have good parents."

"Yes. And so many children have none. That is the subject on which I must dialogue with Kate Barnard and the reason I am determined to reacquaint with her, though I know her time in Talihina will be highly coveted. This explosion of feral children is simply ..."

"*Rebecca of Sunnybrook Farm!*" I pipe up to get her mind off orphans. "And *The Wonderful Wizard of Oz*. Now that's some books I'd like to put my hands on." I've stood and looked at those two books in the Lockridges' library room and had to keep my hands behind my back, since those belong to the Lockridge girls, and you don't touch their things. Sooner or later, they'll outgrow them, just like the two nice dresses I got and my lace boots. Mr. Lockridge likes me special, so it pleases him to bring me pass-alongs from his girls. "But those books are real new. Costly and such."

"Well ... those are *somewhat* new publications. I read them to my students when I was yet teaching."

"That must've been real enjoyable ... for the kids, I mean. I'll bet you made a fine teacher, Mrs. Grube."

"In some ways." Her smile falls. "I did have great love for my students, but it was a lonely life, teaching and caring for a sister who is lovely, but frail, and a father beset with business difficulties. I wanted a family of my own. Unfortunately, once a woman drifts past a certain age unmarried ..."

That sentence ends over a bump in the road and stays hanging. "Well, you got a family now. You got this handsome fella." I hold Baby Beau's chubby hands and clap them together and wonder if I would've done that with my own little brother if he'd lived. Then I remember, he would've been half Tesco Peele's. I don't know how to think about that, so I don't. "And you and Mr. Grube might have more to go with him, soon enough."

"I would have thought so." Propping her feet on the kickboard, she leans forward while the horse lugs us up a hill. She turns her face away.

I mark it in my memory not to talk about babies.

Awhile later, as we rattle along the Old Military Road with the Potato Hills on one side and the Kiamichi River Valley on the other, Baby Beau drifts off to sleep, and I lay him in a padded crate under the shade of the wagon canvas. The time stretches out then. The road has more folks on it. We pass a wagon, plus some farms, and train section houses, and settlement stops, and then two men on horseback. I go stiff, and so does Mrs. Grube. More than once, she feels for the shotgun racked under our seat, then she pushes the horse into a trot till we're out of sight.

When we come into Albion, she pulls her farm hat down low, not looking left or right. I tuck my head to hide my face. It feels like every man on the street and every woman tending a garden or sweeping her yard stops to watch us. I look back at Skedee following behind the wagon, and think, *People won't know me in these clothes, but what if the word is out about a missing medicine hat calico pony?*

Sweat runs under my borrowed blouse. It's too late now to change the plan with Tula and Nessa. *It'll work,* I tell myself. *It has to work.* But over and over, I look toward the Potato Hills and worry.

"We might could slow up some so's not to rattle Baby Beau while he's sleeping," I say after a while. Somehow, I have got to make Mrs. Grube quit pushing that horse. "Maybe you could tell me *The Wonderful Wizard of Oz* to pass the time. Since you know it, I mean. It'd make our ride go by easy."

"Goodness, but what a shame to spoil it for you, though." She turns my way. Her face is sweaty and pale as milk because she's bad nervous, being out on the road like this. "After the library routes are established, perhaps you can take it from the library to read yourself."

"Oh, no, ma'am, you don't touch the books in the library. Those belong to whoever *owns* the library. You don't dare just go in and take it."

She gives me the sidewards eye. "The public library isn't *owned* by anyone, Hazel. It belongs to the community. Surely, your parents have taken you to the library. On a visit to a city, perhaps?"

Careful, Ollie, I tell myself. "Oh, yes, ma'am. I plumb forgot, being as it's been a while. But I figured since there's no library on *this* road, you might favor us with a book review." In the ladies' parlor at the Lockridges,' one of the women stands up and gives a book review whenever there's a gathering. I like to hide and listen at those. Mr. Lockridge knows I do it, and he doesn't care. One time he saw me and just patted me on the head when he passed down the hall.

Mrs. Grube laughs, and it's the first time she's done that since I knew her. "What a wry wit you are, my dear. Well, then, let me see … once upon a time in Kansas, on a quaint little farm, there lived a lovely child about your age, and her name was Dorothy. Because she was an orphan, she resided with her kindly aunt and uncle. She was a good girl, but she had rather a dreamy mind about her, and thusly went on many an imaginary escapade with her little dog, Toto, by her side. One day while she was out about the farm, looking to stir up an adventure, why you will never imagine what happened."

"What?"

She goes on with a tale that's tall as the ones my daddy used to tell. There's a scarecrow that talks, and a man made out of tin, and a lion that's afraid of everything, and witches, but they're a different kind of witches from the Choctaw witches Tesco Peele is scared of.

I forget all about the passing miles and worrying about Tula and Nessa and the little kids. The Potato Hills go away, and my mind is far off in the fields of Oz. The horse slows up and the wagon quiets. Mrs. Grube doesn't even check the gun when we pass by other folks. She just talks, and talks, and talks.

We stop once to change Baby Beau's diaper cloth and clean up a big, stinky mess. It takes a while to get him fixed and rinse the dirties under the water barrel, then hang them off the back of the wagon, downwind.

"I'd be pleasured to hear more of the story," I say when we start out again. "You are a right good teller."

She goes on with all Dorothy's troubles crossing rivers and falling asleep in a field of poppy flowers and almost winding up dead because the flowers smell pretty, but they're poison. Dorothy gets chased by Kalidahs, which have a tiger's head, and a bear's body, and sharp claws. When they try to get at Dorothy, I think of old Gowdy and Tesco Peele and men who hunt children to send to the mines and the mills. I give a cheer out loud after the Tin Woodman chops through the log bridge and dumps those Kalidahs into the water.

Mrs. Grube laughs her breath away, then catches it and says, "And then guess what . . ." The story goes on with more troubles and rivers, which makes me worry again about getting Nessa and the kids into this wagon before we cross the Kiamichi. Truth is, it's all the same difficulties being a orphan in Oz as it is in Oklahoma.

We're right in a whole mess with Dorothy and the Cowardly Lion locked in the castle of the one-eyed wicked witch when Mrs. Grube steers the wagon off the road. We bump down into a clear place along Prairie Creek, where the stone chimneys from a burned-down saw-mill still stand along the bank. "We're here quite early for lunch, but I do believe I'm ready for a respite. What about you, Hazel?"

My mind comes whirling back like that tornado carrying Dorothy clean out of Kansas, and I land in a whole different place. "Oh . . . yes'm. My mercy, that's a good tale!" When I hand over Baby Beau and climb down off that wagon, I can't find my feet at first.

Mrs. Grube nods and smiles. "We mustn't dally too long with our picnic. We have the river ford to worry about yet, and we've a dis-tance to travel after that. I want to arrive in Talihina in plenty of time to stake a camp before the space fills. Kate Barnard draws hundreds, even thousands, with her oratory."

"Yes'm." I study the field around us and then some thorny honey locust brush past that, and the cane grass along the creek, and the Potato Hills, but what I'm hoping for isn't out there. If I don't figure a way to hold Mrs. Grube over long enough, I'll have to part com-pany with her. I can't cross the Kiamichi River without Nessa.

I start whistling while Mrs. Grube lays out our lunch in the shade uphill from the creek, and I water the horse and Skedee from a bucket. After that, I carry Baby Beau back down to the creek to see the minnows. He claps his fat hands while I whistle my tune, and then some bird calls, and then some more of the song.

"That's quite lovely, Hazel," Mrs. Grube calls. "Not too close to the water now. Do be careful down there."

"Oh, yes, ma'am." Looking toward the hills, I whistle my call of *chuck-will's-widow, chuck-will's-widow,* loud as I can.

I listen out. No answer.

Mrs. Grube tells me to come up the hill for lunch, and I dawdle much as I can getting there. I nibble at my food, and play with the baby, and nibble some more, and even get Mrs. Grube to talking about the women's club and politics. When that plays out, which takes a while, I lay back on the blanket and jiggle Baby Beau in the air and say, "It's so pretty here. I feel like I am right by that river in Oz, don't you? We might could finish the story here, don't you think?"

"We'd best get on." She squints up at the sun. "I'll tell more of it on the way."

"Oh, but just for a short while, could we stay? Look at those cotton clouds. I see a pig, and a elephant, and that one there is surely the Cowardly Lion. Don't you think that one looks like him?"

"I suppose it could." But she's getting up and dusting her skirts. "You watch after Beau while I see to my necessary," she says. "Then you'd best do the same, and we'll be on our way. No more stops until we've arrived in Talihina."

My heart goes to thumping. Mrs. Grube being off in the brush might be my only chance to throw the pack on Skedee, grab my things from the wagon, and sneak away into the hills to look for Nessa and the others.

"Yes, ma'am, but could I go first? I need to pretty bad. I don't think I can wait. Also, can I take Skedee down to the water and let him get a good, long drink while I'm over there?"

"You watered him from the bucket before our picnic."

"Skedee never drinks much from a bucket. Silly old thing."

"If you must."

While she folds up the picnic quilt, I take Skedee and walk through the brush to the creek and whistle, and whistle, and whistle.

Nobody answers.

"Hazel?" Mrs. Grube pesters after a while. "Come on up now."

"He didn't drink all he wants yet."

"Hurry him along, please."

"Yes'm!"

But I don't make it quick, of course. I whistle and pace and look down the creek.

I am jumpy as a cat when I hear Mrs. Grube pushing through the scrub brush. "Hazel, really . . ."

I close my eyes and whistle one more time, loud and long, then listen as the wind carries my call into the distance, where it echoes off the sawtoothed hills.

Just when it dies, I finally hear a nightjar's song. *Chuck-will's-widow, chuck-will's wid-dowww, chuck-will's wid-dowww.* Three times.

The thing is, a real nightjar don't sing in the noonday.

CHAPTER 15

Valerie Boren-Odell, 1990

Incident commanders, supervisors, commissioned employees, and their coworkers must all be conscious of the potential for critical incident stress when an employee is exposed to incidents that cause them to experience unusually strong emotional reactions which have the potential to interfere with their ability to function.

—National Park Service Law Enforcement Reference Manual.

"Slow up. Watch where you're walking," I call ahead to Roy and Edwin. "Any evidence on this trail probably washed away in all the rain, but if there is something here, we don't want to blow right by it."

Roy shoots the thumbs-up over his shoulder as the two of them make their way up the muddy track ahead of me with the packable litter. Edwin wears the flat, orange backpack that holds the folded sling portion, and Roy totes the center wheel and assembly. Extracting a live victim from a foot-traffic-only location is no small task. Extracting a body is far worse. Even though the prelim interview with the hikers delayed us at the staging area, Curtis and I, along with Roy and Edwin, are the only responders on site so far. Roy and Edwin must've broken the land speed record to grab equipment from the rescue cache and reach the trailhead.

We'll end up working through our grim task with personnel from the sheriff's office. Parallel investigations: NPS investigates the death. The sheriff's office and medical examiner look at the cause. Oklahoma State Bureau of Investigation could be called to assist if evidence points to a homicide. Since I don't know how the interface between jurisdictions typically plays out here, I've chosen to come prepared.

Despite the rough terrain and high-water debris from floods along Holson Creek, Roy and Edwin bulldoze their way forward, in a rush to get to their first death investigation. Push into an area too quickly, and you run the risk of contaminating the crime scene or missing something you should have noticed.

Quick equals careless.

Curtis must be thinking the same thing. He has slowed so much that he's disappeared from the trail behind me.

"Roy, Edwin, hold up a minute. I see something down there," I call, because I'm afraid to send them ahead to secure the scene while I slog off-trail toward a drainage area that has morphed into a significant backwater slough. The smells of decaying biological matter, moss, and microscopic life envelop me as I work my way downhill, the muck seeping over my boots. Something blue winks at me from beneath a raft of bubbling slime, and I'm so focused on trying to make out what it might be that I miss a step and almost end up in the mire.

"Need help?" Roy pops off, chuckling like we're having a silly college drunk together.

I want to snap, *Hey, you forget why we're out here this afternoon, Roy? Body recovery. Show some respect.* But Roy and Edwin are the closest things to allies I have at Horsethief Trail, and even though their inexperience shows, they mean well. I probably made flippant comments like that myself, once upon a time. Joel and I probably both did. The jokes are a defense mechanism, a way of preparing yourself to experience something you haven't before.

"I'm all right." Mud oozes through my clothes, warm on top, cold underneath, tugging me downward like an undertow. I'm up to my knees in it before I can find a piece of driftwood long enough to reach the unnatural hint of blue.

"What're you after in there?" Curtis has caught up with my crew.

"Not sure. I'll let you know once I fish it out."

"Need anything?"

"Nope. Stay on the trail. It reeks down here."

I snag the blue thing, lose it, sling slime, catch the tantalizing wink of color again. Nylon. A strap of some kind . . . with printing on it. White. Gold. Probably just flood junk, but it could be connected to the deceased. If we move on without retrieving it, it might sink beneath the surface and be gone for good.

My snag finally holds, but the upward heave is an astonishingly heavy lift, the strap either caught on debris or attached to something. With the sludge under my feet slithering downhill toward the water, I feel like I'm wrestling an anaconda and standing on it at the same time.

A guttural growl wrenches from my throat. A wad of moss and dead leaves the size of a volleyball breaks free, my driftwood pole jerks upward, and my quarry sails over my head, showering me with swamp juice on the way. Groaning, I drop my stick, shake the goo off my hands, and wipe my mouth on my shirt.

Curtis and Roy hurry to investigate my find as I trudge toward its landing place.

Squatting down, Curtis clears away moss with a pocketknife. "No wonder this was heavy." He slides the knife blade under a loop of nylon webbing that looks like it could be a dog leash or a . . .

"Lanyard?" I move in for a closer look. A key ring with a half dozen keys emerges from the moss ball, and then . . .

"Somebody's shoe?" Roy peers over Curtis's shoulder.

"Looks like it." Curtis pushes the high-top tennis shoe onto its side, emptying rotten water. The laces are still tied in a bow, a double knot. Someone wanted the keys and the shoe to stay together.

"Came off a canoe or johnboat maybe? Somebody out fishing?" Edwin theorizes.

"Or fell off a four-wheeler at a creek crossing." Curtis clears the shoe sole with his knife blade, tracing the diamond-shaped patterns in the tread.

"What kind of a bonehead ties his key ring to a shoe out on the water, though?" Roy scoffs. "You hook your keys to something that floats."

"Unless you wanted to sink it . . . or you never planned for it to end up in the drink in the first place." Curtis squints toward the water, then at me. "Antlers." He points at the lanyard, smoothing away a smear of mud to reveal white-and-yellow lettering: Go Bearcats! Then he turns over one of the keys, a small, hex-shaped silver one that's symbolic, not meant to unlock anything: Antlers, Senior '91.

A high school kid's keepsake key. Junior class. Graduating next year, the same as Braden Lacey. Same school.

"Roy, grab an evidence bag for this." I force a flat, dispassionate tone, but experience a rush of dread.

"Huh . . . okay but wh—"

"Just bag it." I'm reluctant to speak the thoughts out loud or even think them, but this shoe could have belonged to someone who set up camp in a low-lying area and was caught off guard when Holson Creek flooded. Someone like Braden.

After leaving behind a scrap of crime tape as a marker, I walk uphill, trying to mentally prepare for the sort of thing you can never really prepare for. "Hey, Roy, take a look around the debris line and make sure there's nothing more. We'll go on ahead. Come meet up with us when you're done here."

I hear the faint swish of Curtis drying his pocketknife on his pants as he rises to follow. Ahead, Edwin moves out, his long-legged strides bouncing the litter as he goes.

"I hope that shoe's unrelated to the body," Curtis mutters grimly. I glance back, and his face has hardened. His eyes, resolute and impenetrable, stay fixed on the way ahead. He bears almost no resemblance to the guy who stood languidly in the noonday sun a short time ago, joking about puppies.

"Same."

We make the rest of the trip in silence. Tainted air announces our destination before we get there. In my early years of rangering, that smell would have put me on the lookout for a mountain lion kill or a place where a poacher had dumped cast-off parts of a carcass. Something big. And dead. Today I only wish the odor came from an animal.

"That's it." Edwin points off-trail toward a tangle of flood detritus deposited in a V shape around the stump of a broken-off tree. He turns his attention to extracting the portable litter from its case.

I take the evidence-collection kit and camera from my backpack, grab a pair of latex gloves, shake off whatever grim conclusions my brain is already drawing about the shoe, and the lanyard, and Braden Lacey. Beyond the shallow canyon, Holson Creek shines through a gap in the trees, aquamarine and gemlike in the sun. Peaceful and pure. *Why do people have to come to such beautiful places to die?* The question is a mix of memory and gut reaction. Suicides and pristine views are frequent but incongruous companions. "I hope this death was an accident."

"Guess we'll find out," Curtis answers, but he and I both know that we might not be certain of anything until the medical examiner's report comes in. If they're backlogged, that could take a while.

The two of us make our way downhill, leaving Edwin to wait for Roy and finish assembling the litter. Death's stench wells in my nose and mouth, solid, so that I want to spit it out but can't. The hum of flies and bees fills the air, and nearby a throng of crows and buzzards roost in the trees, driven off by our approach. Fortunately, the body, caged in flood debris, hasn't provided easy pickings.

Bile churns in my throat as I squat down, shine my flashlight into the tangle. A leg lies visible about eight inches in, bloated, shoe missing, the foot so swollen as to be almost unrecognizable. The color is a deep, unnatural red, not yet blackening into active decay. Too recent to be Curtis's missing high-water victim. Too heavyset to be Braden. The hair on the leg is thick and dark. This guy's not a redhead.

I'm too nauseated to be properly relieved. I swallow hard, swallow again.

"This shoe over here isn't a match to the one you bagged up the trail," Curtis offers from the other side of the pile. "He was wearing hunting boots."

I circle to Curtis's vantage point, peer in, catch hints of clothing and bloated skin. No shirt. Camo shorts. "It's not Braden. Not your missing driver, either. Too recent. He's been dead four to six days maybe?"

Curtis nods. "Big guy. That's at least a size fourteen boot."

I focus my flashlight on the waffle sole. "You sure?"

"I worked my way through college at my ex-father-in-law's sports store. I know shoes. This was one big dude. It'll take a crew to get him out of here."

"I'm guessing help will be here soon. Lu probably has half the county headed our way by now." I pull out my pad and pencil and take notes on the body and location, then grab the thirty-five-millimeter camera and begin shooting, multiple shots from each angle. Even though I know better—follow facts, not speculation—scenarios run through my mind. Hunter or fisherman traveling alone? Nobody knows he's missing. Motorcycle rider passing through, stopped off for a swim? Not with boots on, though. Intoxicated camper? Random hiker who underestimated a flooded low-water crossing? Suicide? Overdose? Drug deal gone bad?

Something new catches my attention. "I think he's been in prison." I zoom in on a bloated hand. "There's a dot tattooed between the thumb and forefinger."

Curtis takes a look through the camera. "Incarceration badge of honor."

"Doesn't tell us what he was doing here but it's . . ." The unmistakable rumble of ATVs catches my ear. Curtis and I stand up to listen.

"Sheriff's department, game wardens, or your guys, judging by how fast they're moving." Pointing a finger, Curtis draws an imaginary line toward the noise. "Forest road farther down Holson Creek . . . less than a mile."

I nod. The arrival of the cavalry guarantees that I'm about to get the boot and am probably wasting time by going through the machinations of processing the scene. I'd be frustrated by the inevitable sidelining, but now that this thing is underway, I'm not willing to fight for it. Even in the most clinical of circumstances, death investigations are hard. After the person you thought you'd spend your life with becomes the subject of one, it's never clinical again. Whoever this man turns out to be, he was some woman's son, maybe some-body's husband or father. Some teacher's student in the first grade. A big kid with big feet.

Thoughts like those can't be allowed to show, so I say, "How about we move to where the air's clearer, see who else we've got coming in ... besides Roy." I nod toward our summer ranger, now jogging down the hill, ready for action. By contrast, Edwin has seen ... or smelled ... all he wants. He's purposely diddling with ratcheting the wheel onto the litter.

"Easy there, hoss," Curtis scolds as Roy passes. "You're not going to need to do CPR on this one."

"Better check," Roy answers eagerly.

I let him go. A look at what's in that debris pile should sober him up. "Hands off and watch where you're walking," I yell after him.

"Boy Scout," Curtis mutters, looking back at Roy as we climb the slope. "He's a good kid, though. Learned CPR in middle school gym class, actually pulled a five-year-old girl off the bottom of a hotel swimming pool that summer and saved her life. Been Captain Amer-ica ever since."

"You know everybody around here?" The random chitchat is nec-essary when the job turns brutal. Without it, you start to feel not human.

"Roy's a cousin."

"There anybody around here you *don't* know?"

"Well ... that guy." A shrug indicates the body. "Been trying to think of someone with feet that big. Can't. Nobody who'd have a prison tattoo, anyway."

A clean breeze wafts by, a welcome relief as we return to the litter, where Edwin looks pale around the gills. Picking up Roy's discarded evidence bag, I study the sneaker so Edwin won't think I'm scrutiniz-ing him.

"Sorry, Val," he says anyway.

"Everybody has a hard go of it the first time." Considering his short experience and the parks he worked at as a seasonal during col-lege, he's probably seen a heat prostration or two, maybe a heart at-tack, lacerations, broken bones, but nothing like this. "You get used to . . . well, not *used to* it, but it doesn't sneak up on you the next time. Everyone's that way."

But below us on the hillside, Roy is like Colombo, here and there around the pile, getting as close in as he can without physically disturbing anything.

"Thanks." Edwin swipes a sunburned arm across his forehead, then shakes out his ball cap. Sweat spray flicks through the air.

"Go ahead and make your way down Holson Creek," I tell him, trying not to be too obvious about the reprieve. "We've got ATVs coming in on a forest road less than a mile away. Figure out whether we can get the litter from here to there. It might be easier to do the body carryout that way."

"I'm okay," he insists. "I can stay and . . ." But when I give him *the look,* he's all too happy to depart.

"Well done," Curtis comments after Edwin is out of earshot. "Worst that can happen to a new guy is ending up laid out on the sod in front of everyone. Reputations don't recover from a thing like that."

"The walk will be good for him." I lift the plastic evidence bag into the sunlight. "Looks like I got my feet wet for no good reason. Just unrelated flood junk." Even while I'm speaking the words, I can't get past the feeling that I'm missing something. *What else should I be picking up on?*

"Unless our guy down there and whoever the tennis shoe belonged to got pulled into the water together," Curtis says.

The idea twists into my brain like a corkscrew. It's sharp and painful. "You mean Braden?"

"Maybe." A grimace tightens the muscles around Curtis's mouth. "I don't know what Braden would be doing with a guy like that, and way out here. Partying? Drugs? I never heard of Braden being that kind of kid."

"That's *if* the tennis shoe and keys were Braden's." I squish the mossy mess around inside the bag to get a closer look. "These seem like house keys and . . . maybe a key to a padlock, or a locker somewhere. No car key."

"Braden's car had the keys still in it." Curtis leans in. Our shoulders rub. I can only imagine what I smell like right now. "He could've taken the car key off the lanyard before he tied it to the shoe ... or maybe the quick link came loose when he grabbed the lanyard from the car, and he never even noticed he'd left one ring behind."

"That would explain keys being in the car." I let out a long sigh, set the shoe beside the portable litter. "I'll drop by Myrna Wambles's place on my way to pick up Charlie this evening, ask Sydney what kind of key ring and shoes Braden had."

"Let me know if you find out anything new."

We stand waiting after that, until finally Edwin appears, trailing the incomers behind him. Three from the sheriff's office, one of us. Chief Ranger Arrington has come himself. An incident commander for this death investigation has probably been selected already. I'm surprised Arrington doesn't have the designee with him to take over.

"You're a little ways from home." The chief ranger addresses Curtis first, leaving me standing there like a tourist.

Curtis shrugs. "Caught the dispatch. Thought it might be my missing high-water driver from a couple weeks ago. Not him, though. This fella's all yours." Folding his arms over his chest, he retreats a step and angles my way, silently indicating that whatever else they want to know, they should ask me.

I'm inwardly grateful, but outwardly I keep a lid on it and give the CliffsNotes version of what we know, which isn't much. I barely mention the sneaker and keys. The audience is already getting restless anyway. They want to make their own judgments rather than trusting mine. Every time I say something, they look over at Curtis for confirmation, even though he hasn't answered them once.

I finally decide I might as well let them take the tour. The sooner they do, the sooner we can get this poor guy out of the woods and figure out how he ended up dead in our park.

CHAPTER 16

Olive Augusta Radley, 1909

The charter members of our club were daughters of women who never appeared alone on the street, and had never dreamed of any purely feminine moment—serious, or festive. Affairs for men-only were frequent, but women had to take their pleasure under the chaperonage or guidance of husbands, fathers, brothers, or what have you.

—Tabatha Milner, 1929. Texas Federation of Women's Clubs newsletter.

Talihina is rowdy as ten cats in a tow sack. Before Mrs. Grube and me drove in and set up our wagon camp yesterday, I was worried that folks might turn a narrow eye on a woman traveling in a farm wagon with a baby and a girl and no man. I stopped fretting soon as I saw how many folks had come to get ready for the speaking and dinner on the grounds. It's like a tent-show preaching and a livestock fair and one of Mrs. Lockridge's spring soirees all at once. Wagons are camped everywhere, and stores have tables out front, and peddlers roam the streets with carts.

And the noise of it all! Horses, voices, dogs, piano music, roosters, chickens, and women in their best dresses and big feathery hats. Kids of all sizes and sorts run around everyplace. So much racket went on during the night it was hard to sleep in our camp. But the ruckus is perfect for my plan, which I pride myself on while I help with the baby and the morning work.

When we're done, Mrs. Grube wraps a dozen corn dodgers and six pieces of smoked pork in a cloth and gives it to me. "Look for those poor little children, and if you can find them, give them this food." She straightens the pin-tuck-and-lace blouse and black skirt she ironed the fool out of at home. It's her big day, and she is gussied up for it. I even pinned her hair up pretty, which I know about from helping the Lockridge girls, who are fussy on such things.

"Children, ma'am?" I ask, like I have clean forgot finding four wandering kids on the road after our picnic at Prairie Creek yesterday. When we stopped to ask if they were okay, they talked in Choctaw, and I pretended to understand every bit of it. Then I told Mrs. Grube that they were trying to get to Talihina, and if they didn't get a ride on a wagon, they'd have to ford the river on foot and that'd be awful dangerous.

The plan went perfect. Tula and the little kids had made it cross-country just in time. Mrs. Grube couldn't say no with that terrible water ahead of us, and so onto the wagon they came. We carried them the rest of the way, and then they scampered over the tailgate and jumped off when we slowed down for Jack Crossing, just a few miles out of Talihina. From there, all they had to do was go under the railroad bridge and up the creek a piece to hole up at a good camp spot Daddy and me sometimes used when we'd come down the mountain for supplies.

"You know which children I'm referencing." Her big ol' frown this morning makes me worry that she thinks I was in on it, but I did a good job pretending I'd never seen those kids before in my life, and if Mrs. Grube recognized Tula with no blanket wrapped over her head, it sure didn't show.

Be still, Ollie, I tell myself when I start fussing with the sash on my blue dress, which is starchy and fresh, thanks to Mrs. Grube. *She doesn't know anything.* "Well, ma'am, I'm guessing those ones we carried to Talihina on the wagon yesterday? That was real charitable of you, but ain't you glad they jumped off at that crossing, so you don't have to trouble with them anymore?"

"I certainly didn't intend they just disappear." Her hands go to her hips while she looks up and down the field full of buckboards, hacks, farm rigs, and even a big ox wagon with timbermen who raised Cain all night. Mrs. Grube stares hard at their man camp. "This is no place for a gang of wayward children, especially the girls. It was my intention to feed those little ones and keep them safe, and before I depart for home, to see what could be done about them."

"Done, ma'am?" That's what I was afraid of and why the plan was for Tula and the others to hop off the wagon when they saw the railroad bridge at Jack Crossing. "Reckon those kids are used to doing for themselves, don't you?"

Mrs. Grube frowns so hard her gap teeth poke out. "That sounds rather uncharitable, considering the trouble that befell *you* on the road, and the assistance you've needed. You've been fed and boarded, your clothes washed, and your horse allowed to recover so that you might make your way safely back to your family. Where might you be if some nefarious men had come upon you instead? Haven't you even wondered?"

Blood boils up into my neck and cheeks. "Oh, yes, ma'am, I have. I wasn't meaning to say . . ."

"When we receive a blessing, we should endeavor to pass one along, don't you think?"

"Yes'm, but those kids didn't . . ."

"Most of them thin as rakes, especially the youngest one." Mrs. Grube's voice gets loud enough that Baby Beau stops banging spoons and tin cups on a quilt we've laid out. "Just like those who come to my farmhouse door. Wild creatures. But they are not *creatures*, Hazel, they are *children*. Children just like you. Heaven forbid they fall victim to the fates of the friendless child, carted off to work as burden beasts, or the girls lured into . . ."

She hushes, but I just stand there wanting to hear where girls might get took besides the mills and the factories. It'd be good for me to know.

Mrs. Grube doesn't say, though. "Scores of timbermen, miners, members of the Federation of Labor, the railroad brotherhoods, and the Farmers Union have come to hear Kate Barnard's speech, as she is quite popular among them. Those children, in their obviously wretched state, could wander into one of these man camps and be carted away to serve as laborers or camp hands or worse. Do you understand?"

"Yes, ma'am."

"Bring them here to our fire, if you can spot them. Tell them we'll look after them while we are able. Mind yourself while you go about, though. Dressed as you are, you surely won't be mistaken for a waif, but if anyone should trouble you, tell the person you are being well watched after and are expected back at camp. I'd look for the children myself, but it's imperative that I gain Miss Kate's ear today."

"Yes, ma'am, but after the speeches this noon, you meant to go back home. Where'll you put those kids when you leave?"

"Just do as I've asked, Hazel." She squints at a spoke-wheeled red surrey carrying four ladies in clean white blouses and wide feathery, flowery hats. Sunday best. And there's no man with them. Just four ladies, out in a surrey alone, like they don't mind kicking up a scandal.

Not another word or a look comes my way from Mrs. Grube before she scoops up Baby Beau and follows that surrey toward town.

I watch till she's disappeared into the mess of folks, then I go over behind our wagon where I put Skedee out of sight from folks passing by. "Sore back or not," I tell him. "It's time we get Tula and Nessa and the little kids and start out for the Winding Stairs."

Someplace not far off, music strikes up. A whole band playing, like the parade my mama and me watched from our hotel room window in Fort Smith.

"They got a band for this and everything," I whisper to Skedee, and I can't help but start through the camp flats toward the sound.

That food poke weighs heavy in my hand as I wind past wagons and tents and horses and campfires. I know I oughtn't. Tula and Nessa and the little kids did their part of the plan perfect. My part was to make camp with Mrs. Grube overnight, get her to give me some food for my travels, then pretend my sick mama's medicine was ready at the pharmacy, say my goodbyes, and go to Daddy's old camp spot for the meetup. It's maybe three miles by the road, and a lot shorter through the pastures and trees. I could be there pretty quick. But that band sounds so fancy I just have to get a quick look.

Once I'm past the wagon camps, there's a church building in my way, so I start around it. Soon as I turn the corner, I see two raggedy boys leaning against the wall, one skinny kid with freckly skin and blond hair and one colored kid who's man-sized but still has a boy's face. They're eating turnips with the greens still dangling off the top. From the looks of it, I bet they stole those turnips out of somebody's garden.

We stand there for a minute, just staring at each other, till I notice that one of them's got a poke sack full of turnips in his hand . . . and it's *my* poke sack. Mine and Nessa's.

I walk closer, ask, "Where'd you get that sack?"

The yellow-haired boy looks me over, peels some turnip skin with his teeth. When he spits it out, I can see that one front tooth is broke-off, jagged. Somebody probably whopped him upside the head with a thieved turnip someplace. "Down in the holler, from some girls. Told them I knowed where we could fill it with turnips, but they didn't favor to come along. What's it to ya?"

"It's *my* sack, that's what. Mine and my sister's."

The boy studies on my dress and bonnet and good lace boots. "You a mixed blood? Because them was Choctaw kids." His squinty brown eyes narrow even more. "Amos here's a Choctaw freedman and speaks Choctaw, on account'a his grandpapa and grandmama was slaves on a Choctaw man's cotton plantation before the Yankees won the war. Amos and that Tula gal did a whole heap of conversatin' last night round the campfire." He frowns up at the big boy. "Did she say anythang 'bout this gunny sack belongin' to some high-nosed gal in town?"

"I don't think so, Dewey," Amos says. "We talked about lotta thangs, though."

"You talk about what happens if you're caught stealin' somebody's turnips?" I prop my hands on my hips. "Where'd you get those?"

Amos looks away, nervous. Dewey just smiles and takes a big bite and says with his mouth full, "Nubba yer bid-ned." His mud-brown eyes twitch toward the back of the church, where there's rows of root vegetables growing.

"You *stole* from the parson's garden?" I back up a step or two. "That'll get you struck by lightnin'."

"We gobba eat." Dewey goes to coughing, probably because he's got turnip down his throat.

Amos quits eating, but Dewey comes out of his coughing spell and weighs that half-eaten turnip in his hand. "We all stick together on it," he says, licking his lips, "we'll be fine. That's just what I told them gals down to the crick—you wanna share our camp, well, all right, then. We can partner up. What you got to offer, though?"

"We ain't partnering up with you." That much I know. I don't want anything to do with these boys. These boys are trouble.

"You the one what told them kids to hop off that wagon and hide down the crick from Jack Crossin'?" Dewey asks. "Amos and me seen them do it, and that lady driver hollerin' for them to come back. The kids told us they's waitin' on somebody, and that *somebody* was to be bringin' food. Elsewise, we would'a never let them stay at our camp. That spot is our'n. Ain't that so, Amos?"

"That's right true, Dewey."

Dewey looks at the food bundle in my hand, leans over and gives it a sniff, then stands back with a big ol' slobbery grin. "You are the one bringin' us food, then. You was late with breakfast, but you can gimme it, now."

I hold the bundle away. "I ain't givin' you nothing."

"I reckon you might." His eyes sparkle, mean and sneaky. "Because I've come to wonderin' . . . does that lady wagon driver *know* you told them kids to jump off and hide and wait for you? 'Cause she sure was hollerin' after them yesterday, while you was acting like you didn't even see them go. Me and Amos might just find that lady and tell her all about it . . . unless you turn over them goods."

Of a sudden, I feel like I just swallowed one of those thieved turnips, myself. Mrs. Grube can't find out what I've done. Ever. It'd hurt her too much.

"Don't you *dare*!" I stare at Dewey level-on. He's so scrawny a stiff wind might knock him over, so surely I can. I ain't afraid. Mostly.

"D-Dewey ... Dewey Mullins ..." Amos's voice is deep as a man's, and he stands big as a man, too. I forgot about him. He could pound me flat as a fritter in two seconds, but he says, "We hadn't oughta, Dewey."

"Hush up, Amos." Dewey drops the turnip sack. "I's just fixin' to show her who's boss here. She don't got no—"

"Ohhh, Dewey ... there ... the garden ... he ..." Amos can't even get the words out before across the garden comes the parson in his fine black suit and hat, red-faced and sweatin.'

I feel Dewey's breath on my ear, and he whispers, "Them girls told us y'all was headed up the mountain from here. You let that preacher man think it was *you* that picked his turnips ... or we'll tell that lady everything we know."

Then he snatches the food poke from my hand, and both boys take to running.

CHAPTER 17

Valerie Boren-Odell, 1990

Tipping its summit with silver, arose the moon. On the river

Fell here and there through the branches a tremulous gleam of the moonlight,

Like the sweet thoughts of love on a darkened and devious spirit.

—Henry Wadsworth Longfellow, 1847. "Evangeline."

In the watercolor gray of evening, Myrna Wambles's house looks even less appealing than the first time I stopped by. Every exhausted inch of me wants to continue down the street and leave this for tomorrow, when I'm not covered in dried mud from working a death scene and body recovery. The scent of human decay has secreted itself into the fibers of my clothing and between the strands of my hair—or maybe I just imagine it. I know that the feeling won't stop haunting me until I've showered and run my uniform through the washing machine with just enough bleach to leave the fabric smelling like a freshly treated swimming pool.

I'll need to stop by the store for a bottle of Clorox after picking up Charlie, which will be one more hiccup in the usual evening routine. The poor kid is already stuck at the daycare for supper because I was tied up overtime at the station. With the NPS end of the death investigation expected to be mostly paperwork, Chief Ranger Arrington has left me in as incident commander after all. The general consensus is that the medical examiner's report will eventually come back with cause of death: drowning, manner: accidental. Unless something more surfaces, we may never ID the man, or find out why he entered the waterway, or where. A flood has the ability to carry a body for miles along swollen creeks and rivers.

This trip to Myrna Wambles's place can't really wait until tomorrow—not if I want to sleep tonight. I need some concrete answers about the lanyard and the shoe. Sydney is the one who has those answers. Aside from that, tomorrow is a day off for me, and I've promised Charlie plenty of together time. That will not include dropping by the Wambles house.

By showing up this late in the day, I'm hoping to catch Myrna a bit off guard, and maybe slightly more cooperative. But as I dig through the console for a clean notepad, grab my hat, and exit the truck, I steel myself for whatever might ensue.

The house's front door once again opens before I can get there. A shadowy figure in a housedress steps out. "You got me another one?"

She advances several steps, as people typically do when they don't want you to see what's going on inside. The maneuver rings all my bells, but then again, everything about Mrs. Wambles does. "Heard we had a drop-off comin' this evenin'. You got it in the truck? Boy or girl?"

I hesitate at the bottom of the steps, off balance at hearing a child referred to as *it*. "Valerie Boren-Odell. Park Service. We spoke the other day at the church. About Sydney Potter?"

"Sydney Potter?" The name explodes in a hail of spit. "Oh ... sure, I remember you. How're you this evenin', ma'am? I heard round town that y'all found a dead escaped prisoner today ... and y'all had a mountain fall down last week, with some hikers trapped underneath it, squashed to a pulp. Them mountains claim their price from fools. Always have."

"Fortunately, the rockfall event happened in the middle of the night during the storms." *Sorry to disappoint you, but,* "No one was around and there were no injuries."

"Too many wanderin' spirits up there. Too many bones." Her voice deepens, grows gritty and bizarre. Fisting her dress, she pulls the neckline protectively close. "Y'all hadn't oughta made a park up there, let folks to walk over the graves, wake the spirits. I *know* you government people stole some of the bones off that land. I heard."

A shudder runs under my shirt. Having worked a death scene today, I'm more easily rattled than usual. I thread my fingers around my duty belt, clench down on the leather. "Well, rumors are like flies, aren't they? They feast wherever they land."

Myrna peers in the general direction of the Winding Stair. "My mama used to tell of it. She could see things . . . haints, demon spirits on a person." The bare-bulb porch light casts uneven shadows over her craggy face as she turns my way again. "Was a man round here once. A man-devil. Ran laundry houses from one town to the next, took in little girls to work—orphan ones, or ones with folks that needed the money. He got my mama's half sister, Evelyn. Took her off their dirt farm down near Bald Mountain. Tried to get my mama, too, but Mama seen the devil on him. She cried and spit up and fainted till he wouldn't take her. The family never heard of Evelyn again. That man did bad things. Terrible things. Buried the bodies up in them mountains. Here in Talihina was where he met his end. The men of the town took him from that laundry buildin', hauled him up in the mountains to pay for his sins. Let the coyotes and the wolves tear up his body. Man-devil, he still walks by night, looking for all his parts."

"That's quite a story." I think of the cave, the bones.

Stop, I tell myself. *Don't even listen.* If there are answers to be had, they won't come from this shrew of a woman.

"Wasn't no trial." Myrna *tsk-tsks* under her breath. "So you can't look it up at the courthouse or nothin', but the old-timers still tell it. You best watch yourself up in them mountains."

I pull off my hat, rub my forehead to clear my mind, replace the hat. "Ma'am, I just came by to ask Sydney a few more questions about her brother."

The horror-movie act vanishes, and blatant curiosity replaces it. Myrna's nose twitches my way and her voice normalizes. "The boy in trouble with the law now, is he?"

"Not at this time."

"Because nothin' . . . and I mean *nothin'* would surprise me. That girl I have here, she has got a attitude on her that is nothin' but bad. If I hadn't made room for her when Alton Parker found them kids on their own, Sydney would've ended up in the *real* emergency shelter, throwed in with the teenagers and criminals. But she ain't grateful to me or Mr. Parker. Not one darn bit."

I catalog the scattershot background information. "Kids are hard to read sometimes. I'm sure that's a particular challenge in these situations."

"Oh, yes, ma'am. I could tell you stories!"

I'll bet. "Maybe her case worker could contact . . ."

"She ain't got one. Mr. Parker arranged all this. Like I said, he was tryin' to do them kids *and* Budgie Blackwell a favor. Keep this mess out of the legal system till Braden could get on his feet, workin' and turn eighteen, and be guardian for his sister . . . or else till the grandmama got better and came home. Mr. Parker didn't want the courts to know Budgie had gone off and left them kids by theirselves, so he took care of it as a favor to her."

Even though the story somewhat fits with Sydney's, it sounds exponentially more ridiculous coming from an adult. A flighty seventeen-year-old kid is supposed to become his sibling's legal guardian? A grandmother with resources and connections couldn't have found someone to look after the kids for her?

Myrna's phlegmy cough interrupts my train of thought. Finally she clears her throat and rasps out, "Hon, alls I can tell you about Sydney's brother is, he hasn't been by here in a while, and that is upsettin' for Sydney. But in this business, you learn that folks don't always keep their promises. Not even to fam'ly. It'll only grieve Sydney if you bring it up to her. If she'd heard from her brother, I'd know."

A clamor arises inside the house—kids wrestling or playing . . . or fighting. Squeals and yells and thumps. Somebody blows a whistle. An adult voice rises over the din, but I can't make out the words.

"I'll do my best not to upset Sydney, Mrs. Wambles, but I would like to talk with her. I'll be quick."

"The whole bunch is in their jammies and settlin' down." Myrna shifts foot to foot, the muumuu swinging around her fleshy calves.

"They see you, they'll be climbin' the walls. Anythin' different stirs them up."

"Why don't we have Sydney step out here a minute? I'd like to speak with her in private anyway." Mrs. Wambles is probably wondering whether I have the power to force the issue, but I'd rather not get into the weeds about jurisdictions—better to keep this voluntary.

A June bug whirls past and suffers an unfortunate collision with Myrna's nested-up hair. Savagely plucking it free, she tosses it down and takes a moment to squash it. "All right. But as I have said before, you can't believe a word that girl says anyhow."

The carcass engages in its death throes while Myrna heads inside.

Sydney inadvertently finishes off the writhing beetle when she emerges. "Hey, Ranger Valerie!" Clearly, Mrs. Wambles has prepped her. "I wondered why I didn't see you for a while."

"Well, in general I work in the park, you know? They don't let me come to town much." The joke wins a grin wide enough to show in the dim light.

"Must be tough to get a cheeseburger then."

I laugh. "You have no idea."

"When I get to be a park ranger, I'm never comin' to this stupid town."

And . . . boom. Fun time is over. Threading her arms behind her back, she wanders closer, her tank top riding up. The skinny, slightly arched belly reminds me of Charlie, as do the pajama bottoms and slippered feet. I want to banish the comparison, but I can't. "You'll have to show me what park rangers do, though."

"We'll talk about that sometime." I'm careful to avoid promises, but Sydney continues as if we've sealed a bargain.

"I can do a ride along, like when Braden had his JROTC camp last summer. He got to ride in big trucks and stuff, and planes, too, I bet."

"I didn't know that about him. I think you said he hoped to go into the military, but JROTC—that's really great." *And with that going on in his life, why would he just take off?* Junior ROTC takes discipline. Commitment.

"He's gonna be a pilot." Leaning closer, she cups a hand alongside her mouth and adds in a whisper, "After he springs me from this stupid place." Then she threads her arms behind her back again, rocking onto her heels. Her voice resumes normal volume when she says, "So you could take me on a park ranger ride along up in the Winding Stair Mountains. I can show you some awesome places, too. We used to go there a lot. Well, before Grandma Budgie got sick and stumbly and stuff. That's how Braden knows so much, from her showing us. You run into Braden up there yet?"

"No, I haven't."

"He has places nobody ever goes. He's real smart like that."

"It's a good skill. Hey, so I'll recognize it if I come across his trail or his camp, what kinds of things does he usually take with him? Tent? Backpack? Clothes? Keys? What type of shoes was he wearing? That sort of thing?"

She ponders longer than necessary, which tells me she's inventing at least part of her answer. "Boots, brushpopper shirt, jeans, I guess. He's got keys on a neck thing everybody got free at school. His tent was still at Grandma Budgie's. I bet he borrowed one from somebody, though."

"So, boots then, you're sure?" I open my notepad, take notes. "Not tennis shoes or maybe high-tops?"

"Oh, no, ma'am. He's *got* high-top tennis shoes. Blue-and-white ones for Antlers. But Braden wouldn't go to the woods in somethin' like that. A copperhead snake or a timber rattler could bite right through it. He'd . . ." Her head swivels toward the front window as the curtains shift a bit.

"Hey, hold that thought." I give the words enough volume to carry through the glass. "I need to step right over *there* real quick and check on something in my truck."

"K." A curious look slides toward the driveway.

I've barely made it to my vehicle before Sydney is on my tail. Stretching upward, she peers through the windshield to investigate Charlie's handheld video game, which I'd set on the dashboard while digging out a clean notepad. Charlie lost game rights after trying to sneak the toy into daycare this morning.

"Whoa, radical! Is that the new Game Boy?" Sydney cranes to get a better look.

"Yes, it is."

"Lucky," she grumbles. "Braden's girlfriend, Rachel, has a Game Boy. She's gonna bring it . . . if she ever gets to come see us. After the doctor makes Grandma Budgie all better, she's gonna let Rachel come stay with us a few days, and we could meet her. Mama didn't want Braden's girlfriend to come at *all*, though. She said Braden is too young and Grandma Budgie has enough goin' on at the ranch with the pond dam and the hay barn getting fixed, plus Grandma Budgie's too old for company."

"Your brother had . . . has a girlfriend?" I jot *girlfriend, Rachel* on my notepad. "Where does she live?"

"Around Tulsa someplace. They met at JROTC camp last summer and fell in lu-u-uv."

That could explain some things, like where Braden may have disappeared to, and why.

Sydney returns her attention to the vehicle. "What other cartridges you got for your Game Boy?"

I'm momentarily stumped. The toy was Charlie's Christmas gift from my mom. Video games are not my thing. "You know . . . I can't remember."

Sydney rolls a look my way. "That's your kid's Game Boy, huh?"

"Let's talk about that another time."

"Your kid with its dad right now?"

The question hits like a blind punch. I do my best not to let it show, but I can feel Sydney studying me. "So, about Braden, are there any other family members he might have gone to stay with? His father maybe?"

"Braden's daddy died. He got wrecked on a motorcycle, Mama said. But they wasn't any good together, anyhow. That's because you shouldn't fall all goo-goo in love in high school. Mama told Braden that. Him and Rachel want to marry right off, if Braden makes it into flight school and stuff."

"Do you know Rachel's last name? Or her phone number?"

"Huh-uh."

"But Rachel lives somewhere near Tulsa and they met at a JROTC camp?" I recap.

Sydney shrugs. "Rachel's in college at Oklahoma City now, but if she goes with Braden, her daddy will cut her off. Boom. She hates it anyway, though. College. Her roommate in the dorm is a jerk, plus she misses Braden." As quickly as Sydney became mesmerized by the Game Boy, she disengages. Grabbing my arm, she gasps in a moment of eureka. "*You* could go ask my Grandma Budgie."

"What?"

"You could go see Grandma Budgie at the City of Faith doctor place. That's in Tulsa, too!" A palm slaps her forehead, hard. "And ask *her* where to find Rachel. And ask Rachel where Braden's at, because Braden and Rachel don't go one single day without yakkin' on the phone for-ev-er."

"The City of Faith?" I jot the name in my notes. At least it's concrete information . . . and something new. Last time I talked to Sydney, she claimed she didn't know any details. "And did you *hear* your grandmother say that's where she would be?"

She's slow to answer, careful, as if she's composing on the fly again. "Braden said it."

"So, your Grandma Budgie told Braden?"

"I think so. I didn't talk to him till after I woke up in the morning." Her face turns my way, catches the glow of the truck's dome light. Moisture-tipped lashes close tightly, then part again. "Can you tell Grandma Budgie we really need her to come home?"

My heart shatters into a million tiny pieces and I'm a little girl again, eight years old, terrified that my daddy would never return from Vietnam.

I know I shouldn't, but I reach out and smooth a hand over Sydney's hair. It passes like silk through my fingers. "I'll try." It's the wrong thing to say. If Budgie Blackwell were able to communicate, she would have done so by now. "But I need you to be honest with me. Is there anyone who'd know Rachel's last name or phone number? Or maybe Braden had it written down at your grandmother's house?" *Do I have a pair of young lovers who've run off together? Or a pair of bodies washed away in a flood? Or a breakup that caused Braden to take to the woods . . . or worse?*

A quick head shake, and Sydney's moment of raw emotion evaporates. "If he did, he'd probably burn it, so nobody could get it and call Rachel and break them up, or . . ." Her lips snap shut. She's let out something she didn't mean to. I'm just not sure what the *something* is.

"So . . . who would've called the phone number if Braden had it lying around?" Truth and invention are tangled like multicolored spaghetti here. "Was anyone else there with you the night your grandmother had to leave?"

"Oh, no, ma'am. Sometimes people would stop by to *visit* with Grandma Budgie, that's all. And the housekeeper used to come once a month—Sharla Watson. She was Miss Nosy Rosy. Braden broke up with *her* daughter to go with Rachel, but they moved away after spring break and—"

"Syd-ney?" Myrna Wambles's shrill voice pollutes the evening stillness. "What're you doin' way out there? Did I not say *stay on the porch*? Did I not?"

Wincing, Sydney ducks her head.

"My fault!" I call. "Checking on my truck."

"Time to come in." Myrna has had enough. "*Now*, little missy."

Sydney stiffens to full height, as if that might level the balance of power in this place. "You ask my Grandma Budgie," she whispers before dashing across the yard, up the steps past Myrna Wambles, and into the house.

Myrna stands guard as I climb into my truck, jot down a few final notes, pile all the loose items in the console, then back out of the driveway.

I'm only too happy to see Mrs. Wambles and her house disappear from the rearview mirror. Unfortunately, the eerie feeling and the unanswered questions follow me like a fly buzzing around my head, looking for a place to land. I do my best to brush it off and switch to family mode as I pull up to the daycare. Charlie is sitting in the porch swing, chatting with the owner. He bolts for the truck and climbs into his seat almost before I can wave a thank-you out the window.

"Whew! What stinks?" Pinching his nose, he looks me over, takes in the mud-covered uniform. A dozen rapid-fire questions follow.

He's immediately perturbed when I don't offer any interesting stories from the day—no dumpster-diving bears or raccoons in the camp showers. The only kid-approved tidbit I have is that some of the crew was busy studying the rockfall event that knocked a segment of hiking trails out of service. No, I didn't get to see it for myself, I just heard the chatter. I was tied up in another part of the park.

"But tied up *how?*" he whines as we stop in the dollar store parking lot.

"Just tied up, Charlie. Near Holson Creek. That's all."

"In the water or on the creek bank?"

"Neither. In a backwater off one of the trails."

"Which trail?" He's been studying the park maps incessantly, planning hikes we're going to take on my off days, whenever the schedule settles down. "The one where all the rocks crashed off the mountain?"

"No. Not that one."

"Did the rocks fall all the way to the bottom or just a little way?" He illustrates with his hands.

"I don't know. I haven't been there. That's not where the scene . . . where I was working."

"Working doing *what,* though?"

"Charlie, just hang on a minute while I grab a bottle of bleach."

"For what?"

"Charlie!" My voice reverberates through the vehicle. "Just sit here, all right?" From the console, I retrieve the contraband Game Boy. "Here. If you'll wait patiently, you can play it."

"Can I have the other cartridges, too?"

I fish out the two matchbook-sized accessories. "There you go."

"Can I keep it when we get home?"

"You're pushing it."

"Ohhh-kay," he sighs.

"I'll be right there at the cash register where you can see me." Tweaking the bill of his ball cap, I try to lighten the mood. "Hey, buddy, I'm not mad at you, okay? It's just been a crazy day. Don't unbuckle. Don't get out, all right?"

"I know." With an exasperated eye roll, he hunches over his Game Boy. "I'm not *four.*"

Despite everything, a tender laugh tickles my throat. This kid. Really. "Back in a flash," I say, then hurry into the store.

The three-minute break plus a pile of on-sale dog food bags by the door leave me with an idea as I return from my errand.

"We going home now?" Charlie inquires.

"I need to make a quick stop and talk to someone while things are fresh in my mind."

His curly head falls back and bounces against the seat. "Why-yyy?"

"Long story, and it's not something I can share," I tell him. "But, listen—the good news about this place is, there are puppies."

CHAPTER 18

Olive Augusta Radley, 1909

Looking at her and listening to her, it is impossible not to think of
her as a child, and then one remembers, with a sort of shock, the
work that she has done. She looks like a schoolgirl; she talks like an
idealist; she is, perhaps, a visionary.

—*SUNDAY NEW YORK TIMES* ARTICLE ABOUT KATE BARNARD, DECEMBER 8, 1912.

Kate Barnard is a tiny woman. She's a half head shorter than me,
and I bet I outweigh her, too. The first thing I think when I see her is,
*She doesn't even look big enough for a lady dress yet. That's who all these
people came here to see?*

You'd think the hay wagon hung with flags and striped buntings
was waiting for Teddy Roosevelt hisself. Folks of all sorts and sizes fill
the meeting grounds. There's timber cutters and miners, oil drillers
and farmers, businessmen in fine suits, and ladies and kids and babies. Mrs. Grube must be someplace in that mess, too. I hope she's
got a good hold on Baby Beau because it's so crowded there's barely
room to stand. And folks been standing awhile. First a preacher
talked, then a mayor, then a state congressman for a long, long time.

The crowd has started yelling, "Kate! Kate! Kate..." which is
something like I never heard before. I never would've heard it, either,
except I didn't get hauled off for a turnip thief. When that parson saw
me standing outside his church with the tow sack full of garden

goods at my feet, he said, "Praise God! The women's club sent some-one to gather the turnips."

"Oh, yes, sir, they did," I answered, and stuck my hands in my dress pockets so he wouldn't see them shaking.

He looked the sack over. "That should be plenty. Hurry now, run them to the meeting grounds for the women cooking the luncheon. And no more dallying with boys, young lady. The speeches start soon, and lunch must be ready after. There's a nickel in it for you if you stay to peel and chop the turnips. Go, now, go!"

And so I did, before he could ask any questions about that half-eaten turnip on the ground. Besides, I wanted the nickel.

It never even crossed my mind that by helping the clubwomen fix food at a long row of plank-lumber tables, I'd end up with a good view behind the scrim cloth curtain strung up to hide folks before they go on the stage. Just like Dorothy in *The Wonderful Wizard of Oz*, I got to watch while they fussed with their neckties and wiped the sweat off their faces and checked their pocket watches when they thought nobody could see. The congressman took a nip out of a flask, then handed it to a helper to keep in his coat pocket. Congress-men don't even have to carry their own whiskey.

I'm so close to Miss Kate Barnard, while she paces like a nervous stable horse behind that hank of scrim, that I can hear her talking to herself. Of a sudden, she stops and looks my way and smiles.

It ain't like me to be shy, but I just stand and stare. Even after she turns to shake hands with Mrs. Threadgill, who's headed up the stairs to say her howdies as president of the Oklahoma Federation of Wom-en's Clubs, I don't stop watching Miss Kate and wondering how somebody so tiny can gather this many people.

Up on stage, Mrs. Threadgill goes on about the state federation and a new age for women. Then she says she's sorry that Mrs. McDougal, the vice president of the state federation, couldn't join her right now to talk about the clubwomen's traveling library because Mrs. McDou-gal is riding on the library wagon, and it's running late getting here. It'll surely arrive soon, though, and they should all stay around to see it after the noon meal.

Finally, Mrs. Threadgill comes to the point, which is a good thing because the crowd is getting rowdy. "And now it is my distinct honor and pleasure to welcome a woman who shall require no introduction among you, as you quite fondly regard her as 'Our Kate.' I need not remind you that she is only the second woman elected to a statewide office in the entire country, and by the *largest* majority of *any* candidate on the 1907 ballot! This new state can hold up no finer specimen than our Oklahoma commissioner of charities and corrections. I give you Miss Kate Barnard!"

The cheering goes wild while that tiny woman in a plain black skirt, ivory blouse, and a hat with nothing but one peacock feather for a fancy marches up to the middle of that hay wagon like it's hers. She waves and waves while all the people yell and cheer and hoot and holler. But the minute she opens her mouth to talk, the grounds get so quiet you could hear a butterfly land.

A big voice comes out of that little lady, and I go back to washing and cutting leaf lettuce and carrots, which Mrs. Vernon of the Talihina Women's Club said would earn me a second nickel if I'd stay and do it. I want that money, and besides I can listen while I wash and chop.

Up on stage, Miss Kate says her greetings and tells how, since she took office, she has been all over Oklahoma, but there's no lovelier country anywhere than these mountains in the southeastern part of the state. Then she thanks the mine workers and the timbermen and the farmers for all their support during the statehood campaign, when they stood up for her again and again.

"Vast and powerful forces battled against our campaign to include the planks of worker protection in the state constitution, forces that went far beyond this new state of ours," she tells everybody. "At one point, rousers in Washington were desperate to keep a foothold here, and they sent the attorney general from Washington to stop our progress. Hardly had I started speaking one night when the attorney general and his party arrived and with loud, boisterous remarks attempted to break up the vast assemblage of miners. I addressed the attorney general, and he aimed a stinging rebuke about 'women in politics,' whereupon the huge hulk of Jack Britton moved to the front from out of the depths of two thousand miners.

"Stepping up to the attorney general, Jack asked him to vacate the premises. Jack told the attorney general the miners of Oklahoma respected women as they expected their 'outside guests to do.' Jack Britton has stood faithful to labor in all its storm and stress, and I am proud to call him friend. Must not God look proudly down on such a man, whose soul cannot be bartered for skyscraper or gold?"

The folks lift their flags and streamers and hats and babies and cheer and cheer and cheer. Miss Kate lets that go on awhile before she starts talking again. "Human conservation, then, is the first consideration of true statesmanship. So long as America has one starving child, our governors and statesmen have a right to think of nothing else. Yet there are six million women in these United States toiling for a pittance wage. Many of them are on the road to motherhood, yet their wage will not buy sufficient food, and the child is starved before it is born.

"Shall those who occupy positions as governors and controllers of the destiny of a nation use their influence to conceal this crime?"

The crowd hollers, "No! No! No!"

"I agree!" she says. "And not only is the crime against the mothers and the workingwomen. Two million American children are slaving in mines, mills, and factories while we gather here. It has been my misfortune to visit some of their workshops.

"I tell you of the little children breathing glass dust in the factories of America, seven thousand of them working on day shifts and seven thousand working on night shifts, inhaling fine pulverized glass dust until the thin, delicate lung tissues were cut and bleeding. The little children could no longer get air, so the average life in these factories is three years. I speak of the early graves of these little folks and the tragedy of their short lives. I ask you, is this right? Is it righteous?"

"No!" the crowd yells. "No! No! No!"

"I tell of forty thousand little children in the cotton mills of the South, breathing cotton lint until it wadded in their lungs, and of their working on floors trembling with the vibration of machinery until they succumbed and died of Saint Vitus's dance or lived to be permanent nervous wrecks. I speak of the children in the canneries, in the coal mines, and the coal breakers, buried away in inky blackness where a plant would die for lack of sunlight and oxygen.

"The day that Governor Haskell signed our state's child labor law, only a few short months ago and after a long and weary battle, hundreds of children came out of the black pits of Oklahoma, hundreds more were released from the laundries of the state, and thousands more were liberated in miscellaneous industries. My child labor bill and my compulsory education bill were both written for the conservation of the American home and the American child.

"I tell you that if we are ever to become a great nation of splendid men and women, we must take hold of our little folks. A dollar spent in the morning of their lives is better than a thousand spent in the evening, in shelters and poorhouses. The true wealth of the nation must be figured in terms of child life. If the child grows up to a life of usefulness, the state is clearly the gainer; while conversely, if it becomes ignorant, or a shirker in the world's work, or criminal, or insane, the state must bear the cost of such defection. And so we must . . ."

She talks a long time about why boys and girls both ought to be in school, and how, if a widow woman has to put her kids to work so her family can eat, now she can get help from the state of Oklahoma instead, so long as she follows the new law and keeps her children in school.

It makes me think that when we get up the mountain to the old place, we'll need to have a school. In the cabin, there's the small stack of books Mama brought in her trunk when we left Kansas City for Fort Smith, and then the Winding Stair. I figure I'll be the teacher for Nessa and the younger ones, since Mama showed me how to read and cypher before I was ever in a classroom.

The crowd hoots and hollers again, and I realize my mind's been up the mountain awhile. I go back to washing vegetables and listening at Miss Kate's speech.

". . . appeal for a shorter workday for the workingmen of this state was based solely upon the necessity of permitting the father to reach home in time to have some hours of leisure and some little energy left for the enjoyment of his wife and children. The sanitary workshop law, I endorsed because it would protect the father's health and enable him longer to live and protect his home. The home is the unit of the nation, the keystone upon which the whole arch is built, is it not?"

The crowd cheers and yells, "Yes! Yes! Yes!"

"In this nation," Miss Kate says when they quieten again, "we must fight to preserve the lives of fathers and mothers, so that children may *have* fathers and mothers. For we have made too many orphans, too many friendless children, too many laid young in the grave. All for a profit, can you imagine? Fortunes made from little hands and ruined bodies. I yearn for a day when we adopt a uniform child labor law nationwide, for truly we are playing the Game of Life, and the stake is the destiny of the nation. I shall carry the story to the grassroots and the country districts, telling of the fight some senators and representatives are making to stop me."

She points a finger toward the crowd, like those bad men are out there. Some folks look around to see, and then Miss Kate tells them, "When you get home, you good workingmen and -women, what are *you* going to do about it? What are you going to do to secure a different future for yourself, for the children, and for our newly formed state of Oklahoma?"

She finishes, and the last of her big voice echoes down the valley, then bounces off the foot of the Winding Stair.

Not a whisper breaks the stillness. No talking, clapping, ladies sniffling into their hankies, or men clearing their throats. Even the kids that've climbed trees stay right where they are. Everybody's frozen by a spell.

Her spell.

The magic holds till one man in a plain canvas work shirt hollers, "Hear! Hear! Three cheers for Our Kate, the Good Angel of Oklahoma!"

Noise breaks like a summer squall. Folks yell and clap and blow penny whistles and shake tin-can rattlers.

Miss Kate Barnard stands up there, waving with both hands while the crowd cheers, "Hurrah for Our Kate!"

I wonder what that might be like to have all those people listen at your words and call your name.

When Mrs. Threadgill climbs back up on the stage and tries to take Miss Kate away, the crowd doesn't like that one bit. But there's roast pig cooked in pits in the ground, and big iron kettles of beans and field peas and root vegetables, plus all sorts of covered dishes the club ladies made at home and put on the long tables.

The cost for a plate is twenty-five cents kindly donated to the Talihina Women's Club. That food smells good enough, it's a sure temptation for most folks, and the line grows long right off. I figure I better ask for my pay before all the ladies get too busy. It's way past time for me to head back to Tula and Nessa, so we can make our plans, and get shed of those boys if they're still lingering around. With all the money earning and speech hearing, I've hardly cast a thought toward the hiding place down by Jack Crossing. That shames me some, but we do need the money.

I climb up on a bench to see if I can spot Mrs. Vernon from the Talihina Clubwomen and get my pay. Of a sudden, here she comes, hair sticking out from under her hat all around, and sweat drawing rivers down her cheeks. "Hazel!"

She sounds mad, and I jump off that bench figuring I oughtn't be up there, but soon as she gets within reach, she grabs my arm and says, "There's another nickel for you if you can assist with the toting, serving, and cleaning. We *were* to have students from the Choctaw Female Academy in Tuskahoma as helpers, but only half of them have arrived. Their second wagon met with some trouble on the road. I need girls to work. Will you?"

"Why, yes, ma'am, I most surely will," I answer because all I can think is another nickel. "My mama expected I might be in town awhile, so she won't be missing me at all. I know how to place silver and china, and serve a proper table, and clear it, too."

I cast an eye toward the church building, where a special lunch is set up just for the ladies of the Talihina Women's Club. That's where they're headed with Miss Kate Barnard, if they can ever get her past all the folks.

"Wonderful," Mrs. Vernon says. "Go inside and help as long as you're needed."

I sprint off like a deer, and once I get in that building, a woman shoves a apron my way and points me to two girls in school uniforms from the Choctaw Academy. They're being bossed by a tall dark-headed woman while they chop block ice and get it in glasses. I put on the apron and help with running the glasses to tables before the luncheon guests can crowd up the place.

Once we're done, the woman, whose name is Mrs. Paulson, stands us up along the wall and looks us over. "Straight, straight." She tidies our apron ties and dabs our clothes. "It isn't every day a state politician and the president *and* vice president of the Oklahoma State Federation of Women's Clubs come to visit. Such an auspicious occasion. If we in the Talihina Club are to be taken seriously, we must show that the remoteness here is no hindrance to culture and refinement. Do you understand?"

We all answer, "Yes, ma'am."

"I assume in your classes at the academy you have been instructed in the proper serving of beverages from a pitcher?"

Mrs. Paulson thinks I'm one of the academy girls, and with the apron over my blue ribbon-sash dress, I match them pretty well. "Yes, ma'am," I answer right along, because I am good at pouring without dripping. At the Lockridges' house, dripping will land you in trouble. Only the guests get to mess up the linens or their own dinner clothes.

Soon as Mrs. Paulson leaves us be, along comes bossy Mrs. Tinsley, who I already learned to watch out for while washing vegetables outside. She has us hold our left arms out, bent, and she hangs tea towels on us and tells us to make a comely sight of ourselves. "For the academy! For Talihina! For the federation, and for womankind!"

That makes me giggle inside, but I know better than let it out. So do those academy girls. We stand like statues till she walks away, then those girls and me look sidewards at each other.

We don't even get so far as trading names before a skinny man in a flashy brown-and-blue checkerboard suit comes hurrying in the back door and points his folding box camera at us. "Girls, look this way. Be still, please! One, two, three . . ." He takes our photograph, then squints an eye at us and says, "How's about a bit less stiff this time? This isn't just for the Talihina newspaper. I've been tasked with sending material to Oklahoma City in consideration of a commemorative in *The Daily Oklahoman*."

Right in that minute, I feel pretty important, so I fold both arms behind my back to hide that silly tea towel, and I tip my chin up high. I pretend I'm Miss Kate Barnard, first woman elected to the state government.

The other girls do the same pose. We look so good the newsman takes an extra picture. Afterward, he pulls out a pencil and paper pad and says while he writes, "Girls providing beverage service, left to right . . . names, please?" He looks at me first.

"Olive . . ." I'm just about to add Augusta Radley, when I snap my mouth shut, then finally spit out, "Hazel Rusk."

"Olive . . . Hazel . . . Rusk." The man repeats after me. "Is that R-U-S-K?"

"Yes, but just Hazel Rusk is best. That's what folks call me."

"As you wish. Hazel Rusk it is." He gives me a smile, and he has the prettiest blue eyes. For just a minute I feel like I am the only person in that big room. I never had a feeling like that in my whole wide life. *Someday, when I get grown*, I think to myself, *I'd like to marry a man with blue eyes like that.*

Quick as that thought comes, it scampers off, and my head goes to spinning about my photograph and Hazel's name being in the Talihina newspaper and maybe even *The Daily Oklahoman*. That was stupid of me. Tesco doesn't read a newspaper, but Mr. Lockridge sure does. If he shows Tesco that picture, Tesco will know Nessa and me didn't drown in the river . . . and he'll know right where to look for us.

I step closer to that newspaperman and say, "Girls *visiting* from the female academy *near Tuskahoma*. You should put that in your paper. The academy teachers might be real upset if you don't."

The man nods, then marks over some words and writes new ones. "Very wise advice, young lady. The ire of teachers is best avoided."

"Oh yes, sir. It sure is." I let out a breath. If Tesco does see that newspaper, he'll go looking for me down in Tuskahoma.

While me and those academy girls finish putting out ice glasses, I make sure to let them know I'm on my way to Kansas City to my mama's family, and I leave on the train tomorrow. I tell them about aunts and uncles and cousins up there to make the story seem real, but we only get to talk for a few minutes before the ladies settle in to their tables. Then there's work to do and water glasses to fill.

I don't just pour from the pitcher while I go up and down the tables. I listen at what those women say, more than I ever did at the Lockridges' place. I feel like I'm older now, being on my own with Nessa to look after, and I need to know things. But the biggest reason I mark their words is these ladies talk about more than each other's pretty hats and how to bake a pie.

At the head table, where I dally the most, Mrs. Tinsley gets to jawboning about a man running a new laundry in town, and how he lives in the rooms above the business and has six young laundry girls that never go outside, except to deliver laundry. When they do, they keep their heads down and don't speak to anybody and are even sent *alone* to the homes of *bachelor men*.

"He *claims* they are *all* his daughters." Mrs. Tinsley shakes her head and makes a *tsk-tsk-tsk*. "But I *do* declare. None of them resemble one another *or* him. I fear it might be a circumstance . . . well if you ask *my* opinion . . . *quite* untoward. I will say, though, he has trained the girls at the laundry trade. They do fine work, particularly on the linens, but the girl who brought mine could *not* have been more than ten years old and *certainly* not *fourteen*, as your new child labor law stipulates. I reported it to the Talihina deputy and our city leaders, but nothing was done. *Men*, you know. They do not see the trouble in such things. And, of course . . . they like the starch in their shirts." Mrs. Tinsley hides a giggle behind her hand. "Your department simply *must* look into the situation, Miss Kate."

"I will make note to send an investigator," Miss Kate answers when Mrs. Tinsley finally stops talking. "But in the meanwhile, if the men offer no satisfaction on the issue, the women of the town might form a formidable opposition by doing their own wash at home, wouldn't you say?"

Mrs. Tinsley chokes on a sip of water, and right in that minute every lady at the table has to wipe her face with her napkin to cover a grin. I clamp my lips together and hurry off to refill my pitcher.

Next time I make my way back to the head table, the ladies have started talking about the vote, and Mrs. Tinsley looks like she just bit into a lemon.

Mrs. Threadgill and Mrs. McDougal, the federation president and vice president, sit on either side of Kate Barnard. Mrs. McDougal looks worse for the wear of whatever trouble slowed down that library wagon on its way into Talihina.

"But what say you on women's suffrage in general, Kate?" Mrs. Threadgill wants to know. "Are you a supporter of women having the vote?"

"I do not need the vote for myself," Miss Kate tells her. "As present, I am all smiles because the men of our legislature this year did everything I asked them to do. But if women want to vote, I do not see why they should be denied the privilege. Women pay taxes without representation. Women are wage earners and yet cannot vote for men who will legislate for or against labor. But I say we cannot wait for that time to begin influencing the laws of our new state."

"It is my opinion that many current-day social problems would be greatly diminished if women had the vote." Mrs. McDougal says. She ain't in the pearliest mood, since she missed all the speeches.

"Oh, indeed." Mrs. Threadgill sets down her fork and dabs her mouth. "Women's hearts are naturally inclined toward the poor, the infirm, the feeble-minded, the friendless child. Don't you agree, Kate?"

"To address the suffering of the present," Miss Kate answers, "I find that one must work within the confines of the present. The legislature has authorized me to appear in probate court as 'next friend' to orphans, for example, and I must use my available means to protect them *now*, not tomorrow or on some future day. The starving orphan, the child abused or forced to labor, cannot wait upon political tides. Case in point, the fates of minor children and orphans of the

Cherokee, Creek, Seminole, Chickasaw, and Choctaw tribes in Oklahoma worsen by the day. The congressional enactment of May 1908 having removed the Interior Department from oversight of the Five Tribes, county probate judges are free to do as they please."

Mrs. Tinsley jumps in before anybody else can. "But in truth, orphaned children—especially the *Indian* ones—*should* be managed closer to home. Local administration is most efficient, after all."

Miss Kate sets down her glass hard enough that water splashes out the top. "And I must counter that *efficiency* is not the matter where human lives are concerned, but rather *equity*. Placed under the control of county probate courts, these children are as defenseless as lambs among wolves. They are delivered into the hands of judges who award lucrative guardianships to political donors and heartless grafters who seek guardianships so as to steal the wealth of their wards. Money is spread thick from here to Washington, and the children suffer. This is a travesty, and I tell you, women must stand against crimes such as these *now*, vote or no vote. And so my question in here echoes my question out there, *When you get home, ladies, what are you going to do about it?*"

The table quietens, and of a sudden everybody's busy with their food.

Mrs. McDougal coughs like she's swallowed a bone, and she motions to have her water filled. Just when I step in there, she looks up at me, and I realize I've seen her face before. She's been at the Lockridges' parties out at the ranch.

I get as nervous as those ladies twisting in their seats.

"So many multifarious issues, indeed." For once Mrs. Tinsley busts up the quiet at a good time. "And how do you find the roast pork, Miss Barnard? Is it to your liking?"

CHAPTER 19

Valerie Boren-Odell, 1990

Between every two pine trees there is a door
leading to a new way of life.

—John Muir

T he sound propels me from my bed like a bomb going off. I hit the floor with both feet, stagger around foggy and disoriented.

Where am I?

A moment ago I was pitching a tent along a flooded backwater in Yosemite. Joel was there, the two of us hiking the way we used to on our days off, young, unencumbered, crazy in love.

All of it was so real.

Suddenly I'm in a cabin, an ancient rotary phone caterwauling nearby. I stumble toward it, grab the receiver, blurt out, "Joel?"

"Huh?"

"Wha . . . I . . ."

"This is Curtis. Curtis . . . uhhh . . . Enhoe? Sorry, I'm guessing I hit it a little too early?"

The grogginess evaporates. "N-no. It's fine. I was up." I grab Charlie's leftover bedtime water from the counter, take a drink while Curtis chuckles into the phone, somewhere between amused and embarrassed.

"I was trying to catch you before you went on shift," he adds sheepishly.

I check the woodsy wall clock in panic. The little canoe has its oars pointed straight up and down: 6 A.M.! My heart stutters before my mind catches up, and I say, "Off day."

Dead silence, and then, "Oh . . . geez. Sorry about that. The message you left me didn't say anything about a day off."

"It's fine, really. I was up." I grab another swig of water, swish it around. "I just haven't make . . . *made* coffee yet." With my free hand, I smack my cheeks. *Wake up, already!*

"Well, I can relate there. Morning doesn't start till the coffee's on." He laughs again. It's a nice sound, casual, friendly, unstressed, as if he's in no rush to move into the day. Each thing in its own time, take it as it comes.

It all works out if you just let it. Joel's words. For an instant, my sleepy mind weaves them into the gentle laugh on the other end of the phone. Warmth envelops me, languid and familiar. It's as if I could turn around and Joel would be right here in this kitchen, in his baggy sweats and a T-shirt with the neckband stretched out from hanging sunglasses, ink pens, key rings, and all manner of Joel stuff on it.

I shake my head, drive blood into my brain. Joel vanishes. The sweet warmth gives way to the damp, misty feel of an Oklahoma summer morning.

"So, you got my message, then."

"Bonnie passed it along when I came home. She's a pretty fair secretary. This puppy parenting thing cuts into her efficiency, though."

"So Mama Dog has a name now? *Bonnie* . . . I like it. Tell her thanks for me. Sorry to be so cloak-and-dagger with the message." A blush washes upward from my chest to my cheeks. I feel silly for having deposited a note in the metal kibble storage can next to the dog dishes, but when I stopped by the house, Curtis's roommate, another tribal police officer, was on his way out the door. I hadn't realized anyone else lived there. "Your roommate looked like he was in a hurry. I didn't want to hold him up, so I told him I'd brought Charlie by to see the puppies."

"Good choice. He was probably running late. That's my cousin."

"How many cousins do you *have?*"

Again, that warm, throaty chuckle. "My grandma was one of twelve, so there're a lot of us. Anyway, bring your little guy by whenever. Those puppies can use some people time. Nobody's home around here much."

"Charlie would've stayed in your yard all night if I'd let him."

"Boys and puppies. See? They go together. You take one home with you? It was too dark to do a puppy count when I came in. They were all just one big pile by then."

Even though I've tried to shake off the morning's emotional surge, push my thoughts toward business, the warm sensation slips over me again, tingles on my skin like I've come in from the cold to stand by a fire. I think of tubby little fur balls all flopped together in a pile. How sweet. "No puppies here . . . unless Charlie hid one in his pocket."

"Better check."

"He's still asleep. I'm surprised, because I promised him we'd go hiking today. That usually means he's on the move as soon as his eyes pop open."

"Maybe he's curled up in there with your newest four-legged family member."

"Now you're scaring me. Hang on a sec." I stretch the phone cord far enough to reach Charlie's door, peek in, and scan the maze of bunk beds packed like blocks in a giant Tetris game. Charlie picks a different one each night. "Nope. No puppies. The kid's zonked. He had a long day yesterday. I worked overtime on the incident reports for our John Doe. Then I went by and talked to Sydney Potter for a few minutes. I really need to establish that we don't have a seventeen-year-old kid pinned under flood debris somewhere. Or two kids, for that matter."

"Two?"

I silently pull Charlie's door all the way closed. "Sydney says

Braden had a key lanyard and high-top tennis shoes, but not the color of the shoe we found. She also insisted he would have worn boots to go hiking. I'd like to show her the lanyard and the shoe to be sure, but I'm afraid she'll know what I'm getting at. The poor kid is dealing with enough trauma. She did mention that her brother had a long-distance girlfriend he met at Junior ROTC camp, Rachel ... something? Sounds like they were pretty smitten. Braden wanted the girl to come for a visit, but there had been some family resistance on both sides. Makes me question whether the girlfriend drove down here, and they were camped out someplace in the Holson Creek drainage and ... the flood."

I move farther from Charlie's door, cradle the phone against the kitchen wall. "I'd like to rule out everything I can. I wondered if anyone had mentioned the girlfriend to you. Maybe a last name? She's a college student in Oklahoma City now. Anybody I can talk to at Braden's school in Antlers? Teacher? Guidance counselor? Friends Braden might be close with? If I can track down the girlfriend, I'll know whether she's where *she's* supposed to be and whether Braden has fallen off her radar. That would be a bad sign."

"Let me make a few calls, check with people I know at the high school." Dishes clatter and something jangles in the background as he talks. His voice is muffled. I imagine the phone resting on his shoulder.

Tugging open our ancient refrigerator, I grab the bacon package, plop it onto the counter. "Whatever you can find out, I'd be appreciative. Sydney also mentioned a housekeeper, Sharla Watson, but said she'd moved away after spring break, so I doubt she'd have any recent knowledge. I don't mean to drag down your day with all this. Sounds like you're busy."

"Nah. Getting some breakfast. Long night. Ran into some issues at work."

That explains why he called so early. He's been up all night and he's ready to get some shut-eye. "No rush, really. Charlie's dying to see where the rockfall knocked out our hiking trail. I thought we'd take a long loop and make a day of it."

"Don't forget to have your little guy look for the Dewy trees." Curtis smothers a yawn. "You know about those, right? Not condoning tree graffiti, but it's like an Easter egg hunt, only a whole lot bigger. Kids love it."

"Roy mentioned that." A strangely tender feeling comes over me as I pour a cup of coffee. Roy, Curtis . . . a few people here actually care if Charlie adjusts to our new life, has fun, learns the insider secrets of these mountains. "Thanks for the reminder. I haven't run across one yet, but eagle-eye Charlie will be all over the challenge."

"You'll only find them on first-growth trees, so that means terrain that was too rough for logging," he says. "But I've seen a couple over the years and heard a lot of theories on how they got there. I've had old timers tell me that Dewy was an advance man plotting out operational parcels for the timber companies, a Choctaw Lighthorseman back in the days of the old nations, an outlaw who hid treasure nearby, or a horse thief marking spring pools to water stolen livestock. Take your pick."

I blow softly over the coffee, grab a first sip, feel my anticipation for the day growing. "I think Roy said Dewy was a bootlegger who made wildcat whiskey up there. But I'll give Charlie all the options. The mystery will be right up his alley."

An appreciative laugh answers and then, "Stop over on your way home. I'll fill you in on whatever I learn about Sydney and Braden. Charlie can get in some puppy time. These little rabble-rousers could use settling down."

"Settling down? You've seen Charlie, right?" The joke is a knee-jerk attempt to diffuse the intimate feeling of being invited to drop by. I like it in a way that leaves me vaguely guilty, or off-balance . . . or something. "He *is* a puppy."

"We really *are* getting a puppy?" As is his uncanny knack, Charlie enters the conversation at exactly the wrong time. When I glance over, he's standing in the bedroom doorway in his undies, scratching his scrawny rear end.

"No, we are not getting a puppy."

"Pick one!" Curtis blows my ear out through the phone.

"What'd he say?" Charlie wants to know. "Is that the *puppy guy?*" The last two words come with emphasis, like the name of a super-hero or star athlete. Batman or Michael Jordan.

"Mr. Enhoe," I correct, putting a skillet on the stove and turning on the burner. "And, yes, it is, but we're not getting a puppy." Charlie stares at me over crossed arms, one foot tapping the floor. In court, he'd be the DA who knows the witness can be broken. "Get dressed, okay? We're headed out hiking today, remember?"

The distraction works and Charlie is off to gear up with binocu-lars, collapsible fishing rod, canteen, camera, magnifying glass, bag-gies for trash patrol, and whatever else he can think of.

"That was smooth," Curtis wisecracks.

"Moms know things." The words hit me as a reminder that I'm a mom, not some unencumbered young thing.

Maybe Curtis takes it that way, too, because he's all business when he responds. "Sydney give you any idea about where *she* thinks her grandmother is?"

"Hard to say. Last time we talked, she sounded like she and Braden were on their own. This time, she seemed to expect her grandmother to return from some kind of medical treatments soon. Joanie from the café told me she'd heard that Budgie Blackwell died, then she heard Mrs. Blackwell was in the midst of a health crisis. So the rumor mill is all over the place. Maybe Braden knows but he can't bring himself to be honest with Sydney."

Bacon flares in the wobbly frying pan, shooting grease splatters like Fourth of July sparklers. "Oh shoot-ouch-sorry-bacon." Dragging the fire hazard off the burner, I fan grease smoke with a pot holder. "Breakfast just got a little lively."

"Sounds like I should let you go." The comment comes with an-other stifled yawn. "But, listen, come by on your way back from the hike. I'll give you the brief on what I find out."

We close the call as Charlie exits his bedroom, still in his undies but toting a backpack. "Mom! What did you *do?*" Coughing on the smoke, he rushes to open the front door, then steps out in his skiv-vies, so guests in the other cabins can admire his physique. "Hey, Mom! I see a black bear by the dumpster . . . and I bet it's Zorra!"

Mom fear catapults me to the door, and I stuff Charlie behind me before looking at the intruder across the way. It is indeed black, fairly large, and in the predawn light under the canopy of pines and oaks, it could be a juvenile black bear.

Except that it's a dog—a hefty, hairy, stub-tailed sort. I saw it yesterday with a couple of guys in cabin 6. "Tourist dog, sorry, bud. Good eye, though."

Charlie is bummed, but we have hiking and a day to ourselves to look forward to. That smoothly propels us through preparations, a drive to the trailhead, my filling Charlie in on the hunt for the Dewy trees, and the two of us setting off early to get in some foot miles before the midday heat hits. We'll picnic off trail near a stream, then make a bit of a backcountry climb over a ridge and down the other side to an equestrian trail, where we'll eventually link up with the loop taken out by the freak rockfall.

Charlie hits over-the-top yack-meister mode as we walk. He's ping-ponging back and forth across the trail, asking questions, making observations, and theorizing about whether we might see Zorra the Bear during our junket. A mile or so into our hike, I interrupt him and say, "Hey, bud, I mapped out a long trek for us today. You'll have to pace yourself, or we need to scale back the route—maybe just do this lowlands area."

An over-the-shoulder look of complete horror comes my way. "Mom, I'm just *excited.*" Hooking his thumbs in his backpack straps, he takes a deliberate draft of misty, pine-scented morning air, then exhales. "But I'm calm, too. See?"

"I can see that."

We make it about twenty yards, winding along in the shade of redbuds and dogwoods, cottonwoods and elms, their still-perfect spring leaves cradling diamond pools of morning dew, before Charlie asks, "Mom, did you mean 'hush'?"

Kind of, I think. Of course I don't say it. But between the park opening ceremonies, floods and debris, the rockfall, the death scene investigation, Sydney and Braden and Myrna Wambles with her morbid stories, work has been crazy, and I need . . . peace for a little while. The idea, of course, comes laced with guilt, and a sharp sense of loss, or incompleteness, or vulnerability at being on this journey alone, single parenting. I should be thrilled to spend time with my son. I should be fully present. I have to be. There is no one else.

"You'll see more things if you're quiet, remember? We've talked about that before. It's called *forest bathing*, but there's a special word for it in Japan. It's good for your mind."

I take a deep breath, lose myself in the healing power of feeling the world breathe, water over stones, wind against trees, last year's dry leaves tumbling along expanses of rock, in the play of cloud shadows on mountain peaks, the intricate lace of a dragonfly's wing. The smallest things and the largest. Perspective. To grasp even the faintest bit of it is to look into glory, to feel both insignificant and intricately made all at once. It's a valuable skill, the ability to appreciate that beauty exists even in the most difficult places. My father tried to teach me those lessons, but our relationship was so fraught with complications, I didn't fully comprehend until I met Joel, with his calm spirit and arms-wide-open embrace of life.

If he were here, he'd pass that on to our son. Because he can't, I must.

"Shinrin-yoku." Charlie's voice is quieter, more relaxed and measured, almost reverent.

"You remembered the word." I smile at his lean back and narrow shoulders, watch his small hiking boots find purchase on the path. "Good boy." Stress passes outward through my skin and gratitude settles in. It's hard to imagine that eight years ago an accidental pregnancy seemed like the end of everything.

It was the beginning.

I am so lucky to travel the world with this beautiful, unique little soul. A leftover piece of Joel. Of us, together.

As is commonplace in mothering boys, moments of revelry are like the droplets of nectar in a honeysuckle bloom, intensely sweet but fleeting. We haven't forest bathed for long before Charlie enters into a monologue about leaves and transpiration (which he refers to as *transportation*) the process by which plants sweat water from their leaves in hot weather as an evaporative cooling mechanism. He wants me to know that redbuds aren't very good at it because they have waxy leaves. He learned that on a nature show.

"Yes, but—" I pause as we pick our way around a washout in the trail. "Did you know that when you feel tiny drips falling down on you from a plant, if it's not rainwater or ordinary moisture, it might not be transpiration at all? It might be what's called *honeydew*."

"Honeydew?" He straddle-walks the last few yards, one foot on each side.

"Well, it's a form of sap." I can't count how many times I've amused school field trip kids and hapless park visitors with this obscure factoid. The punch line is the most fun when you're standing under the right sort of tree at the right time of year.

"Does it taste good?"

"It can, but I don't think you'd really want to sample honeydew."

"How come?"

"Because honeydew is produced by insects that eat sap for a living—sometimes tiny insects like aphids, and sometimes larger ones like leafhoppers."

"Soooo . . . when they bite the sap, it drips out from the leaves and falls on people?"

"Not exactly. Remember, I said they *eat* the sap, right? And they are big, big eaters. When something eats a lot and digests a lot, then . . ." Boys love this part of the story. It can send an entire elementary school class into a furious round of squeals, giggles, and whispered words their teachers don't allow them to say.

"It's . . . it's . . . *poo*?" Charlie gasps. "Mom! They poop on you?" Gaping into the trees, he scans the branches with a look of revulsion and insult. "That's bad!"

His horror fades quickly, and we laugh, and walk, and talk. Our morning hike passes with intermittent periods of silence, conversation, and discovery.

Lunch is a stop beside a clearwater creek for wading, cooling off, swimming if you're Charlie, and then we move along cross-country over a ridgeline to see the rockfall for ourselves. The damage is worse than I'd imagined, the rubble field hard-packed and massive.

"What made it happen like that?" Charlie wants to know, and I have to admit I've got no idea.

"Nature does strange things sometimes. We always have to keep an eye out to be safe." But in reality, nobody saw this coming.

"Maybe, I guess." Charlie has moved on to seeking bottle caps, gum wrappers, six-pack holders, bits of plastic, and any other human discards for his trash-and-treasure-collection baggies.

"Not too close." This place sets my nerves on edge. I don't like things I can't explain. Staring at the cataclysmic mess, I ponder potential causes before I realize it's not what I see that's bothering me . . . it's what I hear.

Footsteps. The human kind. With the area closed, no one should be around for miles. I turn my ear, strain against the rustle of leaves and pine branches. "Charlie, be still a minute."

The footstep noise stops, but I hear something else farther away. A voice? A little girl . . . singing . . . or whistling . . . or a flute playing? A radio maybe?

Just the acoustics of wind whistling through rock formations?

It's faint enough that I can't be sure. Goosebumps race up my arms. I think of Myrna Wambles, and murdered girls, and the man-devil searching for his scattered body parts.

You best watch yourself up in them mountains . . .

"Hello?" I call out. "Anybody there?"

I listen again. Silence.

CHAPTER 20

Olive Augusta Radley, 1909

Some attorneys cooperate with "flappers" to ensnare wealthy, young Indian men into matrimony. Soon thereafter a divorce usually follows, and the court allows liberal alimony to the flapper wife, which she shares with her co-partner, the attorney.

—GERTRUDE BONNIN, 1924, RESEARCH AGENT, INDIAN WELFARE COMMITTEE, GENERAL FEDERATION OF WOMEN'S CLUBS.

My heart's pounding, and my legs are near falling off before I make it all the way to Jack Crossing. I'm wore out after serving lunch, then helping the clubwomen clean up the mess. Lucky for me, Mrs. McDougal never did ask where she knew me from, and after the meal, she went to the doctor for her hurt ribs from the terrible trouble with the library wagon on the way into town. Mrs. Tinsley and some of the other ladies walked outside to see about damage to the book crates, and Kate Barnard headed to the Commercial Hotel to rest.

I wound up with five nickels for the day's work, plus Mrs. Paulson loaded me up with pit-smoked pork, roast turnips, and lemon tea cookies to carry home to my ailing mama. I can't wait to give the food to Nessa, Tula, and the little ones. Hopefully those turnip-thieving boys have wandered back into town by now because Tula and me need to talk. Word came this afternoon that the bad men who'd been raiding farms and road wagons north of here had raised trouble farther south now. The Talihina deputy gave orders that folks not leave town except in groups of several parties together. Then he gathered some men, and they galloped off to make sure the academy girls and their teachers didn't meet with trouble on the road home.

Mrs. Grube has to hold over to catch a line of wagons going her way in the morning, and she is in a nervous fit about the whole big mess. I didn't know how I'd get shed of her so as to go to Jack Crossing, till she heard that Miss Kate was staying overnight at the Commercial Hotel, and she decided to try one more time for a conversation.

"You keep close to camp, Hazel," she told me. "I may be awhile."

Soon as she picked up Baby Beau and left, I grabbed the extra food from where I'd hid it and took off cross-country toward Daddy's old camp spot to check on Nessa.

A nightjar's call catches my ear when I start into the brush by the creek, *chuck-will's-widow, chuck-will's-widow.* This late in the day it could be a real nightjar or it could be Tula. I answer back as I push my way through the cedars and grapevines and greenbrier.

Chuck-will's-widow, chuck-will's-widow. The call comes again, and quick as a blink, I'm a little girl, camped here with my daddy on a pack trip. He's got a fire lit and the horses fed. I feel safe as can be while I explore around, looking for lightning bugs and glittery rocks and a place to build a fort where me and my rag doll can have a playhouse.

Chuck-will's-widow. I don't answer, because I want to keep my pretend world real. My daddy is right there at camp, watching over. He's singing old songs while he does the chores. Soon enough we'll sit down at the evening fire for food and stories. I'm not an orphan. I'm Olive Augusta Radley . . . Keyes Radley's girl, and that's a thing to be proud of.

Chuck-will's-widow.

"Tula?" I whisper.

The air goes still, and a chill runs through my bones. Silent as the dawn, a face melts from the brush, a thin face with dark eyes that seem too big, just like the first time I saw her and thought she was a elf child.

"Tula?" I say, because down here in the shadow-light, I'm spooked. "Tula?"

She doesn't answer, just tips her head off to the side and looks at me like she never saw me before in her life. "That's you, ain't it?" My voice goes to trembling. "Y-you better . . . better ans . . . answer me."

Holding the food pack tight against my body, I stumble back a step. Black locust branches grab me with their long thorns, and I gasp, "Where's Nessa?"

Noise troubles the air. Just a slip of sound, but I know it right off. You don't live with somebody for three years and not know her giggle, even if she *is* trying to cover it. "Nessa Bessie! That ain't funny. You get out here right now."

Snickers and laughs come from all directions. Tula and the little kids bust from the bushes wearing big ol' grins, proud of their trick and that I fell for it.

"W-w-where's Nessa?" a voice singsongs, mocking me. It's one of those boys. Tula and the others helped them make me look like a fool.

Something hits my head and bounces off, and they all laugh harder. Up the creek bank, Dewey Mullins sits on a sycamore branch with a handful of pebbles in his hand.

"Sissy," he says, and tosses another one. "We fooled you good."

My face goes from cold to hot. "Why don't you come down here and say that?" Tucking the food bundle by a rock, I get ready for a wrangle.

"No, Ollie!" Nessa scoots from the brush and latches on to my one arm, which I was about to load for a punch. "Them boys are our friends."

"They ain't friends." I try to shake her off while Dewey shinnies down the tree. "I'm mad at *you*, Nessa, but I'm even madder at *him*."

"Here, now, y'all two. All us is friendly-like." Out of the brush comes Amos, his hands pocketed in his raggy canvas trousers. "We's just funnin'. No harm done."

Tula tries to tell me in Choctaw that they didn't mean anything by it. She's all sorry now, of course.

"When did *you* get mean, Tula?" Tears prickle in the back of my throat. They made fun, same way Tesco Peele picks on people and laughs about it. "Here I been running my legs off to bring you some supper and working all day to get money for us. Well, now I'm sorry

I did." I snatch up the food bundle and turn back the way I came. "I'll take my leave and say my goodbyes. Nessa, you comin'?"

"Stay," she sniffles. "I got a book. You can have it, Ollie. All for your own."

"C'mon, stay. Share them vittles." Even Dewey wants to be chums now that he knows there's food.

"Book?" I turn back to Nessa. "Where'd you get a book?"

"Outta the wagon." She's already dancing off down the creek bank, wanting me to come after her. "Come look."

"Nessa, you didn't go into town, did you? I told y'all to stay put."

"They been put." Dewey struts on by. "That book wagon *might've* come through Jack Crossin', and *somethin'* might've spooked the horse into a runaway, that's all."

A breath catches in my throat. At lunch I heard Mrs. McDougal say that right before the wagon horse bolted, there were voices in the woods. Children's voices. And that her and the driver could've got killed in the wagon wreck, except the runaway horse eventually plowed into a thicket and got stuck. It took two men with axes and timber saws to cut that rig loose so it could limp on to Talihina.

"What did y'all *do*?" I choke out.

"They oughta put a better driver on that wagon than a couple womenfolk." Dewey grins over his shoulder, heading down the creek toward the old camp place.

When we get there, I see books all right. A half dozen and a busted crate that's stacked with the extra firewood, plus a ruined silk parasol the same dark purple as Mrs. McDougal's dress.

"You stole their books?" I babble out.

"Them books just . . . fell off the wagon while it was bouncin' around." Dewey lifts his hands, palms up. "Landed in the water, though, so they're ruint. If we knew them crates was just carryin' books, we woulda let that wagon pass. Next time, we'll pick more careful when we jostle a wagon at the crossin'."

"What?"

"Raid it, just like Robin Hood and his merriment. That's a tale I heard, workin' down in the mines, and it's a good'un. What you got to eat in that pack, anyhow?"

He's already trying to grab the food, and so I hand it to Tula. "It's for Tula and Nessa and Pinti and Koi." I look round that fire, where they've all squatted down licking their lips while Tula opens the food pack. "Tales don't fill a belly, or thieved turnips, either. At least they shouldn't."

Dewey's bony shoulders rise and sink under his overall straps. "That reverend's got plenty."

"Point is, it's against the law. Once the deputy is back in town, you better mend your ways, Dewey Mullins. Those clubwomen are mad about the wagon and their books. Ain't my worry, though. Come tomorrow, us girls are leavin', and you can sort it out for yourself."

Tula shares the food around with everybody, and while they're busy, I whisper the plans into Nessa's ear, so Nessa can tell Tula in Choctaw. Tomorrow I'll get Mrs. Grube to hand over some food for my baby brother and sick mama before she leaves out with the other wagons. Then I'll come back here with Skedee and the packs, so we girls and little Koi can head into the Winding Stairs. With Pinti and Koi being so small, it'll take us three days or so to make the trek up the back trail to the old place. Daddy and I could do it a lot faster, but that's all right. I know good camp spots on the way—places where nobody can find us.

Nessa tells Tula the plan, but I notice Tula's not nodding or answering. She keeps her head tucked like she's studying on her food, real hard.

Dewey's the one who pipes up first. "Don't know why you'd want to go way up in them mountains. That's what you're talkin' about, ain't it? Amos here speaks good Choctaw. He learned me some of it." Half-chewed pork meat shoots past Dewey's chipped tooth while he talks. "Ain't nothin' up there. How you mean to make your livin'?"

"Hunt. Fish. Harvest from the woods. My daddy showed me how." I hand my food over to Nessa, because I can get something else at Mrs. Grube's wagon. "None of your business anyway."

Dewey flicks his fingers at me, scattering black grease. "I say we can do fine right here. Jostle us a few wagons. Take from the rich and hand to the poor, like Robin Hood and his merriment. Get back for the wrongs that's been done us. See?"

"What wrongs?" I don't like it that they've been talking so much here on their own.

"Well, Miss Fancy in your nice clothes"—Dewey gives me a pig-eyed look—"just take ol' Amos here, let's say. He is a official Choctaw freedman, so when the gov'ment cuts up the Choctaw lands, few years back, Amos gets his own patch like all the other Choctaw freedmen. Plus after his folks pass on from the malaria sickness, Amos owns their land and the cabin he growed up in. Then one day comes a man who says, 'I'm your ma's half brother. I am to take care of you, 'cause you ain't got no folks now. For you to keep this land, you need to marry up with a woman. I found you a woman, and we'll go to the justice of the peace to marry. Once the knot is tied, we'll all have ice cream and get you a fine horse and saddle and a new rifle, so you can be a husband.' Well, don't that sound good to Amos? Horse, saddle, new rifle, plus you keep your house with your folks buried out back?"

He turns to Amos, who leans his elbows on his knees and hangs his head. "Yeah, it did. I was a fool, though."

Dewey pats him on the back, hard. "There now, it ain't your fault. How was you supposed to know any different?" Fire sparks glitter in Dewey's muddy brown eyes when he looks my way. "So there's Amos. He's only just turned fourteen that month. Off they go in a wagon to some town that's a far piece away. Sure enough, a woman's there waitin'. She's a bunch older than Amos, but she don't seem to mind, and he's wantin' that horse and saddle and gun—and ice cream. They see the justice, say some words, mark some papers, go to the ice cream shop, just like the plans is. Next thing Amos knows, he's all alone there on the boardwalk, waitin' on a horse, saddle, and gun that ain't comin'. He don't have to worry about that land or cabin, either, because by the time he finally finds his way back there, the wife and half uncle have moved in, and she's getting a divorce from Amos and taking the land as her part. So what you think of that, Miss Fancy?"

I look at Amos, slumped over, stabbing a stick into the ground with one hand and rubbing Koi's head with the other. Koi grabs Amos's lemon tea cookie, and Amos doesn't even care.

"Well?" Dewey leans toward me, and I notice that a chunk of his ear is missing on the same side as the broken front tooth. "Ain't that a wrong thing against Amos? Don't he deserve somethin' to pay back for that?"

"But not from stealing." I mean it when I say it, but I also think about Amos, who seems kindly, even if he does keep bad company. I'm mad about the men who tricked him. "He should go to the judge. There's courts and sheriffs and that kind of thing." On Mr. Lockridge's porch all the men talk about is courts and lawyers.

"Only gettin' back for what was stole from me." Amos looks at Dewey when he says it, pulling those words right out of Dewey's mouth.

"Hear that, Miss Fancy?" Dewey snaps his fingers. "And let me tell you what'll happen to Amos if he goes tellin' his tale. He'll wind up dead or in jail. Them people warned him when they run him off. I found Amos hidin' in the Jack Fork Mountains, eatin' worms and bugs and minnows out of the crick. It was a sad sight, and so I told him, 'Since I'm on the road from bad to better, we oughta travel on together. Join up. Ain't nobody in this world cares about a orphan ... *but* a orphan.' That's somethin' you oughta think about, Miss Fancy. Ain't nobody else cares. Them pretty clothes get dirtied up, they'll chase you off their porch, just like us."

"Yeah, that's true." Amos says. "Dewey and me, we joined up. It's good, joinin' up." Perfect round circles of firelight move on his cheeks when he nods. The evening shadows are long and thick, but not so thick that I can't see Amos looking over at Tula and Tula looking at him. Those two are going sweet on each other.

Wonder what Dewey will think when he figures that out.

"See." Dewey grabs up a pine twig. "You tote this lil' stick all by its lonesome, you can't do much with it—bends too easy. Breaks too quick." He fishes around for another twig. "Join these two up, it's stronger, like me and Amos."

Tula squints at Dewey with her thinking look, trying to make out the words. Nessa watches, too ... both the twigs and me, back and forth.

Setting those two sticks on the ground, Dewey points around the circle at each of us. "You take one, two, three, four, five ... and six 'n' seven—" He counts up a handful of twigs and lays them out, seven, then holds them in a bundle. "You take seven together, well, there's no tellin' what you could do."

Tula nods and says, "Ahli" which means she agrees it's true. Pinti and Koi scrabble closer to look at the bundle in Dewey's freckly, scarred-up hand.

Nessa ducks her chin till all I can see is the top of her head, then she says, "C-could dig taters." Her voice is just above the night bugs' songs, but it hits me the same as if she was yelling. They've all been planning this.

"Could scrape a hide for tannin'," Amos pipes up. "If you sharp them sticks on the ends."

"Tunnel out a shelter in the side of a hill," Dewey throws in. "Start a fire for cookin'. Fix a fish trap and catch a fish. You could ..."

He keeps talking, except I don't want to hear it. I push to my feet and turn to Nessa and tell her, "I've got to get back to the wagon camp before it's too dark to see. Don't you go anyplace till I come in the morning with Skedee, Nessa Bessie. You hear? You stay right here in this camp. We're heading to the mountains like we planned, to the old place under the shelterwood trees, you listenin' at me?"

She just stares down at those sticks.

My heart squeezes. All Nessa and I have now is each other. "Hazel left you with me. Remember that. She left you with *me*."

I turn and run for town, and don't stop till I get back to the campgrounds.

When I round the corner to our wagon, there sits Mrs. Grube on her milking stool by the fire, holding a tin cup in one hand and a dinner plate on her lap. She ain't eating alone, either. Across from her on the upside-down bucket that was my seat last night sits the blue-eyed newspaperman.

While I stand there with my chin hanging, Mrs. Grube looks up peaceable as you please and says, "Oh, Hazel, where in heaven's name were you? Well, it's no matter now, I suppose. Come and sit. I've just been talking with Mr. Brotherton about the elf children."

CHAPTER 21

Valerie Boren-Odell, 1990

Many and long are the duties heaped upon their shoulders. If a trail is to be blazed, it is "send a ranger." If an animal is floundering in the snow, a ranger is sent to pull him out; if a bear is in the hotel; if a fire threatens the forest; if someone is to be saved, it is "send a ranger."

—Stephen T. Mather, 1928, director, National Park Service.

"My guess is, the investigation doesn't go much further," Curtis comments. We sit side by side, legs dangling off the edge of his front porch as the sun rests atop mountain peaks of evening blue and pale violet. Charlie and a gaggle of puppies run wild in the yard, determined not to surrender the day. "Unless an ID comes in, he'll end up a John Doe who underestimated what water can do. If he was out there with somebody else for a nonrecreational reason—drug trade, illegal hunting, breaking into private cabins on inholdings—his cohort isn't likely to come forward."

"True enough." I've had no hits so far on a missing ex-convict with a size-fourteen foot. The medical examiner's office is backlogged. The death looks to have been accidental. Speculation was minimal and hushed when I dropped by the station after Charlie and I finished our hike. The only thing that causes more collective angst than an accidental death in the park is a death involving foul play, so the keywords right now are *presumed accidental.*

Curtis twiddles a piece of grass between his fingers, watches it pensively. "Be good if an ID came, though. He might have a family out there who'd like to know."

I'm struck by the decency of that comment. "I hope we'll catch a break on it, but to tell you the truth, my mind's on Braden Lacey—even more since the body recovery. What if he and that guy *were* together, or they had a random altercation out there, or the same weather event that got John Doe also got Braden? You come up with anything else that could help locate him?"

"Not much, sorry." An involuntary tightening of Curtis's jaw muscles indicates an emotional investment. "His school friends knew about the long-distance girl, but Braden was so into her he'd pretty much ditched his buddies. They thought her last name was Walker, Walters, Watson, something like that. Since Braden moved over here to work for Parker, they haven't heard from him at all."

"Dead end . . . again." Sinking forward, I let my arms slide between my dangling knees, stretch the muscles in my back, stiff from the long day hike. In the yard, Charlie is in puppy heaven, literally rolling through the freshly mowed grass while a dozen black-and-white banditos use him as a jungle gym.

"Mommmm!" He laughs when one tries to abscond with the junior ranger ball cap. "H-h-help!"

"You're on your own, buddy." Loose wisps of hair blow against my cheek and glow red in the late-day sun. I'm so used to having it up for work, the sensation of it stroking my skin raises an involuntary shudder. I tuck it behind my ear before turning back to Curtis. "Nobody in Antlers had a bead on whether Braden was depressed, overwhelmed, at loose ends? Whether he might have become involved in something he couldn't handle? Maybe as a way to pick up some quick cash?"

"All I got was more confusion. About the kids and about Budgie Blackwell." Scratching Bonnie's ears as she settles in beside him, he shakes his head. "Things had changed in the past few months. Budgie hadn't been going out much, hardly answered phone calls, sounded foggy. She started keeping the gate closed so visitors wouldn't drop by. Stroke, heart attack, depression, the flu, some sort of dementia and paranoia—depends on who you talk to. A couple people said she went to her sisters' house in Tulsa and died there. No funeral because Budgie never wanted one—just spread her ashes in the Winding Stairs. But there's no death certificate on Mrs. Blackwell. I checked. I'm sure you have, too." Scratching his chin, he runs a thumb along his bottom lip. I catch myself watching.

"Maybe Sydney is right. She's hospitalized or in nursing care up in Tulsa at the . . . City of Faith, I think Sydney said? I have a feeling it's more wishful thinking on her part, but I made a note to follow up tomorrow when I'm back at my desk."

Curtis responds with a skeptical look. "The City of Faith went bankrupt a year ago. It's been all over the news."

"Went . . . what? Sydney asked me to go there and talk to her grandmother. She *begged* me to." I squeeze my knees against my threaded-together hands, tighten a cocoon around myself, frustrated. "The whole thing just doesn't fit."

Curtis nods in grim agreement. "Under any normal circumstances, Budgie Blackwell wouldn't leave those kids, or her house and land, without making arrangements beyond just depending on Alton Parker. Parker's got the money to step in and help, but the man basically eats, sleeps, and breathes his businesses. His wife divorced him years ago, and Parker moved into his warehouse. That's not the kind of situation a loving grandmother would pick for her grandkids unless she really had to leave in a hurry."

"Or she wasn't thinking straight. Maybe she intended to go to the hospital, but got confused? Got lost? Went off the road somewhere, and the car's not visible? Is there anyone else she might have tried to reach? Maybe the kids' mother?"

"Jade?" He looks at me like I've grown a second head. "They haven't been on speaking terms for years. Last I heard, Jade was living out west. Vegas . . . Reno. Something like that."

I mentally page through my interview at the Wambles house. "Sydney mentioned that her mother didn't want Braden's girlfriend visiting, that they had enough going on at the ranch with pond dam and barn repairs. That has to mean Jade was around enough to know about recent events."

"If that's true, it changes everything." The tone of that statement is so ominous it pulls my gaze to his. His expression is dark, foreboding. "Jade wouldn't come there unless she was desperate for cash, a crash pad, or a place to hide."

"Hide from what?"

"Could be anything, but Budgie Blackwell's a tough old bird. Not the kind to take it lightly if somebody came around her place causing trouble. I remember a story about her spotting some yahoos in one of her pastures with an empty stock trailer and a couple of four-wheelers, trying to make off with her cattle. That's been . . . maybe ten years ago. She must've been at least eighty. When the sheriff's department got there, old Mrs. Blackwell was belly-crawling through the high grass with a rifle on her back.

"A few years later, when Congressman Watkins held a public forum about designating Winding Stair as a park, the lawyers and the suits from Big Timber had spread quite a bit of propaganda that it would destroy mom-and-pop timber businesses, hurt the local economy. Mrs. Blackwell showed up with facts, figures, pictures of federal forest land that'd been clear-cut by corporations carting the profits out of state. She let them know they'd better hear her out at that meeting, or she'd be on the TV news next. She made a pretty sympathetic picture, compared to some corporate lawyer in a three-piece suit. So that's Budgie Blackwell. If she caught Jade . . . sneaking around? Trying to pocket things to sell? Or if some ex-boyfriend or drug contact of Jade's gave them trouble? No telling, but it could get ugly."

My thoughts tumble over one another. "And then Sydney is told that her grandmother left because of a medical crisis in the middle of the night? And that she's in Tulsa, under treatment at a hospital no one can call."

"If something happened at home on Budgie Blackwell's land, it could explain the conflicting stories and the lack of any verifiable information." A long exhalation rounds Curtis's shoulders. "It makes more sense than most of what we've come up with, but it's still possible an addled old woman drove away in the middle of the night, or that Budgie really is in a facility being treated, but Sydney has the details wrong. It's worth digging into who *really* told Sydney it was the City of Faith. Was it Braden, or was it Jade?"

"I'll follow up with Sydney."

"I think you're the one she's most likely to level with. She's obviously a Ranger Valerie fan."

"Yeah, there are a lot of those around here," I joke.

That earns a smirk. I hadn't noticed before, but he has dimples.

"Goes with the job," I add flatly. I don't want him to think I'm looking for a defender. I can take care of myself. "You deal with it or you get out."

"Doesn't sound like you're on your way out." The observation comes with a note of appreciation, and we spend a few minutes diffusing the tension with random career talk. He's particularly interested in backcountry life in Yosemite. I'm into a few funny anecdotes before I realize that Joel is part of the story, and the story ends with his death in a rescue gone bad.

I tell the story anyway. I'm not sure why. Aside from family, all of my relationships since Joel's death have been surface only, especially at work. Sharing the hard truth with Curtis, the parts that aren't pretty, feels like opening the valve on a pressure cooker I didn't know I'd left on the stove. And yet somehow, cupped in the palm of the mountains at the day's end, it feels doable, maybe even cathartic. Curtis is a relaxed listener, nodding occasionally and offering a sympathetic comment or two, not advice, but empathy.

"Yeah, it just happened, you know?" A hard sigh escapes as I finish. "There's no saying why. I wish things were different. I wish Charlie had known him at least, that Charlie would have memories."

"Stories turn into memories. You just have to tell them enough." Curtis stares into the distance, a tiny diorama of trees and sky reflecting against his eyes. "I had a brother twelve years older than me. He was killed in a car wreck before I can remember. We had an empty spot in our house when I was growing up, but with a big family, there was always someone to tell another story, and so I knew him that way. You'll give that to lil' Charlie over there. You do a good job telling his dad's story. I feel like I've just been to Yosemite." A fringe of dark hair casts a faint shadow over his forehead as he looks my way and smiles. "And I'm pretty sure I'm not half tough enough to be a backcountry ranger there."

Of all things, we laugh together. The moment carries the unexpected promise of a sudden breeze on a suffocating summer day. It promises life.

I take that with me as we wrap things up, and I separate Charlie from the puppies, one by one, while Curtis slyly keeps cycling them behind his back, so that we've said goodbye to each at least twice before I catch on. Then he threatens to tuck one into Charlie's backpack, wherein he becomes Charlie's hero. In the end, Bonnie follows us all the way out the gate and climbs halfway into the seat with Charlie. They're so cute together I almost give in before I come to my senses and we leave dogless.

But not friendless.

The comfort of that new realization lasts until I drop Charlie off at Edwin's place for safekeeping, slip into an NPS windbreaker and ball cap, and drive the few blocks to Myrna Wambles's house.

Stepping out of the truck in the Wambleses' driveway, I steel myself for another terse greeting, but when Myrna opens the door, she's wearing a smug smile. She's particularly eager to tell me that if I want to talk to Sydney, I'll need to contact Alton Parker—he came and picked Sydney up a few hours ago.

Alarm bells buzz in my head, and I glance toward the tattered curtains over the front window.

"She ain't in there, if that's what you're gettin' at." Myrna's eyes narrow. "You need to do a search, or you just want to take my word for it? Parker showed up right at outdoor recreation time in the backyard . . . said he was set up to take charge of the kids now. Had rooms fixed up for them and all."

"Them? You mean Sydney *and* Braden, both? Braden came home?"

"I reckon. The girl's only got the one brother. That I know of anyhow. Considerin' who the mama is, there's no tellin'." She dusts her palms against one another, *clap-swish-swish-swish.* "Off my hands, anyhow. Parker'll have his plate full with that one."

My stomach roils. "Any idea where I might find them?"

"Parker stays in that apartment off the back of his business. You can't miss the place. Big sign out front."

"Yes, I've been there." I can't picture a little girl living amid the conglomeration of metal buildings, the grounds littered with piles of old telephone poles, empty fifty-gallon metal barrels, and derelict heavy equipment, a chain-link fence and the smell of grease, creosote, and industrial chemicals surrounding everything. "*That's* where he took the kids?"

"Yep. That's it." Grabbing the doorknob, Myrna gives it a loud rattle, effectively quieting a rising interior clamor. Snickering at how well the trick worked, she adds, "But you won't find Parker at that warehouse. He'll be headed out to his huntin' cabin for the weekend by now. Reckon he'd take those kids with him."

"Cabin?" The scenarios grow more disturbing with each new tidbit. "Where is that?"

"Oh, I couldn't tell ya. The Parker family had land from years ago, thousand acres or more. But him and them kids'll be back come Mon-dey, probably with some fresh-killed game." Myrna's smile widens. "Till then, they're someplace in the deep, dark woods. You have a good night, now, y'hear?" She slides through the door and locks it behind herself.

I hurry away, my body so tightly strung I'm at Edwin's trailer before I even realize I haven't caught my breath. An impromptu glow-in-the-dark whiffle ball tournament is happening in the front yard. Charlie begs me to stay and join in, but all I can think about is Sydney, Braden, and Alton Parker's hunting cabin in the woods.

I barely even remember to thank Edwin and his wife before hustling Charlie off to the truck.

"You crack the case?" he asks on the way home.

"What case?"

"About the girl, and her brother, and their grandma in the hospital, but the hospital's closed? And maybe they all had a fight or something?"

I stare at him agape. "Charlie!" I had no idea how much he picked up while playing with the puppies. "You're not supposed to listen to work conversations."

"I didn't listen, I *heard*. I can close up my eyes." He demonstrates by squeezing his lashes tightly to his cheeks. "But my ears don't got lids. Ears don't close, huh, Mom?"

"Yours don't." Then I warn him that he must not repeat any of this—not to the teachers at daycare or the kids.

"K," he agrees amiably, and busies himself with sorting a couple of found coins from his litter collection baggie as we drive the quiet streets back home to Lost Pines.

"New kids!" he observes, pointing to a family unpacking their minivan at the cabin court. "Can I go say hi?"

"Okay, but just for a minute. We've got baths and supper, then off to bed."

He's out the door as soon as we're parked, intent on doing his thing as unofficial welcoming committee for the Lost Pines Cabin Court. Tracking him with the peripheral mom-eye, I unload the hiking gear and carry our lunch trash over to the dumpster.

I'm caught off guard when I look up and the tourist dad is headed my way with Charlie hurrying along beside him. The man has a bearing that denotes either military or law enforcement, and his body language is anything but casual.

"You know he had this?" A calloused palm offers up one of the treasures Charlie sorted from his litter bag on the way home—a metal tube from a hiker's broken flashlight or walkie-talkie.

"He picked that up on our hike today—he always carries a couple baggies for trash and treasure pickup. We like to think of it as voluntary dejunking of federal land."

The man is unamused. "Ma'am." He's still slightly breathless from unpacking coolers and suitcases. "I'm a retired US Army engineer, and this thing your son has . . . this is a blasting cap."

"A *what*?" I grab Charlie and shove him toward our cabin.

"It's an empty. It's inert," the guy assures me. "But it's nothing to play with." Now I know why he's breathing hard and his eyes are bugging out of his skull. He's just gone through a near-death experience, similar to the one I'm currently having. Blasting caps, if they're not inert, are filled with the kind of explosives that trigger a bomb.

"I didn't know-w-w," Charlie wails, shrinking away. "Nobody told me!"

"Charlie, where did you get that?" He's been taught not to touch syringes, needles, razor blades, other sharp objects, anything that looks like medicine or discarded drug paraphernalia. He knows how to watch for loose rocks, slippery moss, snakes, poisonous spiders, scorpions, beehives, bear scat. But blasting caps? My mind runs wild. *That kind of thing shouldn't be within miles of a public-use area. How did it get there?*

I squat down to look at Charlie straight on. "Did you see any more?"

A quick shake of his sniffling head, and then, "No ... 'cause I looked everyplace for pieces, so maybe I could put it back together. I wanted to fix it, but I thought it was something *good*, Mom."

A mental catalog of our hike cycles through my head. The swimming hole where we ate lunch? The parking area? New gravel had been spread there. Maybe that thing was mixed in a delivery of road base material from the rock quarry?

I elect to make our excuses before questioning Charlie any further. Once we're inside, I hold him by the shoulders, say again, "You can tell me. You're not in trouble. Where *exactly* did you pick that up?"

Finally he spills, "At the rockslide."

"You're sure?" He nods, and I hug him close, pull in a long breath, draw back so I can look him in the eye. "So, listen, that isn't something to talk to anybody else about, either, okay? And like the man said, if you ever, *ever* see an object you're not sure of, ask an adult first."

"Oh, I will." Sagging forward, he lets his arms dangle. "Whew. I'm glad that's over."

It's anything but over.

That rockfall didn't just happen. Somebody blew a chunk off the side of our mountain.

The question is ... why?

I hustle Charlie through his bath, supper, and then off to bed. He's out cold before I can take a quick shower, slip on sweats and a tank top, and make a cup of tea. Grabbing my notepad, I jot down words, tear off pages, turn the coffee table into an impromptu evidence board.

Cave bones. Rockslide. Braden Lacey missing? John Doe.
Heard someone near the rockfall area.
Budgie Blackwell missing?
Alton Parker.
City of Faith.
Jade?
Murder? Cover-up?
Sydney . . .

Sinking into the sofa, I stare, chew on my lip and the possibilities, rearrange the board. Finally, I scoot *Budgie Blackwell, murder, cover-up* out of the picture, put *Braden Lacey* at the top, throw my wet hair over the back of the sofa, rest my head, study the remaining cards again.

What if there *was* more in that cave to begin with? Antiquities? Indigenous grave goods? What if the truck drivers who supposedly discovered the site fled as soon as they saw human remains? What if, as the phone tipster indicated, they really were talking about it at a bar? And someone besides the tipster heard the story? Someone who knew the mountains well enough to go hunting for treasure? Someone who, after making one score, was willing to blow the side off a mountain looking for another?

What if . . . that person was . . . Braden Lacey . . .

Some military knowledge or interest . . .

Had access to the Parker Construction warehouse . . .

Explosives?

Familiar with the area . . .

Needed money . . .

Sydney said . . . he was . . . he was going to find treasure . . .

Robbed a . . . a grave . . .

My eyes drift closed and sleep whisks me into darkness. I land in a high-mountain meadow. A spring creek runs past, the water musical, clear, peaceful. Along the banks, three little girls turn in a circle, holding hands and laughing, singing, "... around the Rosie. Pocket full of posies. Ashes, ashes, we all fall ..."

A flash of light, a burst of sound, the earth trembles. The girls lie on a carpet of leaves beneath an ancient oak, their bodies wrapped one around the other. I try to run to them, but my legs are heavy, uncooperative.

Reaching the tree is arduous. I claw through the grass on hands and knees. Thunder echoes against the mountains as I touch the eldest girl, turn her over to check for a pulse. The face is Sydney's.

I gasp, jerk upright.

The meadow disappears. The thunder morphs into a frenetic hammering.

Someone's pounding on the cabin door.

Snatching a can of bear spray off my day pack, I start across the room, saying, "Okay. Okay. I'm coming."

The dream and reality run headlong into one another as I unlock the door, open it a crack.

"Sydney?"

Grabbing my arm, she gasps, "You gotta help me."

CHAPTER 22

Olive Augusta Radley, 1909

The enterprising grafter was aware of the value of orphans. "Professional guardians" began to appear, thrifty geniuses who had secured appointment . . . that they might control the orphans' property.

—ANGIE DEBO, 1940. *AND STILL THE WATERS RUN.*

D ewey Mullins snatches at the burlap sack, but Mr. Brotherton shifts it away. The rest of us wait proper and polite for that blue-eyed newspaperman to keep the bargain he made with me before I led him to the Jack Crossing hideout.

"Listen here, fella." Dewey's face gets narrow and blister red. "Amos and Tula and Nessa *told* you about how they come to be here, so now you *owe* us the food. That was the deal. You get stories for your paper, and we get travlin' goods."

"In due time there, son." Mr. Brotherton stands up and lifts the sack onto his shoulder, where it makes a dirt patch on his clean pinstripe shirt and fancy red suspenders.

Watching him, I wonder, *Was he lying when he said he'd trade food for stories and never, ever let on to Mrs. Grube that I knew where the kids were hiding?* She's planning to write articles about the women's meetings for his paper, so she'll be in touch with Mr. Brotherton, regular. I don't know how she'll manage to keep going to the club meetings, since she was so nervous about getting home ahead of Mr. Grube she had the horse hooked up an hour before the rest of the wagons were ready to go this morning. She wanted *me* in the wagon, too, but I flashed the two train passes and said Mama had me carry them for an emergency, and soon as the medicine came in at the pharmacy, I'd use the passes to get me and Skedee home on the train, not by the road where those bad men might be.

Once she rolled out of sight, I went to find Mr. Brotherton to strike a bargain with him on a story for his paper. A story about elf children. Just what he and Mrs. Grube talked and talked about at the wagon camp last night. Elf children and laundry girls.

"That *was* our deal, Mr. Brotherton," I remind him while Dewey tries to stare him down. "You said a real newspaperman won't pay money for a story, but you *could* bring some food."

Mr. Brotherton winks at me, and then says to Dewey, "Firstly, my young friend, I must be certain you plan to share the food fairly with the others. And, secondly, I don't believe you've favored me with *your* story."

Dewey's lip curls, showing his jagged tooth. "I wouldn't steal what belongs to a pal, *firstly,* and *nextly,* you come askin' after Indian stories. I ain't Indian, but these here Choctaw kids been done wrong by liars and thieves. Tell that in your paper. Why, there's kids all over this countryside turned out to fetch for theirselves . . . and them are the lucky ones. If they ain't lucky, they wind up dead and buried. I heard many a tale and seen things, too. I once run up on a wagon where a man was diggin' holes for four dead bodies wrapped in Choctaw blanket quilts . . . and no place near a graveyard, either. The man went for his rifle when he saw me, and that ain't no lie."

Mr. Brotherton opens his pad and pulls the pencil from behind his ear. "And how is it that you came to be traveling on your own?"

"I got a wanderin' spirit." Dewey cocks back like he's looking for a fight.

The newspaperman taps his pencil. "No family?"

"None that wants a boy who can't be put to work at the mines and the money sent straight home to a daddy that don't work a lick. Since the new laws, them mines won't take a breaker boy if he don't look fourteen. So out you go like trash." Dewey spits on the ground and just misses the newspaperman's shoe.

Mr. Brotherton moves his foot. "The laws are meant to protect children, allow them the opportunity for a decent life."

"Well, this be it, I reckon." Swirling his arms out wide, Dewey takes a bow. "An Irish boy livin' free as a bird, and with all these poor souls here, right under my wing."

"Don't you point at me, Dewey Mullins," I pipe up. The last thing I need is Mr. Brotherton figuring me out. "I *ain't* under your wing or one of your pals, and you *know* that. I was only trying to help y'all get some food."

Dewey and me lock eyes.

He flips his fingers my way. "That one's just some gal we come across in town. But there's lots like me, too. Them men runnin' the mines don't send you home on the train when they can't work you no more. Oh, *there's* men that'll put you on a train, all right, but you'll wake up down South, workin' in a cotton mill, or laundry, or pulpwood plant, or pickin' crops on some farm, where there's no law agin' it. I don't aim to land myself in such a troublement."

"Quite a story." Mr. Brotherton's tongue slides over his pretty white teeth while he looks at his papers. I figure it's time to shift him out of Jack Crossing so Nessa, Tula, the little ones, and me can make our way into the Winding Stairs while there's still plenty of traveling hours in the day. Morning's almost gone already, and it's the kind of weather where storms might kick up later. I still have to go back to town with Mr. Brotherton and then return here with Skedee.

"Well, I reckon that's all there is, Mr. Brotherton." I look down the creek toward the railroad bridge where he hitched his horse.

"I suppose so." He thinks on it another minute before he hands over the gunny sack, says his goodbyes, and starts down the creek.

On my way past Nessa, I lean in and whisper, "Wait for me."

"Tushpa!" she says. *Hurry up!*

I nod without looking back.

"You speak their language?" Mr. Brotherton asks on the way to the horse.

"Only some."

While he mounts and helps me climb up behind the saddle, I start spinning a tale that my great-grandma's second husband was a Choctaw man and they came over the Trail of Tears, back in 1831, when the government had the Choctaws come all the way from Mississippi to Oklahoma in the cold of winter. "She used to tell her children what a terrible thing that was, how people just fell by the way and died and . . ."

That tale does what I want it to do. It keeps us busy almost the whole way back to town, so Mr. Brotherton doesn't ask more questions about Jack Crossing, or where I live exactly, and if I'm safe to make it home with a gang of bad men on the loose.

"A reporter is to remain objective," he says after I run out of stories. "But I find myself infuriated by the superfluity of Choctaw land parcels that have been sold off since the congressional enactment of May 27, 1908. Miss Kate is correct; it is a crime, and the grafters proliferate like vermin. Hazel, does your family live on allotment land?"

"No, sir, we do not. My daddy bought our land." Then I tell him what I heard Miss Kate say at the table, about the men in Washington and that new law. "Miss Kate said that terrible, awful new law was a tra-vesty. I do believe that's what she said." That big word feels strange on my tongue, but I want him to believe I am very grown-up. "Of course, I know I am not to listen while serving food, but it was very interesting, and I could not help it. Nobody should ever be thrown to the wolves by Congress, but not children for sure, I don't think."

"Ah, yes, the wolves. They are here among us even as we speak."

"Truly, they are. I hope Miss Kate goes to Washington to tell those men about it. I'd go tell them, too . . . if I could."

"You have helped to bring attention to it, though you are yet unaware." He twists in the saddle to look over his shoulder at me. "The newspaper stories of the elf children will shine light on this shadowy matter. Miss Kate means to rise against it, and I am told that Mrs. Threadgill has thoughts of appointing a committee of her clubwomen to study the Indian Concern. Whether they will do more than simply express indignation in their parlors remains to be seen, but if unified behind a cause, they will be a force not to be trifled with."

That man's words are so fast and fancy I don't understand the half of it, but I like that he talks to me like I'm grown. "I hope they will. I hope for it all the time."

"The pen is a mighty thing, Hazel, and today you've exposed the faces of the misery behind this political maneuvering of moneyed men living in high places while children survive in ditches. Chased and hunted, left to freeze and starve. And in the twentieth century! This modern age of telephones, electrified lighting, refrigeration, automobiles. It is an abomination, Hazel, that our society can muster the wit and will to create such magnificence, yet not the resolve to do right by a child, don't you think?"

"It surely is." He has himself in a fuss now. His hand flits around enough that it scares the horse into a sideways jig trot. We go the rest of the way into town like that, me bouncing up and down on the horse's rump.

I'm glad when we get to the hitch rail out back of the church, where I left Skedee. "Well, sir, that's my pack pony." I slide off without waiting for help. "I'd best be on with my business now and get home to my mama. It was nice, you giving food to those elf children. I wonder why some folks call them by that name, don't you? It's like the old nursery stories about gnomes and fairies, except these are real kids that just . . . come on hard times. They ain't pretend. It'd be good for folks to know that in your paper."

Mr. Brotherton snatches his pad and goes to writing.

Since he likes what I said, I pat the horse's muzzle and keep talking. "Maybe the reason people call them that is . . . if something ain't real, meanin' it ain't flesh and blood, then it won't need anybody to feed it, or put a roof over its head, or buy it some shoes in the winter. Then nobody feels bad that they didn't do those things. I think that's why folks tell such tales."

Lifting the pencil, he studies on me over his spectacles. "You are quite an exceptional mind for your age, young lady. Perhaps one day you'll follow Miss Kate into politics."

"Oh, I doubt that." Keyes Radley would turn over in his grave at that idea. *The only thing lower than a snake is a politician,* he used to say.

Dewey puts that wrecked purple parasol on his shoulder, and him and Amos follow along, even though I tell them to go mind their own business. I start the long way around Talihina, instead of straight up Railroad Street, hoping they'll peel off.

Dewey complains before we're halfway through town.

"Safer to go this way," I tell him. "And you better toss that parasol into the bushes. If the deputy's back, he'll be watching for whoever shook up the library wagon yesterday. The clubwomen were real put out about it, and they are a force not to be trifled with." That last part comes straight from Mr. Brotherton.

"Deputy ain't got time for a bunch of womenfolk," Dewey pops back at me. "He's out huntin' them road agents. You know the boss of that gang ain't but seventeen year old? That's July Joyner hisself. The others ain't but fifteen, fourteen, and two at sixteen. Been fillin' their pockets full of loot and livin' high. Make fools of the lawmen, every time." Dewey laughs at that, a bunch of bad boys that can't be caught.

"They're stealing and hurting people." Thinking about it sends a shiver over me. I hope that gang has run far away from here by now and that Mrs. Grube and Baby Beau are home safe. "They'll hang when they get caught."

Dewey shrugs and we walk a bit before he pipes up again. "I say we get us some peppermint sticks from the store before we head out."

"Go ahead," I answer. Dewey probably means to steal those, too. "But we ain't. Storm's coming."

"Says who?"

"Says the *sky* . . . and that thunder off south. It'll hit pretty quick." Any fool can smell the rain on the wind. Dewey Mullins must be a bigger fool than most.

He trots on up next to me and starts walking backward, the broken parasol bumping his knees. "I say we take a vote like the miners do in camp. All them that wants peppermint sticks, raise a hand." Up goes his paw, dirty fingernails and all, but nobody else joins in. Tula and the little kids can't understand because Dewey's talking too fast, and Nessa won't dare go against me, plus she's scared of storms. I am surprised about Amos, though.

"Never say never." Mr. Brotherton smiles. "Miss Kate is only t
first. We'll soon see a day when all avenues of government and co
merce will be open to the fairer sex. You mark my words. These clu
women are the beginning of a new era. They'll lobby for the v
until they have it, and that will change . . ."

The rest gets caught up in the noise of the train blowing its wh
tle on the way into town. I untie Skedee's lead rope and make r
excuses, and Mr. Brotherton hands me a calling card with
name—V. R. Brotherton, Editor and Correspondent—on the fro
"Should another story such as that of the poor unfortunates in Ja
Crossing come upon your ears, I would be most desirous to hear
either from you directly or through our mutual friend, Mrs. Grub

"Yes, sir." I tuck the card away. It feels nice in my pocket. Still wa
from his hand.

"You've done good work today, Hazel." He winks at me before
rides away, and my cheeks go prickly pink. I don't even know why
takes a few hard swallows to get the tickles out of my throat, a
right as I do, down the way between the town buildings, I see the t
end of that train, and a red coach car with black-velvet curtain frin
shimmying behind the glass windows. A band of shiny gold lett
catches the sun as it slides toward the station.

Every bit of me turns cold as a icehouse door.

The writing on that private car reads E. N. LOCKRIDGE, but I'd kn
that even without the words. I've gone to meet that coach more th
once with Tesco Peele.

Quick as the car disappears behind the building, I fetch the pa
saddle from where I hid it under the church's back steps, then
Skedee cinched up and start tugging him away from town. It's ha
not to pull him into a fast trot, but I make myself walk like it is a
other day, so no one will take notice of me.

I don't catch a good breath till I've made it back down to Ja
Crossing, and Nessa, Tula, and the little kids are waiting and ready
go. I make Nessa and Tula leave the wet things from the book wag
behind. "If we get stopped going through town, we don't want to
caught with clubwomen's books," I say. "We'll wind up in jail f
thieving."

"What are you doin'?" Dewey's eyes lock on Amos. "We are *votin'* on peppermint sticks and also who's *boss* of this gang."

"There *ain't* any gang," I snap.

Dewey bares his teeth. "Amos, you tell the gals what I said about a vote and peppermint sticks. Say it to them in Choctaw."

Amos's shoulders go up and down. "Can't be votin' today." His bottom lip pushes into his top one as he studies on the sky. "All them clouds come in. Lotta clouds."

"You afraid of some rain, now?" Dewey's voice gets so loud a lady feeding yard chickens outside a shack house turns to get a good look at us. Dewey cusses a blue streak, and the lady's mouth drops open.

"You all right, little girl?" she calls, looking at me. "Them beggar lice troublin' you?"

"No, ma'am. Thank you kindly." Pulling Skedee's lead line, I walk around Dewey and tell him hush up.

"I ain't afraid of that lady," he blabbers, loud. "I'll go tell her to her face."

"Shut your yap," I whisper.

"Not till we make a vote. You're big talk, havin' a horse and all. Well, how's about I just *take* that horse? What're you gonna do about it?" He grabs the lead line, and Skedee balks, yanking the rope out of my hand. Next thing I know, Dewey is flying like laundry on a line while Skedee whirls in a circle.

"You stop that! You come on over here, right now!" the yard lady shrieks above the ruckus. "You lil' beggar lice, you git away from that girl and her hoss. You best beat a path before I knock your noggins into next Sun-dey with this hoe."

"We're just funnin'!" I dive for the lead rope, but Skedee plows me down, and I cover my head while his hind hooves go right over me. Dewey's feet and that purple parasol fly by next. Dust and gravel sling everywhere.

I figure my horse is lost, but Dewey clings on till Skedee finally gives up the fight and stands there snorting. Scrambling to his feet, Dewey raises the parasol like he means to whip my horse with it, and little Koi goes to wailing, right there in the street.

Amos gets to Dewey before I can. He snatches the rope away quick enough that it zips through Dewey's fingers. "Ain't no use in this fightin'. Can't be votin' today. The sun ain't out."

Of a sudden, I understand. Lots of the old-time Choctaws won't do business, or hold councils, or sign papers unless the sky is clear. They've got a belief that the sun shining keeps men honest. More than once, I've heard Mr. Lockridge, and Tesco, and the men on the porch making fun about it.

Dewey's face goes red as a hog plum, and he shakes his hands from the rope burn. "Amos, you idjut! If you ain't with me, well then, you're agin' me and we ain't friends, neither. Have it your own way, then, and see if I care, too!" Throwing down that parasol, he takes off to town, his long bare feet stomping the dust like butter paddles.

Amos looks heartbroke, standing there with his palms turned up, while he calls out, "Sun ain't out, Dewey!"

"Boy! Don't you be puttin' hands on that hoss!" the yard lady howls. "Jubal! Jubal! Fetch me the gun. A colored boy's tryin' to steal a hoss, right there in the street. Come quick!"

Amos drops that lead line so fast I almost miss catching hold.

Tula, Pinti, and Koi take off. They've been chased enough times they know what to do, but Nessa just stands there froze up in the street. Grabbing her dress sleeve, I turn her around, yell, "Run!"

Finally, she gathers her skirt and does what I said, and I pull Skedee into a long trot.

The last thing I do is look over my shoulder and see Amos with his hands raised, like he means to stop the woman from coming after us.

Everything moves like a river under ice—quiet on the surface, things passing underneath. I see Amos look at me, then at the lady, then past me to Pinti and Nessa, their long hair flying, and Tula running heavy with Koi held across her chest. I see the lady come through her yard gate with a garden hoe, and a boy hurrying to her with a gun big as he is. I see the wind catch the woman's dress and the hoe come down, and Amos dodge away, then finally take to running.

A chug hole catches my foot. I turn forward to watch my way.

Then I hear the shot.

CHAPTER 23

Valerie Boren-Odell, 1990

All victims and witnesses of Federal crime . . . shall receive the assistance and protection to which they are entitled under the law. The
type of assistance provided will vary according to the individual's
needs and circumstances. Sound judgment will, therefore, be required to make appropriate decisions as to the range and length of
victim services and assistance given.

—NATIONAL PARK SERVICE LAW ENFORCEMENT REFERENCE MANUAL.

I down another swig of soda. At four in the morning, I need caf-
feine to generate the acuity required for separating fact from fiction,
but I dare not leave the couch to make coffee. For the third time, I say,
"Now listen, Sydney. I want you to go through the story again and
tell me only the parts that are true. Otherwise I have no way to figure
out how to help you."

"I already *did.*" Her face fills with earnest desperation as she tosses
aside the ice bag I gave her an hour ago when she staggered into my
cabin banged up and begging for help. "You gotta call the Feds. The
FBI. Somebody that's not *from* here."

If my alleged victim weren't a frantic adolescent who's just contra-
dicted almost everything she told me in earlier conversations, I
would've been on the phone already, requesting a special agent from
our NPS Investigative Services Branch, as well as contacting the Oklahoma State Bureau of Investigations, DHS, and local jurisdictions.

Instead, I motion to Sydney's bruised elbow and swollen wrist and
say, "Keep the ice on that." I don't think anything is broken, or I'd

insist on a trip to the emergency room. She's vehemently opposed to the idea. The people at the hospital are local, she says, and they'll tell Alton Parker. If I try to take her anywhere, she'll run.

I'm not intimidated by a twelve-year-old, even an athletic, cunning one, but right now the primary task is to sort out where this fantastical tale meets reality. We don't have much longer. I'm not up on all the particulars of the related state law, but within a few hours—maybe three to six depending on interim custody standards—I'm compelled to notify Child Protective Services, whether her story seems plausible or not. My fear is that, if she's inventing these events or embellishing them, she'll end up in a deeper hole than she's already in.

On the other hand, if even half of it is true, it's big. And dangerous.

"It's *all* true." She seems to read my thoughts. "And you can't tell anybody from around here or else they'll tell Parker and he'll get Braden. You gotta come with me. We gotta hurry!"

The uptick in volume causes me to glance toward Charlie's door. Good thing he's a deep sleeper. "All right, Sydney, just for instance, you've given me three different versions of what happened to your arm." I look down at my notepad. "You said Alton Parker grabbed your arm and twisted it. You said you hitched a ride to my cabin with some partying high school kids and tripped getting out of their truck, landing on your arm. You said you got in a fight with one of the boys at Mrs. Wambles's place yesterday morning, and the boy hit your arm with a broken-off branch. Which is it?"

"All *three*. And I landed on my arm when I climbed out the window at Parker's warehouse, too." Pressing the ice bag against her elbow, she winces.

I sift through my notes again. "You're saying that the night your Grandma Budgie disappeared, your mother, Jade Potter, actually *was* living with the rest of you in the house. And Jade took Budgie Blackwell to get treatment after a medical emergency came up?"

"That's right. That's what happened."

"But the other day I asked you if anyone else was at the house when your grandmother left, and your answer was no."

"Braden said to keep my mouth shut till he could find Grandma Budgie and figure it all out."

"So it was your mother, Jade, who told you she was taking Budgie to Tulsa, to this City of Faith place . . . in the middle of the night?"

"That's what the note said."

"Note?" *This is new.*

"Braden was . . . he sneaked out to meet his girlfriend, okay? And I was asleep. I didn't hear anything when Mama and Grandma Budgie left."

My thoughts crumple like a paper wad in a tight fist. I unfold them again. The story is morphing so fast I can't keep up. "All right, so . . . Braden's gone. You're home but asleep. When you wake up, your mother and your Grandma Budgie are both gone, and you find a note explaining what happened?"

"Braden found it first."

"The note?"

"Mm-hmm."

"So, Braden returns sometime in the early morning hours and finds the note, then wakes you up and tells you about it?" Myriad scenarios roll through my mind, none of them reassuringly benign.

What if this really is a murder case?

Family fight? Jade's ongoing drug issues? Inheritance?

Maybe someone wanted Budgie Blackwell out of the way. Maybe Braden didn't go into the park for recreational purposes, but to dispose of a body . . . or to search for one. Could he have been helping his mother with a cover-up, or conversely, trying to uncover the truth about Budgie's disappearance?

In Sydney's scenario, Alton Parker is the villain and Braden the target. She insists that after taking her from Mrs. Wambles's house, Parker searched her belongings, found a *secret book* in which she kept drawings, notes only she understood, and handmade maps of hiding places she and her brother knew from spending time in the mountains. When she wouldn't tell Parker where Braden was, he twisted her arm until she heard something pop, then he locked her in a room and said he'd deal with her later. She's terrified that given enough time, Parker and his guys will decipher the notebook's contents and *get Braden.* And for that reason we need the FBI. Pronto.

You cannot listen to a word that one says. She is very manipulative cycles through my mind in Myrna Wambles's phlegmy voice.

What if every bit of this is fabrication? Sydney climbed out a window of Parker's warehouse apartment because she didn't relish being there, banged up her arm in the process, and sought out the person she thought was most likely to buy into her story.

Me.

Braden, she says, is still hiding in the park and the thousands of acres of adjacent state land—he has been the whole time. All of this has to do with the strange family relationship with Alton Parker. After Budgie's disappearance, Braden went to work for Parker because Parker had, over the past few months, insinuated himself at the Blackwells' ranch in Antlers. Parker was ostensibly monitoring his construction crews working on Budgie's ranch roads, barn, and a pond dam. Braden's feeling was that Parker showed up too often, offered too many favors, and, for a man with a business located an hour's drive away in Talihina, was oddly available to chat with Budgie over afternoon coffee. Jade, having recently moved back home to get her life on track, told the kids to leave it be.

After Budgie disappeared, Braden got it in his head that Parker knew something about it. While working for Parker, he'd been surveilling the business, trying to figure out what the man might be *up to.* Braden had also been to Tulsa looking for Budgie, but with no luck.

And that cave with the three little skeletons? It is part of the story, too. According to Sydney, there *were* indigenous funerary artifacts at the site, including clay eating pots, a river cane basket, blankets, sewing needles and thread, handmade wooden dolls—belongings that would have been buried with female children, which explains why the local rumor mill dubbed the remains as being those of *little girls.* When word of the cave got to Parker, he sent a man there to steal the artifacts and bag up the bones so no one would know, but the man chickened out when it came to handling the skeletons.

Parker then told Braden to go finish the job—a test of loyalty, or possibly a trap. By the time Braden went to the cave, the area was crawling with park personnel.

That's when Braden decided it was a setup—that Parker was *on to him*—and so Braden took to the woods.

It's all very . . . extraordinary.

Unbelievably so.

The story, if even remotely accurate, is a political grenade, especially in a park already plagued with local opposition, an unmarked burial site, a massive rockfall, and a dead body. The first thing you learn, working for a public-facing government agency: Controversy is enemy number one, bad press is number two, litigation is number three.

You're not some twenty-four-year-old kid anymore, Val. You're a grown-up with a son to support. That comes first. The thought injects a dose of bitter medicine. I stare at the wall. An eternity seems to pass. My eyes and everything in me go dry.

You've worked hard for this career.

Charlie deserves stability, a home.

"I need to call someone." The words echo past my ear, a strange out-of-body experience.

"Finally! The FBI, right?" Sydney gasps.

"No."

There's a wary shift at the other end of the sofa. I move, preparing to block the door if she tries to bolt. The problem is, the phone is attached to the wall in the kitchen.

"I knew not to come here. I knew you wouldn't care. You're just like stupid Granny Wambles and all of them."

"No. I'm not." *Am I?*

My stomach roils, churning a mix of soda, bile, and adrenaline. Acid upon acid.

"I shouldn't've told you anything." The words grind out through clenched teeth, the two in front still slightly overlarge for the face they're in.

Like Charlie's.

Stop it. Stop.

"She's got a big leather paddle she whips people with. Granny

Wambles. You know that? She sticks a tube sock over it so it won't leave marks, but it hurts just fine."

The accusation snaps me around. Our gazes collide. Sydney's left eye narrows, gauging my reaction. I suspect there is no leather paddle in a tube sock. I have no way of knowing for sure.

"You don't have much choice but to trust me, Sydney." I stand up slowly, watching her in my periphery as I move to the kitchen. "And if you make a run for that door, I'll get there before you're through it."

"Pppfff!"

"Count on it."

"Mommy?" Charlie's sleepy voice startles me half out of my wits. He's standing at the bedroom door, rubbing his eyes.

"Go back to bed, Charlie."

"I heard the"—a huge yawn stalls the rest—". . . bear . . . was . . . in my dumpster . . . closet . . ."

"Everything's all right."

"No, it's not," Sydney grinds out.

Charlie looks her way. "Hey," he says, as if an adolescent girl on our sofa is completely normal.

"Hey, kid." She repositions to the barest perch on the cushion, the crouch of a cat about to jettison from its hiding place.

"Charlie! Bed. *Now*."

He vanishes, the door rattling behind him.

I make it to the phone. "Calm down, Sydney. Everything's going to be all right."

"No, it won't! They'll read my notebook and *get Braden*!" Sobs wrench the last few words from her mouth.

I barely realize I've dialed Curtis's house before he answers the phone.

"I need you to come over here." There's no time for niceties.

"Valerie?" He's clearly awake. Either up early or just home from work.

"Yes."

"Where are you?"

"My cabin at Lost Pines. First one on the right. I've got a . . ." *situation.* "I just need you to come over here. I'm sorry. Can you?"

"I'll be there in fifteen," he answers, then hangs up.

The tension seeps out through my feet as I hang up the phone. Hopefully Curtis will have a greater grasp of the nuances of the situation than I do. More importantly, I trust him.

I think.

From the living room, Sydney demands to know who I've called. "A friend" is all I tell her. "Just stay put. We'll sort this out."

"We're wasting *time.*" She paces the room, hugging herself and shivering as she passes by the window air unit. I offer her a blanket, but she shakes her head and peers through the gap in the ancient plaid curtains.

"Soon as Parker knows I'm gone, he'll come hunting me," she warns. "He got on the phone with some of his guys after he took my stuff and locked me in the room. If they can't figure out Braden's map on their own, they'll come to get me out of that room and make me tell. I shouldn't have saved the map. Braden told me to learn it by heart, then get rid of it. Burn it."

"*Burn* it?"

"Yeah, but how you gonna do that at Granny Wambles's house?" A narrow look flicks my way. "I had to sleep with it in my underpants at night. *Myrna* looked through all my stuff. She oughta get arrested. She's working for Parker. Him and her are in on it. He handed her a wad of cash when he stuck me in that place. I saw him."

"One thing at a time." Parker could have been legitimately paying for Sydney's care, since she wasn't officially in the foster system. It's possible.

"I *told* you, there's not any time." Sydney presses against the wall, a banged-up, stranded creature, trapped, lost, scared. "You don't cross Parker. Not around here. He'll get rid of you. He'll come *here* when he sees that I got away. He knows you been over at Granny Wambles's talkin' to me. She tells him stuff. That's what she gets paid for."

"I doubt he has any idea where to find me."

"He can find *anybody.* And you got your little boy in there."

We look toward Charlie's room in unison. A lump rises in my throat. This is exactly the reason home life and law enforcement work should never mix.

I walk to Charlie's door, peek inside, pull the door closed again. A shudder runs beneath the hiking shirt I yanked over my filmy tank top and gym shorts after letting Sydney in the door.

Glancing at the clock, I think, *Hurry up.*

An eternity seems to pass before headlights strafe the curtains. Sydney leans close to peer around the edge. "Crap! It's the Choctaw Police. They can't take me outta here. I'm not in the tribe. Don't tell them you saw me. Parker knows all of them, too." She flees to the other side of the room and tries to hide behind the recliner.

"It's okay." Leaving her where she is, I cross to the door and tug it open.

Curtis is alert, slightly guarded. One hand resting near his service weapon, he eyes me quizzically, taking in the unevenly buttoned shirt, gym shorts, bare feet. "Val?" He searches my face, then looks past me to the lamplit cabin interior. "What's up?"

The answer emerges from behind the recliner. "You called *him*?"

Curtis visibly deflates, rubbing his forehead as he crosses the threshold. "*This* is your situation?" He levels a stern look at Sydney, who has already grabbed the back of the chair and turned the seat in his direction as a barricade. "People are looking for you, Sydney. Let's go."

"You can't let him take me!" She sprints to a defensive position behind me, clutches my shirt in handfuls. "I'm *her* prisoner. She called the Feds already."

"No, I haven't," I interject. "Everybody just calm down."

"Come on, Sydney." Curtis is clearly too tired for the drama. "Enough of the fun and games. Granny Wambles reported you missing at least a couple hours ago now. People have been out looking for you." He reaches wearily for his handheld radio to put out the call that Sydney Potter has been found.

A flurry of protests issue forth from Sydney and me.

"Curtis, wait!"

"I wasn't even over there! Parker took me. He locked me up!"

"Curtis, just a minute." My hand is over his before he can push the PTT switch and put out the call.

He looks down at my fingers, then slowly up at me, his readable emotions ranging from shock, to indignance, to bewilderment, to a flash of something else that I feel but can't categorize.

"Curtis ... just ... Listen before you make that call, okay? Hear her out first."

His thumb brushes over mine as he lets off the switch. "That's asking a lot, Val."

"I know. Give us fifteen minutes, all right?" I back away to allow him into the room, and he obliges, closing the door behind himself.

"I hope you know what you're doing here, Val," he mutters close to my ear.

"Playing on a hunch," I admit, and we move across the room, Sydney clinging to my shirt until we're positioned side by side on the sofa. Curtis takes the recliner, knees set in a wide stance, elbows braced, as if he must hold himself in place to do what I have asked of him.

I grab a blanket, throw it over Sydney, say to Curtis, "For one thing, Myrna Wambles shouldn't be reporting this girl missing. When I went by there earlier, I was told that Parker had picked Sydney up hours ago, intending for her to stay at his warehouse with him ... or out at his hunting cabin."

"Who said that?" Curtis is incredulous.

"Mrs. Wambles herself. If she was lying, she was pretty convincing. My guess is that when Sydney went missing from Parker's place, he didn't want anyone to know he'd ever had custody of her." Leaning back, I turn to Sydney and say, "You'd better tell the short version of the story you came here with ... but *only* whatever part is true."

CHAPTER 24

Olive Augusta Radley, 1909

My father, O. N. Tucker, practiced medicine around Doaksville for nine years before losing a case excepting those from gunshots and stabbings, which were plentiful.

—Augusta Tucker, 1937. Indian-Pioneer Papers Collection, interview by Hazel B. Greene.

"Nessa!" I scream. "Tula!" Around me the day has gone black with rain and wind. I can't see anything, and all there is to do is keep running up the wagon road, farther from Talihina, farther from the woman with the gun. Lightning cracks. Sound booms overhead. I tell myself it's thunder, not shotgun blasts, that nobody would keep chasing us with a storm letting loose.

My legs buckle and I tumble forward, fall face-first, and Skedee turns off the road, dragging me through some farmer's field. Water and mud fill my eyes and ears and mouth as I splash through the furrows, hanging on to the lead line. I choke and spit and think, *Am I shot?*

Quick as it started, it's over—not lightning and thunder, but the water and mud and bumping across the ground. The rope slacks up. I feel soft, dry dirt under me. A hand clamps on my arm, and I try to fight it off before I notice it's a small hand. Something damp wipes over my eyes, and when I open them, through the haze and the dim, I see Nessa, cleaning the mud off me with her dress hem.

"You okay, Ollie?" she wants to know, but I can't hear her over the thunder and rain. I only see her lips make the words.

Nodding, I grab her and hug her tight, and she hugs me back just as hard. "We're okay," I say against her wet skin. "I'm here. We're okay."

We hang on to each other that way, and I close my eyes against the burn of tears and mud.

When we let go, I look around and make out that we're in a lean-to shed with log walls and a tar paper roof. It's just high enough for Skedee to get under, and he's wedged himself far back as he could go before the pack saddle hit the log rafters. His head's down between his knees, his ribs pumping and steam coming off him. Tula stands by the open side of the shed. Koi and Pinti cling on her skirts while she puts her fingers to her mouth and whistles into the wind. I guess that's how Skedee knew to come in here. He must've heard what I couldn't.

One more look around, and it's plain enough who she's still whistling for. Amos ain't here. I think of the gunshot, and I can't catch my breath.

Tula whistles, and whistles, and whistles, her calls gone in the storm.

Pushing off the ground, I drag myself to my feet, my blue ribbon-sash dress heavy with dirt and water. I tie Skedee to a hay manger on the wall, then sift through his packs, taking out Nessa's coat and mine, plus Daddy's oilskin slicker. The coats hang like tablecloths over Pinti and Koi, and the oilskin would fit two of Tula. Her skin's like ice when I wrap the collar up high on her neck.

Fresh hay sits in the manger, which means this is somebody's cow-shed. The farmer will come back in the morning or maybe even when the storm breaks.

We can't stay here.

We can't leave till the rain and the lightning let up.

After checking Skedee's legs, I loosen the pack saddle cinches and rub him down with handfuls of hay. Nessa helps, and then we sit against the wall and huddle close together under the mothy blanket from the trainmen, while our teeth chatter and the rain beats on the tin roof.

I don't know how we fall asleep, but when I open my eyes, my dress is half dry and my drawers are pasted to my skin. Nessa's head lays drooped over in my lap. The shed is black as being down a well, but I feel enough arms and legs to know that Koi and Pinti are curled against Nessa. The oilskin slicker covers all of us, which must be how we were warm enough to stay asleep.

It's so quiet I can hear everybody breathing and the frogs singing outside.

"Tula?" I whisper. The little ones stir but don't waken.

I slip out from under Nessa, then creep all around the shed in the dark, my hands splayed. "Tula? You there? Tula?" Skedee's right where I left him, but Tula's gone. From the open side of the shed, I try to see through a night fog that leaves not a slip of stars nor moon to go by. The one light I can make out is a single yellow flicker. A farmhouse is close by. Somebody has the hearth fires burning.

"Tula?" I whisper again. A cow stomps just a few feet from me. A bull snorts and paws the ground, and I jump back. The stock must've wandered up sometime after Tula left, and then smelled us in their shed and got too spooked to come in. That means Tula's been gone a while. Maybe she sneaked over to the house to see if there was a kitchen garden or a chicken coop with fresh eggs?

Maybe she got lost in the dark.

Maybe she got caught.

I don't dare call out again with that house so close by, so I stand at the door and wait for dawn or Tula to show up. Come morning, those cows will go to bellowing for food and a dry place, and the farmer will come see about them.

We've got to be gone before that happens.

Soon as the first gray light breaks, I hurry to get Skedee ready, wake the other kids, and put the two without shoes up on the pack saddle. A shiver runs through me as I whisper to Nessa, "Watch where you're stepping. Rain like that washes the snakes out of their holes."

A dog goes to barking, and there's no more time. Shaking the oilskin slicker at the cows to scare them away, I tell Nessa to keep close, then I lead Skedee over a corral gate that blew down in the storm and pull him into a trot across the open field. We run through the morning dim, around a pond and down behind the spillway, where we can hide while I figure what to do next.

"Where's Tula gone to?" Nessa's voice seems loud, even though it barely stirs the air.

"I don't know. I'm watchin'." Putting a finger to my lips, I hand her the lead rope, then I climb the pond dam, squat down in the wet grass, and peek over.

At the house, the lamps burn bright, cutting circles in the fog. Hinges squeal, a screen door slams. A man's whistling drifts over the field, a soft, lazy tune.

I crawl forward a little, try to see across the way.

The door slams. The whistling is gone.

Has he got Tula in there?

To know anything for sure, I'd have to get closer to that house. Near enough to hear the voices or see in the windows. I can leave the little kids here, but I hope Nessa is strong enough to keep hold of Skedee.

"Nessie," I say when I get back down to her, "I need y'all to wait real quiet and don't move a bit while I go see if ..."

"Tula! Tula!" Pinti whispers, pointing to the road from high up on the pack saddle.

The honeysuckle vines block me from seeing at first, but finally two people melt out of the fog, coming from the town way with a lantern. One's short and skinny, one's tall and big. I know Amos right off, but he's limping and leaning heavy on a stick.

The little kids slide down and run ahead to Tula while Nessa and me work Skedee through the vines and brush.

"Lost y'all." Amos's voice is thick, and he groans with the words. "Had to crawl up in a black haw thicket back down the road. Figure a haw bush ain't the worst place to die. Flowers come sprang, sweet haw berries in fall." He tries a tiny laugh but it ends in a cough and a moan. "Reckon that gun just winged me through the fat, 'cause when I woke, there I was, still upside of the sod. I heard Tula's call, and spotted a lantern light coming through the fog." Even through the dim, I can see him smile at her.

"We best blow out that lantern and move along quick," I tell them, because the only place Tula would've got a lantern was off the porch of the farmhouse. "Amos, we might could get you on Skedee."

"I weigh too heavy for that pony," he tells me, but a whimper comes after the words. "I'll get along all right."

"You let me know if you need it. Skedee's strong."

"I'll do that. But if somebody comes up on us, y'all run. Don't worry about me. Y'all run and git away."

"I don't think anybody's coming after us."

"And you make Tula go, too." He looks hard at me.

"All right."

"Anumpulit issa," Tula whispers, and I know what that means. *Stop talking.*

"We go," Koi says, then gets his skinny little shoulder up under Amos's hand to try and help. We start out walking that way, and as we pass the farmer's gate, Tula leaves the lantern by the post.

The Old Military Road leads us toward the mountains, but it's hard going. Amos catches a breath each step. Even though we try to walk slow, we have to stop and wait, and stop again. We're through the clear and into some trees before morning sun burns off the fog, but with the light comes seeing that it's not just dry blood on Amos's shirt and pants. He's bleeding heavy.

Tula and me and the little kids go to chasing the spiders off their webs and gathering up the sticky threads to make a poultice. Spiderweb will stop a bleed quicker than anything, keep infection out, and help it heal, too. I guess Tula's mama or daddy taught her that, same as my daddy taught me. Tula had good people to show her things, same's I did. And she loved her people, but then they were gone, just like my daddy and my mama. We're not so different, Tula and me.

I think on that while the sun scatters through the new spring leaves and a breeze stirs the branches. Leftover rain drips down like strings of pearls, and the songbirds wake the day with music even prettier than the Victor Victrola phonograph at the Lockridges' house. Sounds and smells wrap tighter around me with every step. Home's getting closer, but going slows when the road turns uphill at the foot of the mountains. Amos's groans grow deeper, and even all the spiderwebs in the world won't stop the bleed. Finally, he wobbles on his feet and stumbles down onto one knee.

Tula and Nessa get up under his arms, but they're so tiny it's not worth much. Time and again, they fall behind, and I wrestle Skedee to a stop, and wait. That pony's nose is pointed toward the old home-place, and he's itchy to go. If I could, I'd strip off the pack saddle and ride him up the backtrail Daddy and me used as a cutoff from the Old Military Road. Horse thieves and outlaws traveled that secret trail . . . and men like my daddy, who lived far from the world of trains, and automobiles, and telegraph lines, and electric lights. One long day's hard climb and Skedee and me could be near our valley, if we went that way. Everything's waiting for us just like it was. Preserves in the cellar, quilts on the rope beds with their soft ticking mattresses, water bucket by the door to run down to the springhouse and dip out all you need. Mama didn't even bring the milk cow and the chickens when we left. She just turned them loose.

Of a sudden, I'm mad at her all over again for making us go. For leaving the cow and the chickens to be eaten by mountain lions and coyotes. For getting tied up with Tesco Peele. For turning to the drink and the powders, for loving it more than she loved me.

I'm mad at that pale, skinny woman with the sunken eyes who stole my mama. No matter how good I was, or how much I begged and cried, or combed her hair and brought clean clothes for her to put on, that woman wouldn't let me have my mama back.

"Get away!" The words bust out of me when somebody grabs my arm. "I hate you!"

But it's only Nessa with wide eyes and her lip trembling because I scared her.

"It's all right, Nessie," I whisper. "I didn't know it was you, that's all."

She points back down the way where the road dips into a gulley. Amos and Tula are too far behind to even see, now.

"He can't go no more, Ollie." Tears spill over her cheeks and run down through the dried mud from last night. "*Stop,* Tula said."

"We ain't come but a few miles this whole mornin'." I look down the road and think about the hanging valley that seemed so close a minute ago. Of a sudden, it feels a far piece. Too far. "We gotta get back—"

"Home," Nessa finishes like she wants it bad as I do. "Hazel's up there?" she asks, and then I know it's not the hanging valley she's hoping for, it's her sister. She still thinks we'll find Hazel in the Winding Stairs. For a long minute, I want to let her believe it. We could make the climb up the old back trail, just us two. Nessa would be like Skedee, eager and fast.

Holding her face between my hands, I squat down and look in her eyes. "Hazel ain't up there, Nessie. I wish she could be, but she's not. I don't know what become of her. We've only got you and me from now on." I fight the part of me that wants to leave it at that, only two people to worry about. But I know it's not so anymore. "And Tula, and Pinti and Koi, and Amos. That's our family now."

Hand in hand, Nessa and me walk downhill and go sit with Amos and the others under a pine tree. The little ones wander, picking dewberries and the first wild strawberries, while Skedee rests with his packs off, and Tula sets out a meal from the goods Mr. Brotherton and Mrs. Grube gave us. Even after the food and some water from the canteen, it's plain that Amos can't travel anymore. Not today. Not for a while. He'll bleed to death if we don't stop.

Tula and me have to make a new plan. Much as I want to be back in that beautiful valley, there's no going up the mountain till all of us can make the climb together.

Standing in the road, I study on the rocks and the trees and the piled stones the soldiers stacked almost a hundred years ago to build up a wagon path to Fort Smith. I try to figure out exactly where we are. *What've I seen before? What's near? Where can we hole up with Amos till he's better?*

A mule's bray splits the air, and every thought in my head scatters.

The little kids run for cover, while Tula and me work to get Amos on his feet.

"Y'all leave me be," he whispers. "Y'all run."

"Ssshhh," I say while we help him farther into the thickets. "I know it's hurtin', but you've got to quieten, now. We'll get you hid and ..."

Before I can do one thing to stop it, Skedee throws his head up and whinnies loud and long.

"Who's out there?" a voice calls.

CHAPTER 25

Valerie Boren-Odell, 1990

That girl was a wild one. She'd ride by whistling like a boy.
—Mrs. Chas. McWilliams, 1937. Indian-Pioneer Papers Collection,
interview by Effie S. Jackson.

I fidget with a pen under the table, trying to keep myself in my chair as the weekly sit-down meeting drones its way through the usual paces. Washouts on trails, flood flotsam, graffiti cleanup, a hazardous material spill from an overturned Parker Construction truck carrying a tank of glyphosate herbicide, an ATV enthusiast flipped a four-wheeler and had to be airlifted, a teenager was rescued from Cedar Lake. Fortunately, he didn't become the second water fatality of the season, following our John Doe, whose autopsy report has finally come in. Cause of death: unwitnessed drowning.

The man is still unidentified and the drive to change that is underwhelming. Enough of a local stir has been created by Sydney Potter's claims, plus the herbicide spill three days later. By happenstance of proximity, I ended up coming upon the overturned spray-tank truck first. The vehicle was unmarked, and the driver was too shaken up to tell me immediately what was leaking into the nearby creek, or to whom the truck belonged. When I called it in, I had no way of knowing Parker Construction would be implicated, or that they hadn't had the truck inspected in years, and the license plate on it belonged to a different vehicle owned by the company. Technically, that is a felony in Oklahoma, but no one has owned up to swapping the tags, and nothing serious is likely to come of it.

Regardless, word is all over the area that I am *out to get* Alton Parker any way I can. I'm abusing the authority of the federal government to blacken Parker's reputation and bring down one of the biggest employers in the area. I'm responsible for an NPS Investigative Services Branch special agent having shown up to look into Sydney Potter's outlandish story, for Parker having to endure the humiliation of being questioned, and for raising the likelihood of trouble between the park and the Choctaw Nation as soon as the new federal laws on indigenous remains and grave goods go into effect.

I *am* guilty, but only of doing my job. While Sydney didn't have the best reputation for truth telling, her story was bound to leak out, and if Braden was somewhere on state or federal land injured, or became injured trying to hide in the woods alone, we would be responsible for not having done everything we could to find an endangered minor. Chief Ranger Arrington understood that on some level, but he had all he could deal with, trying to lay the blame for the mishandling of the burial site on Frank Ferrell, who agreed to quietly opt for retirement rather than returning from his medical leave.

I knew I was teetering on the edge of becoming an even bigger public relations liability than Ferrell, but I thought the Braden Lacey case would end up proving me right, so I pushed it as far as I could.

Unfortunately, a full seven days and one ISB special agent visit later, we have almost no new information. Even with air, surface, sonar, and canine unit assistance from cooperating departments, we've turned up nothing. The dogs found the campsite Sydney described, under a rock overhang where a stacked-stone wall had once been built to form a rudimentary dugout. Someone had holed up there recently, but the ashes in the fire pit were days old. Search dogs picked up scent trails, Braden's, only to eventually lose them at water crossings. One ended at the debris line above Holson Creek. In two days of gridwork along the banks, the dogs were unable to pick up the trail again.

When someone enters a waterway but doesn't exit, it's not good. Given the extensive wetlands acreage downstream, and then the Fourche Maline River and Wister Lake, a body could stay hidden for months or years.

There's still hope, but Braden hasn't shown up anywhere, nor has his mother, Jade.

Budgie's financial accounts are untouched. Nothing at her home is out of order. Her Medicare account shows no activity. No hits from medical facilities on a woman matching her description. Her credit cards are dormant.

Three people from the same family have vanished without a trace.

No matter how I try to explain it, I can't. Even sitting in the weekly meeting while all manner of bizarre human behavior is bandied about, any scenario I come up with seems far-fetched.

Sydney, at least, is in protective custody with people who can be trusted; however, it's a temporary solution, and unless proof of something nefarious is found, it's her word against Parker's. He'll win that battle. He has no black marks on his record, not even so much as a traffic ticket. He vehemently insists that he would never manhandle Sydney or lock her in a room. He consented to a search of his facilities. No evidence of Sydney's imprisonment, escape, or mysterious notebook was found. The place was clean, with new bedding and curtains in two of the bedrooms. Sydney's suitcase sat empty on a chair, her belongings having been neatly unpacked into the closet.

All of this is driving me to the point of madness. I can't sleep. My stomach is a constant whirlpool. My career may be on the line. I'm on the wrong side of some sketchy elements in town, underscored by another weird middle-of-the-night incident at the cabin court. The manager saw someone creeping around outside my place.

I called my mother the next morning and told her Charlie wanted to come visit for a couple of weeks—that work was a little out of control right now. She and my grandmother made plans to meet me halfway on my day off to pick up Charlie.

"Are you okay?" Mom asked as we stood in a grocery store parking lot in the fading evening light. "Why don't you take some time off and come home for a while?"

"I'm fine, Mom. I've just got a couple busy weeks ahead and Charlie's spending way too much time with babysitters. He'll have a lot more fun visiting with you and Gram and the cousins."

"You're *sure?*" Worry lines fanned around her eyes.

I insisted I was, of course. Fine.

While Mom loaded the car, Gram whispered in my ear, "Rip up that postcard I sent to you after you moved, Valerie. I was being emotional. You're a grown woman, and you get to make your own decisions. If this is what you want, don't let anybody stop you." Leaning back, she held my face in her hands like she used to when I was a child. "But call if you need me. I'll be on your doorstep in a New York minute."

I hugged all three of them, then watched my mother's car roll off. When it was gone from view, I felt lost.

Less than forty-eight hours later, after a lonely supper at the Sardis Shores Café, I found a place mat with *Pine Pigs Die* scrawled on it, stuck in the driver's side door of my vehicle. I dropped it into a Ziploc and stuffed it into my pocket.

It's been riding around with me for a day and a half.

Sitting in the staff meeting, I can't decide whether to show the note to everybody or dismiss it as idle harassment from one of the resident grousers.

Across the table, Edwin, Roy, and Chief Ranger Arrington discuss plans for Edwin and Roy to do a horseback patrol now that things have dried out enough. They'll ride to the blocked hiking trail from the back side to assess the rockfall area, and to scour for any further evidence that the trail damage was not a natural occurrence.

Mindy, the clerk typist, slips in the door and hands me a sheet of printer paper. The information on it makes for a paltry report when the meeting cycles my way.

"No new state, local, or tribal hits on anyone matching Budgie, Jade, or Braden," I say. "We got a hit on Braden's girlfriend, at a motel in Poteau. She's gone now, though. She had the room for four days and hung the Do Not Disturb sign, so no cleaning people entered. The manager didn't see who came and went, because the room was around back. He did remember checking Rachel in on the first day. Tall, blond, athletic. So was she there looking for Braden, or coming to pick him up and they're miles from here by now?"

Rachel's driver's license and a still frame from the hotel surveillance video are included on the printout. In the photo, she wears a ball cap. A silky ponytail trails over her camo tank top and cargo shorts. Her combat boots seem too heavy for her long, toned legs. "Looks more like she's dressed for a camping trip than a hotel stay," I add before sliding the page to the center of the table so everyone can take a look.

"How come I never see hikers like that?" the maintenance supervisor wants to know.

"Dang." Roy leans in with interest. "If that was *my* girlfriend, I wouldn't be runnin' off into the woods."

The men around the table chuckle in the way of high school boys spreading testosterone on the football bus.

I roll my eyes and sit back, think, *Really?*

"All right, all right. That'll be enough. There's a lady present," Arrington says, underscoring the point that he's decided the Blackwell case is nothing more than Sydney making up stories to escape foster care. He thinks I've been played by a kid. I'm soft. I'm a woman, with female emotions, overreacting.

Every face in the room silently supports that conclusion. It infuriates me. Blood rises hot in my chest, up my neck, into my cheeks, all the way to the tips of my ears.

Roy glances my way and blanches. His college-kid grin falls slack. "But if the girlfriend came here to look for him and she couldn't find him . . . I mean, if she thought he was lost or drowned, she would've reported it, right? She'd be worried." Fingers interlaced, thumbs up, he affects a serious posture.

Before I can answer, Ranger Arrington moves to close the meeting. "Well, who knows. Young people. Spats. Things happen. Maybe they ran off to Vegas together. Fact is, we've *more* than looked into it. Turned up nothing. Thanks to some adolescent girl with issues, I've got the tribe breathing down my neck, the state ticked off about the manpower we ate up, plus the superintendent and the NPS Intermountain Region Office on my back. Unless something new comes up, it's past time we cool the temperature and move on."

My jaw tightens until my head hurts. This is normally the kind of dressing down that would at least be done in private. Arrington wants everyone to get his message, and my standing among my co-workers is a mere casualty of the usual go along, get along.

"We'd better tell that to whoever left this." I slap the Pine Pigs Die sign on the table before my brain catches up with my mouth.

A pall of silence falls over the room. Hands move to laps, backs straighten, eyes glance at the paper, then fasten forward.

My pulse beats so hard I barely hear Arrington say, "Where'd this come from?"

"Someone stuck it on my windshield yesterday while I was at the Sardis Shores Café. I didn't see who."

His pen hammers the table as he squints at the baggie. *Tap, tap, tap, tap.* "You just now remembering to turn it in?"

"I didn't think it was serious."

"You bagged it."

"Like I said, I wasn't sure."

His gaze circles the table, silently nailing each person to the wall. "Anybody else get one of these?"

Eyes focus downward. Heads shake. I twist in the wind alone.

Edwin finally breaks the silence. "So . . . then, it's true about somebody being outside your cabin the other night?" He adds that Charlie blabbed the information when Shellie was babysitting him at their place.

Arrington directs a frown my way. "That true?"

I'm forced to admit that it is.

"Stay close to the station for a few days," the chief ranger orders. "Check with me before you head out anywhere." Then he gets up and leaves the room.

"Geez, Edwin," I snap. "You could've asked me that in private." Pushing up from my chair, I proceed to my desk, which I can now expect to be strapped to indefinitely. If I'm lucky, I'll get permit patrol in the campgrounds.

I've calmed down a little by the time I walk outside to scrounge up some Tylenol from my glove compartment. Nearby, Roy and Edwin blithely load their gear into a vehicle at the maintenance yard. As soon as they see me coming, Roy hides behind the truck and Edwin ducks under the brim of his ball cap. "Man, I'm sorry, Val. I didn't mean to set off a kerfuffle."

The term *kerfuffle* cools my jets a bit more. Who uses words like that? Edwin is the tall, skinny, idealistic, full-grown wilderness geek Charlie will someday be.

"It's okay, Edwin. I'm over it." My tone is unconvincing, especially considering that I'd give anything to be out in the woods today. "Okay, I'm not *over* it, but I'll get there. Meantime, I'm wondering if I can call in a favor, just between us?" I glance across to Roy, think, *Is this a good idea?* I'm already in trouble and neither one of these two can keep their mouths shut. I've heard more than once that Arrington would like to ship Edwin out—too yappy with the guests, too forthcoming about the kind of stuff that makes tourists wonder if they should head for Disney World instead.

"Anything." Edwin exhales desperately, his kind heart and thin skin painfully evident. He's wounded that I'm upset with him. "Since you'll be out that way on horseback today, could you guys make a little foray up that slope across the valley from the rockfall, get a view from the top?"

"How come?" Roy injects.

"It's just a hunch . . . sort of . . . but I swear I heard something . . . or someone out there the day Charlie and I found the blasting cap." That carefree hike seems like six months ago, but it's only been a matter of weeks. "It's probably nothing, but maybe somebody's hiding a setup back there. Growing weed, boiling meth, or . . . who knows? Just take a look from the ridge, see if you spot anything beyond."

Edwin and Roy quickly agree to the side trip, eager to be on good terms with me again.

"Keep it between us, all right?" I step back from the truck to let them go. "And be a little careful . . . just in case someone really is out there."

"You can count on us." Roy clicks his bootheels together and effects a goofy salute. If anybody inside the ranger station is watching, that gesture will definitely raise questions.

After they drive off with the horse trailer in tow, I engage in my own parking lot pity party, which devolves into a self-doubt session. Everything about this case has a benign explanation. Why can't I accept that?

Because I want it to be more? Because I *need* it to be more?

Because I can't stand being looked at as the token female?

Or because I am the product of a father who refused to leave wounded comrades on the battlefield in Vietnam, a mother who works tirelessly to get veterans the care they deserve, and a grandmother who fought school boards, delinquent parents, and the state legislature to defend the best interests of her students? We Borens have never bowed to bullies, politics, public pressure, embarrassment, name calling, or threats. Not that I ever saw.

The right thing is hardly ever the easy thing, Val. That was one of the last pieces of advice my dad offered before he died. I was home on military leave, wondering about my life decisions. *Anyone who says otherwise is selling something. At the end of the day, you have to look at yourself in the mirror. Don't do anything you can't stand to see looking back at you.*

I won't be able to look at myself in the mirror if I let this go without exhausting all means of uncovering the truth about Braden and Sydney . . . and figuring out what happened to Budgie Blackwell.

I can't do that from my desk, which is where I end up the rest of the morning and into the afternoon, as daily chatter hums along on the station radio, reminding me of my uselessness while I feed forms into a persnickety typewriter that looks like it came from a middle school surplus sale.

I'm opening a lunch I thought I'd be eating somewhere more interesting when a shadow falls across my desk. By the faint scent of the aftershave and creases in the trousers, I know it's Arrington.

I look up hopefully. "Reports done. After lunch, I thought I'd go—"

"Why don't you head out of town for a few days?" he says, pre-empting me. "Take a little time off with your son. I checked your annual leave. You have plenty."

I'm momentarily dumbstruck. "What? I just got here. No. I'm fine. In fact, Charlie is visiting his cousins right now. I've got extra time to keep digging into—"

"That's what I *don't* want." As is his habit, the chief ranger inter-rupts. He's to the point, but the point is *his* point. "I don't like this 'pine pigs' thing. You're under somebody's skin. I need to sort out how serious that is, exactly."

I push up from my chair, not in a confrontational manner, but by way of leveling the playing field. At five-eight, I meet him almost eye to eye. "I know how to watch my back. This isn't my first—"

"It's your first *here*." I expect his gaze to cut right through me, but instead, he has the stern look of a professor schooling an overeager student. "You're an outsider. You haven't had time to form a network locally, to build trust. You've gotten on the wrong side of a man who's well thought of in this county. Horsethief Trail needs a net-positive entry into the local ecosystem. It's our job to give it that. Your job, too. This unit operates as a team. Team players only. No Lone Rang-ers here in the Winding Stairs. Understand?"

Swallowing what I want to say, I briefly entertain the image of John Wayne as Marshal Rooster Cogburn, charging horseback across a valley with the reins in his teeth, guns blazing in both hands as he confronts Lucky Ned Pepper's outlaw gang.

I'm not possessed of such romantic notions, but leave town? Run away until things settle down?

I stare at the wall, try to get my head right. "I understand the issue. But I don't need a vacation, okay? I'm . . . saving up my time."

"Suit yourself." He chews on that for a moment, not fully satisfied with the taste. "But stay . . ."

The sentence hangs unfinished. Both of us swivel toward the sta-tion radio as a barely audible call to dispatch interrupts the drone of daily duty traffic. The codes are rushed, obscured by static: "700–5-7-9, 10-18 . . . 700–5-7-9, 10-18 . . ."

"Five-seven-nine. That's Roy," I gasp, and Arrington and I hurry across the room to turn up the volume. Ten-eighteen is an urgent call.

Mama Lu's response comes in, and radio protocol immediately goes out the window. "You're ten-one, though, hon, pretty bad. Your radio hittin' the right repeater? Check your settings. Was that a ten-eighteen? Go ahead, five-seven-nine."

A pause and then Roy comes back clearer. He's off firing codes so quickly they're hard to discern, but nothing in the ten-fifty range is good. "Holson Valley Road, at forest road number . . . road number . . . uhhh . . . he's . . . red tag. *Red* tag. I need that ambulance, quick."

"Okay, hon, slow down a minute." Mama Lu is both maternal and efficient. "I'm hearin' *emergency*, you've got an *accident* with *injuries* out there on HVR, victim is *critical*, and you're requesting assistance and an *ambulance*. What's your ten-twenty, over?"

Roy tries again to pinpoint his location. I picture Roy and Edwin, giddy with the novelty of a horseback day, chatting, joking, both so caught up they failed to pay attention to exactly where they left the blacktop for the forest roads. But they should be deep into the park on horseback right now. Why would they be back on Holson Valley Road at all? Edwin is senior, too. Why wouldn't he be the one calling in the emergency, and . . .

The thought freezes.

Because Edwin is *the emergency.*

Within moments, Mama Lu nails down a firm location based on landmarks.

I rush to strap on my duty belt, holster my radio, and grab my keys, then follow Chief Ranger Arrington out the door.

The afternoon becomes a patchwork of blurred and sharp-focus moments—arriving at the scene, watching EMTs stabilize Edwin, his uniform shredded and blood soaked, his face swollen, one boot twisted at an unnatural angle, blood and saliva dripping down his cheek, his body going into convulsions as medical personnel load him for transport.

CHAPTER 26

Olive Augusta Radley, 1909

A brisk traffic grew up in "dead claims" land that had become alien-
able through the death of the allottee.

— ANGIE DEBO, 1940, *AND STILL THE WATERS RUN.*

"Where'd you get this from?" I pick up the book after it slips
through a hole in the poke sack and lands in the dirt of the Old
Military Road. "And what'd you mean to do with it? Because we ain't
using book pages to start our campfires, that's for sure." Two weeks
now we been holed up in a broke-down dugout Daddy once told me
some Frenchmen built under a rock cliff while hunting for silver
mines. Every single day since we got there, I've wished we would've
all kept quiet when we heard Dewey Mullins yell from the road,
Who's out there?

But Amos knew Dewey's voice, and he called right out, "Help me,
Dewey!" like they were still best of friends. Then here came Dewey
with a crooked old man on a skinny white mule, Dewey riding behind the saddle. The only good thing was they weren't the law, and
they did help us scout for Daddy's old dugout camp. Without the
mule, we never could've gotten Amos moved there.

The old man is addled and mostly can't remember somebody's
name from one minute to the next, but he and the mule, named

Milk, are both gentle and wouldn't hurt a fly. Dewey said the man stole the mule and escaped from the Confederate Soldiers' Home, where his family had put him out to pasture. He was headed back to the Winding Stair to look for his true love, a Shawnee-Cherokee girl named Angeline, because this is where he left her during the War between the States.

The man's name is Gable. *No mister about it; just call me Gable,* he says every time he forgets he knows you. He's half deaf and goes around our camp singing songs like "Battle Hymn of the Republic" and telling stories about the old days. Dewey says that Gable carried secret papers in the war and knows where all the Confederate treasure is buried, and that's why the old man is *really* headed into the mountains. Dewey says Angeline ain't a lady but a stash of gold and silver.

But Dewey says a lot of things.

"Hush up talkin' so loud!" he growls at me when I snatch that book from the dirt. "What if that July Joyner gang comes along the road and hears you?"

"Don't *say* that name," I whisper, because just speaking it might bring bad luck. July Joyner and his gang of cutthroats have stole, burned, horse thieved, and now shot a man and committed depredations on the man's wife and daughter. Word is all over Talihina.

I wave the book in Dewey's face. "I know how to listen out. I ain't stupid. But *you* are, for stealing, because that's the only way you'd get a book. You're supposed to be working, not stealing. Find *work* in town. That's the plan we voted on during the council meeting . . . us older ones go make money till Amos heals enough to get up the mountain."

"I didn't vote on that part."

"It's your own fault you ran off mad." I walk faster because I'm still sour about the council. Dewey was the reason I didn't get to be president. First, he said a girl couldn't even *be* president. Then he said, *If girls can be president of us all, Tula oughta get a chance, too. She's older.*

Tula won because her brother and sister voted for her, and even Amos did. Nessa voted for me like I knew she would, so I came out ahead of Dewey, who ran off mad before our meeting was even over.

With our camp walkable to Talihina, if we cut cross-country some, getting work there made sense. Tula's clothes were too poor, so that left Dewey and me, being old enough. After what Kate Barnard said about the laundryman, I figured some of the clubwomen might need help doing their own laundry, and I could work at their houses without being around town where people would see me much. I've brought in twice as much money as Dewey, plus most days the ladies send food for my ailing mama and baby brother, who I told them moved closer to town till the Joyner Gang is caught.

"All I know about is workin' the coal mines." Dewey kicks dry leaves as he walks. He's got himself a new pair of brogan shoes, probably snitched off somebody's back porch. He's been trying to mud them up so nobody'll recognize them in town. "These farmers got no need of a breaker boy."

"Learn some farm work, then. If you're mannerly to folks, they'll help you."

"People round here ain't trustable and kindly as you think. Wasn't a week before I met up with Amos, I come upon a old Choctaw woman, cryin' over the grave of her little granddaughter. Somebody poisoned the girl for her oil land. Like you say in them pirate stories at the night fire, I guess, *dead men tells no tales.*"

Even with the hot May afternoon, I feel cold of a sudden. "*You* tell tales, Dewey. And that's a fact."

"You see all them land notices in town?" He snorts. "Why, I could make five nickels a day hangin' up handbills, but I don't feel right about it."

"You don't feel right about working." I've spotted him in Talihina, tossing nickels with other raggedy boys like him. Meantime, I'm taking the chance on getting seen if Tesco still has anybody out looking for me, but we need the food and the money. "And your stealing's gonna land us in trouble. What do you want with a book, anyway?" I know Dewey can't read.

"I brung it for *you.* It's got a pirate ship on it like them stories you tell from Mr. Keyes Radley. High seas and buried treasures and such."

I swallow hard, because I don't want to feel soft toward Dewey Mullins, but on the book cover is a gold ship with sails wide. *Treasure*

Island, by Robert Louis Stevenson. "I bet it's a good one, but you oughtn't have taken it. That library wagon will lend us books for free. I asked."

"Except now this book is ours to keep. You wanted to make a school for the little kids in camp, so there's a book for it."

"Shelterwood Camp School," I say, and I like the way it sounds. That's what I named our hole-up at the dugout: Shelterwood Camp. Since I came in second place for president, I said I ought to get to be a commissioner, like Miss Kate Barnard. Now I'm commissioner of names, plus of the school and the bank because I can cipher and read. The only letters Dewey knows are the ones in his name, because I showed him by scratching it on a rock. He can't be bothered to write the E twice, so he spells it, D-E-W-Y.

When we move up the mountain to the hanging valley, we'll build a real school with writing paper and pencils, puncheon floors and piggy benches. It'll be a church on Sundays, plus a council house for our meetings. I haven't told the others yet, but I plan to name the new place Shelterwood Town, after the grandpappy oak my daddy loved. *The roots spread even farther than the branches, Ollie Auggie, you know that?* he'd say while we lay underneath and looked into leaves and sky. *That's how strong a tree, or a person, or a family is. Strong as the roots, see?* He'd breathe deep, and I'd feel his chest swell and sink under my head. *The old shelterwood trees keep the forest safe from the wind and the weather, from too much sun and heat in the summer, too much snow in the winter. They're strong and pull up the water from down deep in the drought times, hold the soil so everything smaller can grow, and all of that comes from the roots of this big ol' tree. The old take care of the young, just like a family.*

Of a sudden, I feel bad that Dewey never had anybody to tell him about trees and roots and families.

"It's a pretty book." I tuck it in my rucksack. I'll find a way to leave it in town where it'll get found with nobody to blame. We don't need any more troubles in Talihina. We're already careful to stay away from the tatty side of town, where that woman who shot at Amos might remember us, and I leave Skedee back at camp with Gable's old mule because a calico pony is noticeable. I keep one eye out for the lawman and the other for Mr. Lockridge's train car, but nothing's come of it in two whole weeks, so it seems more and more likely that Tesco gave Nessa and me up for drowned in the river after all.

Dewey pulls something else out of his poke sack. "I brung you a newspaper, too. Trade it for a bite of that grub you got from them ladies today. I'm hungry."

"You thieved a newspaper, too?"

"It's a *old* one," he snorts.

"I'll *bet*." I snatch at the paper, and he pulls it away, but I get half of the first page. He's right about it being an old paper because there's a picture of Miss Kate Barnard giving her big speech. *Miss Kate Barnard in Talihina. The recent oratory of Oklahoma's Good Angel charged ordinary citizens to turn an ear to the concerns of miners, Railroad Brotherhoods, workingmen, poor, and friendless waifs*, it says under the picture. The title reads, *Clubwomen Accept the Charge!* There's no note of who wrote the story, but even reading the first sentence, I know it was Mrs. Grube, because it sounds just like her.

She really did it, I think to myself. *But I sure hope Mr. Grube doesn't find out.*

"Give me the rest," I tell Dewey. "I'll read it out loud at night fire."

He slaps me in the chest with it. "You want it, carry it. You might oughta look in the middle. That newspaper man pulled one over on us. He put a picture of us in the paper. *All* of us. See for your own self."

I open the paper and find "Friendless Waifs Relate Woeful Tales at Hidden Encampment," plus a long story and an ink drawing of skinny kids huddled at a campfire. "Ain't much of a likeness, so I guess there's no harm." I don't want to speak bad of Mr. Brotherton. "Nobody'd know us by it. These kids look real pitiful."

"Maybe we do, too." Dewey turns his face away.

We walk on back toward Shelterwood Camp, listening for riders or wagons and watching for pretty bird feathers we can sell to the hatmaker in town. Finally we come to a hollow where the wild blackberry brambles and cow-itch vines grow like walls, head high on both sides of the road. Our cutoff is a toppled elm tree that's hung up on a tangle of briars so snaky and thick no man on foot or horseback would ever go into it. I named that tree Sleeping Beauty Bridge, just like the fairy tale. We climb up the roots and go right over the briars, walking on the trunk. At the other end, the tree's branches make a ladder, and we set our feet in a whole new land. *Our* land, at least for now.

The trek down a rocky, dry wash from there goes easier because we don't worry about riders or road wagons, just snakes. Timber rattlers shake their tails to warn you off, but the copperheads are quiet and the same color as tree shadows and dead leaves. They're sneaky and mean, and they'll kill you dead.

Picking up a long stick, Dewey moves on ahead. "I'll get the snakes away. I got the best eye."

"Tula's got the best eye. She's killed three around camp already."

Dewey pokes under leaves and rocks. "The hatmaker in Talihina makes a fine snakeskin hatband. I'm gonna kill some snakes. Sell him the skins."

"You'd best leave the snakes be if you can." My daddy taught me that.

"Pin the rascal under a stick, cut off the head with my bone-handle Barlow, one quick slice, like butter." Dewey has come up with a two-blade pocketknife, and he's so proud he's either sharpening it, talking about it, or whittling with it every chance he gets. He's made wood spoons, roasting sticks for the fire, and a crooked flute, plus carved his name in every tree he can find.

He won't say if he earned that knife or stole it, so I'm careful not to admire it.

"Cut somethin' in the neck, it's done for." He reaches into his pocket for the Barlow. "I seen one man slice another clean through the neck in a fight one time, blood spraying everywhere."

The way Dewey talks about knives and blood makes my stomach turn, and I tell him to hush up about dead men; I'm tired. That much is true. All day today I've been washing, and starching, then rolling Mrs. Paulson's curtains and dresser scarves through the big mangle iron. Day after tomorrow, which is Monday, we'll start on bed linens. Mrs. Paulson ain't only keepin' her own laundry at home now, she's taking in her husband's father's wash, and a widow lady's laundry, and a bachelor gentleman's, too. The housemaid at the Paulsons' is down with the gout and can barely do the dusting and minding the children, which are three-year-old twin boys. Mrs. Paulson's husband is Choctaw and a lawyer. He travels away a lot to the county courthouse in Poteau to argue for folks in the tribe that got done wrong on land and oil, coal, or timber deals. I'm hoping Mrs. Paulson might hire Tula, too, but first Tula and me would need to figure a plan about what Tula's wearin.'

I'm turning that over in my mind when Dewey yells, "I see a possum! Possum stew for supper!" He goes clawing his way up the side of the draw on all fours, pine straw and leaves flying everywhere. I guess he forgot about snakes, but he'll never listen, and so I keep going along the dry wash till I wind down the slope to our creek, where water music flows in the air so pretty I named it Sweetwater Valley. It's peaceful in the evening light, and I'd like to take off my shoes and soak my tired feet, but there's no time. Before Dewey shows up, I need to talk to Tula about my new plan . . . and get everybody else on my side to vote for it.

Dewey's bound to argue against it because he wants to keep running with those boys in town. But if he's going to bring more trouble than money, Tula and me should go to work and he should stay here to watch after Amos and the younger ones. We can't trust old Gable to do it, because he forgets about us and wanders off on his mule, searching for a magic spring pool where you can look into the water and see your true love. There he'll find Angeline.

I'm not even into camp before all the little kids come climb on me and pester about what have I got in my pack today? They're hoping for some tea cakes, or fresh bread, or cheese, or a cinnamon ball from a scrap of pie dough.

"Let me talk to Tula first." I look around for her, but only Amos is at the cookfire outside our cave shelter. "She go off food gathering?"

"Yeah, she did. Tula will find us somethin' more to put in the stew." Amos's eyes shine in a fond way when he says her name.

I unwind Nessa's fingers from mine, then shake off Pinti and Koi, who are so thin they weigh half what Nessa does. Little children need more food to grow. Koi looks up at me with his hungry face, and I touch a fingertip to his nose. "You been good all day?"

"They been," Amos says from where he's stretched out against a backrest Gable made for him, on account of sitting up still hurts too bad. "They gathered wood, and checked the fish traps, and Nessa caught us a little turtle. We're fixin' up a stew, Ollie. Don't that sound fine?" Propping on one elbow, he leans toward the fire and stirs the pot with a wood spoon Dewey carved from a long stick.

"Sure does," I say.

Nessa grins real proud. "I caught 'im right in the water, Ollie. He tried to bite me, too."

"That was real brave, Nessie. I can't wait for some turtle stew. There's no better kind." Truth is, that stew looks like mostly water again, but complaining only makes a belly emptier, so I don't. I'm better off than the rest anyhow because the ladies feed me at noon-day when I work.

"You little kids take care of Skedee?" I ask when I don't see my pack pony in the brush corral we fixed against the rocks. "You walk him down along the creek, where he can eat some grass and leaves?"

"Gable took him and the mule," Amos answers. All the little kids go quiet because looking after Skedee is their job.

"You let that old man go off with my *horse?*" Quick as that, I go from tired to mad ... and scared. Gable is kindly, but his mind is gone. Some days he helps us build firepits and fish traps and back-rests. Other days, he wanders off mumbling about enemy soldiers and battle marches and spies. "What if he doesn't come back?"

"Tula said it'd be all right." Amos puts more wood on the fire.

"That ain't Tula's choice to make."

"She's the president of all us, ain't she?"

"Skedee's *my* horse."

"Everythin' belongs to the tribe, don't it?" Poking in the coals, he frowns up at me. "Ain't that what we decided at the council? We drawed a circle round the tribe. A circle in the dirt and all us in it."

"That don't go for horses!" Losing that calico pony would be like losing the last piece of my daddy.

"All together was what we said."

I throw my pack on the ground, then turn around and run down the creek, all the way to Lookout Tree, and climb up. From high in the branches, I try to spot old Gable and the mule and my horse, but there's not a sign of them anywhere.

Tears blur Sweetwater Valley while the sun sinks to the mountaintops, burns the sky, and finally shushes the land in deep blue and purple, pretty as the ruffles on the Lockridges' silk party frocks when Mrs. Lockridge would bring the girls down from the city for the soiree on the lawn of the big house. The men and the women danced and whirled to "The Blue Danube" and the "Willow Waltz" while the fiddlers fiddled and a stand-up piano played right out there on the porch. By late in the night, those new dresses from Paris were so ruined by dew and damp and sweat that Mrs. Lockridge and her girls would shuck them off by the bedroom door, and there the dresses would stay. After three days of the fun, the pile got shoved in a trunk and carried away on Lockridge's private train car, so nobody could make the dresses over and show up in them at the party next year.

I always wished Mr. Lockridge would give me one of those extra party frocks, so I could play princess in it. He loved bringing me good things his girls didn't want anymore—clothes and boots and coats and bonnets and such. I even got two pretend teacups and a tiny china teapot with the handle broke off, but much as I hoped for it, none of those silk soiree dresses ever came my way.

Standing in the Lookout Tree, I want my calico pony back more than I ever wanted a silk dress. But the sun falls, and hills go black, and fireflies sparkle like stars falling from the sky. Still, there's no sign of Skedee.

Down in the valley, Tula and the little kids holler for me. Nessa screams, "I'm sorry, Ollie! Come back, Ollie!"

The glow from the night fire rises up the cliff above our dugout and draws a face there, like the man in the moon. I watch the shadows shift so that his mouth moves. I hope he's calling Skedee home.

Even Dewey finally joins in, yelling, "Possum-turtle stew! Possum-turtle stew! Smells mighty good. Ollie, Ollie, Ollie, where is you-ooo-ooo-ooo?" I cover my ears because I don't want to come down. They can't find me up here. I made this tree my special secret after I didn't get elected president of Shelterwood Camp and I needed a place to be mad awhile. From these branches, I feel like I can almost see clear to the old homeplace. It's right there under my same stars.

"Wait on me," I whisper, so that the Lookout Tree can send the news through all the trees, till the old spreading oak hears in the hanging valley. "I'm coming."

I nestle into a crook where one branch hooks back on another like the number four, and I wait for the moon to rise. It's past full and waning again, which means we've been gone from Tesco Peele's house about a month now. I wonder, does Mama ever think of us? Or are powders and wildcat whiskey still all that matter? Does she miss me, or is she glad I'm not there to bother her anymore? Maybe liquor and opium powders dry up love the same way they dry up a body, leave it brittle and thin and pale, till it turns to dust and blows away and is gone.

Maybe everything's gone. Even Skedee.

Time and again, I sit up and look for the glow of the moon against white hide, Skedee's or the mule's, and I listen for old Gable singing one of his songs.

Time and again, there's nothing.

Finally, I close my eyes and see my calico pony, running free from his halter and headed up the back trail to the homeplace. I jump from the tree onto his back and we race toward the sky . . .

A scream wakens me, jerks me so hard I almost come right off the branch. My mind clears in a hurry, and I remember where I am. Someplace down below, a panther calls out again, its cry sounding like a woman's death wail.

Another panther answers, so close my hair stands on end. I listen at their screams back and forth from both sides, getting nearer, so they can find each other to mate.

I get out of that tree so fast I'm half falling, then I stumble and slide down the slope while branches claw my clothes and my face and hands and legs, and I hope not to step on a snake. I don't even catch a breath till I cross the creek near our dugout.

In the dark, the wails come one right after the other, but at camp, everybody's sound asleep, even Amos, who's supposed to guard at night. The fire's banked and burning, but I put more wood on, then shake Amos and whisper, "You best keep an eye peeled and the fire fed. There's panthers close by."

He feels for the spear, and the pine-knot torch, and my daddy's hunting knife, then he stretches his neck and turns an ear when the panthers cry again. "I been watchin'," he says.

"You ain't watching with your eyes closed." Hiding in that tree hasn't gotten rid of my mad. I want to hurt somebody. *It's your fault,* I want to say. *If you hadn't gotten shot, we'd be up the mountain by now, and no crazy old man would've run off with my horse.*

Amos's eyes turn away, like he can see all that in me. "I feel real sorry." His voice is mournful. "Real sorry about your pony."

His eyes pool up, and a tear rolls down his cheek. I should tell him I know he didn't mean any of this to happen. Between Skedee and Gable's mule, all the forage nearby is used up, and the little kids can only go so far before they might get lost. Tula has to hunt for food, and Amos can't help, and Dewey and me need to get work and money in town.

I ought to tell Amos, *We're all just doing as best we can, and every one of us is bone-tired, and it's not fair you got shot. Not fair that my pony is gone. Not fair that the little kids are so hungry they're used to it.*

Not fair that some girls get china dolls and silk dresses.

Nothing is fair.

But all that comes out is "He was my daddy's."

I go to my pallet behind the dugout wall and lie down and cover my ears against the screams.

CHAPTER 27

Valerie Boren-Odell, 1990

In the mountainous region lying east of Talihina, where, owing to the vast lumber industry which was developed in that region upon construction of the Frisco and Kansas City Southern Railways, shady characters were wont to congregate, the presence of law enforcement officers was constantly in demand.

—H. Lee Jackson, 1938. Indian-Pioneer Papers Collection, interview by Gomer Gower.

"I wasn't alone out there." The map I brought with me to Curtis's house crinkles as I trace a fingertip from Edwin's accident site to the location where I found his lost horse. "And I'd bet you a fish dinner that Roy and Edwin weren't, either. That loose horse ran a long way, lame and banged up. Something . . . or someone set him off."

"I'd take that bet," Curtis says. "Except we'd be on the same side of it. So I guess we'd have to split the fish dinner."

We look up at the same time and realize we're in awkwardly close proximity, studying the map from opposite sides of his kitchen table. One of those unexplainably transfixed moments occurs, intensified by the fact I came on lunch break to make this appear to be a casual puppy-shopping trip . . . in case anyone should be looking on.

Curtis saw through the puppy-shopping ruse instantly, of course. He invited me inside, closed the door, and said, "Now tell me why you're really here. Because I know it's not for a puppy."

"Sorry. I didn't mean to raise your hopes." The words carried such strong potential for a double meaning that I blushed.

"You didn't." He was kind enough to keep things on a professional level, following along intently while I pulled out the map, described the recovery of the horse, and the fact that waning daylight plus the slow pace of the injured animal prevented me from taking an up-close look at the place where Edwin's fall started. I didn't dare stay long enough to climb the ridge.

No details have been gained from Edwin. Four days have passed with him under sedation, following emergency surgery to drain fluid off his brain. Officially, the horse balked, lost footing, and fell. Random bad luck. Unofficially, a lot of people know that horse to be experienced and unflappable. He's a sturdy, agile Choctaw pony of the breed the tribe once raised wild in these mountains, a horse with a steady gait and too much good sense to spook at his own shadow and go tumbling end over end.

There's a quiet suspicion that Edwin and Roy may have been targeted by someone looking to make a point. A disgruntled local, irked about tourists, pine pigs, and government regulations? An operation growing weed or running a backwoods methamphetamine lab? One of Parker's supporters sending a message?

In any case, I was the first target via the note, but the repercussions caught Edwin. I am, as Arrington put it, "on thin ice." He wasn't one bit pleased that I'd gone after Edwin's escaped mount alone. "Bad idea, given the trouble following you lately, Boren-Odell." Beneath the reprimand lay the unspoken warning—*stir the pot too much, you'll land yourself a lateral transfer to some other unit, only it won't really be a lateral. Your next location will be an NPS armpit. If you have a next location at all.*

Yet here I am, against all good sense, looking for advice . . . or maybe perspective from the one ally I've been able to count on. "It wasn't only that I was losing the light, though," I admit. "I *know* I was being shadowed. I heard . . . something, more than once. But whenever I stopped to get a bead on it, it would stop, too. Animals don't do that. People do. I ended up taking a look at the slope through my field glasses, then moving on, since I was by myself."

"Good call."

"The thing is, I saw plenty of evidence of a disturbance below where the fall started, but looking upslope, I couldn't tell what caused the fall, at least not through the glasses." I touch the map again. "If a rock tumbled from up there and it was enough to set the horse off, seems like there would be visual evidence, you know?"

"Seems like it." Folding his knuckles under his chin, he pushes a thumb against his bottom lip. I realize I've come to know he does that when he's thinking. When his interest is piqued.

"Roy told me he heard what he thought was a rock bouncing downslope, then Edwin's yell." I've mentally analyzed it over and over, and I keep coming down to one scenario. "But Roy didn't actually *see* the rock fall. If someone took a shot at Edwin with a small-caliber rifle...maybe a .22 with a sound suppressor installed, you could *think* you're hearing stone striking stone, especially out there. Maybe Roy didn't hear a rock falling. Maybe he heard a bullet strike a rock, and then the echo."

I attempt to gauge Curtis's reaction, but he doesn't make it easy.

"Am I off base here? I trust you to give it to me straight." *I trust you.* I haven't said those words to a person outside my family since... since Joel died, and the investigation into his death was short and shallow, weather deemed the cause, not poor decision making by the incident commander.

"It's possible."

"That I'm off base or that I'm right?"

"Either." He's given me what I asked for—honesty. It stings. "But you have good instincts, Val. I think you're right about Sydney, and I think you're right about Alton Parker, even though I've known the man my whole life. The problem is, no matter how many ways I draw the lines, I can't connect the dots. You may not want to hear this, but you have to face the fact that a break in the stone wall might not happen. If this investigation comes crashing down, the fallout will land on you."

I turn away from him, from the map, let my gaze wander through the window to a hollowed-out place under an elm tree, where Bonnie has bedded down for a midday nap with her three remaining puppies. She gently offers tongue baths, checking each of her little ones. I think of Charlie, of all he's counting on from me.

And of Sydney, who has no one to count on.

I think of those three little skeletons in the cave, girls who could have fallen victim to something so sinister I struggle to comprehend it. My packet from Mr. Wouda arrived yesterday. I opened it, scanned the material—a report written in part by Gertrude Bonnin, a research agent for the Indian Welfare Committee of the General Federation of Women's Clubs, and several newspaper pieces about Kate Barnard's efforts to stop crimes against oil-wealthy children of the Five Tribes. *The women of Oklahoma came early to the fight,* Mr. Wouda's handwritten note read. *Women such as my aunt, Alva Grube, but you won't find that in the history books. Had they won the battle, your mountains would have far fewer ghosts.*

As always, I'm torn in two—the mother half and the professional half: the part that promised Charlie a good life here and the part that swore an oath as a law officer.

What's right?

"I just . . ." There's no quitting for me. Not yet. "I have to check the accident scene. To be sure. If it's a dead end, I'll let it go."

Curtis exhales slowly. "Not by yourself, you don't."

"Curtis, I'm not asking . . ."

His hand covers mine, warm, strong, compelling. I want to fall into that touch, but at the same time I want to pull away from it. I can't seem to do either. I sit there, frozen.

"Look, Val," he says, and I turn away from the window, meet the intensity of his gaze. "I *get* that you're a professional. You don't need to be looked after and all that. But you do need backup. Just in case." A hint of irony tugs one side of his lips, forms a dimple there. "Where else are you going to get it?"

Either my resolve goes to mush or he's right. I'm not sure which. "When you put it *that* way . . ." Maybe it's just nerves, but the words come out sounding snarky. We both laugh. "S-sorry," I gasp. "I didn't mean it . . . like th-that."

"Yeah, you Feds," he quips. "All attitude. Hope it doesn't rub off."

I feel the slightest, almost imperceptible squeeze before he releases my hand. Or maybe I imagine it.

In the next moment, he's full-on business, taking a pencil to the map. "Let me see if I can find out who owns the land that juts into the park here. It's weird that I can't say right off. I know most of the families around, plus a lot of the out-of-towners who come and go to hunting and fishing places. I've met the absentee owner who has the property with the road frontage there, a hundred acres maybe, some old hunting blinds and a cabin, but I'm not sure what's behind that place. Looks like it could be a four-, maybe five-hundred-acre piece? If it's landlocked, that might explain an interloper using park land to gain access to the acreage . . . and being kind of sensitive about it."

"Sensitive enough to *shoot* at somebody?"

Resting his palms on the table, he pushes to his feet. "Depends on what they're doing back there."

CHAPTER 28

Olive Augusta Radley, 1909

The report shows that the department has intervened in the cases
of 137 orphan children. Out of 232 Indian orphan children in state
institutions, 137 were being robbed by the guardians.

—*The Daily Ardmoreite* article regarding Kate Barnard's annual report,
January 10, 1911.

Tula and me whisper and giggle while we dash from Mrs. Paulson's screen porch to the washhouse out back. A misty rain falls, so
we run with our bundles held close. If you drop anything in the
mud, Mrs. Paulson will take it out of your pay . . . at least that's what
the housemaid, Flannery, says. Mrs. Paulson seems more kindly than
that, but we don't see her much since the doctor put her abed after
the big women's-club luncheon. Mrs. Paulson is in a family way, and
she's lost a baby once before.

"Quiet and quick, that'll keep ya hired on here" is what Flannery
says. She's a round ol' Irish woman and talks in a Irish way. She's too
gouty to do all this wash, and the washhouse is hot as a teakettle.
"Y'aren't much use to me," she tells us. "Ragamuffins, that's what y'are."

Truth is, Tula and me together come cheaper than one full-grown
washerwoman would, and Flannery knows it. Plus, we both look
right respectable, me in my red pinny dress and Tula wearing Nessa's
bonnet and the blue-ribbon sash dress I wrecked the day Amos got
shot. Me and Tula took up the hem and mended the rips with a

needle and thread I borrowed. Then we made a boiled walnut-bark dye to color it brown and hide the stains. It doesn't look half bad, except for being too big because Tula's so skinny and small from giving her food to Pinti and Koi.

Nessa would give to them, too, but I make her eat hers. "Nessie, you have to be grown and watch over the little kids. You need that food," I told her. Then I held her hands and reminded her she's the oldest girl in camp now that we voted for Tula and me to work in town and Dewey to go out with old Gable to hunt food and take the horse and mule afield to graze. That way, Dewey can make sure Gable and the mule *and* Skedee come back by dark. Not like the first time, when Gable was gone for three days with my pack pony, then came wandering home, singing a song that's been in my ear ever since.

I sing it now while we set down our bundles in the washhouse.

My feet they are sore, and my limbs they are weary;
Long is the way, and the mountains are wild;
Soon will the twilight close moonless and dreary
Over the path of the poor orphan child.

Why did they send me so far and so lonely,
Up where the moors spread and gray rocks are piled?
Men are hard-hearted, and kind angels only
Watch o'er the steps of a poor orphan child.

Yet distant and soft the night breeze is blowing,
Clouds there are none, and clear stars beam mild,
God, in his mercy, protection is showing,
Comfort and hope to the poor . . .

Tula nudges me with her bare foot. Shoes were the only thing we couldn't get her, but lots of kids don't have shoes in the summer.

"What're you kickin' me for?" I say while she rubs the bar of fancy store-bought Fels-Naptha across the grater, the muscles tight as ropes in her arms.

"Oh, where have ya been, Billy Boy-ee, Billy Boy-ee?" she sings, and she's got the tune just right. We been working on words and songs, Choctaw ones and English ones. Tula's learning fast, and I knew more Choctaw words from old Isom at the horse barn and the Choctaw kids at school than I thought. "Where have ya been . . ."

"Charmin' Billy-y-y," I chime in, figuring she wants a happier song, so we go on and sing "Billy Boy" together. "I have been to seek a wife. She's the joy of my life. But she's a young thing and cannot leave her mother. Oh, where . . ."

Tula stomps her feet on the wet floor while we work and sing. One thing about Tula, she loves music. When she can't think of a word or two, she hums or whistles. We go all the way through "Billy Boy" three times and pour the boil kettle into the big washtub before we carry the steamy-hot copper back to the cistern to fill it again, so we can boil all the sheets and doilies and clothes and underclothes to whiten them best before they go in the wash water.

"She'll be comin' round the mountain when she comes . . ." I start up while we stumble across the yard, lugging the full kettle betwixt us. I figure that's enough singing about Billy and courtin' and house-wifin', since Tula and Amos are too sweet on each other already.

"Keyu," Tula complains as the kettle sways like a fat man after too much bootleg whiskey. "Pol-lee put the kettle on, Pol-lee put . . ."

I laugh so hard at her coming up with that song I almost drop my side of the copper. I'm about to throw my head back and join in when Flannery walks out the back door to toss the breakfast scraps to the birds.

"Paid for singin', are ya now?" She gives us a mean look. "Be gettin' the copper on the boil and quick. I need ya to fetch my marketin' in town while the rain's slackened. Missus is after a peach pie for supper."

Tula and me give each other the wide-eye. Peach pie means sticky-sweet tin cans in the rubbish. Me and Tula are gonna have us a treat from the burn bin after Flannery gets the twins down for their nap and makes that pie.

"Yes'm." I stretch my neck to see what breakfast leavings are headed over the fence, where climbing roses grow head high all the way around the house.

Looks like bread toast with jam, oat mash, and ham.

"And fetch the soiled linens from ol' Paulson while y'are out, as well," Flannery says on the way back. "Leave *that one* for tendin' the washhouse." She won't ever call Tula by name.

We've barely got the kettle in place when Flannery rings the bell on the back porch to tell me she's hung the market list on the black iron clip where the dairyman posts his bill for milk, cream, cheese, and eggs.

"I'll hurry," I promise before leaving Tula to tend to the boiling batch. "You know how to do it, right? Out of the copper, into the wash water, take the wash dolly and poke it in there and up, down, around, up, down, around. The dump water goes out that hatch in the back wall, so it'll run down the drain tile into Mrs. Paulson's roses."

Tula stops and puts a hand on her hip. We're already on our third week doing laundry here. You don't have to show Tula something more than once.

"I'll grab those breakfast leavings off the ground first. You watch out for me, all right? Whistle a bobwhite call if Flannery's comin'."

Nodding, she moves so she can see out the window screen to the house.

I hurry and get the market list, then duck through the overgrown rose arbor at the back gate and gather up the food scraps into a flour sack from my pocket.

In the honeysuckle bushes across the way, a field cat or stray dog or a nosy squirrel rustles around, wanting to get at the food. Tula's bird call warns me off before I'm done, and so I wrap up the poke sack, toss it over the climbing roses to the back of the washhouse, and leave the rest for the birds or whatever's in the bushes.

I keep my bonnet up as I run to the market, dodging men and horses, wagons, wandering chickens, and some Choctaw ladies set up to sell pashofa stew to folks off the train. Four of those rotten boys Dewey liked to go around with are squatted down in the shade nearby, probably waiting to steal something.

A thin-faced girl looks out the window of the tall red-rock laundry house as I pass by. She's dressed in just a white shimmy, her shoulders bare and her arms skinny. Her long red hair hangs in wet strings. It must be hot as blazes in there, worse than Mrs. Paulson's washhouse by a lot. The girl's eyes follow me, but when I turn my head, she doesn't smile. I wave, and she presses a hand to the glass. Her fingers are chapped and raw.

I hope Miss Kate comes for her soon, because even with the club-women doing their own laundry, that place won't close up. Talihina ain't the sleepy town it was when Daddy and I used to come down from the mountain. There's more trade in Indian-owned land every day, and more folks that've brought their wagons and their grub-stakes, hoping on a good deal. There's ten buyers for every horse that can pull a wagon or carry a rider. By tomorrow, there'll be eleven, and the next day a dozen, and every man wants a wife. Marriage brokers have hung their shingles right alongside the land brokers, and some men will stop a girl right in the street if her hair's down, showing she's not married, and they'll ask her if she'd like to marry, even if she's too young yet.

All these new people make me itchy to be on the mountain, where we'll build our own town. I draw it in the old logbook from Daddy's rucksack, dreaming up plans. But buying tenpenny nails and twine and sacks of flour, sugar, and garden seed takes money. So me and Tula keep putting coins in Shelterwood Bank, which we hid in the knothole of a big tree along Sweetwater Creek. If we can work the rest of the summer, we might even buy a couple laying hens and a rooster.

That's worth hauling boiling kettles and taking the chance on going around town to fetch marketing and laundry, if I have to.

I'm out of breath before getting to the store where Mrs. Paulson trades. I hurry around back and ring the bell on the screen door, then hand the man my list and tell him who it's for, and, no, sir, I'd best wait outside.

Mrs. Tinsley comes in the front door not long after, and so I stay pressed to the wall out back. That woman will talk your ear off, and she is full of nosy questions. She'll also hire you for work, then come up with reasons not to pay you as much as she promised. I learned the hard way about Mrs. Tinsley.

It's a relief when the goods are ready and I can get out of there without her seeing me. While I walk down the alley to pick up the dirty clothes from Mrs. Paulson's father-in-law, I peek in the grocery box at the canned peaches. I can't hardly wait to pick a sassafras twig and swirl up whatever's left in the can once we get it out of the rubbish. Thinking about it makes my mouth water as I knock on old man Paulson's back door and holler that I'm here for the laundry.

He smiles and tells me, "Halito!" when he opens the door. Setting the bundle atop my box, all tied up in a bedsheet, he asks if I'm sure I can carry that much.

"Yes'ir, I can," I tell him, and he grins and leans on his cane. Then he reaches out to check my arm muscle and says he doesn't know if I'm that stout.

"Stout as a timberjack," I say. "I'd go to cuttin' trees instead of washin' clothes, but I don't want to put the men out of work."

He throws his head back and laughs. Then he takes a brown caramel candy from his shirt pocket and sets it on top of the laundry bundle and winks at me. He's a sweet old widower man who was high up in the Choctaw government in the Indian Territory days and also ran a traveler's hotel. He loves to tell stories of the people who came to stay there. I like to listen at his stories, but rain's on the way, so I tell him "Yakoke" for giving me the candy. I try to say *I better get on before the rain comes* in Choctaw, which makes him chuckle. He pats me on the head and tells me to keep at it, then sends me on my way.

I'm in such a rush going back through the alley, I almost don't notice when somebody steps right in front of me. I look up, from two bare feet in the mud, past a plain brown skirt, to a pair of arms wrapped round a basketful of folded clothes, and right into the face of one of those laundry girls. Both of us catch a breath, each surprised by the other. This girl is blond headed with skin as white as a china cup, but she's sad and sickly looking, just like the one in the window.

"You all right?" I ask, even though I know all we did was scare each other.

"Be about your work, Evelyn." The laundryman's voice is so close I stumble back a step. I turn my head to see past my bonnet bill, and there he is on the back stairs not five foot away. He's a tall, skinny man with rolled-up sleeves and long hands. I don't dare look into his face.

"*Evelyn.*" He says it sharper and steps off the stoop into the wet. "Deliver the man's laundry. I'm certain he's eager to see you. And take care not to track up the carpets while you change the linens. He's a good customer." The girl hurries on her way. I hear her feet squishing in the mud and my own heart beating, and then the man says to me, "And who have we here?"

Taking a better grip on my box, I move back a step, keep my head tucked.

"Oh, now, don't be shy." He's got a soft, friendly laugh. "Evelyn didn't mean to startle you."

His boots take long steps toward me. One, two, three, four. They stop right in Evelyn's tracks.

I open my mouth, but no words come out.

"There now, you're unharmed." Coins jingle in his pocket as he squats down to see under my bonnet. "But we *have* given you a fright, haven't we?"

I shake my head, turn and look down the alley toward old Mr. Paulson's back door, wish he'd still be there on the step. But he's not.

The laundryman's fingers land on my arm, light as a bird, then close in a tight circle above my elbow. "Steady there. Come, sit until you regain yourself. It's dry inside."

I suck in a breath, tell him, "M-my mama n-needs me home," but it comes out as no more than a whisper.

"Of course," he answers. "However, I can't let you go like this." He tugs my arm. I lean against the pull. His eyes grab on to mine. They're pale blue-gray, icy like a winter sky. "I know *you*," he says. "I never forget a pretty face."

The grocery box tips. I clamp my chin over the laundry bundle, shake my head, say, "No, sir."

"It will come to me." He leans so close there's not a foot of space between him and me. His fingers snap, one, two, three. On the third time, a silver half-dollar pops up between his thumb and first finger, like magic.

I catch a breath, think, *I saw somebody do that once. But where?*

"Perhaps I'm mistaken?" The coin disappears, then it's back, then it disappears again.

I stare, trying not to blink. *How can he do that?*

Finally, the coin's in his other hand, and I realize he's turned loose of my arm to work the trick. *Go,* I tell myself. *Run.* But I just stand there with my eyes crossed, looking at that silver half dollar.

Then that half dollar is double, one in each hand.

"I need a girl of *exactly* your size," he tells me. "I've some dresses to alter. The pay is fifty cents, and all you must do is wear the dress and stand very still while I work. Can you manage that for me? We'll begin tomorrow ... shall we say, three o'clock? And if you're suitable, we'll continue with the next dress."

I swallow hard, stare at coins that could buy everything we need. Easy. No more boiling wash in the heat. "How many?"

"Dresses?"

"Yes, sir." I hitch up the market box. My arms ache.

"A dozen, at least. Perhaps more."

Six dollars!

"Fine silk party frocks," the man says. "Oh, and we wouldn't have to tell your mother. We'll keep the arrangement ... just between the two of us."

You'd finally get to see what a silk dress feels like, Ollie, I tell myself. *And six dollars!*

"The dresses are for a soiree." His mouth smiles, but his eyes don't. "Have you ever been to one?"

My mind snaps back, hard and quick. I take a big step sideways, pretend it's because I almost lost hold of the grocery box. "Mama promised me to a widow lady for the next two weeks."

"Is that so?" Thunder rumbles overhead, and a raindrop comes out of nowhere, lands smack on my bonnet bill, then drips off.

"Yes, sir, and I'm sorry for it. I'd best get ... get h-home before the storm." I back up too far for him to reach, turn away with my heart pounding.

"Olive."

The word snaps me around so fast I can't stop from it. My caramel candy slides off and lands in the mud. I don't dare try to pick it up.

The laundryman smiles wide. "The first dress ..." He stares into my face, nods like he's answered a question for himself. "The color is olive green. Just right for you. I'll see you in two weeks, won't I?"

I swallow hard, say, "Yes, sir."

A cold wind kicks up, and hailstones hit tin roofs, *ping, ping, ping.* Clamping my chin over the laundry bundle, I go to running and don't slow down till I'm through Mrs. Paulson's gate.

Flannery stops stringing laundry lines on the porch and looks at me when I run up the steps. "Got the devil on yer tail, gal?" she asks.

Tears push into my eyes, but I know she means the weather. I set the market goods on the bench by the door, then take up old man Paulson's bundle and hurry back to the washhouse without a word. Inside, I press my back against the wall and look up at the rafters and gulp air. *Olive ... The color is olive green. Just right for you.*

I know you.

Does he?

I never forget a pretty face.

Where did I see somebody do that money trick before?

Laying a hand on my shoulder, Tula asks if I'm okay. I don't even know afterward if she asked in Choctaw or English. I just nod. I can't tell her about the laundryman. I can't tell anybody.

A noise from under the worktable in the corner pushes through the clatter in my head. *It's the laundryman. He's come after me.* But I know that's foolish. He didn't see where I went. He can't find me here.

The noise comes again. I'm across the washhouse in two big steps, yanking up the cloth that covers the table. A face with big blue-gray eyes looks out at me from under a mop of dark hair that's curly but so matted it sticks out in all directions. Then I see there ain't one kid back there, but two. The smaller one has straight hair and might be Choctaw. The bigger one, I ain't sure, but I think it's a girl even though it's wearing boy overalls that're tore off at the knees.

Tula starts babbling English and Choctaw all mixed together— something about rain and the food poke and Mrs. Paulson's roses.

That must be what I heard in the bushes a while ago. Not squirrels or cats. Two kids. "Tula, what are you doing? Why'd you let them in here?"

"Omba chito." She points out the window while the wind whips tree branches in circles and lightning cuts the sky.

"If Flannery sees them, she'll run us all off and give us a bad name." *The laundryman will find out, and I'll have to go to work for him.* "You tell them to crawl out the dump hatch, there at the end of the table. They can't stay."

"Jus' a lil' while," the bigger girl whispers. So she does talk.

A hammer beats inside my ears. I want to waken from this day and have it be just a worrisome dream.

"We be real quieten," the girl whispers, and reaches for the cloth to pull it back down. For a minute, we're like two yard dogs in a tug-of-war.

"Let go," I tell her.

"Ssshhh," she whispers.

"You can't . . ." The sky breaks and dumps buckets of rain, and that's that. We'll have to wait till the storm stops, or the day's work is done.

I let the cloth fall back down and try to pretend those girls aren't there, but all afternoon long, while we wash, wring, and hang laundry on the porch, I'm too scared to think. When I finally stand at the back door getting our pay, Flannery fists her hands on her hips. "Y'are a right chance taker today, eh? I've a mind to clean the washhouse, but I'm thinkin' I'd not like the filth in there, are ya hearin' me now, gal?"

I nod and grab the coins, then stumble down the steps on wobbly legs. No telling how much Flannery saw, but I've got to keep those kids away from here for good.

That's how Shelterwood Camp gets Cora and Effie, who're Choctaw freedmen like Amos. A lawyer came and told their auntie and uncle they couldn't be guardian over the girls after the parents had died, and the court had picked a guardian to protect the girls from being robbed of their land and timber money by their own relatives. Next thing Cora and Effie knew, they wound up in an orphan asylum. They climbed out a window and down a drainpipe to get away. Now they don't know where their family is, or if they still have a family, or where home is and how to get there.

That makes ten of us in all, counting old Gable, or nine when he's out wandering with Milk the mule. Cora is smart at setting deadfall traps and snares to catch wild game, so she ain't bad to have around, except she's bossy and hardheaded and cusses if she feels like it. She hasn't got good enough clothes to work in town, but with a mouth like that, it don't seem likely anyhow.

Dewey ain't happy because there's two more girls for voting, and not even a week passes before he leaves Gable in the woods one day and goes to town on *my* horse. Full dark is almost on us when Dewey comes back with a fat lip and a black eye, peppermint sticks in his pocket, and a handful of coins he won gambling at tinks and cards. Trailing behind Skedee come two boys who saved Dewey's hide when some town kids decided to give him a thrashing. I don't like the look of Finnis and Fergus one bit. They're older and bigger than anybody except Amos, and they're runaways from a farmer who rented them out of a poorhouse in Arkansas. I feel sure the law looks for runaways, especially rented-out ones.

But the worst thing is that when Dewey went off to town, he left Gable under a tree napping while the mule grazed. Even way into the night, there's no sign of Gable. The mule comes back alone by morning, but we look everywhere for Gable, and all we find is the leather pouch he carried over his shoulder. Inside there's a tiny fife flute with brass tips, a faded black ribbon with a baby's silver ring on it, a fold-up candle lamp, and a little book that's been read so many times the pages crumble when you touch them. *Evangeline: A Tale of Acadie,* by Henry Wadsworth Longfellow. On the first page, handwritten words are almost too faded to make out,

> *To my Love,*
> *Read this tale again*
> *and think of us.*
> *No journey is impossible*
> *for the heart.*

Below that, the paper is rubbed clean through, so we never know who signed it.

That's all we have left of Gable.

Dewey says the mule must've got loose, and Gable caught a ride on a road wagon to someplace. But I hope Gable finally found that spring pool he talked about sometimes . . . the magic one where you'd look into it and see your true love. I hope he laid his old body down for good, and he's with Angeline.

After that, Tula and me take to riding Skedee and Milk to town. Behind every rock and tree, I see the laundryman. I feel safer on a horse's back, but I know it's risky to be riding the road at all. July Joyner and his gang have laid up somewhere to hide, with $4,000 bounty on their heads. Some folks say they went north into the old Cherokee Nation. Some say they're in the Winding Stair. Travelers still move in groups, and the library wagon has stopped its routes. I hope that gang is caught soon.

My two weeks till I meet the laundryman are running short, and I tell myself he probably found some other girl my size by now, and he doesn't really know my name at all, that the first dress really *is* olive green. But at night in my dreams, he's after me, or Tesco Peele is, and I try to run, but I can't. I wake up on my pallet in the dugout, sweating and gulping air. I curl close to Nessa and think, *We've got to go up the mountain. We've got to go soon.*

Trouble is, we're eleven mouths to feed now, and the coins you can get for woman work add up slow, just like Miss Kate said in her speech. Every morning, I feel more desperate. A shadow hangs over me and I worry, *This will be the day something bad happens.*

Of a sudden one afternoon, the front door of the laundry house hangs open as I hurry up the other side of the street. All the windows are raised, and the place is quiet as the grave. A loose dog trots out while I stand and watch.

I duck into Mr. Brotherton's newspaper office, and he tells me the laundryman slipped away in the middle of the night and took the girls with him. At the Paulsons' house the next day, Flannery says the townsfolk and some of the old Choctaw Lighthorse got the laundryman, after he tried to take two little girls into his road wagon when he thought no one was looking. Flannery squeezes a hand over her neck, making the motion of a hanging while she lolls out her tongue. Then she smiles and marks a cross over her chest and says, "Dark justice for the doin' of the devil's deeds. 'Tis fittin' his soul have no rest." She tells Tula and me she won't need us anymore, once a respectable laundry starts up in town.

But Mrs. Paulson keeps us on the next week, and the next. She says she likes having the laundry done at home, and besides that, there's window washing and the yard to care for, and other chores that're still too much for Flannery.

By middle of July, there're notices in the newspaper wanting men and strong boys to harvest crops and hay, and cut, split, and stack firewood by the cord. When I count up the money in Shelterwood Bank, it's plain that to buy all our traveling supplies before fall, the boys need to leave off hunting, fishing, and looking all over the mountains for the July Joyner gang, hoping to strike it rich on the bounty money.

On a Saturday after Tula and me have finished cleaning up from a clubwomen's tea, we sit on the back steps of the church, waiting for the parson and nosy Mrs. Tinsley to clear out so we can pick through the trash. I pass the time by reading work notices from the newspaper one of the ladies wrapped around her tea cakes.

"The Good Woman?" Tula wants to know if Mrs. Grube has an article in the paper. We been reading them pretty regular at our night fire. After the newspaper readings, Tula tells old Choctaw stories, and Dewey tells coal miner tales, and Finnis and Fergus talk about the work farm, and Cora and Effie cuss about the orphan asylum. I share Daddy's stories of lost gold mines and the big stone head we saw on a treasure hunt. Daddy said it was one of the forest giants that fell in a hole and never could climb out.

"We'll see about Mrs. Grube's writing later," I tell Tula. "But listen at this . . ." I read the work notices out loud, then point. "Men and *strong boys*, that's what it says."

I don't even have to look at Tula to see her mouth puckering up. She knows what I'm getting at.

"Keyu!" She shakes her head so hard her bonnet slides off. "Just you 'n' me go town-workin'."

"Listen at me a minute. The money ain't—"

"Ffff!" She throws the back of her hand at me. Her knuckles are so red and raw she looks like one of those laundry girls. "Listen at *me*. Us only." Then she says she's president, so it's her choice. The real problem is, Amos is healed enough to work now, and Tula's afraid if he goes to town, he'll get shot or put in jail.

I stomp a boot to hush her up, but I'm sorry right off because my feet grew so much this summer, my toes are curled over and blistered. "Well, I am here to tell you, we've got eleven of us to take up the mountain. *Eleven*. It can't be just two of us working for money." I rub my toes through the boot leather. "And these shoes are too tight, and only half of us even *have* shoes, and we can't winter on the mountain without shoes."

I feel Tula's mind turning, so I just keep on talking before she can argue. "More have to work. And any girl without proper clothes can't, so that lets out Cora. Nessa, Pinti, Koi, and Effie are too young. Boys don't need good clothes to work in the hayfields, or shoes, either. Lots of farm boys don't have shoes."

I've got her thinking, so I let her be. After the parson and Mrs. Tinsley go out the front door, I scoot over and check the rubbish barrel. There're some half-eaten tea cakes, a couple tin cans, a hank of jute twine, two mostly burnt candles, some cheesecloth, and two glass jars with chips on the rim. Those are the best prize of all because I know just how to use them. When you want a vote to go your way, you need to grease the wheels ahead of time. I learned that from reading Mrs. Grube's news reports about Kate Barnard's big deeds in the statehouse.

That night, instead of telling stories, I get all the kids to catch lightning bugs, and we gather them in the two tin cans with the cheesecloth over the top. Once we've got enough, I slip off the cheesecloth, pop the jar mouths into the cans, and up come those lightning bugs, under the glass.

"Magic lanterns," I say, and tie the twine round the whole thing like Christmas ribbon, with a double-knot bow at the top for a handle.

"Well, I'll be." Finnis puts his nose right up to the jar. "I ain't ever seen nothin' like it."

"It's purdy." Cora twists her head, her hair going every which way, and her gray eyes crossing. "Let me hold it."

We pass the lantern jars hand to hand in our circle, lighting up one face after another. The air fills with laughs and giggles, and I tell the story of the Lightning Bug Gang and their daring train robbery, which I stitch together like a quilt from tales Daddy told me. I don't think he'd mind.

On Sunday morning, Tula calls all of us to a council. Once she sits down, she points at me and tells everybody that Ollie's got something to say.

All the heads turn my way.

"Why's *she* get to talk?" Dewey gets tetchy right off, trying to scare me quiet, but I stand up and speak my piece about the work notices and the boys. Dewey and his gang don't like it. Finnis and Fergus ran off from a farmer who hit them with a buggy whip and a hoe handle. And Dewey only wants to run in the woods, looking to find the treasure caves he's sure old Gable came here for.

"I'd work," Finnis says finally. "But not for somebody that whips ner does other bad thangs." Beside him, Fergus's eyes rim with tears, and his hands tremble, even though he's twelve years old and a big boy. He's been jumpy here lately. Amos says Dewey, Finnis, and Fergus came upon something bad when they were out hunting treasure caves. It gave Fergus nightmares, but they won't tell what it was.

"We'd only take work from good people." Amos pats Fergus on the shoulder. "Folks that don't whack on nobody, ner shoot nobody."

"Me and Tula can ask around town, see who's good to work for," I say, because I can feel things moving my way. "With six of us drawing pay, we'll get the money for a grubstake *and* some chickens and a rooster. Then we'll head up the mountain and build Shelterwood Town." That's the first time I've said the words out loud, and it feels like speaking a piece of a dream into the big, wide world. "That's the name I picked for it."

"It's purdy, Ollie," Amos says. "Shelterwood Town."

I show them my drawings in Daddy's book, and everybody smiles except Dewey.

"We boys'd need the mule to do farm work in Talihina." He hooks eyes on me.

"You ain't getting the mule."

"We hire out with the mule, we'll make more money."

"You don't know beans about farming with any mule, Dewey. And the mule is too old, besides."

"You ain't the boss of—"

Tula bangs the hollow log and says that's enough talking and we should vote.

Before she calls for a show of hands, I slip in one more thing. "Also, I think we should give the mule a new name besides just Milk. I think we ought to name him Lightning Bug, after those magic lantern jars I made for y'all. Can we vote on that first?"

Tula says we can, and I look over at Dewey and smile and think, *That's how Miss Kate would've greased the wheels.*

CHAPTER 29

Valerie Boren-Odell, 1990

There were many tricks played here, and in fact all over the Territory, regarding claims.

—GEORGE B. SMITH, 1937. INDIAN-PIONEER PAPERS COLLECTION,
INTERVIEW BY W. T. HOLLAND.

"I didn't track down much. Looks like the property was old allotment parcels from when the tribal land was broken up through the Dawes Commission. It's 480 acres total. On the tax rolls it's listed under the name Hazel Rusk, with a post office box up in Jenks." Curtis talks over the window breeze as we wind along Holson Valley, headed toward a utility right-of-way that will take us into the park. From there, we'll hike cross-country to the location where Edwin's horse went down.

The mission involves risks, both personal and professional. If this little foray goes bad, I may still be NPS green and gray on the inside, but I won't be on the outside. On the other hand, if I can prove that Edwin's fall was no accident, both the playing field and the players change. Everyone from the chief ranger, to the superintendent, to the brass and rank-and-file in cooperating branches of law enforcement will want in on whatever comes next. We take it personally when one of our own ends up in the hospital.

"The name on the 480 acres anyone you know?" The sweltering air sweeps my voice out the window as I focus on navigating a curve in the road.

Curtis shakes his head. "The taxes are paid up. That's about all I got before it was time to meet back up with you. Never heard of a Hazel Rusk. Like I said, I thought I knew everyone around here. Maybe today will tell us whether we've got a property holder involved in something shady, or squatters using a piece of land the owner doesn't keep an eye on."

I note that he doesn't add, *Maybe today will tell us nothing,* but that's the reality. I don't know what's next after that. I promised Curtis I'd let it go if this hike yields no new information, but can I?

"Thanks for coming." I loosen my grip on the steering wheel, tighten it again. "But, listen, Curtis, I understand if you . . ."

"It was *my* idea, Val. Coming with you." His sideways look silently admonishes me. "Trust me, right?"

"Yes."

"We're settled then."

"Right. We are." We're not, I know. I'll circle back to this uncertainty again and again. Maybe it will always be this hard. To trust. To let anyone in after losing Joel. The people you're close to aren't guaranteed. They can be gone in an instant.

An uneasy quiet carries us the rest of the distance up a forest road and into the woods, where silence is necessary. From this location, we're a lot closer to the accident site than Roy and Edwin were when they parked the horse trailer.

Curtis takes the lead. He knows these mountains better than I do. I shadow his steps to keep the noise down. My ears strain toward any sounds that don't belong in the mountains. Every bird call, every rustle in the duff pricks my senses. A startled deer snorts as we push our way through a watershed, and I nearly jump out of my skin.

Ssshhh, I tell myself, but touch the butt of my handgun. Reassurance.

My nerves settle as the afternoon shadows lengthen. We move up a slope, down a slope, again and another. We've planned this hike to give us time to reach the accident site while we still have plenty of light, but hopefully late enough that if someone is up to no good there, they've already made their rounds for the day. Even criminals like to be home for supper.

Despite the blazing late-afternoon heat, Curtis sets a brisk pace, moving through thickets and across traverses where we plant our feet carefully to keep from sliding. He seldom looks back, silently acknowledging that he's not here to babysit; he knows I am as competent as any partner. The realization circles, then whisks away. I focus on the immediate. Steps, silence, sounds.

The rumble of farm machinery—or maybe construction equipment—echoes from someplace far off as we navigate rock outcroppings at the top of a slope, then go over the crest. Curtis taps an ear, motions toward the noise.

I nod. *I hear it, too.* But the view affords nothing more than mountains, one folding toward another, the angled sun laying shadows over the valleys. Traveling downward from there, we pass into thick shade and slightly cooler temperatures. Curtis pulls up for a water break, and we sit against a monolith of stone, striking in its naturally formed headlike shape. Around us, the valley offers only birdsong, the swish of breeze through shortleaf pine, the soft flutter of oak and elm.

"You get a bead on that back there?" Curtis whispers near my ear.

"I heard it, but no. Couldn't pin down any source." I grab another drink from my canteen, let my eyelids drift low as water slides down my throat. "Might be a lot farther off than it sounds."

"Or closer. Your people doing any work around here? Roads and trails? Contractors? Anything like that?"

"We're shut down in this section since the rockfall event." I push off the ground, cap my canteen, make ready to go again. "If somebody's running equipment . . . or a generator back here, it's an unauthorized activity."

"My favorite kind." He tugs his ball cap over the bristle of dark hair, outstretches a hand, waiting for an assist in getting to his feet.

Shaking my head at him, I oblige, and we're off again.

By the time the creek below Edwin's accident site comes into view, I've decided we imagined the machinery sounds. Either that, or we've timed it right and hit the area at the end of a clandestine workday.

Before climbing the slope to investigate, we walk the creek bed and the trail Edwin and Roy rode in on, checking for signs of recent activity—ATV tracks, footprints, trash, drug paraphernalia, cigarette butts, food wrappers, anything left behind by humans passing through. I catch a slight whiff of something chemical . . . maybe? As quickly as it's there, it's gone. I decide it must be coming off my clothes or gear. Bug spray on hot, sweat-soaked fabric.

The valley yields no evidence, and so we move upward, trying to keep to cover, but there isn't much. The nearby mountainsides are thick with mature pines and hardwoods, but this particular slope succumbed to fire ten, maybe fifteen, years ago. The trees are sparse and scrawny due to soil erosion and wind. The old growth that would have protected them lies rotting on the ground.

Curtis motions to let me know he'll look farther up while I check the accident site. I take note of his location, then go to work. No rain has fallen since the accident, so the details are painfully clear—where the horse scrambled at the trail's edge, where one hoof lost purchase, started a tumble downslope, end over end, man and animal, an ugly, uncontrolled descent. A trail of blood, hair, split leather, and torn cloth reveals the trajectory. Looking at it is like watching the accident in painful detail.

What I can't see is evidence of the cause—fragments from a bullet bust-up, a ricochet mark on the rocks, the minicrater of an embed in gravel or dirt. Slipping latex gloves from my pocket, I sweep carefully through dead leaves, pine straw, pebbles, twigs. It's a needle in a haystack. If Roy heard a ricochet, the bullet could be nearby or hundreds of yards away, but I continue until it's clear there's nothing to find.

Adjusting my camera for the odd afternoon light, I snap a few photos, but doubt I'll see anything new when they're developed. The trail is completely undisturbed. Pristine.

Pristine? That's virtually impossible. The realization solidifies with the quick, definitive click of the shutter opening and closing. A thousand-pound horse wearing cleated iron shoes must have scrambled desperately in this spot, trying to regain footing, to avoid a fall. The surfaces *on* the trail would have been disturbed, the ground churned up *here,* not just downslope.

It's been swept clean.

Someone made sure no evidence would be found. The only person who'd do that would be the one who caused the accident in the first place—or an accomplice.

I glance toward Curtis to motion him closer for a look, but he's gone.

Where is he?

A hawk takes to the air, shatters the silence with a deafening complaint. Its movement guides me to the scantest disturbance in a thicket of scrub and vines. Curtis emerges, then pauses at the edge of a bare upthrust of rock. If he continues, he'll be exposed. With a glance my way, he raises a fist, then opens his hand and lowers it flat, signaling me to stay put, stay low. A quick motion toward the ridgeline, and his fingertips touch his ear. He's heard something up there.

I squat down, thumb the strap loose on my handgun, watch him climb higher.

The minutes pass in slow motion. I scan the territory above and below him for anything out of the ordinary—a hint of color, a flash of metal on a belt buckle, backpack . . . weapon.

The forest gives up nothing. Whatever Curtis is chasing, I can neither hear it nor see it from here.

A measure of relief hits me when he's into minimal cover again, but then he vanishes over the ridgeline, and only the sound of blood rushing in my ears remains.

I check my watch, monitor the time elapsed. One minute. Two. Three.

Five.

Seven.

At ten, I'm going after him whether he wants me to or not.

Before I can make the call, he reappears and motions for me to follow him up, but stay low and quiet. I duplicate his climb, making no noise. At the crest, we move along the backbone of the mountain, traversing an upward grade of exposed boulders and fire-kill timber. It's slow going, and every turn is blind.

Something crinkles under my boot, the sound muffled but easily recognizable. An empty can lies half-buried in the duff. Its former owner sat here long enough to finish a beer, then clumsily attempted to conceal the evidence. A gap in the rocks offers a clear view of the accident site. Was this the shooter's hole?

"Pssst." I catch Curtis's attention, then point. Giving the beer can little more than a glance, he indicates that what lies ahead is more important, and we're losing the light. We move on, progressing more quickly as the terrain eases. Finally, it's evident that we're on a path, a throughway cleared with a machete or an axe, the vines and detritus pushed aside to facilitate travel along this ridge.

Someone knows this ground much better than we do—someone who might go to deadly lengths to prevent intrusion. We're making more noise than we should, but at every gap in the rocks, I see the light dimming in the valleys, the ridges melting together. Whatever Curtis saw from the overlook ahead might be hidden soon.

As we draw near the edge, he lowers his profile, creeps behind a rock outcropping, then slides over to allow space for me. When I fold in, press my back against the stone, he whispers, "Hear that?"

With the noise of our own movement gone, I pick up the rumble of machinery and the hiss of hydraulics. Though a distance away, it travels on the wind. Another sound revs above it, then disappears, then rises again, also unmistakable. "They're cutting trees." The reality hits like a gut punch. I'm sickened, then furious. Suddenly everything makes sense, even the slight chemical smell I picked up at the creek. Commercial logging operations use herbicides by the tankful. "They're poaching timber."

"Get ready." Curtis hands me his field glasses. His grim expression blackens the dread in my stomach. "It's not a pretty sight."

In the fading amber light, with the sky afire in silver-lined clouds and the Winding Stair bathed in velvet hues of violet, indigo, sea green, I peer through the glasses. I take in all that is not serene—all that is sharp, and scarred, and wrong. Beginning near the border of the park and stretching across the inheld parcel, hundreds of acres lie in ruin, the soil bare. Slash piles of saplings, cut branches, dirt, and rotting leaves dot the hillsides, piled two stories high, heaped wherever was convenient. Dozer tracks wander everywhere, roads cut haphazardly to facilitate the loading and passage of log-hauling trucks. A waterway through the property runs brown with silt.

Around the edges of the scar, hiding the devastated interior from view, stands a ring of tall timber, pristine and undisturbed, a buffer to conceal the operation. Other than from the ridges in this area of the park, no one would ever catch sight of it. Working late in the day and at night, they likely wouldn't be heard, either. If people did catch the sound, they'd be hesitant to try tracking it down in the dark. No wonder these guys wanted to keep interlopers away. They've taken a fortune in timber, without having to follow any restrictions on cleaning up the land or preserving the watersheds, and undoubtedly without paying the property owner one thin dime.

They've decimated everything.

"They've . . ." I change the trajectory of the field glasses, adjusting the focus.

"They've cut roads into the park, too." Curtis finishes the sentence before I can.

The brazenness of it should be shocking, but it's not. Sketchy logging outfits cross property lines all the time, make excuses about bad maps, claim that they didn't know. Usually they get away with it. The landowners are either too poor to hire lawyers or too scared of the loggers to report the crime. The shifty underbelly of the timber industry hires some dangerous people, but it takes an especially brazen thief to move onto government property. If caught, they're facing federal charges. I've been on resource and timber theft cases before, but these guys are running a particularly sophisticated—and profitable—operation. They're determined to protect it.

That makes them especially dangerous.

"I should've thought of . . ."

A branch snaps behind us. Curtis wheels around first, aims, identifies himself. I do the same, just in time to see a tall, thin figure in head-to-toe camo freeze in place.

"Hurry. We've gotta go." The hushed voice is female, and whoever she is, she's young, nervous. Behind the face mask, brown eyes dart left, then right, scanning the maze of rock and debris. "They know you're here. Don't get on the radio. They listen."

She turns, hands raised, then moves out slowly. Curtis and I stand in a moment of indecision before choosing to follow. Ahead of us, the stranger keeps to one side of the path, staying on the stone, where she leaves no tracks. She's clearly familiar with the area, but she passes through like a soldier on alert.

Or an operative on a mission. Is she baiting us into a trap?

Curtis's posture says he's thinking the same thing. How far do we go before forcing her to tell us who she is, why she's here, and why she wants us off that ridge?

A quarter mile into the thick timber on the opposite side of the mountain, another camo-clad, face-masked figure melts from the shadows. My hand twitches toward my service weapon, but the incomer makes no threatening movements. By appearances, he's unarmed.

"What're you *doing*?" He sounds as young as the girl does. "That's not the plan."

"They walked across a trip wire," she snaps. "What'd you want me to do? Leave them up there?"

I'm struck by the idea that we've stumbled onto a couple of teenagers using the park for ... what ... some kind of war games?

Are there more of them? Because this would be a bad location for high ... school ... kids ...

My mind screeches to a halt. "Braden Lacey?" The red hair protruding from his face mask ties all the clues together. "Rachel?" After searching for these two so long, it feels surreal, almost impossible.

"Take off the masks," Curtis orders.

They do as they're told, and even in the dim light, both Braden and the elusive girlfriend are easy to ID.

"We've been looking for you two for *weeks*." I'm somewhere between overjoyed and incensed. I can't count the man-hours these kids have cost, not to mention professional credibility, and potentially my career. "I've got a lot of questions, and the answers better be good."

"Not here." The tremor in Braden's voice hints that he might be about to make a run for it. "I promise we'll tell you everything, but we can't stay here."

"You hit their trip wire. They'll be coming." Rachel's fear rings genuine. Somewhere in the distance, an ATV engine rumbles. A dog barks. "We've gotta go. Now."

Neither Curtis nor I argue. If I have to put my trust in someone, I'd rather not bet on whoever's guarding the timber operation next door.

We double-time it down the rest of the slope, sliding in peat, gravel, and pine straw, grabbing tree trunks and branches for support as we put distance between us and the timber camp. From there, Braden and Rachel lead us along an intricate network of unmarked switchback trails, watersheds, and dry washes.

Dusk has thickened to darkness by the time we lose the sound of motors and dogs. Braden and Rachel slow the pace, each of us gulping air as Curtis and I pull flashlights off our belts and the kids retrieve headlamps from their gear bags.

"This is far enough." Curtis aims a beam at Braden. "What the heck are you two doing out here?"

"It's just a little longer to our camp, okay?" Braden motions deeper into the woods.

He sounds so young, so desperately earnest. My first instinct is to excuse everything. My second instinct is to slap handcuffs on him and Rachel both. "I think *right here* is good." The more I dwell on it, the madder I get. "You know how much trouble you've caused? Your sister *ran away* trying to find you. You triggered a *missing person's* search, and . . ." Spotlighting him, I unpack the whole thing, then finish with "So if you've got some good explanation, spill it. Because I'm about to cuff both of you and march you out of here."

"We'll show you all of it, I promise. At our camp."

"All of *what?*"

"Look," Rachel pleads, shrugging off her gear bag and grabbing the zipper. I touch my pistol, and she stops. "It's just pictures, all right?" Carefully she fishes out a half dozen photos bound by a rubber band. "We had to get proof on them. That's what we've been doing."

I snatch the pictures, wedge my flashlight under my chin.

Curtis leans close, mutters, "You've been . . . running surveillance on that timber operation?"

"*You* two took these?" I'm equally stunned. The photos are good. They're proof of a lot. Judging by the progression of the timber cuts and the multiplying slash piles, Braden and Rachel have been at this for a while.

"Why didn't you report it?" Curtis sounds as disgusted as I feel. "This could've been stopped before they clear-cut the place."

"We had to figure it all out," Braden asserts. "That was the reason I went to work for Parker to begin with. I wasn't really there for a job. I had to find out what they did with her."

CHAPTER 30

Olive Augusta Radley, 1909

There was an old bridge a half mile south of the new bridge on
Coal Creek ... that was called Hold Up Bridge and it deserved the
name.

—LeRoy Ward, 1938. Indian-Pioneer Papers Collection,
interview by Grace Kelley.

I sink down on the steps out back of the church house and let my
head fall against the wall. I'm numb to the bone from serving the
women's club meeting and washing the dishes all by myself. Tula
went with Amos to help some old lady finish picking field peas and
okra before the August dry comes and burns it all to nothing.

My hands are raw, my arms are skinny as a hen's legs, and my good
pinny dress looks poor, even though I try to wear an apron whenever
I can borrow one. Mrs. Grube made her way to the meeting today,
which must mean Mr. Grube is away working the trains. Her eyes got
big when I wobbled on my feet, carrying a teapot.

"Why, Hazel!" she said, and leaned back to get a better look at me.
"Good heavens. I hardly knew you. Are you quite all right?"

"Yes, ma'am. Just workin' hard."

"Too hard, I'd say."

"Oh, no, ma'am. Not *that* hard." Then I saw she was looking at my
hands, so I stuck them behind my back.

Her lips pushed together over her gap teeth, and she grabbed my chin, moving my face this way and that, studying on me. "How is your mother's health, child?"

"Oh, it's better. Better every day."

"And your little brother?"

"Growin' like a weed. He likes it real well at the house Daddy moved us to till Mama gets past her ailment." I wanted to tell Mrs. Grube, *I been reading your articles in the paper,* but the handbell rang, calling the ladies to take their seats.

Mrs. Grube ignored the bell. "I would very much like to speak with your mother," she said before finally turning loose of me. "Today the women's club will be discussing the fundraising to provide scholarships for girls of good manners and fine potential. Girls such as yourself, Hazel. It's imperative that young ladies in this new state of ours have the opportunity to remain in school. A society is only as good as its women."

"Oh yes, ma'am. My mama says that very thing."

"Does she, now?"

The bell rang again, and I was never so glad for a bell in my whole life. I took two steps back to get away from Mrs. Grube's questions. That put me close enough to grumpy old Mrs. Tinsley to hear her saying that restarting the library wagon's visits would have to be postponed. Even with the July Joyner gang finally in jail, the roads were still not safe. Just days ago, a widow woman's wagon got held up at Jack Crossing by wild boys wearing masks cut from sackcloth. One of them threatened the old woman with a pocketknife and took her lunch basket before galloping away on a scrawny calico pony.

I could hardly keep on with my work after that. My hands shook, and all day long I waited for one of the ladies to ask, "Hazel, don't *you* have a spotted pony?"

Nobody did, but all alone on the church's back step, I can't help thinking how wrong I was to let the boys keep the mule *and* Skedee after they made good money working on a hay crew. The first chance Dewey got to split off from Amos, he took Finnis and Fergus, and instead of hunting for more work, they went hunting trouble.

From the sound of Mrs. Tinsley, they've found it.

Soon as I see Tula, we'll call a council and make a vote on what happens to liars and stealers. But if we throw them out of Shelterwood, we'll have to give back their hay money. If we give back their hay money, we won't have enough to buy some used shoes, plus food stores and seed. We already don't have enough.

I think on it while I wait for the last clubwomen to leave so I can pick through the trash. Maybe we don't need so much, if everything's like we left it at the old place—crocks and shelled nuts in the spring house, sacks of seed corn hung in the cabin rafters, buckets, hoe, rake, and shovel. Saws and hammers. Quilts and beds. The pretty blue-and-white china canisters that read Flour, Sugar, Salt, and Tea. Daddy carried those from Fort Smith to surprise Mama, and her with her hand on her hip saying, "Keyes Radley, you shouldn't have done that. I've got no more need for such fine things."

"Sadie-gal, you *are* a fine thing," he teased, and grabbed her up and swung her around. "We'll make a good life, you and me. Like I promised when we planned to come up the mountain."

The remembering makes me smile and hurt at the same time. I want that cabin with the whole family in it, not just dishes and quilts.

My eyes go closed, and I get lost in thinking I can want it bad enough to make it real. For a minute, it *is* real, but then I hear, "Hazel ... Hazel ... come in here, please." It's old Mrs. Tinsley. The back door of the church is open, and she can see me sitting on the steps.

"Hazel! Come *here* please!" Now it's for sure there's trouble. She's figured out about the pony. I hop up quick, but the rucksack's weight throws me off, and my foot goes from wood step to nothing.

I tumble through the air and hit the stone walk flat on my back. The breath goes out of me. Black specks swirl around my eyes as I stare up at the sky and listen at Mrs. Tinsley running down the steps.

"Oh, good heavens!" Her shadow blocks the sun. "*What* have you done, now? You are such an ungainly little thing."

A hand clamps over my arm, a man's hand, big and strong. It lifts me up like I weigh nothing at all, and I figure I'm in for it from both Mrs. Tinsley and the parson. Stumbling up the stairs into the church house, half carried, half dragged, I try to think of what I can say to get past this trouble, but soon as we're in the door, I know that's not the parson who's got me by the arm.

I smell fodder and manure, whiskey and sweat.

And W. E. Garrett snuff.

The stink of all the times I got hauled to the barn and had the fire whipped out of me by Tesco Peele. I know him even before he dumps me on the floor, and I push to my hands and knees, my elbows buckling and my ribs aching while I gulp for air. My bonnet's come off, and my hair hangs in a dark curtain. Through it, I see his boots, bullhide bottom, tall roughout tops stained with the blood and sweat of horses he's torn up with his spurs.

Mrs. Tinsley's black button shoes are behind his, one toe tap-tapping on the floor. "Well, there you have the girl," she says. "Deal with her as you will." She leans over me. "Runaway! And a liar, as well. Shame! For *shame*. Sir, I suggest you take her in a firm hand, lest she continue in her wayward behaviors."

"And I plan to." Tesco thanks her kindly for the help before she leaves. The door slams shut, and then it's just him and me.

"C'mon, now, you ain't all *that* hurt," he says like always, so you'll know he can hurt you a lot worse. "Git up and tell me how you come to be here, Ollie Auggie ... because I been lookin' a-a-all over for you."

Where usually I'd stand my tallest and face him for the stubborn of it, this time I stay down, cough and choke, try to figure out how I can get away.

"I *said*, stand *up*." Squatting beside me, he clamps a hand over the back of my neck. "There you go, get a breath. Now answer me, Ollie Auggie. What are you doin' here? Yer mama's been missin' you real bad."

"Muh ... muh-ma?" I wheeze.

"There, see, you can talk after all." One finger traces along my cheek, pulls my hair away so I can see him leaning close. "She's been bad worried. Walkin' the floors night and day, waitin' on you to come home."

My heart cracks open. More than anything, I want to believe Mama's at the window, not facedown in the bed from her powders and whiskey. She's watching for me. The house is warm, and there's food. My bed is waiting up in the attic . . .

"Everything's gonna be different now." Tesco's voice goes soft, friendly.

I nod. I'm worn out of being bone-tired and scared and trying to make it on my own.

"Nobody's mad at ya."

I nod again, finally catch a real breath.

"That's a good girl," Tesco says, syrup-sweet. "Now, where's our lil' Nessie Bessie? 'Cause we been missin' her, special."

Where's our lil' Nessie Bessie . . .

. . . missin' her, special.

I think of him standing over Nessa's bed. I think about what happened to Hazel. Every word from Tesco Peele's mouth is a lie. If Mama did have her mind back, she wouldn't send Tesco to look for me. She wouldn't even be with him at all. She'd leave him and come find me herself.

Nessa can't go back there, ever.

I lift my arm, point a finger like I mean to show where she's at. "Over th . . . there."

The minute he turns, I slam my hands into his knees, push off, scramble up and run as he topples onto the floor. The dry goods store isn't far. If I'm lucky, the screen door's still open in back. I can . . .

I don't even finish thinking it before Tesco's on his feet, his long legs splayed out like he's hazing a wild heifer in a cattle pen.

A smile slides under his thin, hay-colored mustache, but it ain't a nice smile. "Where you goin', Ollie? Tryin' to get back to the whorehouse? You been whorin' like your mama? Runs in the family, after all."

"You shut up!"

"Oh, now"—Tesco wags a finger—"surely Keyes Radley did you the favor of tellin' you the truth about your mama. But then, it *is* Keyes Radley we're talkin' about; Keyes and the truth wasn't close travelin' partners."

"Don't talk about my daddy like that."

"Your *daddy?*" Laughing, he looks me over head to toe. "And I always thought you was a smart little girl, Ollie. Do you see *any* part of you that looks like Keyes Radley? Next time you git at a mirror, study on whether you look more like Mr. E. Niles Lockridge's two pretty little daughters. The ones that's *got* his name. Keyes Radley ain't your sainted papa. He's just a two-bit hustler and sometime fur trapper. Only real job he ever had was bein' a body man for Lockridge, and he couldn't even do that honest."

"You stop it! You stop!"

"You know what a Lockridge body man does, Ollie? He gits rid of them dead Indians . . . the ol' widows or little kids that's killed off by a sickness . . . or . . . well, say . . . some *accident* happens after Lockridge has his name on their land papers, oil papers, guardian papers. Ain't gonna be the high-and-mighty mister that dirties his hands haulin' away the carcasses. He needs somebody else to take the dead ones off into the mountains, bury them where nobody will ever know. That's what Keyes Radley was."

I push back against the wall, dig my fingers into wood and stone. My mind spins. "That's a lie! You shut up! Anumpulit issa! Anumpulit issa!"

Tesco's head ticks side to side like a rooster's. "Why, Ollie, you been talkin' Choctaw since you left us? Because that's where I hunted for you after we seen your picture in the paper with them girls from the Choctaw boardin' school. You gave ol' Lockridge a real toad choker when he read that name printed, *Hazel Rusk.* He thought lil' Hazel had come back to git him, but there was your sweet face instead. You fit right in, though. Kind of figures you would. Folks say there's some Choctaw blood in the Lockridges, but you'd have to ask your *real* daddy if that's true."

"You stop it! Keyes Radley is my daddy. You're a liar. You always lie."

"I'm your only friend, Ollie," Tesco coos. "I am your one friend 'cause I'm the only thing keepin' *Miz* Lockridge from packing you off to someplace far away. And that's because I *swear* up and down that I am married to your useless mama, and I sired you. I claimed the baby boy, too, but he wasn't mine, either. That's what I git paid for, Ollie

Auggie. To keep your mama and you nearby because the old man likes it. I guess I can thank Keyes Radley for the job, since he was fool enough to run off to the mountains with Lockridge's whore *and* Lockridge's pretty lil' whelp in tow, plus try to steal oil money out from under Lockridge's nose. It was a brassy plan; I'll give Keyes Radley that much."

I know Tesco's lying then. I know all of it is a lie. It's filthy, like he is. "My daddy didn't steal anything."

Tesco's laugh fills the church room. "What? You think he took in Hazel and Nessie out of kindness? He found out them two little girls was soon to become money orphans, and he made a plan to get to them before Lockridge could hear about it. Keyes thought he could hide them on the mountain and work a backroom deal to be their guardian. He only done it to get at their money. Keyes knew Sadie wasn't gonna stay with him unless he could keep her in high style."

I think of the pretty blue-and-white canisters, of Mama saying, *Keyes Radley, you shouldn't have done that. I've got no more need for such fine things.* "They loved each other. Mama waited for him all the years he was away in the army."

Tesco shakes his head. "Keyes never even *knew* Sadie back then. That's why you don't remember him being around when you was small. Tell you the truth, I doubt the man's name even *was* Keyes Radley, but he sure wasn't your papa." He makes the soft, mean sound that lets you know you're about to get hit, and he's looking forward to it. "It's time to stop believin' in fairy tales, Ollie Auggie. Keyes was a liar *and* a fool. Ain't nobody gonna git away with crossin' E. Niles Lockridge. Radley got what he asked for, and your mama's just lucky ol' Lockridge wanted her back, or she'd be buried in the same hole with Keyes."

"*You* killed him." I can see through Tesco clear as glass now. That's why he was at the Commercial Hotel in Talihina when Mama took us there. He knew she'd have to leave the mountains before winter because he knew my daddy wouldn't ever be coming home. "What did you do to him?"

"Now, Ollie—" He makes a soft *tsk, tsk* against his teeth. "I'm a ranch foreman, not a hired gun. I ain't the killin' kind. But Keyes

Radley did it to hisself, anyhow. Died of a overdose of stupid. The big men get the oil, and the coal, and the timber . . . and the money. The little men do the sweatin', and the shootin', and the buryin'"—his eyes, sharp as a snake, settle on mine—"and the fetchin' home brats that belong to the big men. Now let's git Nessie Bessie, and I'll carry y'all on back to your lovin' mama."

Think, I tell myself. *Hurry, think of something.* I know, sure as I know daylight from dark, that I can't take him to Nessa.

"I'll . . ." I stop and clear my throat because my voice is squeaky with fear. "I'll go get her and bring her back here. The lady at the house where Nessa is, she can't abide strangers."

"Oh, I think we'll be just fine."

"That lady shoots at people." I try to cypher the distance between Tesco and the wall without turning my eyes that way. *I might could make it past him . . .*

"That's why I got you. To talk to the lady. Tell her you're nothin' but a couple runaways, and I am here to claim you both." He comes another step closer. I wait for my chance. "After that's all done, we'll stop by the Talihina Jail and grab that scrawny pack pony you stole outta my barn. I had ol' Gowdy put out the reports for a thieved medicine hat calico gelding months ago. It's about time the rascal turned up."

"That pony is *mine*!" My heart pounds wild. *Dewey, Finnis, and Fergus got caught with Skedee? What'll happen to them? How much did they tell?*

"You know what they do to horse thieves, don't you, Ollie? Because there's some half-growed boys that'll find out soon enough."

"I *rented* them my pony. Twenty-five cents for all day." I swallow hard, tip up my chin. "We best stop by the jail and tell the deputy. Then we can go to that lady's house for Nessa." Letting my head sag forward, I start toward the door.

"Good girl." Tesco's hand slips under the rucksack straps, his long fingers circling my neck again. The muscles twitch like they want to do more. "But you oughta know better than to play with boys, Ollie. We'll fetch our Nessie Bessie *now.*"

The last of the valley light blinds me as we step out. Back in Shelterwood, everybody will be wondering where I am pretty soon. Tula and Amos probably made their way home already and checked how much wood the little kids gathered and whether they got a fish or two. Maybe Cora's caught something in her snare traps and skinned it for supper. The younger kids are playing and laughing and jabbering around the fire, waiting on food.

They're looking for me, watching the footpath that goes to Sleeping Beauty Bridge and the sandbar we use when we come in along the creek with the horse and the mule. Treasure Island, that's what I named the sandbar.

That's where I hid our coins in the sycamore tree . . . the grubstake for Shelterwood Town. Tears sting my throat. I swallow hard, blink my eyes clear. All of it can't die because of Tesco Peele. I'll find a way to get back to camp. We'll gather everything and go up the mountain.

"So, where you been all summer, Ollie Auggie?" Tesco asks as I lead him through the streets, past the dry goods stores, and the land brokers, and the empty laundry building. Mr. Brotherton is sweeping glass off the boardwalk at the newspaper office. The front window looks like somebody bashed it with a rock. Maybe they didn't like the stories in his paper about Miss Kate, and women wanting to vote, and grafters, and guardians, and children who had to run away to the woods.

He told Tula's story, and Amos's, and Dewey's in his paper. *Why, just recently a kindly woman who had come here to enjoy the political speeches expressed concern over wretched waifs appearing at her farmhouse, begging for food. Emaciated wanderers dressed in rags, left to live alone in the forest, to forage like animals. "People tell stories," this woman remarked, "of elves which inhabit the woods, but they are not elves. They are children, hiding in unthinkable conditions for lack of help, for fear of men who would take them as tiny prisoners, rob them of their land estates and their very lives, all for a profit . . ."*

"Hello, Hazel," Mr. Brotherton says as Tesco steers me over glass pieces that glitter in the late-day sun. "Careful there, it's sharp." He looks tired, but he's still got those pretty blue eyes.

I want to scream, *Help me!* Instead, I say, "Those boys at the jail. I lent them my calico pony for twenty-five cents. They didn't steal that pony. They didn't." Tesco's fingers nearly pinch the life out of me, and he pushes me along.

"Hazel . . ." Mr. Brotherton calls after us.

"Mind your business," Tesco barks out, and we walk on.

I go roundabout through the streets, this way, that way. I drag my feet.

"You're tryin' my good nature, Ollie," Tesco finally says against my hair. "Quit circlin', or we'll find us a woodshed, and I'll give you some of what you got comin'."

"I . . . I was lost a minute."

"This town ain't that big."

Through the gaps between buildings, I see the Winding Stair, tall enough to hold up the whole sky. I stare so hard I stumble over my too-small boots. Hauling me up by a handful of rucksack straps and hair, Tesco gives me a hard shake. "Ain't nothin' up there gonna help you. That mountain where Keyes Radley built his hiding place? Lockridge Timber Company is gonna cut it bare, drag the logs down over Keyes Radley's mangy bones."

I think of our hanging valley, of the old spreading oaks. "No!"

"Hazel?" Mr. Brotherton's voice calls out from someplace nearby. He must've got worried and tried to follow us. "Hazel, is that you? Are you quite all right?"

Tesco pulls my dress collar so tight I choke. His mustache brushes my ear. "One more word, and I won't just hurt *you*. I'll hurt lil' Nessie Bessie, too. You be good to me, Ollie, and you can keep her safe, just like Hazel did. You understand what I'm sayin'?"

I nod, but my mind scrabbles for a way out. I can't do what he says. I'd rather be dead in a ditch. No matter what it takes, I've got to get away from Tesco, find Nessa, and run.

I look where we're at, and a plan rushes in . . . one that might work if I'm lucky. "The house is there at the end. The one with the pretty red roses grown up all around, see? I should go to the door by myself, though. Like I told you, that lady shoots at people."

"I *ain't* turnin' you loose."

"She won't like it that a man's with me . . . a man she's never seen before."

"You lyin' to me, Ollie? Because if Nessie ain't in that house, I *am* gonna take it outta *you*."

My heart pounds and my breath comes shallow and hurried. I try to steady it. *A good tale is all it takes to outwit most folks, Ollie girl,* Keyes Radley says in my mind, while he tosses a fat katydid into a yellow garden spider's nest to show me how fast the spider can wrap up a meal. *Spin your yarn quicker than a slow mind can move. Speedy and smooth, like that spider. See?*

"She's a old Choctaw widow woman, and she's *real* strange. Dresses all in black and with a long black veil over her face. I ain't dared to ask her why. She shot at the milkman because he woke her from a nap in her chair. Only reason she keeps Nessa is because Nessa's quiet as a mouse and talks Choctaw. That lady even gave Nessa a new name, *Pinti.* That's *mouse* in Choctaw."

Tesco's fingers loosen a little on my neck, so I keep spinning spider silk. "And all day long, that lady says, 'Mouse, get me some water from the dipper,' and, 'Mouse, bring me my shoes,' and, 'Mouse, go chase the crows away.' Crows settle in that lady's yard by the dozens. Buzzards, too. I heard she buried three different husbands out there. All dead of poison." Tesco is fearful about things like buzzards and witches and poisons.

The dress collar goes slack at my neck, and he shifts behind me when we reach the front gateway, where Mrs. Paulson's roses grow so thick over the trellis they're tangled together halfway down the arch.

"I'm real scared of her," I whisper. "She casts spells. I only left Nessa here because I was afraid if I didn't do like she said, she'd turn me into one of them elf children with the bony arms and *all-black* eyes."

I make my shoulders quiver to work his grip even looser. Tesco doesn't seem to notice. It's like he's forgot where his hand is. He just looks up at that house.

"I best call to her from here," I whisper. Then I take in a big breath and push my shoulders up high. Loud as I can, I belt out, "Mrs. Paulson! Mrs. Paulson!"

The noise scares a half dozen crows from the big elm tree and startles Tesco so bad he loses his feet. When he tries to catch himself on the fence, he grabs thorns instead. Quick as a wink, I'm out from under his hand, down on all fours through the bottom of that arbor, and then up and flying across the yard, fast as my legs will run.

"Mrs. Paulson! Mrs. Paulson!"

Behind me, Tesco roars as he tries to push through that gate and the brambles grab his clothes. Ahead, Flannery steps out the door with an iron pot hook in her hand. Crows cackle and take flight from the porch rail when I run up the steps, duck around Flannery, and keep going right through the house and out the back. I fly across the yard, shove open the alley gate, then dart to the washhouse, all the while thinking, *Don't look back.* Cat quick, I push the rucksack through the little washwater dump hatch, and I scramble in after it.

Far back under the corner table as I can get, I wrap my knees to my chest, bury my head, and think, *Please, please, please.*

Outside, there's Tesco hollering, and Flannery telling him who-ever he is, he better get out of Mrs. Paulson's yard, and then I hear the twin boys squalling at the back door. Finally, Mrs. Paulson's voice joins in, and things quieten down.

"I got a runaway girl here someplace, and another one inside!" Tesco is right across the washhouse wall from me when he says that.

I squeeze hard into myself. *Don't move. Don't breathe. He'll hear.*

Mrs. Paulson tells him he must have the wrong house. "Now, I'll ask you kindly to leave, sir, before I am forced to involve the law. My husband would never approve of a man on our property while he is away. We have had girls to do the laundry, yes, but none today."

My heart stops at the word *laundry.* What if he thinks to check in here?

He pounds the wall with a fist, and the whole building shakes.

"Sir!" Mrs. Paulson says. "You will leave this instant, or I will have you escorted away."

"Be gone with ya now," Flannery says. "Yer runaway, she's legged it out the gate and left it hangin' open. A little scapegrace, that one. Knew it all along."

Tesco growls and pounds the wall again, and then his bootheels dig the ground as he runs out the back. I hear Flannery gathering the twins and arguing at Mrs. Paulson to go back to bed. Finally their voices fade, and the screen door slams, and the air quietens.

Even the birds settle after a while.

Inside the laundry house it's hot as a cookstove with all the doors and windows shut, but I sit there and wait and sweat. If I try to get away in the daylight, Tesco . . . or somebody . . . will find me before I ever make it out of town.

My stomach rumbles and my head swims and sweat soaks my clothes. Seems like three days pass before dark sets in and I climb out the dump hatch. The night air slides over my skin like cool water as I take a few steps, stop, listen in case Tesco is someplace nearby. Everything in me wants to go find Skedee, to get him free, but I know I can't. It's too much risk. That stubborn old pony will belong to Tesco Peele now. Skedee's been a good friend to me, and he deserves better. Nothing should belong to Tesco Peele, ever.

Tears sting my eyes, but I have to wipe them away and keep moving shadow to shadow, through the alleys and along the fences. I smell food and cookfires, hear horses rustling in their stalls and chickens bedding down for the night. I hear pans clanking and voices talking and a baby laughing. The sounds of people who have places they belong. Even their animals have places to be.

Something in me pulls and tugs. I shouldn't do it, but I cut loose and run, right down the middle of the shanty street, past the house where they shot at Amos, and all the way out of Talihina.

I know every step of the way to Shelterwood, but it's different in the woods at night, alone. Dark birds fly from limb to limb and animals rustle in the thickets and slide across the pine straw. I think of Tesco and the laundryman and outlaws. But the stars cut a path through the trees, bright and sure, and the lightning bugs come out to show me the way home. Over Sleeping Beauty Bridge and into Little Snake Creek I go.

The dark is so much thicker there. A timber rattler shakes its tail way too close. I back up, then climb the branches to Sleeping Beauty Bridge again. Without a torch to see by, there'll be no getting home till morning. All around me, lightning bugs sparkle in thicket vines while the hours pass and I wish for Tula and Amos, and Nessa and Cora, and all the other kids at our dugout.

Maybe the boys are there, too. Maybe Mr. Brotherton got them free, and they brought back Skedee. We'll call a council and then we'll start up the mountain. Tesco lied about cutting down the trees in the hanging valley, just like he lied about my mama and daddy. The old place is waiting, the shelterwood standing with arms stretched wide and tall, touching a blanket of stars.

By the dark of the moon, I wish and wish and wish. A hundred wishes. A thousand.

I fall asleep wishing and go to a place where wishes come true. I see all of us together in the hanging valley. I see our church and school. Two chickens and a rooster scratch around the garden.

The cabin door is open, and Mama comes to stand in it, and she smiles at me.

"You're here," I say. "You came back."

First light wakens me, and the words are still on my lips. I whisper them into the morning air, and tell myself that all the wishes really are true. Everyone is waiting at Shelterwood Camp, safe.

They'll come running from the morning fire, so happy when they see me. We'll gather our things and go up the mountain.

I think on just how we'll do it as I make my way down the branches of Sleeping Beauty Bridge, and along the dry wash.

"I'm almost home," I whisper when I hear Sweetwater Creek making her music.

But as I turn from the dry wash, no smoke hangs above the low fog. There's no smell of logs banked and burning low, no coals ready to be stoked for morning.

Amos wouldn't let the night fire go out.

I throw down my walking stick and run the last of the way, afraid of what I'll find.

And what I find is the thing I was afraid of.

Horse tracks litter the ground. Shod horses, different size shoes. Boot tracks, different size boots. Men's boots. Everything's been taken away. Our packs. The food pokes we hang in the tree branches so bears and other critters can't get them. The water can.

Even the money we hid in the tree for Shelterwood Bank is missing. The boys must've known where it was. They told. They told all of it.

I stand there with my heart banging in an empty shell, my body numb.

"Nessa," I whisper. "Tula, Amos, Cora . . . anybody?" Their names echo into the dugout, come back at me, but nobody answers. I run inside anyway. The pallets are torn up, everything scattered and trampled.

Back at the fire pit, I turn a circle, see a blur of leaves and rocks and water. A flash of light catches my eye, and I stare down at broken glass and smashed tin cans and twine. All that's left of our magic lanterns. Ruined like everything else.

Sinking into the dirt, I strain glass from ashes, watch the thin gray dust fall through my fingers and run away on the morning breeze.

Everyone's gone.

I'm the only one left.

"Nessa!" I call out, and the sound bounces off rocks and trees. Who took her? Tesco? The Talihina deputy?

Someone else?

Where is she now?

A rustle in the brush jerks me upright. Scrambling to my feet, I whisper, "Who's out there?"

I think of Gable and Milk the mule way back last spring, of Dewey calling, *Who's out there?* while the rest of us hid in the thicket. I tell myself the same thing happened when these men came to ruin Shelterwood. The boys got here ahead of them and warned everybody to run. Hide. Don't make a sound. Now they've heard me call for them, and they're coming up the trail, like magic, like a fairy story.

But when I turn around, only two shadows sift from the morning dim. They move slow and careful, joined at the hands.

I know them even before I can see their faces.

"Nessa!" I cry, and she lets loose of Koi and comes running.

CHAPTER 31

Valerie Boren-Odell, 1990

Risking his life to save that of another is something that every ranger must be ready to do.

—HORACE ALBRIGHT, THE FIRST SUPERINTENDENT OF
YELLOWSTONE NATIONAL PARK AND THE SECOND DIRECTOR
OF THE NATIONAL PARK SERVICE, 1928.

Picking my way up and down slopes, around rock outcroppings and deadwood by flashlight and a fingernail moon, I'm acutely aware that our circumstances could change in a heartbeat. We might be walking into trouble, or trouble could be one step behind us. If Braden and Rachel have evidence stockpiled at their camp, they are in danger, and so are we. No one will be safe until this thing is made public. Maybe not even then.

Alton Parker is a big man in this county. He is on hand-shaking, shoulder-slapping terms with everyone important, and it looks like at least some of his business dealings are much shadier than I'd imagined. Who are his cohorts? Who's aware of this but looks the other way? Anyone I've worked with? Any of the people who watched as Edwin was loaded into an ambulance? Did they know?

I ponder the depth of it downslope after upslope after water crossing, amid star-blanketed meadows, over firefly-lit ridges. Parker beat me at this game the last go-round. He thinks he's beaten me for good.

We put the Feds in their place, he's telling himself. *Lady ranger, she'll know better than to mess with ol' Alton Parker.*

If evidence exists, I want it. I'll do almost anything, go anywhere to get it.

Even in the dark, I've begun to recognize territory from the missing person's search for Braden. He was right under our noses all along. I want to wring his neck and congratulate him at the same time. As he leads us along a softly trickling creek, smoke tinges the air, the smell of a cookfire being tended nearby.

Curtis glances back at me, points upward. His senses, like mine, are on high alert.

We turn the corner, and the camp is exactly where I thought it might be. Firelight casts flickering shadows on the rock formation above, drawing a cratered face. I already know what we'll find after we pass through the underbrush and boulders ahead—the remains of an old dugout, shielded by what's left of a stacked-stone wall built in some long-ago time. We were here during our search. We saw the evidence of recent habitation. Braden and Rachel must have been moving their hideout from place to place to avoid being found.

Braden and Rachel . . . and whoever is tending the fire in that camp.

Braden whistles a nightjar's call. The person in the camp whistles in return.

Curtis visibly tenses. I do the same, think, *We're ready.*

But neither of us could be ready for what awaits when the campsite comes into view. By the fire, a woman sits cross-legged on a woven straw mat, her body shrouded in a colorful blanket. She turns silently to watch us, the fire's glow outlining the contours of a face that is old, but not ancient. Her cheeks are still fleshy and round, her lips full. Her dark eyes reflect the dancing light as she studies us. She projects no apprehension upon seeing our radios, uniforms, handguns.

On the whole, what I feel from her is an unexplainable sense of . . . peace. She seems as if she has grown from the forest itself and has always been in this place. I know that's not the case, and in the moment, I can't imagine how she could have gotten here, except that these kids must know an easier way in.

"Come," she says. Her voice is both commanding and gentle, compelling in a way I can't explain. "I've been wondering about you."

"Mrs. Blackwell?" I ask. But I've seen photos of Sydney and Braden's grandmother. She's a tall, stern-looking woman with a gray braid and a cowboy hat, robust even in her old age. The sort of woman who would wear a nickname like Budgie as a badge of honor.

This tiny, soft-spoken sprite in the blanket shawl can't be her. When she answers, her voice carries a hint of an accent I can't place. "Budgie is safe with Hazel now."

"With . . . Hazel? Hazel Rusk?" My mind reaches for connections. "That name is on the land where the loggers came in. By the looks of things, I'm assuming they didn't have permission to cut the timber."

"No, of course. It is a terribly wrong situation. I only came to see about it yesterday."

"So . . . then you are a relative of Hazel Rusk's?"

"Yes and no. This depends on which Hazel you mean."

My exhausted legs groan in protest as I squat on my bootheels. I'm not in the mood for riddles.

"Sit," the woman says. Then she motions to Curtis, as well. "Hattak himitta . . . binili."

Chuckling under his breath, he moves to settle himself by the fire.

"I apologize. My Choctaw is not very good," the old woman says to him. "Many years I've been away. Very far away. But you *are* young to me. You are all himitta, young. And this is a battle for the young, this business of the trees. I left here so long ago, when I was not even your age. But I suppose, had an old woman called me young then, I would have laughed, too. I could have called you handsome, instead, but I don't remember the word. I left here so long ago. My Choctaw is not good."

Curtis shakes his head, seeming almost embarrassed. "My Choctaw isn't good, either. But *young* is fine. I like it better every year."

"Ha! Wait until you are my age!" She smiles serenely, her gaze resting on the fire. For a moment, she seems mesmerized. "I knew a very old man here once. He told stories and sang songs from the War between the States. That was *his* war. I grew older, and I had *my* war. These trees, this is your war, and their war." She indicates Braden and

Rachel, who are busy digging up a metal canister of the sort campers use to cache food and supplies. "But my sisters would never forgive me if I had failed to come back for the fight."

"So . . . Hazel Rusk is your sister?" I take out my notepad and pen, turn to a blank page.

"Yes . . . and no."

"But she is a relative?"

"That is a long tale." Her eyes gather the flickering light, direct it my way. "Let these young people show what they have found—they're very clever soldiers—and then, if you still have an ear for it, I'll tell you my story . . . and the story of this place."

"At this point, I think we're here until morning," Curtis interjects.

I start to protest, but the truth is he's right. Extracting two teenagers and an elderly woman from the woods, while making sure we aren't ambushed, will be more feasible in the daylight. Aside from that, I want to hear this woman's story. All of it.

"I'll divide up the stew." She reaches for a camp pot suspended over the fire. "I've brought my wooden spoon. Dewey carved it from a branch all those years ago, right in this very place, but I have cooked with it in many places. He was sometimes a bad boy, that Dewey, but he carved a good spoon."

Braden and Rachel beckon us into the remains of the rock shelter, where their sleeping bags lie atop a lightweight rain tarp. There they open the cache can, begin setting out photos, handwritten notes, diagrams of the logging camp, the throughways.

"We always kept the stash buried here," Braden explains, his face shockingly boyish. "That way if we got caught, they wouldn't have all our evidence, you know? Sydney could find her way to this place if she needed to. Grandma Budgie used to bring us a lot."

"Sydney sent me here looking for you," I say, astounded by the mass of documentation Braden and Rachel have collected. "But she didn't tell me to look for anything else."

"If Sydney came herself, she would've found it. My sister and me have our signs. We used to play a treasure-hunt game, bury stuff, and give each other clues to find it. But Sydney was supposed to stay at Mrs. Wambles's place and keep her ears open and her mouth shut unless she knew for *sure* I was out of commission. Sydney is tough as a mule, but she's as stubborn, too, and she talks too much. That's why I told her, 'If people ask you questions, just make stuff up.' It's also why I didn't tell her everything about what Rachel and I were really into out here."

"She knew enough to be scared to death for you," I point out. "She hitchhiked to my house in the middle of the night, looking for help."

Worry etches Braden's features, aging them. "She wasn't supposed to end up involved in it all. I thought Parker would just keep hunting me, but he was looking for me in the end of the park where I left the car, and that's not where Rachel and I were operating from. The car was a decoy."

"This isn't a game," I say. "Parker took your sister from Mrs. Wambles's place and tried to strong-arm the details out of her." I'm still struggling to figure out the details myself. How have Braden and Rachel managed all of this? The photos in their cache were shot with a good zoom lens, sometimes close enough that people's faces are recognizable. These two teenagers are incredibly lucky they didn't get caught.

While I'm awed by their work, I'm also frustrated. "What are you *doing* out here? Why didn't you come to the Park Service with this?"

A silent debate passes between Braden and Rachel. They frown at one another. He inclines his head, she nods.

"Because of Grandma Budgie," Braden answers when he turns our way again. "I knew Mama was lying in the note she left about Grandma Budgie having a stroke and about taking her to the City of Faith in Tulsa. When I called Rachel, she was like, 'Seriously? That hospital's closed down.'"

Pulling off her ball cap and unleashing a bedraggled blond ponytail, Rachel jumps in eagerly. "I told him, 'Braden, that witch of a mother of yours is full of crap. She's just trying to get money again.' And then I thought, what if she's trying to get *all* the money, you know? Like, *forever*? But Braden said that his Grandma Budgie's last will leaves everything to him and Sydney."

Curtis turns his attention from the pictures. "Did Jade know that?"

"Everybody knows. It's not any secret." Braden combs a hand

through his thick red hair, sags like he's being forced to recount embarrassing family details in the principal's office. "Every time Mama would come around, Grandma Budgie would tell her if she'd get her life together, things could be different. Mama would do it for a while, then she'd leave again and stuff would be missing from our house. A few months back, Mama knocked on the door all banged up, she said from a car wreck. We hadn't seen her in . . . maybe four years? Grandma Budgie told her, 'Jade, this is the last time. I'm too old for this and so are you. These kids need a mother.'"

Braden snatches a piece of bark off the ground, shreds it in his lap, watches the splinters fall. "Mama told us she was starting into AA meetings and she'd found a job at a nursing home down in Hugo. Her and my grandma would sit up in the evenings and drink tea and talk about the ranch, and buying some new furniture, making the kitchen modern and stuff like that. They decided to have Parker fix the barn and the pond dam. Sydney was happy, and I was glad my grandma and Sydney wouldn't be alone when I left for college or the military. We all got to believing it, you know?"

Braden's mouth trembles almost imperceptibly. He swallows hard before speaking again. "It was dumb. Sydney is just a kid and Grandma Budgie's old, but I knew better. I could tell something was up with Mama. She kept coming home later and later after her shifts, and she'd be in a weird giggly mood. Sometimes I'd walk into the kitchen and catch her on the phone, and she'd hang up real quick and say, 'Oh, that was just work.' I never should've left the house that night I went to meet Rachel."

"You didn't know, Braden." Rachel's hand finds his. "Everybody wants to love their own mama. *Jade's* the one who did wrong. Not you."

Braden stiffens, resisting absolution. The weight of an entire family rests on his seventeen-year-old shoulders. "Mama was just looking for a chance to get my grandma out of the house, and that night I was gone, she went for it. She got drugs from the nursing home or somewhere, and she tricked Grandma Budgie into taking some, and she left us a note about going to the City of Faith. Then Parker came by later, saying all this stuff about 'Oh, Jade took such good care of my poor old mama at the nursing home. I owe Jade big time for that. She and Budgie are like family to me now. I promised I'd be here for you kids if you ever needed it.'"

I scribble notes furiously by the dim light of a camping lantern. "So he wanted you two to go with him, and you agreed, hoping to find your grandmother?"

"Parker wasn't taking no for an answer." Braden's reply comes through clenched teeth. "He had a paper *signed* by my grandma. He said he didn't want us to be scared or worried, and it was all legal. Sydney was crying and having a fit. I dragged her off to the bedroom and made her pack a suitcase and said, 'If we're going to get Grandma Budgie back home, this is what we've gotta do. We have to go along with it.' I asked Parker if I could grab my fishing stuff out of the barn, and I called Rachel from the barn phone and told her what was going on."

"That's when we started trying to figure it all out." Rachel shifts a few photos closer to the lamp. "Braden told Parker he wanted to quit school and go to work for Parker Construction to make money for an apartment, and I came down here and got busy driving around towns and campgrounds, and hospitals, and nursing homes, looking for the Chevy Suburban that Jade left the ranch in when she took Miss Budgie away."

I stop writing, look at Curtis. "The hotel in Poteau," he says.

"That's why you were there," I add.

"Not at first," Rachel replies. "I tried Antlers, then Hugo. No luck. Jade was really laying low, but I figured if she showed up anyplace, she'd be looking to party. I ended up in Poteau after I started going to bars at night."

Curtis coughs like he's got gristle stuck in his throat. There are some rough backwoods hangouts in the area. This college girl doesn't belong in any of them.

Rachel treats him to a death stare. "I'm *eighteen*. I can't buy drinks, but I'm legal to get in."

"There's legal . . . and there's just not a good idea," Curtis remarks.

"I can take care of myself. And I did spot Jade, so it worked." The response comes with a haughty chin wag. Rachel will not be cowed.

"So, I'm in this middle-of-nowhere dive, and there she is, living it up with some guy. They leave the bar in a brand-new Ford F-150, so I follow them all the way back to a junky little duplex across the street from that hotel in Poteau. Next day, the guy leaves in a log-hauler truck, and later on, I follow Jade to a food drive-through, then to a big old white house outside town. When she leaves, I drive back past the old house, ask some dude down the road about that place on the corner. He tells me the lady there runs an adult-care home. So I go knock on the place's door, say, 'My car broke down. Can I use your phone?' They won't let me in. After that, I follow Jade a few more times. Every day, morning and evening . . . to that same house with a takeout meal."

"To feed my grandmother more drugs, so she wouldn't have a clue where she was," Braden adds.

My alarm level ratchets up. "Is your grandmother safe now?"

"Yes, ma'am, but it took my great-aunt and a lawyer to get her out of that place, day before yesterday. The owner said Mama had checked Grandma Budgie in with all the right paperwork, and they had copies in their files. But our lawyer put the fear of God in those people and they wheeled Grandma Budgie to the door and we left."

"Why didn't you call the police?" I demand again. "County sheriff? DHS? *Somebody?* When we were combing tens of thousands of acres looking for you, why didn't you come to us?"

Braden's countenance turns ominous. "Parker knows *everyone*. You cross him, you're likely to wind up under the asphalt of some new driveway. He wanted the timber from my family's land, and he needed us out of the way."

I stare at my notepad, read, *He needed us out of the way* . . .

Parker was after a small fortune in timber. And the parcel allowed hidden access to federal land, a bonus opportunity too lucrative to ignore.

"Parker arranged it all. Jade was his accomplice," I whisper. Jade, who was shacked up with a log truck driver. Jade, who was suddenly cruising in a new Ford pickup. Jade, who didn't stand to gain by inheritance, but who could cash in by helping to steal a half million dollars or more in timber. "So your grandmother is the one who looks after that land? But it belongs to a family member?"

"It's a long story. We always took care of that land, so I thought it was Grandma Budgie's. I didn't know the whole truth till my great-aunt came down from Tulsa to help us get Grandma Budgie to some-place safe." Peering over the tumbledown wall, Braden indicates the woman in the shawl. "She can tell you."

Reluctantly, we leave the evidence cache and return to the fireside as Braden apologizes for the trouble he's caused and for the fact that Parker's men shot at Edwin's patrol horse. "We didn't mean anything like that to happen. We just . . . we had to get proof on Parker—pictures of him or his business trucks at the logging site. I crossed him, you know? The only way to keep us all safe was to have proof. No telling how many people he does this stuff to. Old folks or people who've got land they don't live on . . . Parker's crew comes in, takes their timber, and gets out. The trucks and equipment he uses are all painted over."

"The spray tanker that hit the ditch on Holson Valley Road," I mut-ter. "I knew something was off. Nobody needs that many gallons of glyphosate to spray weeds for a landscaping business." I'm angry to the core of my being. Incensed. I want to be back at my desk with the photo evidence, and on the phone bringing back that ISB special agent, the FBI, OSBI, and every other applicable means of breaking this thing wide open. Aside from state and local, we can go after Parker on the federal level, where he doesn't have political friends to rely on.

Potential charges spin through my head as the old woman offers stew in wax paper coffee cups, which she regards with a disdainful frown. "These things you use and then toss in the rubbish. It is very bad, don't you think? When I was small, if we found a tin can, we made a cooking pot, or a bowl, or a bucket to gather berries, or a toy to play in the dirt. If a bit of sweet syrup was left in the can, we ate it. If we had a glass jar, we filled it with fireflies to create a lantern. Now, people just throw it all away."

Braden and Rachel accept their disposable cups sheepishly.

My stomach has tied itself in so many knots I wave mine away. "No, thanks. I can't eat."

Curtis runs interference on the cup, hands it to me, mutters, "Eat," and gives me the eye.

I take the cup. It's warm in my hands, which feels good. "How did you *get* here? To this place? Braden, how have you been coming and going to get photos developed?"

Braden's mouth is full, so his great-aunt answers instead. "The old wagon trace. Those of us who traveled it when it *was* a road are still able to find the way here. But you don't even know where *here* is. Where *you* are."

I fight the urge to get defensive. "I haven't been with the park very long, but roughly I do, yes."

"You couldn't possibly." Her tone is gentle, even slightly blithe. "All these years, it was a secret."

"What, exactly, is the ownership situation on the inholding where they're cutting the timber? Braden said you would explain the details. It's important." I move to set down my stew cup again. Curtis nudges it back toward my body, gives a little shrug that whispers, *Eat the stew already.*

"No one else knew about Shelterwood," the woman says.

Pushing my ball cap back, I rub itchy, tired skin. *Shelterwood* is an obscure forestry term for older, larger trees that protect the smaller, younger growth beneath. I know the word. I can quote the definition, but it won't help me build a case.

Curtis seems as bewildered as I am.

"A long time ago," the woman begins, "three girls lived in an attic. Two of them were little Choctaw girls, Hazel, who was thirteen, and Nessa, who was six. Hazel and Nessa were orphan wards of the parents in the house, and they shared the attic room with Olive, who was eleven. Ollie lived there with her mother and a new stepfather, the ranch foreman of Mr. E. Niles Lockridge, a man whose name you will find on the facades of buildings and in the history books. Perhaps you know of him already? But one must never believe what can be read in the history books about powerful men. The wealthy have the privilege of writing their own stories as they like. Tonight I will tell you what is true. What was lived by these three young girls, if you would like to know."

Her gaze catches mine and tunnels inward. I think of the packet from Mr. Wouda—of the corrupt probate courts of the statehood era and the children whose land and mineral rights were stolen. "I know about the guardians and the grafters . . . the whole filthy system," I say.

A long breath settles through the woman, as if she means to drink her story from the night air. "Then you know this was a dangerous time for landowners among the Five Tribes. With local probate courts now in charge, in came grafters by the score, seeking to build their fortunes through leases and guardianships. Children were especially prized, as dominion over the child meant dominion over the child's land and proceeds. In this way, Hazel and Nessa came under the control of people who were not their relatives. The first were kindly people who lived in a high-mountain valley, but the man was murdered, and the wife married Tesco Peele. The two sisters and Ollie found themselves in a house filled with fear and shouting and hitting and yelling. Yet even there, Hazel and Nessa still had one another.

" 'I will always take care of you and protect you,' Hazel promised, and Nessa, being very small, knew no better than to believe it. 'One day, we will go back home to our family,' Hazel said, but the longer Nessa was away from her blood relatives, the less she could remember of the little farm where she had lived with them. But she clung to her sister, and they played and laughed and tried to be children when they could. Sometimes they allowed Ollie to join their circle, but Tesco Peele did not much permit such things. Ollie, who still grieved the death of her own father, had no one . . . not even her mother, who had taken to the opium powders, as did many women in that place and time, when doctors encouraged it as a tonic for nerves and melancholia.

"For this reason, the house wasn't a safe place for little girls . . . even ones who were not orphans or Choctaw. Do you see? Tesco Peele was a very bad man, in the employ of another bad man. Niles Lockridge had, through the courts, gained guardianships over dozens of Choctaw children, and thereby control over a king's ransom in land, oil, and timber. He built grand homes, commissioned private railroad cars, purchased fine new automobiles, dressed his wife and daughters in fashions from Paris. In the young state of Oklahoma resided thousands like him, their wealth built at the expense of people who were, quite frankly, often more easily managed dead than alive. The three little girls in the attic did not understand any of this, of course. How could they? And then one day, Hazel disappeared . . ."

The old woman's words hit like a physical slap, and both Curtis and I jerk upright as she goes on to weave the narrative of two runaway girls, a calico pony, and elf children who scavenged food from passing trains, and a farm wife who helped them, and Ollie using Hazel's name to disguise her own identity, and more children joining them.

The night around us deepens as the storyteller plaits her tale together, bringing the children to Talihina, where Ollie comes upon a newspaperman with blue eyes.

"Oh," the old woman laughs. "Ollie was quite taken with him! She would have told you she wasn't, but she was. She brought him to meet the elves. Amos, and Nessa, and Tula with little Pinti and Koi, shared their stories, and he told them of Miss Kate Barnard, the first woman elected to office in the new state, who would take on the land grafters. Miss Kate had been to speak in Talihina, invited by the Oklahoma Federation of Women's Clubs. The railroad brotherhoods, the coal and asphalt miners, the workingmen, the clubwomen, had come to Talihina by the thousands. All sorts of people—the Choctaw and the freedman, the Oklahoma boomer, and the immigrant still speaking a language from a homeland across the sea. Miss Kate had words for each of them, and with those words came hope. The people cheered so loudly the sound could be heard for miles. Perhaps all the way into these mountains."

She sweeps a hand to the air around us, where an audience of fireflies glitters in the trees, and the pines whisper as if they already knew the story, as if they've been telling it all along, we just couldn't hear them.

"It was grand to think this tiny woman would rescue all the friendless children of Oklahoma," she goes on. "But little ones must eat while newspapermen write and politicians debate." Her smile fades quickly, and the story takes on a darker hue. She tells of a woman with a garden hoe and a boy with a gun, and a terrifying flight in a storm, and a friend being shot.

"This is where they came when Amos could travel no farther. Ollie knew of this place, an old dugout hideaway where she had camped with her father. Here the little ones began to build a world of their own. A world for a tribe of children who could trust no one."

Pointing into the darkness, she locates the schoolroom, the horse corral, the bank, Ollie's Lookout Tree. She talks about voting for leaders and making firefly lanterns. She tells of an old soldier searching for a lost love.

"The children lived here all summer." A smile overtakes her and she stirs the fire, watching the crackling embers. "The bigger ones worked in town for money, and the younger ones gathered wood and wild foods. After dark, they sat here in this very spot and told tales around the night fire. All sorts of tales . . . for *every* orphan has a story."

Overhead, night breezes comb the branches, stirring thin shards of moonlight that dart about like forest spirits raised by an alchemy of moonlight, wind, and story.

"They were more than just a word, *orphan* or *elf child,* all those little citizens of Shelterwood Camp—that is the name Ollie, being the elected commissioner of names, chose for this dugout. But Shelterwood Camp was only meant to be a temporary place. The children planned to climb high into the mountains, come autumn, to the little cabin constructed by Ollie's father in a beautiful hanging valley. There they would build a new home, with a church and school, and call it Shelterwood Town. It was a dream. A beautiful dream. They believed these things as only dreamers can. As only a child would. It sounds so very fanciful, doesn't it?"

Staring into the flames, she's hypnotic, yet also hypnotized. "But do not let the fairy tale name mislead you. Children abandoned by the world live a hard life. Bellies were often empty, and the longer the elves remained in Shelterwood Camp, the scarcer the wild foods and firewood became. The young ones ranged farther and farther each day in their work, searching for edibles and wood to burn. Yet, being children, they even made a game of the labor, dividing into teams and trekking off to see who could return with the best goods. They were often tired, carrying their wood bundles miles through the forest on weary legs."

I stare into the woods, imagine children here alone, struggling to survive in this place with all its dangers.

"But it is an eternal truth . . . and you young people remember this, if you remember nothing else I say." The storyteller locks eyes with each of us, one by one. "Your burden will often become your salvation. It was only for this reason, the burden of a remarkably heavy load of wood, that those two girls from the attic, Ollie and Nessa, were not separated forever the evening Shelterwood was destroyed. On that day, Nessa was yet making her way home with little Koi in tow, both of them bending beneath their wood bundles, when they heard horses, and dogs, and screams. Men had come to round up the elves and take them away. Nessa and Koi crawled under a fallen tree and hid themselves in the leaves. There they remained all night, afraid to come out.

"In the morning, they heard Ollie calling to them, but Shelterwood Camp was gone. All the work, ruined. All the dreams, destroyed. Yet there was not time to cry over it. An orphan soon learns that crying does not benefit."

Gathering the shawl closer around her shoulders, she shudders. "Ollie, Nessa, and little Koi simply gathered what they could—an upturned cookpot, a wooden spoon that Dewey had carved, a walking stick, a few fishhooks and matches, and together they started north over the mountains, not knowing where they would go. 'Far from here,' Ollie told the little ones. 'Away from the Winding Stair, where those men can never find us.'"

The air falls silent, and we sit frozen, staring into the dichotomy of night and fireflies, darkness and light. I think of the skeletons in the cave, realize the alternative to Shelterwood was far worse. The man-devil of Myrna Wambles's story existed. He walked this territory in myriad forms.

I imagine Charlie, off in the world alone. My heart wrenches.

"They traveled a long distance," the woman explains. "But it was difficult on foot with nothing. In the woods, they scavenged. At farms or cabins, they begged. The more they traveled, the more ragged they became. The more ragged they became, the fewer people were inclined to help them. The fewer people helped them, the more ragged they became. The more ragged they became, the colder they were, because the weather was changing."

Beside me, Curtis rests his elbows on his knees, slumping forward. I glance over and see him staring at the ground. The world we left only hours ago seems far away. I ache to take those three little children by the hands and say, *You're safe now.*

"Isn't it true that life can turn a circle at times?" The old woman looks my way again, and I meet her eye. "That all things, all people, move within the circle, unaware?" Her face fills with empathy, as if she feels the need to apologize for the sadness her story stirs in me. *Ssshhh,* her expression seems to say. *Listen, now.*

"That winter of 1909, Miss Kate Barnard received a report of elf children living in a hollow tree, begging for food at farmhouses nearby. She came to see and found them sleeping, curled together against the wind on a cold November day. They trembled when she touched them and were so frightened they were thought mute when Kate asked who they were.

" 'This little boy is Koi,' " the oldest girl finally found the courage to say. 'And this girl is Nessa Rusk, and I . . . I am Hazel Rusk.' "

"So Ollie continued using Hazel's name?" My mind sharpens again.

The woman smiles wryly. "Nessa knew this was not true, of course. She knew Ollie *wasn't* Hazel, but she would never tell. Ollie had saved Nessa once, and this was Nessa's chance to save Ollie from being returned to that very bad house. They became sisters in every way that mattered, Ollie and Nessa. And they pleaded that Koi be reunited with *his* sisters. Miss Kate was a venerable woman of good heart and great power in that year of 1909, and with the help of Mrs. Grube, Tula and Pinti were found. Together with Koi, Nessa, and Ollie, they were transferred to the Whitaker Orphanage at Pryor, Oklahoma, with a group of Cherokee orphans Miss Kate had taken there for safekeeping. In that place, the children drew a circle around a new tribe, where, twice each year, Mrs. Grube rode the train all the way from Pushmataha County to see that they were well taken care of."

Laughter slips softly from her, as if there is more to that portion of the story, but she'll forgo it for now. "On occasion, they also saw Miss Kate, who came to make inspections of the facilities or to gather information about the children and their rightful land holdings. Her

Department of Charities and Corrections began prosecuting the grafters and guardians, as well as the lawyers and probate judges who enabled them. Some men were reported to have more than one hundred court-appointed guardianships. Many children had disappeared, been housed in asylums, or chased into the woods . . . or murdered. Some were spirited away as soon as they came of legal age, forced into marriages, or plied with drink and drugs, held prisoner until they could be coerced into signing away their fortunes."

The old woman pauses to draw breath, and I stare in the direction of the bone cave. What did those three little girls own that was worth killing them?

I barely hear the story continue at first. My mind is across the hills.

"Hazel's land parcel was among the cases in which Miss Kate was successful," the woman says. "As was Nessa's, and one of the Dawes parcels inherited from their parents. The lands with oil were gone to the wind. Miss Kate fought the good fight as the years went on, but digging too deeply into what the clubwomen spoke of as The Indian Concern would eventually be Kate's undoing. The oil kings drummed her out of office and left her broken by the failure of her life's work, tormented at the thought of all the young ones she could not help. But she made a difference to many, including Hazel, and Ollie, and Nessa."

"Kate Barnard found Hazel?" Curtis asks before I can. "The *real* Hazel Rusk?"

A smile twists the old woman's lips. "Quite the opposite. Hazel found Ollie and me. My sister came home." For the first time, she places herself within the story. She is Nessa. "But not until I was a college student and Ollie a married woman. Hazel had fled all those years earlier to save herself. At only thirteen, she'd become pregnant with Niles Lockridge's child after going to him to plead for relief from Tesco Peele's indecencies. She ran away in shame and fear and eventually came to a wayward home run by the Methodists, who took her in. She joined the missionary service when she was old enough, leaving behind the torment of her past. Many years went by before she could bear to come home and search for me. Even then, she couldn't stay, and so when she left, I followed her into the mission service overseas. I do not think Ollie could fathom at first why I would abandon her for the sister who had once abandoned me. She worried that I loved Hazel more, but it was only that I loved Hazel, also."

Taking Braden's hand, she pats it gently, as if to reassure him that his Grandma Budgie is as dear to her as her sister by birth. "Over years, and visits, and letters sent home to Ollie from the far corners of the world, I think she understood. Had she not been a young married woman with a dashing husband she adored, ranchlands to manage, and political goals of her own, I do believe she would have come along with us. Inside Ollie and me, there was always this forest, that one summer in the wild, and the vision of building a new place, a better place, a place where children could be safe. The monies Budgie produced through our land here, from cattle grazed on the meadows and timber thinned in the forests, allowed Hazel and me to help the little ones we found in our work."

Moisture gathers at the corners of her eyes, glitters in the uneven light, as if tiny fires burn there, also. "So you see, the small dream that was born among the children of this forest did not die here. It grew as the dreamers grew. Its branches stretched through air, to places far and near, to forests and deserts, across rivers and oceans. Evil could not poison it. Men could not cut it down. Floods could not wash it away. It grew into a tree of life, of *lives.*"

A log snaps in the fire. Watching the sparks spin up, and up, and up, Nessa smiles as she finishes her story, and Ollie's. "Many have dwelt beneath it . . . labored, and rejoiced, and rested, and lain down to watch the sky through its magnificent shadow and light. Through a thousand eyes of a thousand colors, we have seen our Shelterwood."

EPILOGUE

Valerie Boren-Odell, 1990

THE CHAIRMAN. "What do you know, personally, about the reputation of the people who signed this report?"

MR. HOWARD OF OKLAHOMA. "She is a research agent of the Federation of Women's Clubs of America, which is an organization in practically every little town."

MR. HASTINGS. "It has been given to the press everywhere, and it not only complains about the irregularities in the probate court of Oklahoma, but it criticizes Congress very severely."

MR. ROACH. "To whom do they make the report?"

MR. CARTER. "To the newspapers."

MR. SPROUL. "Now, we are asking for $10,000 here to ... go out and make an investigation upon a report of some women folks. Well, now, that is not sufficient, in my judgment. If they know of wholesale mistreatment of the Indians or misappropriation of their money ... they can tell us of it, and then we can take an intelligent action."

MR. CARTER. "The country is already stirred up about it. The charges have been made. They have been carried in almost every paper of consequence in the country, and therefore Congress can no longer ignore the matter."

—SUMMARY FROM US CONGRESS, HOUSE REPORT OF THE COMMITTEE ON INDIAN AFFAIRS, WITH HEARINGS, 1924.

A ticker-tape parade of autumn leaves clatters along the Muskogee Federal Building steps as we exit into a bright November afternoon, leaving behind the cloistered scents of oiled wood and aging paper, polished stone and human struggle. Outside, the sun has long since chased away morning's chill, painting the Muskogee streets in a golden hue that belies the imperfect search for justice housed behind the weighty stone facade. We don't always get what we seek in places like this. I've been involved in enough court cases to know that justice is not the idealized woman on the statues, blindfolded and draped in flowing robes. She's battered and chipped, and she has picked herself up from a million hard falls, dusted off her scales, and gone back to work.

But she's a tough old girl, and on this bright fall day, I'm heady with the notion that we did right by her. After months of investigation, witness testimony, and evidence presentation, the US Attorney for the Eastern District of Oklahoma has obtained a grand jury indictment. The federal case against Alton Parker and his co-conspirators was significant enough to warrant a press conference following the arrests.

The details were like a racketeering checklist—theft, wire fraud, money laundering, illegal kickbacks, conspiracy, aggravated kidnapping, arson, bribery, and obstruction of justice, with a heavy dose of false imprisonment, felony elder abuse, depredation of government property involving the stolen timber and blown-up hiking trail, and violation of the Archaeological Resources Protection Act, involving the removal of Choctaw funerary items from the burial site in the cave. Parker had wanted the place wiped clean to avoid having park personnel, archaeologists, the Bureau of Land Management, the Choctaw Nation, and possibly the press in his operational area. For the same reason, he had my unfortunate John Doe, who is now Jack Sieg, blow a hiking trail off the side of a mountain. Sieg was a convicted felon fresh out of prison. This time his foray into explosives landed him in a flooded waterway and cost him his life.

Thirteen of Parker's minions and associates are also named in the indictment. Their crimes will lead to prison sentences or the kind of financial pain capable of bankrupting most people in this part of the world. A handful of others flipped and agreed to testify for the prosecution. The slippery thing about Parker is, he did business not by dealing in overt orders, but by offering suggestions like, *Well, I guess we'll just have to hope the side of that mountain falls off and buries that hiking trail, won't we? I'd give a thousand dollars to see that.*

Sieg thought he'd earn himself an easy grand. He'd learned a bit about explosives working for a demolition business.

The beauty of the racketeering charge is that it allows federal prosecutors to go after Parker and his cohorts for the crimes committed by others on their behalf. Parker's victims will also be able to use the outcome of the federal trial to sue for civil damages. Those three girls from the attic may yet receive a round of financial justice for the destruction of their timberland.

"I hope the RICO charge sticks. You know Parker's got good lawyers," Roy says as we stop at the bottom of the steps, watching Budgie, Nessa, and Hazel make their way slowly up the wheelchair ramp from the lower level. Budgie leans heavily on the handles of Hazel's chair, and Nessa follows behind, a brightly colored shawl over her shoulders. Edwin trails farther back, moving with a slight limp, his wife at his side. He has a metal plate in his head and a leg full of pins at this point, but he's healing.

"The RICO charge is as solid as they come," I assure Roy, and look around for Curtis in case he managed to slip in at the last minute. The rest of us barely had enough time to get here when the press conference was announced, but Curtis was on shift at work. He may have been tied up with something or too far afield.

"I hope so." Roy stares down at his feet, shakes his head. He looks like a college boy in his T-shirt and jeans. "Man, Alton Parker used to bring us candy bars at the football game. Whole *packs* of candy bars. The big ones, not the little Halloween kind. And he'd buy stuff from all the team fundraisers and donate things to our church youth group. We all thought he was so nice to do that. Now I wonder where the money came from, you know?"

"Hard to say." The striking thing about Parker's crimes is how well he adopted the techniques of the old-time grafters from the statehood era. He had ears on the ground in three counties, trolling for news of old folks moving off their land and into nursing homes, families caught up in divorces, substance abuse issues, drug prosecutions, medical problems, financial struggles. When he found opportunities, he bought or leased timberland for pennies on the dollar, then pillaged it. When he couldn't obtain title or permission, he just moved in and stole the trees outright.

"I picked up a forest conservation class this semester." Roy gauges my reaction. "Like, how do you fix the land after it's been clear-cut, and all the slash piles left everywhere, and the watersheds are mud . . . that kind of thing. I think I might do forestry, not law enforcement."

"Seems like a good idea." I have a hard time picturing this kid, with his big heart and soft-spoken demeanor, going into law enforcement. "Somebody has to plant the trees."

"Somebody's gotta keep jerks from plowing them under, too." He lifts a hand for a high five, and I oblige.

"Team," I say. "See you next summer."

"Aren't you supposed to be in school?" Sydney's voice echoes into the street like a train whistle. She bounds down the sidewalk and gives Roy a playful shove.

"Aren't *you?*" he retorts.

The girl's hands go right to her hips, all attitude. "Grandma Budgie said I could come hear the press conference."

"Some of that isn't appropriate for children." Roy shrugs toward the courthouse.

"Whatever." Sydney turns her attention to me. "Where's Charlie? You make him stay at school instead of coming here?"

"What Roy said." Part of me would've loved to let my junior ranger see that sometimes the good guys do win, even if it's hard work to get there. But Charlie lives in the world of a brand-new eight-year-old, and Parker's sleazy deeds don't belong there.

"Geez," Sydney huffs. "That's lame."

"Matter of opinion," I say, then remind myself that Sydney is sadly accustomed to dealing with things far beyond her years. Her grandmother is in fragile health and her mother is now a fugitive from justice. Jade and her boyfriend have disappeared off the map, possibly into Mexico.

"You sound like Braden and Rachel. They wouldn't even let me go to the *bathroom* by myself in there. They said creepy people hang around courthouses, and . . ." Noting that the three old women have worked their way within earshot, she snaps her lips closed. Sydney may be loaded with bluster, but she has respect for her Grandma Budgie. And love. It's evident as she jogs over to help the ladies make their way up the sidewalk.

"Fifty-seven-count indictment," I say when we are finally all in one place. "Parker and his cohorts will have good lawyers, but those charges are going to be hard to beat."

"*We* have the National Park Service." Budgie clasps my hand in both of hers and leans on me rather than on Hazel's wheelchair. "And we have you. I'm brimming with confidence." Looking into her dark, age-clouded eyes, I see a skilled politician who hasn't lost the ability to shake hands and win hearts.

I also see who she was long before she earned the nickname Budgie. She was Ollie, the commissioner of names in Shelterwood, a campaigner even then, a little girl determined to make her own world, and she did. I learned a few things about her while helping Charlie do his first project of the new school year, which involved writing a ten-page construction-paper book about a famous Oklahoman. Ollie spent a college semester in Washington, DC, under the wing of one of the first women elected to the US House of Representatives. By thirty, Ollie won a seat in the Oklahoma State Legislature. She was revered for being skilled in the art of persuasion and unafraid to speak her mind. She became known as Budgie because she hung on mercilessly once she sank her teeth into something . . . or somebody.

Parker thought he'd found an easy mark, but he should have done a little more research. That handle, *Budgie*? It was short for *Bulldoggie*.

"You'll get 'em." She offers me a wink and a sly smile. "I'd do it myself, but I'm old, you know."

"It doesn't show."

"I hide it well," she teases. "But it's for you young gals to fight the battle now. Be smart and tough, like this one." She smiles at Sydney, then moves to put an arm around the girl's shoulders. When Budgie's hand pulls away from mine, I notice that she's left me with a folded piece of paper. She winks slyly, and I close my fist as she hugs Sydney close. "We'll take care of each other when our Braden goes off to fly those military planes, won't we?"

"Yes'm." Sydney's head rests on Budgie's stooped-over shoulder.

The light between them outshines the November day. My heart-strings tug, and I want to call my mother and my grandmother, the women who built me—who implanted the idea that whatever path I chose for myself, I could conquer it.

What a gift that was. What a gift that still is.

"You'll come visit us in Antlers, though, right?" Sydney's query parts my thoughts. "And I still want to see all those new trails in the park and stuff, and you could take me on a ride along . . . and Bonnie, too." Curtis's stray mama dog has found the perfect home, complete with acres of ranchland and a girl child to look after. Curtis is finally out of the puppy business.

"Sure thing. I'll let you know next time Charlie and I plan a hike. He'll be glad to see Bonnie again."

"I'll bet, since he doesn't got a dog of his own." A reproachful frown punctuates the comment.

"I might just join you on that hike," Nessa interjects. "If the trail is not too demanding. Hazel and I have decided to stay for a time. At least until all the legal proceedings are completed . . . and until Budgie is fully back on her feet."

"I'm glad." In truth, Budgie needs the help, and so does Sydney. "It's a perfect season to be in the mountains." The trees have donned their fall colors and the Winding Stair is just plain showing off.

We chat a bit more before Braden and Rachel bring the ranch vehicle around. Budgie lingers beside me as the others make their way to the SUV. They're so preoccupied with how to load everybody they don't notice that they're missing someone.

Budgie taps a finger to my closed hand.

"Those little ones who were laid to rest in the cave? My father put them there, I think," she says quietly. "Keyes Radley was not a bad man, but on behalf of bad men, he did wrong things in the days when Choctaw people with land rights were apt to die of sudden illnesses or meet with accidents. I don't mean to say that he had any hand in the killings. A man who'd place the bodies so carefully, gather the proper grave goods for little children before laying them to rest, couldn't possibly have been so wicked. I'll always believe that

Keyes Radley brought Hazel and Nessa up the mountain to save them from a far worse fate, to keep them safe with my mother and me. I think he dreamed of beginning a new life, and in that place under the spreading oak, he thought he could leave behind the evil he'd seen, the things he'd done for money."

She fixes a steely gaze on me, as if challenging me to contradict her. "In the record book in his rucksack, he'd kept a list—names and how the poor souls perished. I've never shown it to anyone, not even my sisters. Perhaps he meant to use the list as leverage against power-ful men. Perhaps he meant to go to the government with it. I'll never know, but there is only one notation of three girls: Ara, Alma, and Addie Crooms. He wrote beside their names, *Killed in a wagon acci-dent,* with a question mark. Their burial was the last time he did such terrible work. Perhaps he couldn't stomach it after that. I think he would want to see their names returned to them." With a squeeze of my hand, she steps away.

The group at the SUV is growing restless now. Braden jangles the keys as he holds the back door open. "Everybody's in, Grandma Bud-gie."

"Coming!" she calls, then turns to me again. "If you have some space on one of those . . . those signs in the park where tourists stop to see maps and gather brochures and such . . ."

"The notice boards?"

"Yes, notice boards. Perhaps you could tell the visitors about Shelterwood—that once a community of children lived in these woods, and they fished and gathered wild foods and played and learned. And this is why they did it: Because they had no one to save them, and so they had to save themselves. People called them *elves,* as if they were spirits or myths, but they were just children. They found an advocate in one tiny woman only five feet tall, Miss Kate Barnard of Oklahoma. Had the oilmen not caused her office to be defunded and her name ruined, the plundering and the killing might have been stopped years before Gertrude Bonnin and the clubwomen fi-nally took it to the newspapers with their report. People should know what happened here and who fought against it."

"Yes, they should." Having that story placed in the park is not in my purview, but I'll find a way to put it out there.

"Being that I was Shelterwood's commissioner of names, I commission you to do it. And you might want these." She slips a yellowed envelope from her pocketbook and leaves it in my hands before turning to Braden, who has come to fetch her. Taking his arm, the woman who once was Ollie winks at me and then departs, leaving me to open the envelope and unfold the musty newspaper clippings inside. When I do, I take in a photograph of a woman in a high-button blouse and black skirt, standing amid buntings and banners on a hay wagon, speaking before a massive crowd. *Miss Kate Barnard in Talihina,* the caption reads.

The second clipping is a pen-and-ink drawing that looks like something from a Dickens novel, gaunt children with sunken cheeks and bowed backs, seated around a campfire. *The mean estate of our elf children,* the commentary beneath offers. *Who will help them?*

Staring at the sketch, I imagine the children as more than lines on paper. The grand jury indictment feels like some measure of justice for them, too. A modern-day grafter will face his day in court. But amid the thrill of victory, a hollow spot remains. Curtis isn't here. The celebration won't be complete until we share it, which means my next move will be to track him down. The idea teases a smile as I tuck away the clippings and start down the block toward my car.

When I turn the corner, his vehicle is pulling in next to mine.

"I was wondering about you," I call across the space between us as he steps out the driver's side door. "You're late by an hour, Officer Enhoe." I try for scorn, but the comment comes out sounding giddy.

Grinning, he takes me in. "Looks like the news was good. That's a cat-ate-the-mouse smile if I ever saw one."

"This time I think the mouse ate the fat cat," I say as I close the distance between us. "Fifty-seven-count indictment."

"Fill me in?" Leaning against the car, he crosses his arms over his chest. His sunglasses reflect the downtown Muskogee street as he waits for me to join him. "Hated to miss it. Couldn't be helped, though."

"Bad shift?" We settle in side by side, crimson and amber leaves tumbling past our feet.

"Yeah." He rubs a hand through his hair. Every strand settles right back into place. I smile to myself because I knew it would.

"Anything big?"

"Gave the game warden an assist over by Clayton Lake. Took some bad actors into custody. Three."

"Three? That's a load." I understand that when duty calls, it just does. But I wish today of all days it hadn't.

"They were cute, though."

My brain does a noisy skid, then a quick 180. "Cute? What? The *bad actors?*"

The smallest dimple forms in his cheek. "Blonds . . . well, one's sort of blond-and-white-spotted-ish."

I don't know whether to laugh, talk some sense into him, or hug him for being the man he is. "You have *got* to be kidding me."

"Leaving them running around in the middle of nowhere wasn't an option. And they're golden retrievers . . . I mean mostly . . . I'd say."

"You're *back* in the puppy business?" Slapping both hands over my face, I shake my head. "Curtis Enhoe!"

"Curly little blonds. Just the right kind for a towheaded boy about . . . yay high."

"Not a chance."

"Perfect time for it. I heard *somebody's* finally about to settle into permanent housing."

"Where did you hear that?"

"I have my sources." A grin widens beneath the glasses and the scrub brush hair. "And the bad actors told me to tell *you* that a home's not a home without a dog."

Home. It warms me to the core. I want that for Charlie . . . and for myself. Joel would have wanted this for us—to make a home, a life. A good life.

"We could talk about it over that fish dinner you owe me." Curtis harkens back to the wager we made when everything was falling apart.

"I think we ended up on the same side of the bet." That day feels like years ago. We've come so far. *I've* come so far. I hardly recognize the woman who drove into Talihina with a car and a life full of baggage she was afraid to unpack.

"We might have, after all." Shifting to his feet, he winks at me and adds, "But this one's on me, Ranger Boren-Odell. If you're up for a little walk, I've got a cousin who runs a place right around the corner."

"Of course you do." Laughing, I push off the car, and together we pass from the shadows into the light.

Nashville Banner newspaper

JANUARY 9, 1915

At one time, the department of charities was informed that three "elf children" were sleeping in the hollow of an old tree and eating at neighboring farmhouses. An investigation proved that these little ones were actually living in this homeless, friendless fashion, their hair so matted that it had to be cut from their heads. They were under the "protection" of a "guardian" who had fifty-one other children under his protecting care. These three children had valuable lands in the . . . oil fields. The guardian was charging up large amounts for "schooling" and "general care," yet he did not know where the children were, had "lost all track of them," and it was with difficulty that the department of charities located the guardian.

For me, Oklahoma, with her streams and rivers, her lush green hills and mountains, her caves and lakes, her legends of Vikings and treasure, and her tumultuous and unique history, was home. I grew up in areas that had been governed by the Cherokee, Creek, and Choctaw Nations in the decades before statehood. While the Horsethief Trail National Park in the book is fictional, its development, land mass, and historical features mirror those of the Winding Stair Mountain National Recreation Area, a 26,445-acre southeastern Oklahoma gem managed by the US Forest Service. Such places were the campgrounds and adventure lands of my childhood.

By the 1970s, those regions of the state were a patchwork of property still owned by tribal enrollees and property that had been sold or inherited into the hands of nontribal owners. This reality was the legacy of the 1887 Dawes Severalty Act, through which vast swaths of land that once had been under tribal control in common were systematically divided into allotment parcels and assigned individual members. The eventual result was the breakup of tribal lands and the loss of millions of acres. Along with land, an untold wealth of coal, oil, asphalt, and timber found its way into the hands of land barons, settlers, oil companies, industrialists, dishonest politicians, and opportunistic grafters.

In C. D. Foster's 1923 tongue-in-cheek commentary *Foster's Comic History of Oklahoma,* these words described the ongoing land grab in Oklahoma more than three decades after the passage of the Dawes Act:

"Since Statehood . . . the term real estate dealer, in Oklahoma, is a synonym for grafter, and the specie is not extinct at this late date."

Of course, as kids growing up in Oklahoma in the 1970s, we knew none of this.

I don't remember back then whether highway markers delineated the borders of what had once been known as the Indian Nations. Road signs, tourist opportunities, cultural sites, and tribal boundaries are prominently marked now, but during my childhood, the intertwined bits and pieces of nationhood seemed more a routine part of life in Oklahoma. We hung out with friends who were enrolled members of various tribes, went with them to powwows, festivals, all-Indian rodeos, and occasionally waved at them as they rode on parade floats dressed in traditional regalia.

Living on the edges of the suburbs, we occupied much of our free time riding our bikes and ponies on seemingly abandoned tracts of property that everyone referred to as *Indian land.* This, to our understanding, meant that via generational inheritance, the property now belonged to dozens of heirs in common, making it almost impossible to sell. We rested secure in the idea our favorite fishing ponds, bike trails, and enchanted forests would not be plowed under to make way for new housing complexes. It never crossed our minds that when the profit potential of the land finally became high enough, developers would find a way to get their hands on it.

On a few occasions in those golden years of childhood, we went along on trips into the countryside to visit someone's grandmother or grandfather who still lived on land that traced back to the family's original Dawes allotment. Often, those places were remote and unbothered. There were horses and old barns and wooded spaces to excite the minds of kids with healthy imaginations. Sometimes the grandparents pointed to ancestors' photographs hanging in homes, or iron wash kettles now used as yard ornaments, or the remains of tumbledown log cabins, and then told us fascinating long-ago stories. More often, though, we chatted about TV shows, sports, what grade we were in, and whether we thought some boy was cute.

Each year in school, from the third grade on, we studied Oklahoma history. We learned about what were then referred to as "the Five Civilized Tribes"—the Cherokee, Chickasaw, Creek, Choctaw, and Seminole, all forcibly removed by the US government from their homes in states farther east such as Georgia, Florida, Mississippi, and Tennessee. We learned that the brutal marches, beginning with the Choctaws in 1831, became known as the Trail of Tears, because thousands starved, died of sickness, or froze to death. We learned about Sequoyah, who developed a written syllabary of the Cherokee language. We reveled in spicy tales of trouble between the old tribal governments, outlaws looking for places to hide, squatters seeking land, oilmen lusting for "black gold," and eventually the residents of Oklahoma Territory eagerly pursuing the combining of Oklahoma Territory and Indian Territory into the forty-sixth state of the union in 1907. In elementary school, we reenacted the Oklahoma land runs as a class project, lining up on the playground with our makeshift covered wagons and claim flags, prepared to run forth in a mad rush of jostling humanity, to stake out our homesteads before all the land was gone. Little was said about why so much land was suddenly open to incomers.

Toward the end of each school year, we went on field trips to museums housed in the lavish mansions of old-time oil barons. Along the way, we rode school buses down streets named after those same men, and ate our sack lunches in parks they had funded. Museum docents told us about wildcatters and oil gushers that spewed hundreds of feet into the air. We were told of the men who came to the state with a few dollars in their pockets and made themselves into millionaires. Those men became governors, and congressmen, and senators. Men whose names lived beyond their mortal lifetimes, their legends growing larger with the passage of time.

A name never mentioned was Kate Barnard. In all the years of Oklahoma history classes, I do not recall ever hearing of her. If she was part of the curriculum, the brief glimmer of her was so insignificant as to become a footnote. It seems remarkable now not to have ever known that the politician who had the broadest influence on the state's constitution and then went on to be elected to statewide office by the largest majority of any candidate on the ballot was . . . a woman? In an era when women couldn't even vote? Yet by the time I came along, the Sooner State had long since moved past her life and legacy. The things she believed in, the battles she fought, her influence on lives of ordinary working men, women, and particularly children had disappeared into the dust cloud of history.

I came across Kate purely by accident, when research for a previous novel dredged up an old newspaper mention of a woman who found "elf children living in a hollow tree" in Oklahoma. That propelled me on a winding quest to discover the rest of the story. Who was this woman? Who were these children? Why were they living in a hollow tree? Why did people call them *elf children*? Why had I never heard of all this?

Uncovering the *how* and *why* of it became a winding excursion through the rampant graft and mind-boggling land grab of the statehood era. I sifted through mountains of historical documents—Federal Writers' Project Indian-Pioneer History interviews from the 1930s, available as part of the University of Oklahoma's Indian-Pioneer Papers Collection, old newspapers, maps, books, court cases, congressional hearing transcripts, guardianship papers, and reports like the 1905 *USGS Gazetteer of Indian Territory* and *Oklahoma's Poor Rich Indians*, written in part by Gertrude Bonnin, herself a member of the Ihanktonwan Nation (or Yankton Sioux Tribe), and at the time a revered speaker among women's clubs and an advocate for the rights of indigenous people. By the time Bonnin worked on the report in the 1920s, the abuse of land rights and landowners, particularly minors and orphans among the Five Tribes, had been in flood stage for decades. It had continued virtually unimpeded, save for a brief period from 1907 to 1915, when Kate Barnard, as Oklahoma's newly elected commissioner of charities and corrections, tried to put a stop to it.

Kate was a fighter—Irish by extraction, fierce in temper, incredibly talented in the arts of oratory and persuasion. She was brash, determined, confident, and she loved a fight, which she often referred to as "a good shindy." Unfortunately, she had no idea what she was up against when she fired the first shots across the bow in 1909, the year she rescued the "elf children" from the hollow tree and discovered that their court-appointed guardian was living lavishly on the children's oil monies, while the children survived in the woods, begged for food, and became so malnourished and ragged people thought they were elves.

The guardian had, in total, court-sanctioned control over fifty-one allotment-wealthy children, many of whom he had no means of locating. Kate's department prosecuted the man and sought to regain the children's money and property. In the process, Kate and her small staff exposed a system of graft, greed, and political favors that included not only the guardians themselves, but everyone from local merchants to lawmen and probate court judges. Kate's attempts to put an end to the graft were foiled at every turn, and she was eventually steamrolled by forces more powerful than she could ever have imagined. After her second term, she was drummed out of office, her name maligned in newspapers now owned by wealthy oilmen, her crusade silenced and left to fade. Years later, she would remark, "To this day . . . hardly a voter in Oklahoma knows that my office was wrecked and my life work ruined by the very men they returned to office. . . . I was ostracized because I would not surrender the fight to return to Indian orphan children the oil lands stolen from these little ones."

Fortunately, the noted Oklahoma historian Angie Debo, whose papers are now housed in the Angie Debo Room at Oklahoma State University's Edmon Low Library, had admired Kate Barnard in her prime. Debo researched and wrote extensively in the 1930s about the sordid history of the land grabs, grafters, corrupt judges and lawyers, the Five Tribes, and Kate Barnard's ill-fated fight to protect orphans and minor children of the tribes. When Debo finished her book *And Still the Waters Run,* no one was willing to publish it. She would spend years seeking a publisher before finally seeing the book in print via Princeton University Press. In this now-classic volume, Debo honored and preserved the dark legacy of Kate Barnard's battle.

Entire novels could be written about Kate's tumultuous childhood and eventual rise to political stardom. She was, quite literally, a woman who invented and reinvented herself. But my interest in her began with her report of the elf children, and researching that topic led ultimately to Kate's deepest passion: the battle to protect "little ones" and to ensure quality of life for all children. She saw around her a world in which millions of children had become—through greed, abuse, or family necessity—sources of labor and income for adults. The systems that should have protected them instead turned a blind eye to their suffering, sickness, injury, ruined health, lack of education, and in some cases, wholesale exploitation.

Most of those children had no choice but to endure their young lives any way they could and hope to survive to adulthood. A few of them were ancestors of mine, including two little Irish immigrant boys, nine and eleven years old, listed on the census as "papermill workers." They were, at the time, the sole breadwinners for their recently widowed mother and three-year-old sister. Within a year, their mother was also dead. I do not know what happened to the boys and their little sister after that—where they might have lived, or toiled, what they might have eaten, where they may have slept, whether they were hungry, or frightened, or unloved, or even whether all of them survived. One lived to become my ancestor.

For a short time, millions of children like them found a champion, a brash and unrelenting "next friend to orphans" in a tiny woman with a big voice. She was determined to reclaim for them their childhoods, and for at least some, she succeeded. I hope the children of *Shelterwood* help to tell their stories.

ACKNOWLEDGMENTS

Shelterwood began with a wrong turn on an ordinary day, as the most fascinating journeys often do. Having known Oklahoma most of my life, I thought of it as an old friend whose stories were already familiar to me. Then the vintage newspaper mention of "elf children" hinted that my old friend may have left some parts of the story untold. My expedition into that hidden history became this novel.

All books are the product of many hands, or at least I believe that to be the case. Countless friends, neighbors, colleagues, and kind strangers contributed to transforming *Shelterwood* from an idea into a novel. Now you, dear reader, are the final link, for no story is complete until it finds a listening ear. Without you, these many years of writing, storytelling, and grand adventuring would never have happened. I'm thankful for each of you whom I've met either in person or long-distance over thirty-three books and twenty-odd years, and I'm grateful to the readers, library folks, and booksellers who have brought so many others to join us in our story circle.

I am also grateful to the organizations, volunteer history buffs, and professionals who helped with the research, editing, and vetting of this book. Years of digging, researching, reviewing, and reworking went into the process. Any mistakes that may have slipped through the cracks are human foibles, unintentional, and mine entirely. To all those who helped and advised me along the way, I owe a huge debt, and I would be remiss if I didn't take a moment here to express my appreciation.

Thank you, first of all, to my family in Texas and in Oklahoma for sharing stories of southeastern Oklahoma "old timers," for connecting me to resources in the Winding Stair area, and for encouraging me to pursue this story, even when the research materials seemed almost impossible to find. In particular, thank you to my husband, Sam (of Antlers High School alumni fame), for answering endless questions about Pushmataha County, the Kiamichi River, plants, trees, animals, people, and places, and for tromping around the Winding Stairs and Le Flore County with me, tracking down the hidden remnants of a bygone age. Thank you, also, to my mother, to my writer friend Judy Christie, to my sons and daughter-in-law for listening to endless chatter about unbelievable new history bits— and an equal amount of whining about history bits I couldn't find— and for reading early copies of the manuscript. This story would not exist without your having helped me to tell it.

Thank you also to family members, friends, employees, and officials within the Cherokee Nation and the Choctaw Nation of Oklahoma. Thank you in particular to Brian McAdams, author Stacy Wells, Randy Hammons, Stacy Shephard, and Dr. Ian Thompson for pointing me in the right direction when I came asking. Thank you to Dora M. Wickson at the Choctaw School of Language for generously helping with Choctaw language words. Thank you to the staff members, guides, and cultural educators at the Choctaw Cultural Center and the Choctaw Nation Capitol Museum for going above and beyond to answer questions, offer hospitality, and bring history to life. No one passing through southeastern Oklahoma should forgo the chance to spend a day visiting the historic Capitol Museum and the Cultural Center. These are incredible places focused on preserving and sharing the history of the vibrant and multifaceted people whose story in southeastern Oklahoma, and far beyond, continues to grow.

In terms of general Oklahoma history, as well as the history of Kate Barnard, Angie Debo, the women's movement of Oklahoma, and the early days in Pushmataha and Le Flore counties, I am grateful to the generous folks at the Pushmataha County Historical Society Museum and the LeFlore County Historical Society and Museum. I am also deeply grateful to Oklahoma State University, Edmon Low Library, and Dean of Libraries Sheila Grant Johnson for treating me to a personal tour of the Angie Debo Room and for sending a mail packet of pertinent materials from the Debo Collection. What a joy to know that Angie Debo's pioneering work in preserving Oklahoma's untold history, and the history of the Five Tribes, is housed at the university that once greeted me as a starry-eyed computer science student who secretly wanted to be a writer. No matter where I wander, OSU and its grand old library will always be home.

In the category of Val's job among those finest of America's heroes and servants, the protectors and caretakers of our state and national parks, monuments, preserves, forests, seashores, historical sites, and wilderness and recreation areas, I am thankful for all of you and the difficult work you do among sometimes unbelievable human and environmental conditions. In researching Val's career and daily duties, I learned that rangering is, quite literally, not a walk in the park. Thank you to National Park Service and Forest Service personnel from Winding Stair National Recreation Area (site of the fictional Horsethief Trail National Park in the novel), Chickasaw National Recreation Area, Big Bend National Park, and Yosemite National Park who kindly answered questions and offered ideas about how to accurately render Val's work life and career.

Thank you a thousandfold to Retired Major Jody Lee, State Park Police, Texas Parks and Wildlife, for reading and rereading Val's story, then sitting down to go through all the fine points of park life and law enforcement. The multicolored sticky notes on the manuscript were terrifying, until I realized that some of them were actually a thumbs-up. I looked forward to "good job," "yes, that's how it is," and "good line," and quickly realized that where the sticky notes meant the story needed clarification or correction, you were there to help think it through. I can't imagine a better way to spend an afternoon than over coffee, snacks, sticky notes, and ranger stories. It was further proof of Stephen T. Mather's 1928 quote, "They are a fine, earnest, intelligent, and public-spirited body of men, the rangers. Though small in number, their influence is large. Many and long are the duties heaped upon their shoulders.... If a bear is in the hotel, if a fire threatens a forest, if someone is to be saved, it is 'send a ranger.' If a Dude wants to know the why, if a Sagebrusher is puzzled about a road, it is 'ask the ranger.'"

As it turns out, if a book about a park is to be written, it is also "ask the ranger," and the ranger will give you answers plus real-life tales to illustrate the point. For that, I, and the characters of *Shelterwood*, remain indebted and greatly obliged.

Last, but in no way least, I'm thankful for the incredible publishing crew behind this book. Thank you to my amazing agent, Elisabeth Weed, for encouraging me through the writing of *Shelterwood*, to Kara Welsh and Kim Hovey at Ballantine for believing in this book, and to Jennifer Hershey and Wendy Wong for shepherding the story through an editorial process that strengthened both Ollie's and Valerie's stories. I am also immeasurably grateful to the talented teams in design, art, production, marketing, and publicity at Penguin Random House, and in particular Quinne Rogers, Allison Schuster, Emma Thomasch, Jennifer Garza, Karen Fink, and Brianna Kusilek. Without you, books would arrive on shelves in plain brown wrappers, or not arrive at all. You not only bring color to bookshelves everywhere, but on a deeper level, you facilitate the eternal person-to-person connection of story. Long may stories continue to bind us together in bookstores, in libraries, in book clubs, in reading groups, and in all the other places we gather to share the adventures we've found between the pages.

What lucky people we readers are that we live not just one life, but many, and diving into yet another is as easy as opening a book.

—LISA

PRIMARY RESOURCES AND FURTHER READING

Albright, Horace M., and Frank J. Albright, *Oh, Ranger! A Book About the National Parks.* Redwood City: Stanford University Press, 1929.

Angie Debo Collection. "About Angie Debo" page. Edmon Low Library, Oklahoma State University, Stillwater, Okla. https://library.okstate.edu/search-and-find/collections/digital-collections/indians-outlaws-and-angie-debo/about-angie-debo.

Barnard, Kate. "Working for the Friendless." *Independent,* November 28, 1907.

———. "Oklahoma's Child Labor Laws." *Sturm's Oklahoma Magazine,* February 1908.

Bonnin, Gertrude (Zitkala-Ša). *American Indian Stories.* Washington, DC: Hayworth Publishing House, 1921.

Bonnin, Gertrude, et al. *Oklahoma's Poor Rich Indians: An Orgy of Graft and Exploitation of the Five Civilized Tribes—Legalized Robbery.* Philadelphia: Office of Indian Rights Association, 1924.

Carlile, Glenda, and Bob Burke. *Kate Barnard: Oklahoma's Good Angel.* Oklahoma Statesmen Series. Edmond, Okla.: University of Central Oklahoma Press, 2001.

Cronley, Connie. *A Life on Fire: Oklahoma's Kate Barnard.* Norman, Okla.: University of Oklahoma Press, 2021.

Debo, Angie. *And Still the Waters Run: The Betrayal of the Five Civilized Tribes.* Princeton: Princeton University Press, 1940.

———. *The Rise and Fall of the Choctaw Republic.* 2nd ed. Norman, Okla.: University of Oklahoma Press, 1961.

Debo, Angie. *The Five Civilized Tribes of Oklahoma: Report on Social and Economic Conditions.* Philadelphia: Office of the Indian Rights Association, 1951.

Ducker Finchum, Tanya, and Allen Finchum. "Not Gone with the Wind: Libraries in Oklahoma in the 1930s." *Libraries & the Cultural Record* 46, no. 3 (2011).

Dunkle, W. F., ed. "A Choctaw Indian's Diary: Diary of Willis F. Folsom." *Chronicles of Oklahoma* 4 (1926). PDF retrieved from the Oklahoma Historical Society website. gateway.okhistory.org/ark:/67531/metadc2191566/.

Edmondson, L., and M. Larson. "Kate Barnard: The Story of a Woman Politician." *Chronicles of Oklahoma* 78 (2000). PDF retrieved from the Oklahoma Historical Society website. https://gateway.okhistory.org/ark:/67531/metadc2016803/.

Finchum, Tanya, and Juliana Nykolaiszyn. "Oral History Collections in Oklahoma." PDF. Retrieved from Oklahoma State University Library, https://library.okstate.edu/oralhistory/oral-history-collections-in-oklahoma-survey/oral-history-collections-in-oklahoma-directory.pdf.

Foster, C. D. *Foster's Comic History of Oklahoma.* Oklahoma City, Okla.: The Publishers Press, 1916. www.loc.gov/item/16014911/.

Gannett, Henry. *A Gazetteer of Indian Territory.* US Geological Survey, Department of the Interior. Washington, DC: Government Printing Office, 1905.

Haag, Marcia, and Henry Willis. *Choctaw Language and Culture: Chahta Anumpa.* Norman, Okla.: University of Oklahoma Press, 2001.

Habecker, Tom. *Send a Ranger: My Life Serving the National Parks.* Helena, Mont.: Falcon Guides, 2023.

Hafen, Jane P., ed. *Help Indians Help Themselves: The Later Writings of Gertrude Simmons Bonnin (Zitkala-Ša).* Lubbock, Tex.: Texas Tech University Press, 2022.

Indian-Pioneer Papers Collection. The University of Oklahoma Western History Collections. https://digital.libraries.ou.edu/whc/pioneer.

Kickingbird, Kirke, and Karen Ducheneaux. *One Hundred Million Acres.* New York: Macmillan Publishing Co., 1973.

Kidwell, Clara Sue. *The Choctaws in Oklahoma: From Tribe to Nation, 1855–1970.* Norman, Okla.: University of Oklahoma Press, 2007.

Lankford, Andrea. *Ranger Confidential: Living, Working, and Dying in the National Parks.* Helena, Montana: Falcon Guides, 2010.

McKelway, A. J. "Kate the 'Good Angel' of Oklahoma." *The American Magazine*, October 1908.

"'Miss Kate,' Livest Wire in Prison Reform, Visits Us." *The New York Times*, December 8, 1912.

Mould, Tom. *Choctaw Tales.* Jackson, Miss.: University of Mississippi Press, 2004.

Muir, John. *Our National Parks.* Layton, Utah: Gibbs Smith, 2018.

Musslewhite, Lynn, and Suzanne Jones Crawford. *One Woman's Political Journey: Kate Barnard and Social Reform, 1875–1930.* Norman, Okla.: University of Oklahoma Press, 2003.

Odell, Marcia. *Divide and Conquer: Allotment Among the Cherokee.* New York: Arno Press, 1979.

Peavy, Linda S., and Ursula Smith. *Women Who Changed Things.* New York: Scribner, 1983.

Rafferty, Milton D., and John C. Catau. *The Ouachita Mountains: A Guide for Fishermen, Hunters, and Travelers.* Norman, Okla.: University of Oklahoma Press, 1991.

Rainey, Luretta. *History of Oklahoma State Federation of Women's Clubs.* Guthrie, Okla.: Co-operative Publishing Company, 1939. https://digitalprairie.ok.gov /digital/collection/culture/id/8159.

Rhea, John M. *A Field of Their Own: Women and American Indian History, 1830–1941.* Norman, Okla.: University of Oklahoma Press, 2016.

Saferstein, Mark J. ed. *Oh, Ranger! True Stories from Our National Parks.* New York: American Park Network, 2007.

Sprague, Donovin Arleigh. *The Choctaw Nation of Oklahoma.* Charleston, S.C.: Arcadia Publishing, 2007.

Truman, Margaret. *Women of Courage.* New York: William Morrow and Company, 1976.

US Congress, Senate Report of the Select Committee to Investigate Matters Connected with Affairs in Indian Territory, with Hearings. November 11, 1906–January 9, 1907. 59th Cong., 2nd Session Report no. 5013, vol. 1.

US Congress, House Report of the Committee on Indian Affairs to Investigate Administration of Indian Affairs in the State of Oklahoma, with Hearings. February 21, 1924, 68th Cong., 1st Session on H.J. Res. 181. Washington, DC: Government Printing Office, 1924.

US Congress, House Report of the Subcommittee of the Committee on Indian Affairs to Investigate Five Civilized Tribes in Oklahoma, with Hearings. March 22 and 28, 1924, 68th Cong., First Session on H.R. 6900. Washington DC: Government Printing Office, 1924.

US Congress, House Report of the Committee on Agriculture, Nutrition, and Forestry, to Consider Winding Stair Mountain, Oklahoma Wilderness Bill—S.2571, with Hearings. September 7, 1988. 100th Cong., Second Session on S.2571. Washington, DC: US Government Printing Office, 1988.

US Congress, House Report of the Committee on Oversight and Government Reform to Examine Misconduct and Mismanagement at the National Park Service, with Hearings. September 22, 2016. 114th Cong., Second Session. Serial number 114-164. Washington, DC: Government Publishing Office, 2016.

Yosemite Conservancy, ed. *The Wonder of It All: 100 Stories from the National Park Service.* San Francisco: Yosemite Conservancy, 2016.

ABOUT THE AUTHOR

LISA WINGATE is the author of the #1 *New York Times* bestseller *Before We Were Yours,* which has sold more than three million copies and been translated into over forty languages worldwide. The co-author, with Judy Christie, of the nonfiction book *Before and After,* Wingate is a Goodreads Choice Award winner, an Oklahoma Book Award finalist, and a Southern Book Prize winner. She was named as one of the 2023 Distinguished Alumni of Oklahoma State University. She lives with her husband in Texas and Colorado.

lisawingate.com
Instagram: @author_lisa_wingate
Facebook.com/LisaWingateAuthorPage

ABOUT THE TYPE

This book was set in Sabon, a typeface designed by the well-known German typographer Jan Tschichold (1902–74). Sabon's design is based upon the original letterforms of sixteenth-century French type designer Claude Garamond and was created specifically to be used for three sources: foundry type for hand composition, Linotype, and Monotype. Tschichold named his typeface for the famous Frankfurt typefounder Jacques Sabon (c. 1520–80).